Elvi Rhodes was the eldest of five children brought up in the West Riding of Yorkshire in the depression between the wars. She won a scholarship to Bradford Grammar School and left to become the breadwinner of her family. A widow with two sons, she lives in Sussex. Her other novels include *Opal, Doctor Rose, Ruth Appleby, The Golden Girls, Madeleine, The House of Bonneau, Cara's Land, The Rainbow Through the Rain, The Bright One, The Mountain, Spring Music* and *Midsummer Meeting*. A collection of stories, *Summer Promise and other stories*, is also published by Corgi Books.

Portrait of Chloe

Elvi Rhodes

CORGI BOOKS

PORTRAIT OF CHLOE
A CORGI BOOK : 0 552 14577 7

Originally published in Great Britain by Bantam Press
a division of Transworld Publishers

PRINTING HISTORY
Bantam Press edition published 1997
Corgi edition published 1998

3 5 7 9 10 8 6 4 2

Set in 11/13pt Plantin by
Hewer Text Composition Service, Edinburgh

Corgi Books are published by Transworld Publishers
61-63 Uxbridge Road, London W5 5SA,
a division of The Random House Group Ltd,
in Australia by Random House Australia (Pty) Ltd,
20 Alfred Street, Milsons Point, Sydney, NSW 2061, Australia,
in New Zealand by Random House New Zealand Ltd,
18 Poland Road, Glenfield, Auckland 10, New Zealand
and in South Africa by Random House (Pty) Ltd,
Endulini, 5a Jubilee Road, Parktown 2193, South Africa.

Printed and bound in Great Britain by
Mackays of Chatham plc, Chatham, Kent.

For Shirley Hall, secretary and friend

Acknowledgements

I especially wish to thank Chief Superintendent (retd) Norman Cooper for his unstinting help on police procedures in the 1950s. Any errors I might have made are mine, not his. Also I thank my many friends who have helped me with their memories of Brighton at this time.

Prologue

The baby stands close to the sofa on which her mother is sitting. Today is her first birthday. She has been able to stand unaided, but somewhat unsteadily, for more than two weeks now, but she has yet to take her first step.

The floor is strewn with presents – a teddy bear, a rag book, a golliwog with fuzzy hair and striped trousers, a brightly coloured shiny ball, a pile of wooden bricks. She has played with them all briefly, and with the fancy paper in which they were wrapped. She had seemed more taken with the paper than with its contents, crumpling it in her hands and throwing it around, but in the end she has tired even of that.

She looks around, her deep blue eyes taking in everything: the discarded toys, the tabby cat asleep on the hearthrug, her tall father standing with his back to the fire, not quite obscuring the dancing flames. Her mother, she knows, is behind her, her grandmother in the armchair at the far side of the room. And there, on the floor by her grandmother's feet, she sees the duck!

The duck is of bright yellow felt with a black beak, large black feet and circular embroidered eyes. It has been made by her grandmother from a pattern in a magazine. It is tightly stuffed with old socks, cut up small, and is pleasingly curved. The baby stares at the duck. It is, she thinks, though she doesn't know the words, sublimely beautiful. Why hasn't she noticed it earlier? It is the object of her desire and she must have it.

It comes to her exactly what she must do, even though she has never done it before. She removes her hand from her mother's knee where she has been resting it to balance herself. Then, with careful confidence, she puts one foot in front of the other. And again, and again, and again.

Her parents and her grandmother look at each other, then watch in amazement, hardly daring to breathe in case they should distract her and cause her to fall, as this little girl in her best white and pink embroidered dress walks across the carpet.

The child continues to walk. Momentarily the coloured ball is in her path, but the side of her foot touches it and it rolls away. Her gaze is fixed firmly on the duck. As she nears it the grandmother holds out her arms, pleased as Punch that the child should make for her with her very first steps, ready to catch her when she falls. The baby has not even noticed her grandmother. She has only one thought in mind. She continues on her way until she is within reach of the duck, then she drops to the floor, stretches out her arms and grabs it, holding it tightly to her chest.

'Wonderful!' the mother says. 'My clever little Dora!'

'Splendid!' the proud father cries. 'And on her first birthday! We shan't forget this!'

'She knew just what she wanted,' the grandmother says with approval. 'And she went after it! Mark my words, this one will let nothing get in her way!'

I

'You don't seem to be taking much with you, Dora,' Elizabeth Branksome said. 'Are you sure you'll manage?'

Perhaps the fact that her daughter was travelling light meant that she wasn't leaving home for good. Perhaps, before long, she would return. She was grasping at straws.

'Quite sure,' Dora said. 'When I need more, I'll buy things out of my wages.'

She knew what was going through her mother's mind, she could read her like a book but, as so often, her mother was wrong. There was no way she would ever return to Akersfield. Years ago, while she was still at school, she had planned to leave, though she had confided in no-one. She had kept it to herself, saved for the event in pennies and rare sixpences from her pocket money and in larger amounts once she had left school, completed a secretarial training course, and found herself a job – or, rather, taken the job her father's influence had gained for her in the Town Hall.

He was Medical Officer of Health then and had connections everywhere. She had hated the job – Secretary to the Deputy Surveyor – and stuck it only because of the money she could pay into her savings account at the end of every month. It was her leaving home money. She knew exactly what she would do, her goal was fixed. When she had saved the sum of fifty pounds she would give the required month's notice and she would quit.

She would quit the Deputy Surveyor with his boring planning applications, his preoccupation with sewers, road widening and street lamps; she would quit her comfortable, constricting home – Royal Lodge, Mount Grove, a very good address her mother often said with quiet satisfaction. It would be no effort to tear herself away from what friends she had. If such a thing were possible they were even more boring than the Deputy Surveyor. Their goal in life was marriage to a man with a nice steady job and, as soon as possible, two or three children. The war had been over for nearly seven years now. Everyone, especially everyone in Akersfield, was for settling down, putting down roots.

Everyone except me, Dora thought. No way was she going to settle down, not for a long time, and specifically not here.

'Why go so far away? Why Brighton?' her mother asked for the hundredth time.

Dora, not bothering to answer, wrote the luggage label for her suitcase in a clear, firm hand.

Miss D Branksome
C/o Blenheim House
Sussex Square
Brighton.

It looked good, but was she going too far in putting
the address where she was, after all, only going for
an interview? Was it tempting fate, courting disappointment? She shrugged her shoulders. What harm
could it do? In any case, you made your own fate.

'Why?' her mother persisted.

'I've told you. The job advertised happened to be
in Brighton. It sounded what I wanted.'

'A mother's help,' Mrs Branksome said. 'Why
would you waste a good education *and* a secretarial
course on looking after someone's children. Your
father must be turning in his grave!'

If he turns in his grave every time you mention
it he must be like a spinning top, Dora thought.
She didn't say so, there was no point. She had had
this conversation with her mother a dozen times and
got nowhere with it. She had been quite fond of her
father, sorry when he'd died of a heart attack two
years ago, but the people who said, after his funeral,
'Life must go on' were quite right.

She had seen the advertisement for the job in a
most respectable women's magazine. 'MP and wife
seek help with children aged 5, 3 and 4 months. No
housework. Must be adaptable'.

It had sounded interesting. She didn't mind
children as long as they were someone else's and
she reckoned she was adaptable, though she would

have to approve what she was required to adapt to. Also, a Member of Parliament and his wife sounded fine. She had no more interest in politics than in planning applications, but at least she might get to meet some interesting people.

Mrs Branksome glanced at the luggage label.

'You're being a bit premature, aren't you? What if you don't get the job?'

'Then I'll try for another,' Dora said. 'There's sure to be something.'

She would be paid her travel expenses and she had at least enough money for a week or more in a boarding house, should that prove necessary. She had no qualms about landing a job of some kind.

'You're always telling me it's impossible to hire anyone to do anything. I'm not worried about finding something.'

'Who knows what might happen to you in Brighton? It does *not* have a good reputation,' her mother warned. 'Quite the reverse, in fact! It's not like Akersfield.'

'Good!' Dora locked the suitcase and put the keys in her handbag.

'Oh, Dora, what am I going to do with you?' Elizabeth Branksome wanted, at this moment, to take her daughter in her arms, but she had never been a demonstrative woman, it wouldn't come naturally to her, nor to Dora for that matter. She had moved forward on an impulse, and now stepped back again. It was too late.

'Oh, Dora!'

How I hate that name, Dora thought. Who in the

world would want to answer to 'Dora'? It sounded old-fashioned, flat, uninteresting. One thing was certain, if she had a child, if *ever*, it would not, definitely not, be called Dora.

She fastened the luggage label securely to the handle of her suitcase. She had bought the suitcase out of her own money and it was not of as good a quality as she would have liked, in fact it was hardly more than cardboard. A person could be judged by the quality of their luggage, but her mother had refused to let her have either of the good pre-war leather cases they had always taken on family holidays. If it turns out that I ever do much travelling, Dora thought, one of the first things I shall buy is a decent suitcase.

Her sister came into the room. Her round face was pale, her eyes red-rimmed. She was dressed in her school uniform, which did not become her, Dora thought. At fourteen Marilyn was plump, bulged in all the wrong places, and was not helped by being short in stature.

'It's not fair!' Marilyn said dismally. 'I shouldn't have to go to school this morning, not when Dora's leaving.'

'You can't just stay away from school,' her mother said. 'Not with exams coming up.'

Tears welled in Marilyn's pale blue eyes, and brimmed over, running silently down her face. Dora moved across to her and put an arm around her sister's shoulders. Parting from Marilyn was the only thing she minded about leaving Akersfield, though they did almost nothing together, except share a bedroom, and that Dora disliked intensely. The four-year gap between them was, at this stage of their lives, too wide, but since their father's death Marilyn had chosen to be dependent on her rather than on their mother or their elder brother. In any case, after the honeymoon Maurice and his new bride had moved smartly out of Akersfield. He was no more than a dozen miles away but in spirit, and even in the flesh, since he seldom visited, he might as well have been in a foreign country.

'I want to go to the station with you!'

Marilyn pleaded in the same voice she had begged Dora for the last ten days not to leave. That had been a request there was no question of granting, but really why shouldn't the child go to the station?

'Please let her go with us, Mother,' Dora said. 'What does a half-day off school matter? Just as long as you don't make a scene,' she added to Marilyn.

'Oh, I won't, I won't! I promise!' Marilyn took a crumpled handkerchief from her pocket and dabbed ineffectually at her eyes.

'Oh, very well!' her mother said.

It was going to be a bad day. So many of her days went from one defeat to another. 'A blessing you have three children to comfort you,' her friends had said when her husband died. It wasn't true. Her children had never been the blessings she had expected; she had not found the delight in them other people seemed to in theirs. In her widowhood so far they had given her precious little comfort, and she didn't know why.

'Then we'd better be off,' she said.

They got into the car, the sisters sitting in the back, and she drove the two miles to the station.

Dora, sitting with her back to the engine, watched her mother and sister walk away down the platform. Passing the barrier they turned and gave last waves, her mother's restrained, Marilyn's frantic. She acknowledged a pang – not of guilt, nothing like that – about her sister. She wished the child had not been so upset, but then that was Marilyn. She would write to her, send her a comic seaside postcard the minute she was settled in. In fact, she would write to her regularly.

When they were out of sight she moved to the seat opposite, facing the way she was going. It was not only that she preferred to travel thus, it also symbolized her feelings – face to the future.

The train gathered speed through the blackened, stony landscape of the West Riding town. She would be happy never to see this again, never to see another mill chimney etched against the sky. She wondered what Brighton would be like. No-one she knew had actually been to Brighton, though everyone had heard of it. She liked the name.

It was at Doncaster that she saw the man. As the train, drawing into the station, slowed down and then stopped, he was standing on the platform scanning the compartments. He was tall, more than six feet. He had dark hair and his face was tanned as if he had been in the sun. His well-cut, dark grey suit fitted to perfection over his broad-shouldered slender figure, his white shirt gleamed, his silk tie, grey, red, black, was elegance personified. By his side a porter carried a tan leather suitcase and a matching leather briefcase. All the man carried was a neatly-folded newspaper. He was the picture of elegance.

He is not from these parts, Dora thought, that's the kind of suitcase I will have one day, as well as a matching handbag.

As he scanned the train for a moment his gaze met hers. Then the porter spoke to him and they moved together along the platform.

It was clear, she thought, that he was looking for a first-class compartment. Never had she set eyes on anyone more suited to first-class surroundings. She craned her neck but it was impossible to see where he had joined the train. She settled back in her seat and opened her book.

She couldn't read. So many thoughts jostled in her head, so many bright visions of the future. And what was it like, she wondered, to travel everywhere first-class, to have a porter at one's beck and call, dealing with every last piece of luggage, so that all one was left to carry was a newspaper? She had peered into the first-class compartments as she had walked down the platform at Akersfield, had noted the dark, rich-looking upholstery, the white linen antimacassars on every headrest, the shaded light over each seat; and in the dining-car the tables laid with white cloths and gleaming cutlery. What wouldn't she give to eat at one of those tables as the train sped through the countryside?

'And one day I will!'

She said the words out loud, which didn't matter because there was no-one else in the compartment and somehow it made more of a promise to herself, not just a wishful thought, when the words were actually said.

They had left the towns behind now. The smoke-blackened buildings, the chimneys, the slag heaps, had given way to open country with flat, green fields stretching away to a distant horizon. The landscape was so unlike that of her home, where every viewpoint which was not taken from a hill was bounded by one. Resolutely she turned her thoughts away from what, after all, was no longer her home. She had left it. She would think only of what was to come.

So what was the first-class man doing, ensconced in his first-class compartment? Was he gazing out of the window, as she was? Or was he reading his newspaper, which would undoubtedly be *The Times*? So why don't I find out? Dora asked herself. What was there to lose? She had only to walk down the corridor and who was to stop her doing that?

She opened her handbag and took out a small mirror and a lipstick. Carefully, because the train was swaying, she filled in the generous curves of her lips with clear scarlet lipstick. Her mother disapproved of the colour, said it was far too bright, almost common, but Dora knew it suited her, added life to her appearance. With her almost-black hair and the surprising contrast of her fair skin, the redness of her lips made a striking whole. She surveyed her image in the mirror with satisfaction, smoothed the dark arch of her eyebrows with a damp finger, smiled at herself to show the evenness of her white teeth. She would not use her powder compact; the faint shine on her skin was not unattractive. She ran her fingers through her thick hair which, though most people seemed to admire it, was too curly for her liking. She would have preferred straight hair, it was smarter, more sophisticated, but there wasn't much she could do about that.

She rose to her feet, moved towards the corridor door and then, as a fresh thought struck her, turned back and picked up her suitcase.

It was not easy, negotiating the corridor, case in hand, on the swaying train. She swore that it had put on speed the minute she'd started to move. Will he be alone? she wondered. If he's in a compartment with other men, will I enter? She knew what she was going to say. It had come to her in a flash, which was why she had turned back and picked up the suitcase. She would rather – oh *much* rather – say it to him alone, but if it didn't turn out that way, then it couldn't be helped. They would probably *all* be sympathetic and she'd get her ride in the first-class, hopefully all the way to London.

Luck was with her. Halfway down the first-class corridor she saw him. He was sitting, back-to-the-engine, by the window, he was alone, and he hadn't seen her. She paused, took a deep breath, then summoned up the saddest thought she could possibly think so that tears came into her eyes. It was a talent she had had – and had the good sense to cherish and cultivate – since she was a small child and it had seen her around many a tight corner.

She took a firmer grip on her suitcase and with her other hand quickly opened the sliding door to the compartment, pushed her way in, and sat down, breathing heavily.

The man looked up.

'What . . .'

'I'm sorry! I'm sorry!' Dora gasped. She threw a nervous glance towards the corridor. 'I thought he was following me!'

The man sprang from his seat, crossed to the corridor, looked both ways.

'There's no-one in sight,' he said. 'Not a soul! Now get your breath back and tell me what this is all about!'

He has a beautiful speaking voice, Dora thought. It goes exactly with his appearance.

'What if he comes after me?' She was all apprehension and the man was clearly interested. I'm doing rather well, she thought.

'Who is he? And why should he come after you?' the man asked. 'Come over here and sit opposite me. I will see that no-one annoys you.'

She moved as he instructed, dragging her suitcase after her. Sitting opposite him she could study him more intently. She liked what she saw.

'I don't know who he is,' she said. 'Just a man in my compartment. He came and sat by me. Then he . . . he made advances. I had to get out. I was frightened. I'm sorry!'

She spoke in a low voice, in disjointed sentences.

The man was concerned, which was interesting because she had thought of this approach only on the spur of the moment.

'Don't be sorry,' he said. 'You were quite right to move. You were quite right to come in here.' He opened his briefcase, which lay on the seat beside him, and took out a small, silver flask. 'Now I'm going to give you a little drink,' he said. 'It's whisky, and you might not like it, but it will do you good, calm you down.'

He filled the cap and handed it to her. She sipped at it, pulling a face, though that was all right because she sensed he would prefer her not to like it and drinking it would give her a good reason to get back to normal, so that they could have a proper conversation. She wasn't sure how long she could sustain the role of a terrified young lady.

'There!' he said. 'Is that better?'

'Oh, it is!' she said. 'Thank you very much, Sir. I wonder . . .'

'Yes?'

'Do you think . . . I mean, is it possible I could stay here a little longer . . . just until . . .'

'You can stay as long as you like,' he said.

'But this is first-class, isn't it? My ticket's third-class,' Dora said timidly.

'Don't worry about that,' he replied. 'If the ticket inspector comes I'll explain it to him.'

'Oh, thank you!' she said vehemently. 'You're very kind!'

'Not at all! I'll be glad of your company. Train journeys can be quite tedious, don't you find?'

They almost always were, he thought, especially when he had to visit his constituency, which he did as seldom as possible. It was not the constituency he would have liked, it was too far from London and the Home Counties, but his father-in-law's influence had got him the seat, and at least it was a safe one.

'Oh, I do!' Dora agreed. It wasn't true. She'd made very few train journeys in her life and this one, so far, was proving a long way from tedious.

'And when did this young man who annoyed you board the train?' the man asked.

'Right at the beginning. In Akersfield. And he troubled me from the word "Go", but I was determined to sit it out . . . that is . . . until . . .' Her voice trailed away.

The man had a sudden memory of this girl's face looking at him from her compartment when he was standing on the platform. Their eyes had met and, for a moment, locked. Her eyes had not been those of a woman in any way troubled, annoyed, distressed. There had been no call for help in those eyes. They had been happily provocative. Is she having me on? he asked himself. And if so, for what purpose?

'I think,' he said smoothly, 'I think, don't you, that it might be a good idea if we reported this to the guard? The man must still be on the train.'

She looked at him with wide-open eyes, eyes of a blue so deep as to be almost navy, yet as bright as speedwells. Her look was one of great innocence, but it did not deceive him. However, it might be amusing to play her game.

'Oh, no, Sir!' she said swiftly. 'Please don't do that! Men always stick together. He might think . . . he might think I'd encouraged him!'

Which I daresay you would have if he'd existed, the man thought. So what was she up to? Probably any minute now she'd ask for money, spin him a yarn about that. In the meantime he was enjoying the situation, she was fun. He might, in the end, give her a little something. Entertainment value.

'I'm sure the guard would never think that of you,' he said. 'But as you wish. So shall we talk of other things? For instance, what's your name?'

Dora hesitated, but not for long. Wasn't this the perfect moment for throwing Dora out of the window? Would there ever be a moment as perfect as this?

'Chloe!' she said firmly. 'Chloe Branksome.'

'Chloe! A beautiful name and it suits you perfectly!'

It was also interesting because he had seen the label on her suitcase and it clearly stated 'Miss D. Branksome'. Oh well! He wouldn't call her bluff. It didn't matter.

'And you are Mr . . .?' Chloe ventured.

'Hendon. Charles Hendon.'

'Oh! Well that's a nice name, too. In fact,' she blushed prettily, 'Charles is my favourite name!'

'Thank you. And are you going to London, or somewhere else?'

She told him she was going to Brighton, hoping to land a job. She told him the man of the house was a Member of Parliament and she thought that would be most interesting.

'It will be. It is,' Charles Hendon said. 'And what is this MP's name?'

'Mr Portman.'

So John Portman was going to take on this little beauty, Charles thought. There was no denying she was a beauty. Ought John to be warned, or shall I let him find out for himself? And will even Miss Chloe be any match for Moira Portman? But I'll let them find out whatever there is to be found out, he decided. The thoughts raced around in his mind. Certainly, he would pay the Portmans a visit before too long.

'You'll like Brighton,' Charles said. 'I'd say it will suit you down to the ground.'

'I hope so,' Chloe replied. 'But anywhere's better than Akersfield.'

'And how many broken hearts have you left behind there?' Charles teased. 'Don't tell me you didn't have a string of boyfriends!'

Chloe shrugged. There wasn't one she wasn't happy to leave, but she wouldn't say that in so many words. Men didn't like you boasting about other men. They preferred to think they were the only one you'd ever had, or ever would have. She'd learned that ages ago.

'So you're not going to tell me?'

Chloe smiled and shook her head. 'There's really nothing to tell, Mr Hendon.'

The door slid open and a man in uniform popped his head into the compartment.

'Lunch will be served in the restaurant car in

ten minutes,' he announced. 'Will you be taking lunch, Sir?'

'We both will.'

The man was off before Chloe could say a word – not that she intended to protest too loudly, only as much as good manners dictated.

'Oh, Mr Hendon, I can't do that! I shouldn't really be in here at all! What if . . .?' Her voice faltered. She sounded quite overwhelmed.

'Nonsense!' Charles Hendon said. 'You must be my guest. I can't have you going hungry, not after your unpleasant experience! Not that it will be the best of lunches these days.' He gazed straight into her lovely eyes and the look she returned was as innocent as a baby's.

'In fact,' she admitted, 'I do have a sandwich my mother made for me. I could eat that.'

Mousetrap cheese and pickle, she thought. How very common!

'Now do you want a minute to pretty yourself up?' Hendon asked. 'Not that you need it – in which case you can join me in a few minutes in the restaurant car.'

'I'll go with you now,' Chloe said. She saw herself, Chloe (late Dora) Branksome, walking into the restaurant car by the side of this most attractive man, fussed over by waiters, fed and cosseted. It was an attractive picture.

Everything exceeded her expectations, especially the waiter, who was more than attentive.

'I'm afraid the food isn't all that much,' Charles Hendon said. 'Blame rationing!'

'It is to me, Mr Hendon,' Chloe told him. 'I have never been in a restaurant car before. It's wonderful to me!'

She was at her best when she was honest and simple, without airs and graces, he thought. Alas, he doubted she would believe that.

They spent a long time over the meal, drinking endless cups of coffee while the waiters hovered around, wanting to clear away. By the time they returned to the compartment they were nearing London, though Chloe only guessed at this by the density of the buildings, which seemed to go on for miles.

Charles Hendon looked at his watch.

'We should be on time at King's Cross. I'll see you into a taxi. Since you don't know your way around it's the easiest way to get to Victoria.'

Stepping off the train, he had only to lift a finger to summon a porter. Chloe half ran to keep up with his long strides as they followed the porter to the taxi rank. She was disappointed that she was going no further with him but it had been fun while it lasted.

'There you are!' he said, helping her into the taxi. 'Take the lady to Victoria.' He pressed money into the driver's hand.

Chloe held out her hand.

'Thank you very much, Mr Hendon. You've been so kind.'

'Not at all,' he said politely.

'I don't suppose I'll see you again?' Her tone was a question.

'Who knows?' he said – and was gone. Who knows, he thought as he hurried away. I'll make a point of it, see how Portman is getting on.

I would like to see him again, Chloe decided, sitting in the train on the way to Brighton. I think I might get somewhere with Mr Charles Hendon. But when she thought about it further it came to her that she had told him a great deal about herself yet, beyond his name, she knew nothing of him.

2

The train slowed, and finally stopped. So at last this was Brighton! The hour's journey from London had seemed almost as long as the journey from Akersfield to King's Cross, possibly because this time there had been no-one to talk to, no adventure, no Mr Charles Hendon who had so enlivened the earlier part of the day. He had been gracious to the last. She had half-hoped – they had got on so well – that he might just have arranged to see her again, but nothing had been said beyond his cheerful farewell.

'Thank you for your company. I enjoyed it.' He'd smiled at her. He had a beautiful smile in which his whole face took part, his rather large mouth widening to reveal a set of strong, perfectly even teeth, his eyes narrowing, crinkling at the corners.

She picked up her suitcase and left the train, following the crowd to the barrier. Giving up her ticket she thought how odd – but how lucky – it had been that the ticket collector on the train to London had never put in an appearance once they'd left Doncaster behind, nor had there been anyone to check at King's Cross. Not that it had bothered her at the time. If there'd been any trouble she was sure Mr Hendon would have dealt with it.

She walked out of Brighton station half expecting to be met by the sight of the sea but alas there was no sign of it. Buildings on either side lined the broad street which led from the station, though that was the only resemblance to Akersfield. Here the buildings, though still shabby from wartime neglect, were clean; in Akersfield they were blackened by smoke and soot. As a child she had thought that stone came out of the ground coal-black.

So where should she go from here? Mrs Portman had given her no directions whatever, simply the address, that she would be pleased to interview her at whatever time in the afternoon she might arrive, that her travelling expenses would be paid. Does that, Chloe asked herself, mean that I can take a taxi? What if Sussex Square was miles and miles away and it cost pounds to get there? Perhaps she should investigate the trolley bus which was standing a few yards away?

'No I won't,' she decided. 'I'll do no such thing. Why should I?'

She joined the short queue for taxis. 'Blenheim House, Sussex Square,' she said grandly to the driver when her turn came.

A posh address, he thought, but with that suitcase she's going for a skivvy. There would be no tip from this one so he wouldn't bother to help her with her case. On second thoughts, though, she was young and pretty, so he got out of his cab and heaved it in for her.

'Is it far, Sussex Square?' Chloe asked.

'Ten minutes at most,' the driver answered.

He drove down the street, past office buildings, assorted shops, a cinema, hotels, and suddenly there was the sea, the English Channel, bluer by far than the sea at Morecambe or Scarborough. When they reached the bottom of the street where it led into the promenade, two piers – one to the left and one to the right – came into view. The latter they left behind as they turned left.

This was more like it, it was the Brighton she had imagined! On the clear May day with the sun shining on the water and fluffy white clouds scudding across the sky, and scores of people strolling on the seaward side of the promenade, it lived up to its name. She couldn't have thought of a better one.

'What a lot of people about,' she said to the driver.

'Not really,' he said. 'It's out of season now. Just you wait until July and August, *then* you can talk! All coming back since the war, the visitors. Practically walking on each other's heads they are in August.'

Beyond the pier – Palace Pier the driver informed her, the other one is the West Pier, a bit more posh – he drove past terrace after terrace of elegant houses and hotels built of cream-coloured stone or perhaps painted cream, she couldn't tell which. Either way, they looked wonderful. That they were in need of repainting didn't detract from their style. Then, with a sharp left turn, they were in Sussex Square and the taxicab drew up.

'Here's Blenheim House,' the driver said.

It wasn't the first time he'd been here. He often picked up a bloke from the station and brought him here. An MP, he was.

It was a tall house, several storeys high, and the last word in elegance and style, with its large windows and a porticoed entrance. Chloe (as she already thought of herself), opened her purse and, to the driver's surprise and her own – but she was in such a good mood at the sight of everything – gave him a sixpenny tip on top of the fare, for which he carried her case to the very doorstep.

She pressed the doorbell and waited. No-one answered, though she could hear it ringing in the house. She lifted her hand to ring it again and at the same moment the door was opened by a young woman holding a baby in her arms and with a small child standing behind her.

The woman smiled at the sight of Chloe, but it was a strained smile which did not reach her eyes. She looked pale, and there were blue shadows under her brown eyes.

'You must be Miss Branksome,' she said. 'Dora Branksome.'

'Chloe. Dora *is* my name, but everyone calls me Chloe. I don't know why.'

So far, she thought, no-one had called her Chloe, but from now on they would. Dora was done with.

'I'm Moira Portman. Please come in.'

The first thing Chloe saw, even before she had shaken hands with Mrs Portman, who stood on the other side of it, was the large doormat, sunk into a brass-bounded well, into which the name

'Blenheim House' was woven in capital letters. She was impressed. When she had greeted Mrs Portman she allowed her gaze to wander to the spacious entrance hall from which a wide staircase rose to the upper floors. The elegance of the hall, with its elaborately moulded cornice, and a ceiling rose of similar design from which hung a crystal chandelier, was somehow mitigated by its untidiness. Toys – a kiddie-car, a discarded doll, a picture book, several bricks and a jigsaw puzzle – made an effective obstacle course across the floor. A child's coat was draped over the newel post, a school hat occupied the chair.

'Will you come down to the kitchen,' Mrs Portman said. 'I was just giving the children their tea.'

She led the way to the back of the hall and down a flight of wooden stairs, less elegant than the main staircase. Chloe followed.

'I'm afraid this is a house with lots of stairs,' Mrs Portman said. 'We would like to have the kitchen moved on to the ground floor, but it's impossible at the moment. There's such a shortage of materials – and labour – since the war. I expect you know that.'

Chloe murmured agreement.

'My mother says she can never get anything done to the house.'

'My mother disapproved of the children eating in the kitchen, and even more of us having our dining-room on this floor,' Mrs Portman said. 'But it's easier. When my mother lived here she had a cook, two maids and an odd-job man. I keep telling her, those days are gone for good. All I have is Mrs Wilkins who comes for two hours every morning to tidy up. Not that anything ever stays tidy!'

'Does your mother live here?' Chloe enquired. She devoutly hoped not. She didn't like the sound of her.

'No,' Mrs Portman said. 'The house is mine, now. Mama has more sense. Since she was widowed she lives in a nice little service flat in Hove.'

A little girl sat at the large kitchen table with a glass of milk and a plate of bread, spread with Marmite, in front of her. This must be Janet and if so she was five years old, Chloe thought. Mrs Portman had said little about the children in her letter, just their names and ages. The little boy keeping so close to his mother was Robert and the baby in his mother's arms was Edward. They looked like perfectly normal children, Chloe thought. She didn't think she'd have much trouble with them. Well, she wouldn't put up with it. If they behaved well she'd treat them well and if they didn't they'd soon find out what they were up against.

'This is Janet and this is Robert and the baby is Edward,' Mrs Portman said. 'Say hello to Chloe, you two!'

Neither child said anything. Janet's clear grey eyes met Chloe's in an unblinking stare; Robert, eyes downcast to the floor, continued to stand beside his mother. He is far too quiet for a three-year-old, and Miss Janet Portman is far too bold, Chloe decided. Nevertheless she favoured Janet with a dazzling smile. If the children showed no liking for her she'd not get the job, and what she'd seen of Brighton, and the house, told her she wanted it. At least to begin with. Afterwards, who knew?

'Please sit down,' Mrs Portman said. 'Perhaps you'd like a cup of tea? You've had a long journey.'

The baby began to grizzle, then to whimper.

'He's fractious,' his mother apologized. 'It's almost his feed time. You wouldn't like to hold him, would you, while I put the kettle on?'

'Of course! I'd love to!' Chloe's voice was eager, which was not at all how she felt. The truth was that, aside from Marilyn, who was after all only four years younger than herself, she had no experience of small children, let alone of babies. She presumed, and fervently hoped, that babies slept most of the time. But what she lacked in experience she made up for in confidence. She'd learn, and hopefully so would the children. When you looked at the people who *were* parents, she consoled herself, it couldn't be all that difficult.

She held out her arms and Mrs Portman put the baby into them and, wonder of wonders, he stopped whimpering at once.

'My goodness!' said his mother, 'you have the right touch. Are you used to babies, then?'

'Oh, yes!' Chloe said with confidence.

I might just have found myself a treasure, Mrs Portman thought, filling the kettle, switching it on, carefully measuring the tea into the pot. And a beautiful one at that, for the girl's looks were quite simply stunning, with her combination of almost

34

black hair, deep blue, wide-spaced eyes, and a bone structure which would last her for life. The painter in Moira Portman, for that was her profession which she followed whenever she could get time away from the children, which was hardly ever, felt her fingers itch to set up a palette, to put this girl's beauty on canvas. She would dress her in red, her looks were enough to stand against it. Or, perhaps better still, she would paint her in the nude.

Of course someone, especially in a place like Brighton, which swarmed with theatre folk, would snatch her up and put her on the stage, or in a film. In the meantime, she thought, I reckon I'm going to be happy to have her looking after my children.

She made the tea, poured it.

'I'll take the baby now,' she said, 'while you drink your tea. It's no use putting him down. At this time of the day he would just cry.'

Chloe handed back the baby. She hadn't done too badly on that one.

'Now, tell me something about yourself!' Mrs Portman invited.

Chloe put down her cup, sat demurely upright in her chair, and prepared to tell whatever the lady might like to hear.

'So, I think the first thing is, are you fond of children? You'll agree that's important?'

Chloe opened her eyes wide, nodded her head.

'Absolutely, Mrs Portman. Of course I *adore* children. Why else would I have applied for the job?'

Why? Well if you knew Akersfield you'd know

just why! Without speaking, she turned her head and smiled in the direction of the children.

'Quite. But it's such a distance to come. All the way from the North of England to Brighton. Are you sure you won't be lonely, won't get homesick?'

Her husband had queried the wisdom of it when she'd written to offer an interview to a girl from the North.

'It's too far away,' he'd pointed out. 'She'll mope for the moors and all those mill chimneys. And she'll have a terrible accent. You'll have the kids speaking broadest Yorkshire in no time at all.'

'Not necessarily,' she'd told him. 'I had a friend at school from Bradford and she spoke perfect English. As good as yours or mine.'

'She would,' he'd countered. 'Yours was an expensive boarding school in Kent. This girl won't be like that.'

In fact, Mrs Portman thought, listening to Chloe, the girl's voice was quite pleasant. True, there *was* a Northern accent, but was that any worse than a London or a Brighton one? And the fact that she was a long way from home meant that she wouldn't be tempted to run back too quickly. Just as long as she didn't mope – and she didn't look a moper. She was far too bright.

'With three children to look after I won't have time to be lonely,' Chloe said virtuously. 'As for being homesick . . .' Her voice trailed off. How could she admit that homesickness was the last thing she'd suffer from. 'I think I shall feel at home here in Brighton. It seems a lovely place.'

'Well certainly *we* love it, the children, especially Janet and Robert like the beach, the rock pools. Of course they have to be watched.'

'Of course!'

'And we have a flat in London, because of my husband's job, that is. Sometimes we spend a week or so there. Would you like that?'

'I'd just love it,' Chloe said with complete truth.

Mrs Portman looked around the kitchen as if searching for inspiration, which she was. She was no good at this sort of thing. It embarrassed her, asking people personal questions. She wished Johnny had been at home. He always knew what to say.

'Well then,' she said, her eyes coming back to Chloe, 'that all seems satisfactory. And your vicar gives you a good reference.'

Which was a miracle in itself, Chloe reckoned, since they had never seen eye to eye and she had only ever gone to church under protest. He had no doubt done it for the sake of her mother, who was one of the pillars of St Mary-the-Virgin.

'Are you a churchgoer?' Mrs Portman asked.

'Oh yes!' Chloe replied, mentally crossing her fingers. Who knew, it might get her a few Sunday mornings off-duty?

'We aren't, not particularly, but of course I approve of it. I think we might suit each other, what do you think?'

'Oh, I'm *sure* we shall!' Chloe was all enthusiasm.

They discussed wages, and hours. Chloe accepted what was offered. Time enough to negotiate when she had made herself indispensable which, she thought, looking at Mrs Portman's tired face, wouldn't be all that long.

'Of course my husband will want to see you, but I'm sure he'll agree with me. So shall we say a month's trial?'

'Thank you, Mrs Portman,' Chloe said.

'My husband will be home this evening, though I never know quite when. Members of Parliament work strange hours.'

And what will *he* be like? Chloe wondered.

'Then I'll show you to your room. And could I have your ration book? And you'll have to register. It's a nuisance, isn't it? I hate rationing and it's worse since the war ended. You'd think it would be better, but my husband says we're feeding Europe now.'

Chloe, carrying her suitcase, followed Mrs Portman, who still held the baby. The other children continued to sit at the table, Janet watching Chloe closely as they left the kitchen. Mrs Portman led the way up the stairs, through the hall and up the main staircase. After the first flight, where the steps were wide and shallow, they became steeper and narrower and were less thickly carpeted. Mrs Portman stopped on the second floor.

'The children sleep in this room. At the moment Janet and Robert share a room. They'll be no trouble to you. Thank goodness they sleep through the night, except that poor Robert sometimes has bad dreams. The baby has his cot in our room on the floor below, but when he's stopped the night feed I want him to move out. And here's your room, right next to the children's.'

The two women stood in the doorway, surveying the room which was to be Chloe's. It was all right, Chloe supposed: a single bed with a coloured counterpane, a chest of drawers painted white, a wardrobe, a small dressing-table, a comfortable armchair: a faded flowered carpet on the floor and chintz curtains at the window. Except for a wireless set on the chest every surface was bare, the room was impersonal. I'll soon change that, Chloe thought. And at least she'd have the room to herself. No more sharing.

Mrs Portman crossed to the window and looked out.

'You have a nice view of the sea from here,' she said.

Chloe went over and stood beside her. There it was, blue and sparkling in the sun, white horses dancing in the breeze. And just think, at the far edge of the sea which was visible from her window lay France. She had never been abroad. She didn't know anyone who had, except to fight in the war, which didn't really count, but one day she would. Anything could happen now. The sea which stretched before her, whose boundaries were just beyond the horizon, was an invitation to adventure.

Mrs Portman broke in on her thoughts.

'I'll leave you to unpack then while I go and feed Eddie. Come down when you're ready.'

'I won't be long,' Chloe said.

She was soon unpacked. She had brought very few

clothes with her, they no more than half-filled the wardrobe, partly because she disliked what she had – every garment purchased in Akersfield had been a battle between herself and her mother whose taste in dress was, her daughter considered, dowdy and her feeling for fashion non-existent.

Chloe had not always won the battle because her mother held the purse strings.

Not to worry, she thought, putting her underwear away in the drawers. Now that she had landed the job – and all found, her wages simply pocket money – she would dip into her savings and buy a dress, or even a suit, in Brighton. It would be something plain and very well-cut which she could dress up as the mood took her. Thank goodness clothing coupons were no more!

She scrutinized herself in the dressing-table mirror. I'll get black, she thought, even though my hair *is* black, for which reason her mother had said it was a colour she should never wear because it offered no contrast, but Chloe knew that the skin of her face and neck was sufficient and indeed in striking contrast. Appraising herself in the mirror now, she happily acknowledged the creamy fairness of her skin, the uncommon colour of her eyes, the frame of her silky hair. There was no point in false modesty. She knew her good points. She took a lipstick from her handbag and filled in her curving wide mouth with its full, almost pouting underlip.

'You'll do,' she told her reflection. 'At least for the moment.'

She was not over-keen on the blue cotton dress

she was wearing, with its demure white collar, but it had seemed suitable for her interview. And she had not, she realized, discussed the question of whether she was expected to wear uniform, which if she was Mrs Portman would have to supply. Probably not. She wasn't a nanny, was she? On the other hand a becoming uniform could have great sex appeal. Look at nurses, and the way they were always marrying doctors.

She smoothed her eyebrows down with spit, and pinched them into shape, then gave a final tweak or two to her hair, arranging a few careless-looking curls to fall over her forehead, thus enhancing her eyes, and she was ready.

In the kitchen Mrs Portman was feeding the baby, quite unselfconsciously, her breast exposed and the baby sucking vigorously.

How primitive, Chloe thought. Even if I ever had children, which I won't, I would never breast-feed them. It was not that it embarrassed her, it was just – well – prehistoric. She tried not to look.

'I thought it might be nice if you took the children for a little walk before they get ready for bed,' Mrs Portman said. 'If they get some fresh air at this time they do sleep better, but it's not often I can manage it.'

'Of course!' Chloe said.

'Can we go on the beach?' Janet pleaded.

'Oh no. The tide's coming in. Just take them around the Square, Chloe, get your bearings. Robert can take his kiddie-car. He prefers that to walking.'

It was pleasant in the Square. The early evening

sun shone on the houses, turning their cream to gold. Such beautiful houses they were, dignified and well-proportioned, though it was evident by the number of bell-pushes outside the doors that many of them had been divided into flats. Robert pedalled furiously in his kiddie-car, though his progress was slow. Janet dawdled a yard or two behind, reluctant to take part in this walk.

'Hurry up, Janet!' Chloe said.

Janet kicked savagely at a pebble.

'I'm bored!'

'That won't do at all!' Chloe said. 'I don't allow little girls to be bored. Shall we play not treading in a nick?'

'What's that?' Janet said suspiciously.

'You mean you don't know? "Tread in a nick, you'll be buried under a brick".'

'What's a nick?'

'Really! It's the line between the flagstones. You can only walk on the stone.'

'It sounds stupid!' Janet said. Nevertheless she began to play the game, reciting the lines as she jumped from flagstone to flagstone.

'Will I be buried under a brick?' Robert enquired anxiously. 'I can't stop my kiddie-car going over the nicks.'

'No you won't,' Chloe assured him. 'It doesn't count with anything on wheels, only if you're walking, and never when you're only three years old.'

Chloe walked, Janet jumped and Robert rode around three sides of the Square and then around the crescent on to which the Square opened, until they were back at the door of Blenheim House.

When they entered the house Mrs Portman was coming down the stairs.

'Did you have a nice walk?' she enquired. 'I've just put Eddie to bed. He went out like a light.'

'We didn't tread in the nicks but it doesn't matter if you're riding a kiddie-car,' Robert volunteered. 'You won't be buried!'

Mrs Portman looked at Chloe.

'A game,' Chloe said. 'We used to play it when we were children.'

'I won,' Janet said. 'I didn't tread in any nicks, and I had to jump. Robert didn't.'

'You both won,' Chloe told them.

'That's fine then,' Mrs Portman said. 'Now Chloe's going to give you your baths and you might see Daddy before you go to bed.'

He had said that, barring some emergency in the House, he would be home for supper. He hadn't phoned, so presumably there were no emergencies which required his presence. He was, after all, not a minister but a backbencher, though an ambitious one who wanted to be around, wanted to be noticed at the right moment.

She went into the dining-room and began to lay the table. On the days, only too frequent, when her husband didn't arrive home for his evening meal she ate on her own in the kitchen. But that wouldn't do for Johnny. Johnny wanted everything to be correct, wanted his home life to run like clockwork no matter how hard pressed she was looking after the children since Nanny Bates had left. Keeping up standards, he called it, and since she loved him and wanted to please him she did her best.

She finished laying the table, looking with satisfaction at the silver arranged on the mahogany table. The cutlery was a family possession which her mother had handed on to her when she'd moved into her flat. She placed the damask napkins in their silver rings in position and then returned to the kitchen to prepare the meal. It was a pity the food wouldn't live up to the standard of the table-setting. What could one do with one-and-tuppence worth of meat each, to last the week? The butcher had saved her some small cutlets, two for John, one each for herself and Chloe. Not enough. She hoped that Chloe wasn't going to be difficult about food. She would eat *en famille*, except when they had one of their very rare dinner parties, because, well, a mother's help wasn't quite a servant these days, the world was changing fast. Also, she didn't like to think of the girl sitting down alone at the kitchen table.

It had been different with Nanny Bates. Nanny Bates was of the old school; she knew she was a servant, though on the highest rung, and she did not expect to be treated otherwise. In any case, when Nanny Bates had ruled there had also been a housekeeper, so the two of them ate together. It was a pity they had both left more or less at the same time.

Mrs Portman, when she had prepared the meal as far as she could, left the kitchen and went into the sitting-room to see that all was neat and tidy. She plumped up the cushions, tidied some magazines, then glanced out of the window in time to see a taxi drawing up outside and Johnny getting out, paying the driver. Her heart still leapt at the sight of him, as it had on the very first occasion she had set eyes on him. He had been the parliamentary candidate at the by-election in the village where her grandmother lived; she, following her grandmother's true blue example, had been on hand to help with his electoral campaign. In spite of the previous year's Labour landslide, he had held the safe seat with ease; after all he had fought honourably in the war, had been demobbed with the rank of captain; he was just what the party in opposition was looking for, and he would be a useful man when they came into power again. The fact that he was also tall, lithe, and quite handsome was no drawback either. They had married immediately after his election.

She watched him as he strode up the path to the door, then rushed to meet him in the hall.

'Darling, how lovely to see you, so early for a change,' she said.

'I know!' He kissed her. 'Are the children in bed?'

'Eddie is, and fast asleep. The other two are being bathed. I engaged the girl: Chloe.'

John Portman frowned.

'Was that wise? You know I wanted to see her first.'

'Don't worry! She's on a month's trial. Anyway, I'm sure you'll like her. Why don't you go up while I see to supper?'

He ran up the two flights of stairs and went into the bathroom.

Janet was out of the bath and drying herself. Chloe, enveloped in a large white apron, was on her knees with Robert in front of her, being dried with a large fluffy towel. The bathroom was steamy, the floor wet. Chloe's hair, which curled all the more when the atmosphere was damp, hung down over her forehead and clung around her neck in dark, twisted tendrils. Her cheeks were flushed with the heat and with the effort of bathing two small children who were as slippery as eels. It was not as easy as it looked.

As John Portman came into the room she looked up at him with wide eyes, then started to rise to her feet.

'Please don't get up,' he said. 'You must be Chloe. I'm John Portman.'

She was astonishingly beautiful. What was she doing here bathing his children?

He smiled at her. It was the smile which had won Moira's heart nearly seven years ago, and still did. He extended his hand.

'I'm pleased to meet you,' he said.

Chloe held out her hand. 'I'm sorry, I'm a bit damp!'

John Portman, MP. She had wondered what he would be like. She was not the least bit disappointed. Quite the reverse.

3

Janet gave a sudden twist away from Chloe, escaped the bath towel and flung herself at her father.

'Mummy made me go to school!' she complained loudly. 'I hate school! You tell Mummy I don't have to go to school – ever. Tell her!'

He picked her up, held her close, smiling at her furious little face, stroking her silky skin.

'What's all this about? I thought you liked school. You liked it last week. You even wanted to go on Saturday!'

'Well I don't like it any more! I hate it! I hate it!'

'So what happened, Princess?'

'It was carrots at dinnertime. Everybody knows I hate carrots. She made me eat them!'

'Mummy did?'

'No! I told you, it was school dinner. It was Miss Tempest. I hate Miss Tempest. I won't go to school tomorrow.'

'All children have to go to school,' John said. 'How would you grow up to be a clever girl if you

47

didn't go to school?' In his arms her face was on a level with his, a face full of defiance, pouting lips, angry eyes.

'Robert doesn't go to school!' she said.

'Of course not. You didn't when you were three. He'll go when he's old enough.'

'Tell Mummy she's not to take me.'

He put her down gently.

'Get into your pyjamas, Princess. I expect Chloe will take you to school tomorrow.'

Chloe, John thought, looking across at her. A beautiful name and it suited her. She was beautiful all right, but there was a hint of something deeper than that.

'I won't go! I won't go with Chloe!'

'Oh yes you will, my girl!' But because John Portman was there, and his daughter was clearly the light of his life, Chloe bit back the words which rose to her lips. All the same, the little minx would go; she will go if I have to drag her kicking and screaming, Chloe promised herself. This was a battle young Madam wouldn't win, but now was not the time to protest. With an effort, she smiled sweetly at Janet as she handed her her pyjamas.

Yet though Chloe had managed to say nothing, John Portman read her feelings. Her mouth had curved in a smile while at the same time her eyes sparked with anger. Did she realize how her dark eyes gave her away?

He felt a tug at his trouser leg and looked down to see Robert patiently waiting for his turn to be noticed. He hauled him up in his arms. It took no effort at all, the child was so lightweight. He never seemed to put on an ounce of flesh; he had none of the chubbiness of a three-year-old.

'So what about you, son?' John asked. 'What have you been doing with yourself?'

'I didn't fall down the nick, but you don't on a kiddie-car. Chloe said so.' The words rushed out of him.

John Portman looked at Chloe, raised his eyebrows in a question.

'It's just a game,' Chloe explained.

'Can we play it tomorrow?' Robert was eager.

'Of course!' Chloe promised.

John kissed his son, then put him down.

'Let me put your pyjamas on, Robert,' Chloe said.

'I can put on my own pyjamas,' Robert replied. 'I *am* three years old!'

'Of course! How silly of me!' Chloe apologized. Though she wasn't mad about children, Robert was a dear little boy. She'd have no trouble with *him*.

'You seem to have everything in hand,' John Portman said. 'I'll leave you to it, talk to you later.'

'A story, Daddy!' Janet demanded. 'A story!'

'When Chloe tells me you're tucked up in bed I'll come up and read you a story. What shall it be?'

'*Thomas the Tank Engine!*' Janet said.

'*James the Red Engine*,' Robert demanded.

'Very well,' their father agreed. 'I'll be back shortly.'

When he had gone Chloe saw the children through

their teeth-brushing operation, Robert compliant, Janet somehow imbuing every movement of the toothbrush with defiance. She tidied the bathroom then marshalled the children into their beds, where they each arranged a small army of stuffed toys around them.

'They take up more room than you do,' Chloe said.

'They have to be comfortable,' Robert said. 'They've got to get a good night's sleep or they'll be cross-patches in the morning.'

'Tell Daddy we're waiting,' Janet ordered.

'What's the magic word?' Chloe prompted.

'Abracadabra!' Robert said quickly.

Chloe laughed.

'It usually is, but this time it's "Please"!'

She was saved from a tussle with Janet by the sound of John Portman's tread on the stairs, and then he came into the room.

'We've got the books ready, Daddy!' Janet cried. 'One for me and one for Robert.'

John Portman grinned.

'I'll let you get away with it this once, but don't think I'm going to read two books every night, Princess!'

'You can't,' Janet retorted. 'Because you're not home every night, are you? Other people's Daddies are.'

She knew where to aim the blow, this five-year-old, John thought. He doubted whether either his wife or his children knew how much he cared about not being there for them when he was needed. And he *did* care.

He knew what he was missing. He knew that facets of his children's lives were missing from his because of the demands of his job. He also acknowledged, and had done so from the beginning to Moira, that he loved his job, could not help but be immersed in it, and that there was no job in the world he would rather have than that of being a Member of Parliament.

I'll stay and hear him read, Chloe decided. She obviously needed to know Thomas and James, neither of whom had so far entered her life. But it was not to be.

'My wife said, would you go downstairs. She'd like a hand.'

John Portman smiled pleasantly as he spoke which, Chloe thought, made the words more like a request than an order. She would have to learn to take orders, especially at first, but she would keep a sharp eye on just what she was ordered, or requested, to do. She was *not* here to do housework. Before going downstairs she went to her own room, took off her apron, changed her dress, combed her hair and brightened her mouth with lipstick. Perhaps her appearance would give the hint that she was now off-duty.

'Oh, there you are!' Mrs Portman said as Chloe entered the kitchen. 'Did everything go all right? I usually come up but there were things to do and in any case it's a treat for the children to have their father.'

'Quite all right. They were very good,' Chloe said smoothly. 'Mr Portman is reading them a story.'

'*Thomas the Tank Engine*, I've no doubt! I hope

you like Thomas. You'll certainly get a lot of him!'

'Oh, I do, very much!' Chloe said.

'Everything's about ready,' Mrs Portman said. 'Will you take in the cheese and put it on the sideboard and then you can dish up the vegetables while I finish off the cutlets.'

I suppose, Chloe considered, that's reasonable, as I *am* to eat with them. She would, however – should she ever be asked – draw the line at taking part in the cooking. About washing-up she would reserve her opinion, see what Mrs Portman suggested. She might lend a hand, but no way would she do it every evening. Start as you mean to go on!

Carrying the cheeseboard, on which rested one minute piece of cheddar, into the dining-room, she caught her breath at the sight of the table. It was so elegant, everything laid out with such precision. Most women, considering the small amount of food which would grace the table, wouldn't have gone to the trouble, but Chloe thought Mrs Portman had the right idea. However meagre or monotonous the food might be, it couldn't but taste better in such a setting.

There was a wine glass at each place, including that which must be hers. She had never, ever drunk wine with a meal, and seldom on any other occasion either. Her family was as near teetotal as made no difference, though a glass of sweet sherry, obtained from where, no-one asked, had been served after her father's funeral for those who chose to partake. Otherwise it was water on the table at mealtimes and a bottle of ginger wine at Christmas.

She returned to the kitchen. At Mrs Portman's request, she drained the potatoes and was transferring them to the tureen when John Portman popped his head around the door.

'Nearly ready darling? I'm starving!'

'Just about, Johnny,' his wife said. 'Take the potatoes in, Chloe. Oh, I sometimes think I'll splurge the whole of my butter ration on a dish of potatoes, and eat dry bread for a week! Don't they look naked without butter on them? How I loathe and detest rationing!'

She arranged the small cutlets on a dish, and walked into the dining-room behind Chloe. John Portman took his place at the head of the table, with his wife and Chloe on either side of him. He poured a half glass of wine for his wife.

'What would we do without the wine your mother left behind for us?' he asked his wife. 'But we must go carefully with it. There's not that much left.'

'You did say wine was beginning to come in from France,' Moira said.

'It is, but in no great quantities, yet.' He turned to Chloe. 'Do you like red wine, Chloe?'

'Oh, yes!' Chloe said firmly. 'Thank you.'

She was enjoying this. She felt as if to the manor born. She raised the glass to her lips and took a generous sip, then quickly suppressed a shudder. It was awful! So strong and sharp, so incredibly rough on the edges of her tongue. But if this was the thing to drink, and by the reverential look on the faces of her employers as they sipped it she could tell it was, then she would just make herself get used to it. Like it she never would, but no-one need know that.

She hates it, John Portman thought, observing her shudder. Poor kid, she's probably never tasted it before.

Mr and Mrs Portman conversed easily over the meal, which they ate in a leisurely fashion. Am I supposed to join in, Chloe wondered, or should I wait until I'm spoken to? She did not have long to wait.

'And did you have a good journey from Akersfield?' John Portman enquired.

'Very good, thank you.'

'And how did you get on, crossing London?'

'I took a taxi from King's Cross to Victoria,' Chloe said. 'It was expensive, but I've never been on the underground and I wasn't at all sure which bus to get. There were so many.' She would say nothing of Mr Hendon's generosity. It might not go down too well.

'Quite right,' John Portman said. 'And we will reimburse you. London is not the place for a young lady who doesn't know it to be wandering around.' Especially one who looks like you, he could have said. The wine had quickly brought a flush to her cheeks and she looked lovelier than ever. He had intended to use the dinnertime to interview her, politely of course, and informally, just asking a few questions, but as she looked at him – she had such a direct look – the questions went out of his head.

'We shall go to London for the Queen's Coronation next year,' Mrs Portman said, changing the subject.

Chloe opened her eyes wide, caught in amazement. There were very few occasions on which she couldn't hide her feelings, but this was not one of them.

'The Coronation? Do you mean . . .' She hesitated. 'Oh, Mrs Portman, do you mean we shall *all* go?'

'Why, certainly Chloe. I wouldn't dream of allowing the children to miss it. I hope it will be something they'll remember for the rest of their lives.'

'As *you* will, Chloe,' John Portman smiled at her. 'Indeed, we all will! We have a young Queen now. She'll reign for a long time, as Victoria did. And with the war behind us, and we the winners, we have a golden future.'

As always, he looked forward with confidence, and in his all-embracing optimism he saw no reason why this girl, sitting at his table, would not be part of that future just as long as the children needed her. After little more than an hour's acquaintance he felt sure she would pass her month's trial with flying colours.

'Of *course* you will go with us,' Mrs Portman said kindly. 'I'll need you there to help with the children. I daresay Mr Portman and I will have some social obligations, it will be a busy few days, but I'll see you have some time to yourself.'

'We might give a party ourselves,' John Portman suggested. 'What do you think, Moira?'

'I think it's a long time ahead. But if we *are* to do it then we must arrange it in good time. Everyone will be choc-a-bloc with invitations. And there'll be the caterers to think of. We can't possibly raise enough food to do it ourselves. It's not too soon to book them.'

Chloe listened as they became caught up in suggestions: who they would invite, whether it would be held in London or whether they'd return to Brighton for it.

'London, I think,' John Portman said. 'We've so many friends there.' He would also wish to invite one or two influential people from the House.

'We've lots of friends in Brighton. Perhaps we could have two parties? If we could get the food, that is.' Moira Portman preferred Brighton. People in the Arts, of which Brighton had more than its fair share, were more fun than politicians.

'That would cost a lot. But then it *is* a special occasion. I suppose we could push the boat out.'

If he had to rely on his parliamentary salary as some members, particularly the Opposition ones, did, it would be impossible. Fortunately, that was not the case. He had his own income from the family business, a chain of medium-sized hotels, mostly in the south-west but now expanding, and picking up real business since the end of the war in which most of them had been commandeered by the government. He was a director, but the day-to-day running now fell to his father and his two brothers. Should the worst happen, should he one day lose his seat in the House, he had a secure bolt hole.

He saw it as the most unlikely thing in the world that he would ever run to it, for even if – and heaven forbid such a happening – his party should fall from power, he would be there on the Opposition benches, and hopefully on the front bench.

Mrs Portman served the cheese.

'It looks so meagre!' she apologized. 'The French cheeses are coming back, but I missed them this week. You have to be up at the crack of dawn to get things. I think I'd sell my soul for a piece of Camembert!'

It was awful the way her mind was always running on food. Doubtless it was something to do with the fact that she was feeding the baby. It was what she wanted to do, she would not give it up until she had to, but some days she felt that all her strength was being sucked out of her.

She finished her cheese to the last crumb, as did her husband and Chloe, then pushed her plate away.

'We don't have to wash the dishes,' she said to Chloe. 'Mrs Wilkins will do all that in the morning, thank goodness.'

Thank goodness indeed, Chloe thought. So what was she to do now? Go to her room, probably; but she didn't fancy that, it was still early, still daylight.

'Feel free to go for a walk if you want to,' Mrs Portman said. 'I'll go up and look in on the children. I expect they'll be fast asleep.' She turned to her husband. 'You weren't wanting to go for a walk, were you?'

He shook his head.

'You know I'd love to, darling. I've brought papers home to deal with. That's the price of getting away early.'

'It doesn't matter,' Moira said. She was far too tired to go for a walk. Bed was what she craved. Bed and sleep. And when they went to bed John would want to make love to her, and she was also too tired for that.

'I would like to go for a walk,' Chloe said. 'Perhaps I'll go on the beach.'

'The tide's in,' John Portman told her.

'Oh! Then I'll walk along the promenade and look at the sea.'

'Do that,' Mrs Portman said. 'Don't be too late, will you? It drops dark quite quickly and you don't know your way around yet.'

'I'll be back soon,' Chloe assured her. She hoped Mrs Portman wasn't going to keep tabs on her, wasn't going to treat her like a child, because she wasn't one, and she'd not allow it. But softly, softly. Everything in good time.

She left the house a few minutes later, a pale pink cardigan slung around her shoulders in case the evening should grow cool. Cardigans were the thing in Akersfield – her mother had them to match every dress, all hand-knitted – but she wasn't sure that they were right for Brighton. She would find out.

She walked to the bottom of the Square and around Lewes Crescent, then crossed the road to the sea. There she stood, debating which way to go. To the right lay Brighton, the beautiful seafront houses, the Palace Pier. To the left the land on the seaward side sloped slightly upwards to green cliff tops. She decided to go left. Although Brighton beckoned, she would save it until she had more time to explore its delights, which she was sure were there for the taking.

She walked to the highest part of the cliffs, then sat down on the close-cropped grass, her hands clasped around her knees.

Oh, but it was so beautiful! The sea was so wide, and on this early summer evening reasonably calm, though with the tide at its height she could hear the waves breaking against the foot of the cliffs far below. Seagulls whirled and dived and circled close in to the shore, calling with raucous, painful cries like souls in distress.

Out away from the shore there were fishing boats and, though not making much progress because there wasn't enough breeze, she also saw two white-sailed yachts.

To her left the cliffs continued into the distance, now dipping into a small valley, then climbing higher again. Where the land curved, the chalk faces of the cliffs were visible, gleaming white when she first sat down, but now becoming tinged with pink as the sun started sinking.

She turned her head to look towards Brighton. The sun was a red ball now, dipping in the sky, with the Palace Pier silhouetted against it. When it finally dropped below the horizon the sky was a sheet of flame – orange, red, purple, mauve – and on the pier and around the curve of the coast to the west the lights came on, a few at first, then more and more until the whole scene resembled a string of jewels against a now almost dark sky. She was amazed at the speed with which the light had faded.

In the North of England the days had lingered on in a long twilight, reluctant to give way to the night.

She rose to her feet, feeling the dampness of the grass against her body, and began to walk back towards Sussex Square. When she reached Lewes Crescent she stood for a moment, looking towards Brighton, before crossing the road. Tomorrow, somehow, she would get to Brighton. It looked so exciting, its bright lights so inviting.

It was quite dark when she reached Blenheim House. When she rang the bell John Portman opened the door.

'Ah, there you are! I was beginning to wonder what had happened to you!'

'I'm sorry, Mr Portman. Was I too long? I didn't know the time – my watch has stopped.'

'That's all right, Chloe.'

She stepped into the hall and he closed the door behind her.

'I think I sat too long on the cliff top,' she said. 'It was so beautiful.'

'It is,' he agreed. 'I often walk in that direction – when I have time, that is.'

They were still standing in the hall. Where do I go now? Chloe asked herself. Do I go to my room, or what?

'Come into the sitting-room for a minute,' John Portman said. 'There are one or two questions I'd like to ask you. My wife has gone upstairs to see to the baby.'

She followed him into the sitting-room. It was, by her standards, a big room, furnished with comfortable-looking armchairs whose floral chintz covers had seen better days. The large window looked out to the Square's substantial gardens.

'This is where we spend most of our time,' John Portman said. 'It's cosy, doesn't take too much heating. The drawing-room, which is on the first floor, is very large, very beautiful, and like an ice-box in winter. We don't use it a great deal but when my wife's parents lived here they used to entertain a lot.'

'This is a lovely room,' Chloe said. 'It's nice to look across to the gardens. Can anyone go into the gardens?'

'No. There's a key. You have to be a resident, pay a few pounds a year. People moan about what they have to pay, though we don't. It's such a safe, handy place to take the children. Now do sit down.'

She sat on the edge of a low armchair, and he took a seat opposite her. She looked up at him expectantly.

'What did you want to ask me, Sir?'

She managed to sound apprehensive and just a little fearful, so that he instantly felt sorry for her.

'Nothing much,' he assured her. 'Nothing to worry about. In fact I expect my wife has asked you all the questions. Have you looked after children before, then?'

'Not as a job, not as a *paid* job, that is.' Her eyes were wide with honesty. 'But of course I have a younger sister, and then there are cousins and so on. And I am *very* fond of children, which I think counts for a lot. I hope you agree, Mr Portman.'

'Oh I do, I do! And do you think you'll be happy here? Will you settle?'

'Oh I will! I'm sure of it!'

About that she could be quite honest. She liked what she had seen so far. She looked forward to staying here quite a while, but if things didn't turn out right, she'd move on!

'Well, then.'

He smiled at her. She was susceptible – well, perhaps not exactly susceptible, but she appreciated smiles, and John Portman's was one of the best, equal to that of Charles Hendon on the train.

Chloe returned his smile. She had a nice line in smiles herself. She remembered that her grandmother had said, when Chloe was a little girl, 'That child's smile would fetch the ducks off the water and the birds from the trees'. She had not understood what her grandmother meant. She had tried smiling at the ducks on the lake in Akersfield Memorial Park, but with no effect whatever. Since then, however, she had learned something of the power of her smile. She knew now what her grandmother had meant.

'Well, then!' John Portman repeated. 'That all seems satisfactory and I hope you'll be very happy here!'

Chloe rose to her feet.

'Then if you think Mrs Portman doesn't need me for anything, I'll go to my room.'

In the bedroom, Moira Portman looked down at her baby. He looked so small in the large cot in which she herself had slept as a baby. He was well away now, with the pallor of a young baby in a deep sleep. She pulled the coverlet over his shoulders, touched his cheek gently, then turned away.

Crossing the room, she caught sight of herself in the mirror, and stopped short. What a mess you look, she thought crossly. She absolutely must do something about her hair – perhaps now that she would have time to visit the hairdresser she would have it cut, re-styled. And her skin was dull, free of the make-up which might have given it life. She must pull herself together. Staring at herself critically in the long mirror she acknowledged that basically she was all right, it was just that she had let herself go. But she had not lost her figure. She remained trim and slim, in spite of having borne three children in less than six years. Oh well!

As she left the room she met Chloe on the landing.

'I was going up to my room,' Chloe said. 'Do you want me for anything?'

'I don't think so,' Mrs Portman said. 'You might look in on the children before you go to bed. I did so half-an-hour ago but sometimes they throw the bedclothes off, especially Robert.'

'I'll do that,' Chloe said.

In the bedroom she stopped briefly to check on the children. Both were fast asleep, Janet smooth-faced, rosy, her dark lashes splayed against her perfect skin. She's a pretty child, Chloe admitted. Robert, even in sleep, looked worried, restless. Was he having a bad dream? Chloe wondered.

She went back to her own room. Before getting

into bed she, too, studied herself in the mirror but, unlike her employer, she was reasonably satisfied with what she saw. She gave herself a wide smile and her reflection smiled back at her. So far, so good!

She jumped into bed, put out the light, and lay there thinking of what she would do next day until, quite quickly, sleep claimed her.

4

Without opening her eyes Chloe reached out to silence the alarm bell which had disturbed her. Her hand encountered, not the round, chunky clock with the oversized bell on top which for the last two years had called her to get up and face another day in the Borough Surveyor's office, but a much smaller, square affair on which her fingers refused to locate the switch which would cut off the unwelcome sound.

Where was she? Was she still dreaming? Reluctantly, she opened her eyes and was met by the sight of the unfamiliar room. It took a confused second or two, in which she lay back on her pillow, to realize that she was in Blenheim House, Sussex Square, Brighton. She sat bolt upright, picked up the clock from the bedside table and silenced its din.

Seven o'clock? She could do with at least two more hours' sleep, she always could, but it was impossible. Mrs Portman had laid out the timetable last night: rouse the children, see them through washing and dressing, give them breakfast – cornflakes and toast – take Janet to school.

She got out of bed, stretched and yawned, then crossed to the window and looked out. Yes, the scene was every bit as lovely as it had been yesterday evening; more so in fact, since the back of the house faced east and everything was now bathed in the morning sun. She located the cliff top where she had sat the previous evening, noted a man walking his dog there, then she turned back into the room.

There were no surprises from the children. Robert was compliant, Janet was truculent, but somehow she urged them through their dressing and accompanied them downstairs. Mrs Portman was in the kitchen but there was no sign either of the baby or Mr Portman.

'Where's Daddy?' Janet demanded. 'I want to see Daddy!'

'Where's Eddie?' Robert wanted to know.

'Daddy's getting ready to go to London. You'll see him for a minute before you go to school,' Mrs Portman promised. 'Eddie, I'm pleased to say, is fast asleep, which is more than he has been for most of the night.'

She was deathly tired. All she wanted was for everyone to leave the house and to go back to bed and sleep and sleep. Of course that was quite impossible. Eddie would waken. He'd have to be changed and fed. Any minute now Mrs Wilkins would arrive, and though Moira was glad to have help in the house, Mrs Wilkins had to be talked to, listened to. Especially she had to be listened to, with her long recitals of the vagaries of Mr Wilkins and their brood of five children. Once, visiting the Wilkins's small house in Kemp Town, when Mrs Wilkins had been temporarily out of action with a poisoned foot, Moira had met the children. Every inch of the tiny living room was filled by them and by their possessions, strewn everywhere, but there was no denying that the chief impression of the Wilkinses was that they were a healthy, happy, bright lot, and that Mrs Wilkins, her bandaged foot propped up on a stool, was in command.

So why do I, with three children plus help, find it so hard, Moira had asked herself – and still did.

As if summoned by thought, there was a knock on the door, followed by Mrs Wilkins's entrance. She wore a flowered scarf, tied turbanwise around her head, and carried a brown paper carrier bag. Every woman in the land, sick to death of them, had abandoned turbans. Not so Mrs Wilkins, though she did ring the changes by having several scarves.

'Good morning all,' she said. 'And how's everyone this morning?'

'I think the baby is cutting a tooth,' Mrs Portman said. 'He's too young, but I think that's what it is, poor mite.'

'Well, my Alfie had two teeth when he was only three months old! Enough to spear a pickled onion, my hubby said!' She laughed heartily at the thought.

And a full set at a year, I wouldn't wonder, Moira Portman thought. All popping through his gums without inconvenience either to himself or to anyone else.

'Like pearls, his teeth was!' Mrs Wilkins mused.

Janet looked up from her breakfast, spoke up in a crystal-clear voice to her mother.

'If Eddie cuts a tooth he'll bite your titty! You'll bleed!'

Chloe hid her mouth behind her hand, tried not to smile.

'Tut, tut, tut!' Mrs Wilkins said.

'I don't want you to bleed, Mummy!' Robert wailed. 'I don't want him to bite you!'

'It's all right, my darling!' his mother assured him. 'I won't let him!' She turned to Janet. 'And that is not a word polite little girls use! Where did you learn it?'

'What word, Mummy?' Janet was all innocence.

'You know!'

'Titty,' Janet said. 'Titty, titty, titty! Peggy told me. She knows lots of words. She knows . . .'

'That will be quite enough,' Mrs Portman interrupted. 'Finish your breakfast. It's time you were setting off for school.'

Mrs Wilkins, taking her pinafore out of the carrier bag, tying it around her, sniffed. It was what came of sending children to private schools. You paid good money to have them learn bad language.

'I'll see to Robert while you take Janet,' Mrs Portman said to Chloe. 'It's not more than ten minutes away, but it takes double that for Robert.'

'I won't go to school 'til I've seen Daddy!' Janet said.

Mrs Portman was spared an argument with her daughter because at that moment her husband came into the kitchen. Chloe lifted her head and smiled at him. How wonderful he looked in his dark suit, his immaculate white shirt, with his hair – a rich, golden brown, ever so slightly curly, and perfectly cut by his London barber. His own smile took in everyone in the room.

'Good-morning!' he said pleasantly, taking his seat at the table.

'I know a new word!' Janet announced.

'Janet!' Moira warned.

'Titty!' Janet declared. 'Titty! It means . . .'

Mrs Wilkins, about to leave the room to pursue her duties elsewhere in the house, paused.

'Thank you, Janet,' Moira Portman said. 'We all know what it means. Get down and go and wash your hands!'

Wash your mouth more like, Mrs Wilkins thought.

'Well what *am* I supposed to call it when you feed the baby?' Janet asked. 'Miss Tempest says everything has a name. Everything in the world!'

Moira looked at her husband but he refused to meet her eyes.

'What word?' Janet persisted.

'Well . . . bosom,' Moira said.

'Chest,' Mrs Wilkins said firmly. 'Chest! And I can't stay here talking all day. There's work to be done!'

'Quite right!' John Portman called after Mrs Wilkins's retreating figure. 'And that goes for you, young lady,' he said, turning to Janet. 'Give me a kiss, and then off to school with you or you'll be late. And don't forget, you have a special duty this morning, you have to show Chloe the way.'

Chloe stood up and moved away from the table, ready to leave with Janet. Janet remained stubbornly seated until her father abandoned his breakfast, lifted her bodily from her chair, gave her a kiss, pointed her in the direction of the door and gave her a small shove.

'Off you go, and no more nonsense! Otherwise you'll go straight to bed the minute you get home from school!'

All very well, Moira thought, but you'll not be here to carry it out.

'Wear your blazer,' she called after Janet. 'And don't leave it behind when you come home.'

Janet, it seemed to Chloe as they left the house and set off for school, had taken a vow of silence. She refused to speak, even to answer a question. Fortunately, Mrs Portman had told Chloe how to get to the school. It was quite straightforward, impossible to get lost.

'When I was a little girl,' Chloe said conversationally as they crossed the Square, 'I used to decide not to speak to anyone for a whole day.'

It was quite true. That much she had in common with Janet. It had been quite an effective weapon, had driven her mother mad.

'On the other hand,' she continued, 'I did know a girl who didn't speak for two whole days. She pretended she was a horse, so she could neigh and whinny, but she didn't speak a single word . . .'

Janet, with tightly closed lips, looked up at Chloe.

'You're wondering what happened?' Chloe said.

'But you can't ask, can you? Well, I'll tell you. At the end of two silent days, not a word spoken, she went to bed and when she awoke in the morning she'd lost her voice altogether, couldn't speak at all!'

It was a neat little story, Chloe thought. Not true, of course, but she could tell by the expression on Janet's face that she didn't know what to believe. She pressed home the point.

'It happens all the time. Think of all those people in fairy stories, and in the bible, who were struck dumb! I wouldn't care to risk it myself!'

They were at the school now. It was housed in a handsome double-fronted building. Chloe took Janet into the entrance hall, which was crowded with small boys and girls, with two teachers in attendance.

'Good-bye Janet!' Chloe said pleasantly. 'I'll be back for you at three o'clock. I do hope you'll have found your voice by then.'

Janet faced Chloe squarely, gave her a venomous look, then opened her mouth and uttered at the top of her voice, 'Titty!'

There was a sudden silence, of which Janet made full use.

'And *bum*! Titty and bum!'

When Chloe reached Blenheim House there was a taxi drawn up at the kerbside and Mr Portman was just leaving the house. He stopped to speak to her.

'How did you get on with my daughter?' he asked. 'No problems, I hope?'

'No problems at all!' Chloe said. She had no intention of telling him, or anyone else, about Janet.

That was a relationship she would sort out for herself. And sort it out she would.

'I thought so! She's a nice little girl, really. A wee bit headstrong, but a nice child. And I'm sure you'll know how to deal with her!'

Chloe treated him to a dazzling smile, combined with a gentle, almost demure voice.

'Oh, I will, Mr Portman! I'm sure I will!'

'Well, I must be off,' he said. 'Don't want to miss my train!'

He sat back in the taxi, looking forward with pleasure to the day ahead. Sometimes he almost felt guilty about the alacrity with which he left his home each morning and the speed with which he was able to put out of his mind all that he had left behind there, concentrate on what awaited him in the House. He felt guilty because he knew Moira was finding things difficult. She hadn't seemed to get over Eddie's birth as quickly as she had the other two. But she'll be all right now that she's got the new girl, he thought. Chloe. I do believe Chloe will be exactly what they all need, he told himself, all of them.

He was still thinking of Chloe when he boarded the Brighton Belle, returned the attendant's greeting, took his usual seat in the usual first-class carriage.

'You look mighty pleased with life,' his usual friend in *his* usual seat remarked.

'Why not?' John said. 'The sun's shining, the sea's sparkling blue. Why not?'

He settled back in his seat and opened his *Times*.

It was going to be a good day, he could feel it in his bones.

By the time the Brighton Belle had reached Victoria Eddie had wakened, been changed and fed, and was about to have his morning bath.

'I knew he wouldn't sleep long,' Mrs Portman said. 'It was too good to be true. I never knew a baby need so little sleep.'

Holding Eddie, she sat down on the low nursing chair, the papier mâché baby bath on the floor in front of her, a toilet stand with all the paraphernalia of infant bathtime – soap, flannel, cotton-wool, lotions, ointment, scissors – to hand. On the brass rail of the nursery fireguard, the same one which formed part of her own very earliest memories, hung clean towels, napkins, pristine tiny garments, at present being warmed by the gas fire, turned low. Robert sat on the floor, quietly playing with a Dinky car.

Mrs Wilkins stood at the table, ironing the children's clothes, banging the iron down with unnecessary but impressive force. She would let it be known, and before too long, that ironing the kiddies' clothes was not, and never had been, part of her duties. She had done it only to oblige Mrs P while she had no other help. Now that there was a mother's help *she* must take it over. Chloe, she thought. What a silly name! Who would christen a little baby 'Chloe'? She gave a long, hard look in the girl's direction, followed by an extra thump with the iron. Chloe received the message and understood, and at once occupied herself re-arranging the clothes on the fireguard.

'Perhaps *you* would like to bath Eddie, Chloe?'

Mrs Portman made the suggestion in the pleasantest of voices. In four months she had grown so used to doing everything for the baby that she had overlooked that there was now no need to do so, though in fact, bathing Eddie and feeding him were the two tasks she enjoyed most, the ones which gave her deep satisfaction.

'Oh! Well . . .!' Chloe was politely hesitant. 'Of course I'd just love to, he's so sweet. But to be fair to Eddie it might be better if he got used to me for a day or two. That is, if you agree?'

She had never bathed a baby in her life. She supposed she must have seen her mother do it to Marilyn, but she didn't remember. She would hardly know which bit to start with, which end to do first. Added to which, she was terrified she might drop him.

'That sounds sensible,' Moira Portman agreed.

'But I'd just love to be here while you do it,' Chloe said. 'I'd like him to get used to me.'

She would watch every move Mrs Portman made. I am, after all, she thought, a quick learner. If I can persuade her to do it for the next day or two I'll learn all about it.

She stood close by while Mrs Portman gently lowered the baby into the shallow bath, supporting his shoulders and head against her arm. She watched while the mother washed and dried the baby's face – no soap for that, she noted, then soaped his front, washing his incredibly tiny feet, and finally lowered him backwards and washed his hair, at which he cried, briefly. It was clearly just a matter of routine.

'Pass me a warm towel,' Mrs Portman said, lifting the baby out of the water.

Mrs Wilkins slowed down her ironing, watched Chloe as Chloe herself watched her employer's every move. Miss Toffee-Nosed Chloe doesn't know how to bath a baby, she thought suddenly. That's easy to tell. There was something fishy here!

Mrs Portman laid the baby on the fluffy towel and patted him dry. Happily contented now he gurgled and spluttered, and vigorously kicked his legs. 'Who's a strong little boy then?' his mother asked. She chucked him under the chin then gently ran her fingertip around the curves of his round, plump cheeks. She loved her children at this age, even if they did keep her awake at night. Of course I love them at any age, she thought guiltily. Robert was no trouble, except that the poor lamb was so timid, but with Janet she seemed to have lost control. It was no doubt a phase the child was going through, but how long would that awful phase last?

When she had dressed Eddie she enveloped him in a shawl, from which he immediately freed his hands to wave them in the air.

'Now he can go in his pram in the garden,' Mrs Portman said. 'He should sleep for a while, which will give you time to do a few little routine jobs.'

And what will *those* be, Chloe wondered, following Mrs Portman out into the garden. It was not the large communal garden to which one had to use a key; this one was at the back of the house, behind high walls, up which roses, the buds showing pink, red, white, climbed. It was small in size, not nearly as spacious as the Branksomes' garden in Akersfield, but still quite pleasant.

'We'll put his pram under the greengage tree, in the shade,' Mrs Portman said. 'Do you like greengages? We usually get a good crop.'

'I like greengage jam,' Chloe said.

'Well you'll certainly get plenty of that!'

When she had tucked her son into his pram Moira stood and looked at him, then she gently rocked the pram and in a minute or two he was fast asleep.

'Now,' she said, turning to Chloe, 'what next? Well, normally at this time you would wash through those of the children's clothes which don't go to the laundry. There are always some, especially baby things. Mrs Wilkins has been doing it so far, and she'll continue to do the nappies.'

Thank heaven for that, Chloe thought. Anything as gruesome as nappies had not entered her head.

'For today I think it would be a good idea if you were to take Robert for a walk. He'd enjoy that.'

'Could we go on the beach?' Chloe asked.

A frown creased Mrs Portman's forehead.

'I think not,' she said. 'You see, Janet would be rather disappointed if she missed the beach.' That was putting it mildly. There would be hell to pay. 'Perhaps you might take them both on the beach after school,' she suggested. 'For the moment take Robert somewhere close, maybe in the gardens.'

'Want to play ball?' Robert asked.

'We'll do that,' Chloe promised. 'Just give me five minutes. Oh, there was one other thing, Mrs Portman . . .' she hesitated.

'Yes.'

'Well – and I hope you won't think I'm cheeky – but you did say I could have two hours off a day, as well as my full day. When would you like me to take them?' There was no way she was going to give up her rights even for one day. Do it once and it was the thin end of the wedge.

'Of course! I'd overlooked it. It needn't always be at the same time. We could vary it. Today, would you like to take it straight after supper. Or if you like you could have tea with the children then you'd be free as soon as they were in bed.'

Do I want to have tea with the children? Chloe asked herself. Do I want to miss supper at that elegant table? Do I want to pass up the chance of Mr Portman's company? The answer to all three questions was 'No'.

'I think it might be better if I waited until after supper,' she said kindly. 'Then I could give you a hand.'

'Very well,' Mrs Portman said. She didn't particularly want to eat with Chloe every evening. She was a nice enough child, quite pleasant and seemingly willing, but I would rather have John to myself, she thought.

The gate to the gardens was almost opposite Blenheim House. Chloe felt quite important turning the key and letting herself in, being careful to lock it behind her. Robert stood close beside her, clutching a large, multi-coloured ball to his chest.

'Where shall we go?' Chloe asked him.

There was a wide area of well-kept lawn with several shrubs, some of them in flower, and a few small trees. The trees and shrubs had been bent and shaped by the prevailing wind so that they looked as though they had been sliced along their tops into a regular pattern, low at one end, higher at the other. There were several benches in the garden, placed in strategic positions, some sheltered, some facing the sea, others back to the sea and the main road to Brighton which bordered the gardens on the south side. A few of the benches were occupied, mostly by one person, as though the residents preferred to keep themselves to themselves rather than to congregate. There were, at the moment, no other children, but it was still early, perhaps they would arrive later. Or perhaps the residents didn't bring children into the garden.

'I'll sit on a bench and you can throw the ball to me and I'll throw it back,' Chloe said to Robert. 'Which bench shall I choose?'

'Down at the bottom.' It was a firm decision.

'Why?'

'It's near the road. I can see the cars. I like watching cars best.'

'Very well,' Chloe said, 'but we must be careful throwing the ball. If it goes into the road I expect we'll lose it.'

Between them they chose a seat which was close to the road but protected by a bed of shrubs. Chloe sat down, having positioned Robert a dozen yards away, and they began to throw the ball back and forth to each other. It did not go well. When Chloe threw the ball to Robert he could seldom catch it; when he returned it to her he was wildly erratic so that most times she had to leave her seat to retrieve it. For Chloe, it quickly became boring.

'He'll never play for Sussex, that's for sure!'

Chloe looked up at the sound of the voice – she had not known that there was anyone near – and saw a girl walking across the lawn towards her, a girl of about her own age who held the hand of a boy only a little older than Robert.

'You're right!' Chloe said. 'I don't think his heart's in it. He'd rather watch the cars.'

'Same with this one,' the girl said. 'So why don't I sit with you and we'll take it easy while these two watch the traffic to their heart's content?'

She suited her actions to her words and came and sat beside Chloe on the bench.

'This is Peter,' she said. 'He's nearly four years old. I look after him in the daytime because his mother's what she calls a professional woman. She gives piano lessons. She lives at Walmer House but I don't live in. My name's Josie, short for Josephine, of course. What about you?'

'I'm Chloe, and this is Robert. He's just gone three. His family live at Blenheim House. I do live in. I only arrived in Brighton yesterday.'

Less than twenty-four hours in the place, she thought with satisfaction, and already I'm meeting people.

'I thought you didn't come from round here,' Josie said. 'You sound different. Have you been in service before?'

'I'm not in service,' Chloe said stiffly. 'I'm a mother's help. Well, more of a companion-help, I suppose you'd call me. I was a personal assistant to quite an important man before I came here.'

In two short sentences she promoted herself in both jobs.

'So why did you leave him?' Chloe was soon to learn that when Josie wanted to know, she asked.

'I wanted a change of scene,' she said truthfully. 'Of course I don't intend to be a mother's help – companion-help – forever. I shall do better.'

'Me too! I definitely intend to marry a rich man and be kept in comfort for the rest of my life! I'll be a good wife, of course. He'll have no cause to complain, whoever he is.'

I want to be rich, Chloe thought, but I don't want to be married. All the marriages she had seen so far seemed exceedingly dull. In addition, she was not keen on domesticity, or even children, come to that, though Robert was all right, standing there at the moment with his new-found friend, the two of them watching the traffic, both of them reeling off the makes of every car which passed.

'What do you do in your time off?' Josie enquired.

'I haven't had any yet,' Chloe said. 'But I'm off this evening. I thought I'd go into Brighton.'

'Would you like me to show you around?' Josie offered. 'We could go on the pier.'

'Thank you! I'd like that.' The Palace Pier,

which she could see from where she sat, looked so enticing.

'The Palace Pier is the best one,' Josie said. 'There's more going on.'

'I watched the cars with Peter,' Robert announced as they sat at lunch, he, his mother, and Chloe. They were eating in the garden of Blenheim House where a small table had been set up under the greengage tree. The day was hot, the sun at its zenith, but under the greengage tree, thick with summer foliage, there was shade.

'Peter? Who is Peter?' Moira Portman asked. 'And where were you watching the traffic?' She turned to Chloe. 'I thought you were in the gardens, playing ball.'

'Oh, we were, Mrs Portman,' Chloe said. 'We played ball for quite a time. Robert was very good at it. But when Peter came the two boys wanted to watch the traffic. We didn't leave the gardens.'

'I'm pleased to hear that,' Mrs Portman said. 'The traffic on the coast road is quite dangerous. I wouldn't want Robert to be standing on the pavement there.'

'Peter knows *all* the cars,' Robert said. 'He knows more than I do,' he added generously.

'You haven't yet told me who Peter is!'

Robert looked to Chloe. All *he* knew was that Peter had appeared. It had been fun, much better than ball games.

Chloe explained.

'I don't know his last name, nor Josie's; only that

he lives in the Square and his mother teaches music. They live at Walmer House.'

'Oh yes, I think I know,' Mrs Portman said. 'They haven't lived here long and I rather think she's French. I didn't know she had children.'

'He seems a nice little boy,' Chloe said; not that she had taken much notice of him.

'Then we must ask him to tea,' Mrs Portman said to Robert. 'But I don't think the mother is just a music teacher. From what I've heard she's a concert pianist.'

'I don't know,' Chloe admitted. 'Josie didn't say.'

'So what about Josie?'

'She seems very nice. She lives in Brighton, I think. As a matter of fact she's offered to take me on the pier this evening; after supper, that is – if it's still all right with you.'

'Of course,' Mrs Portman said. 'But if I were you I'd be a little bit careful on the pier. I wouldn't stay after dark.'

'You have to be careful,' Robert said. 'Because you could fall through the gaps between the planks. You could fall right down into the water and be drowned. You can see it through the spaces.'

His mother laughed.

'I don't think even you, my darling, could slip through those narrow gaps!'

5

When Chloe returned from school that afternoon with a still-silent Janet in tow there was a sleek, silver-grey car standing outside Blenheim House. In spite of her resolve never to speak to any living soul in authority ever again, unless certain matters, such as going to school, were sorted out to her liking, Janet was caught off her guard. She opened her mouth and the words came out.

'Grandmother's car!'

The words caused Chloe a slight sinking of the heart. She did not look forward to meeting her employer's mother who, from the few things which had been said about her, sounded a formidable woman. But never mind; she would deal with the difficulties, if difficulties there were, as they arose. No old woman, however fearsome, was going to get the better of *her*.

'How nice!' she said to Janet. 'I look forward to meeting your grandmother!'

Janet, back to scowling, replied only with a look. Perhaps she inherits her lack of charm from her grandmother, Chloe thought. Certainly it was not from her parents. They were, so far, the most amiable people in the world. Dead easy. Perhaps Grandmother would prove better than expected.

Janet rushed into the house ahead of Chloe, straight into the sitting-room where Moira and her mother were drinking tea. Robert was playing on the floor, Eddie was lying in his carrycot beside his mother's chair. Janet flung herself at her grandmother, who hastily put down her cup on the low table. Chloe stood just inside the doorway.

The old lady was not at all what she expected, at least not to look at. For a start she was not old – well old, but not very old. About fifty. Her hair, elegantly coiffured as if she had just come from the hairdresser, was brown, not grey, and she was narrow and thin, her shape not a bit like that of Chloe's own roly-poly mother. She wore a mauve dress, and round her neck a single string of pearls.

'Janet darling, do not rush into the room in such a manner. I almost spilt my tea!' Her voice was clear, clipped, with a beautiful accent just like a lady announcer on the wireless.

'Grandmother!' Janet cried. 'They made me go to school! I hate school, they know I do! Tell them I don't have to go!'

'Calm down, child! Who is "they", who is "them"? Don't they have names?'

'You *know* who I mean,' Janet said impatiently. 'Mummy and Daddy. And Miss Tempest as well. She's just as bad. She tried to make me talk but I wouldn't.'

'Come in Chloe,' Moira Portman said. 'Mother, this is Chloe. Chloe, this is my mother, Lady Stansfield.'

'How do you do,' Chloe said politely. She wondered if she should shake hands, but Lady Stansfield gave no sign of it.

'Good-afternoon, Chloe. I hope my naughty granddaughter hasn't been difficult?' But her tone, when speaking of Janet, was indulgent.

'Not in the least,' Chloe lied.

Lady Stansfield, dismissing Chloe, turned to her daughter.

'I think I would like another cup of tea, darling.'

'Of course, Mummy.'

They were using, Chloe noticed, the most exquisite china, decorated in red and gold. Before pouring the tea Moira turned to Chloe, who stood there not sure what to do next.

'Chloe, will you take Janet and Robert into the kitchen and give them tea? And if you would like to have yours with them, so that you can go out earlier this evening, please do so.' It would save an argument, or at least postpone it. Her mother was staying to supper and Moira knew exactly what she would say, albeit not in the girl's presence, about employers sharing the same table.

'Oh no, Mrs Portman!' Chloe said, her eyes wide and innocent. 'I'm in no particular hurry!'

'Well,' Lady Stansfield said when Chloe and the children had left the room, 'she seems nice and polite. One hopes, of course, that the children won't pick up her North Country accent.'

'She doesn't have much of an accent,' Moira said.

'That's true, but even a little is too much. However, all that will be taken care of when they go away to school.'

'I'm glad to have her. She'll make a difference to my life. I just hope she'll stay, that's all. We intend to treat her as one of the family.'

'One of the family?' Lady Stansfield paused with her teacup in mid-air. 'What do you mean by that?'

'Well . . .' Moira hesitated. '. . . Well, she'll go where we go, helping with the children, of course. And she'll eat with us.'

'*Eat with you*? Do you mean she'll share your evening meal?'

'All our meals, Mummy. As you well know, I take most of them in the kitchen these days. All except dinner, and even that if I'm on my own. People do since the war.'

'I don't!' Lady Stansfield spoke sharply. 'Someone has to keep up standards!'

'I think we can rely upon you for that!' Moira said. There was an edge to her voice. They had had this particular conversation far too often. 'I make an effort when you come, but do you think, for instance, that I use this precious tea service every day of the week?'

'This china has been in my family – which is *your* family – for four generations,' Lady Stansfield said. 'I hope yours is not the generation which stops using it.'

'Don't worry, Mummy,' Moira raised a smile. 'I'll use it whenever you visit!'

'Do I take it that your mother's help is to grace your dining table this evening?'

'Yes. I think you'll find she doesn't *disgrace* it. She knows which knife and fork to use! In fact, I think she's quite well brought up.'

'And what does John say to all this?' Lady Stansfield demanded.

'Oh, he's all in favour, Mummy.'

Lady Stansfield shook her head. 'I don't understand it. If he were a *Labour* MP it would be different. What is the Party coming to?'

Moira laughed out loud.

'Oh Mummy, you're priceless!'

'You may laugh at me,' Lady Stansfield warned. 'But it's the thin end of the wedge. You're making a rod for your own back. Don't come to me when it blows up in your face!'

'I won't!' Moira promised.

Lady Stansfield lifted the lid, peered into the teapot.

'We need more water, dear.' She stretched out her arm to press the bell at the side of the mantelpiece.

'It's no use doing that, Mummy,' Moira said. 'There's no-one to answer the bell.' She was too late. Her mother's finger was firmly on the bell-push.

'Of course there is, dear. Chloe's in the kitchen with the children.'

'Chloe is not a housemaid,' Moira spoke as patiently as she could. 'She is a mother's help. She has no duties which aren't to do with the children.'

'Surely to goodness she's not going to object to bringing in a jug of hot water?'

'She might not. I don't know. It's early days and I'd rather not ask. She's on a month's trial, but so are we.'

'*We are on trial*? I never heard such nonsense! What *do* you mean?'

'I mean if she doesn't like us she won't stay. She can easily get another job. And from what I've seen of Chloe so far I don't want to lose her. So please don't interfere, Mummy.'

'You know I *never* interfere, Moira,' Lady Stansfield said.

Moira rose, picked up the jug.

'I'll get the hot water.'

In the kitchen the bell rang loud and clear. Chloe, scrambling eggs for the children's tea, looked up at the panel which indicated from whence the call came – and ignored it. Would I answer it if it was Mr Portman ringing? she asked herself as she stirred the eggs. Yes I would, she decided, and perhaps, just this once, even if it was Mrs Portman, but she suspected the finger on the bell-push was Lady Stansfield's and there was no way she would obey that.

'Grandmother is ringing the bell,' Janet said. She could tell.

Chloe gave no answer. A minute later Mrs Portman came into the kitchen.

'I told Chloe Grandmother was ringing the bell,' Janet said quickly.

Moira looked at Chloe and their eyes met.

'I was scrambling the eggs,' Chloe said. 'I didn't want to burn them.'

She spoke quite politely, but the message in her eyes was clear. I am not here to answer Lady Stansfield's bells.

'Of course not,' Moira said, answering the spoken and the unspoken words.

'My mother is a most remarkable woman,' she added conversationally, turning on the tap, filling the kettle. 'You wouldn't believe the things she did in the war! Worked her fingers to the bone on behalf of other people. Anything, anyone – it didn't matter what it was.'

Chloe smiled a slight acknowledgement as she piled scambled eggs on fingers of toast and served it to the children. So what? The war was over!

'But now that the war is over,' Moira continued, 'she thinks that everything should be just as it was before!'

'My mother says nothing will ever be the same again,' Chloe said, though not admitting that her mother bewailed the fact every bit as much as did Lady Stansfield.

'I hope, Mummy,' Moira said tentatively, just before they went into the dining-room, 'you'll be nice to Chloe. For my sake.' She had immediately seen through Chloe's excuse for not answering the bell.

'Nice?' Lady Stansfield queried. 'What sort of a word is "nice"? Naturally, I shall be polite. I would be polite to anyone sitting at your table, whether I approved or not. I hope I know how to behave!'

'Of course!' Moira said.

'But don't expect me to make a fuss of her,' Lady Stansfield added.

As far as Chloe was concerned, though she made her point by being there, supper was disappointing, not least because John Portman telephoned to say he would be late and they were not to wait for him. Lady Stansfield spoke mostly to her daughter on matters which did not include Chloe, throwing Chloe the occasional question about her family, or about Yorkshire, which was as remote to her as the North Pole and in about the same state of civilization. Moira did her best to keep an even flow of conversation but it was a relief to all three when the meal ended.

Chloe escaped to her room, dabbed powder on to a skin which was so perfect that no art could possibly embellish it, emphasized her mouth with 'Heavenly Red' lipstick, and surveyed herself in the mirror. She needed brightening up. Perhaps it was her hair, too tight, too orderly. She brushed it into a looser style and thought it improved her. If she had eaten with the children, she thought, she could have been out of the house much earlier, had time to look around before meeting Josie, which she had arranged to do at the entrance to the pier.

When she went downstairs Mrs Portman was in the hall.

'You look very nice,' she said to Chloe. She thought the girl looked bright and beautiful. Perhaps it was the prospect of an evening out.

'Thank you, Mrs Portman!'

'You won't be late back, will you? Actually, I

think you should be in by ten o'clock. You don't know Brighton yet.'

'I won't be late,' Chloe assured her. All the same, she would make no promises about exact times. No-one was going to stand waiting for her, stop-watch in hand. But easy did it. She would conform, or somewhere near it, at least this once.

She closed the door of Blenheim House behind her and stepped out into the wondrous evening, immediately feeling as free as the air, as fresh as the breeze which came off the sea and blew her hair back from her face. With a spring in her step she walked quickly down the Square and around the elegant curve of Lewes Crescent, crossed the coast road to the seaward side, and turned west, walking quickly, every step taking her nearer to the pier. Bright, white and shining in the evening sun, it straddled the narrow strip of pebbled beach and thrust out enticingly into the water. Chloe had a sudden longing to dip her feet into the water, to let the waves break over her feet. One day soon, she would.

So eager was she now to reach the pier that she broke into a run, dodging past those who strolled leisurely ahead, side-stepping those who came towards her. Within minutes she was at the entrance to the pier. There was no sign of Josie.

It didn't matter too much. There was plenty to see, no shortage of things to watch. The wide area in front of the entrance was busy. There were people buying, or just looking, at the souvenir stalls, a short queue for ice-cream cornets, a small crowd around a man demonstrating a piece of magical kitchen equipment which would do everything, it seemed, except feed the cat. It was also the hour when the population of the pier changed. Mothers, bedraggled and weary, dragging fractious, overtired children, were leaving the pier; young couples arm-in-arm, trendily-dressed youths with the latest in haircuts, vying in fashion with the young women in their summer dresses, nipped in at the waist, full-skirted almost to the ankle, feet shod in high-heeled court shoes, were going through the turnstile on to the pier. The men and girls were in twos or threes, with friends of their own sex, though most of them hoped to leave, by the end of the evening, with a member of the opposite sex.

To begin with, she moved around, inspecting the souvenirs, wondering whether to buy something for Marilyn from her first wage packet; watching the man with the kitchen gadget. If she bought that for her mother, would it ever be used? Then she turned her attention to the placards and notices. 'You simply cannot be dull on the Palace Pier . . . The finest pier in the world!'

Three fully licensed bars; it offered open-air dancing nightly, Fridays excepted. The Palace of Fun, the Palace Pier Theatre (presenting London's most successful plays). Madame Binnie . . . Advice on Health, Happiness and Business. There was no end to the delights. Channel Cruises, Sailings to Eastbourne, to the Isle of Wight. Palace Pier Café. Dodgem cars, Ghost Train – it was unbelievable, wondrous.

But then, she thought in the end, glancing up at the clock over the gates, she had better stop moving around, stay in one place so that Josie could find her. And where was Josie? She should have been here ten minutes ago but there was no sign of her.

Chloe took up her stand by the entrance, close to a board which gave details of the show in the Palace Pier Theatre, studied it. It sounded lively; perhaps she and Josie would give it a try, though not this evening, of course. This evening she wanted to experience as much as possible of everything the pier offered. She was ready, indeed longing, to plunge into the midst of it all.

Absorbed in the notice, she was only vaguely aware that there were other people close by, so that when the man spoke to her she jumped.

'It looks good,' he said. '*You* seem interested.'

He was close by her shoulder, his voice in her ear. She turned her head and looked at him and he saw the surprise in her eyes.

'I'm sorry if I startled you!'

He had a cultured voice, not rough or common, and indeed he was pleasant to look at in a lean, spare way, taller than her by several inches, with a thin, craggy face, bright eyes, and a smile hovering around his mouth.

'I just thought you looked interested.'

'Oh, I am,' Chloe said. 'It seems as if it would be a good show.' She tried not to sound *too* enthusiastic, as if she had never seen such a thing before.

'I think so . . . So I wonder . . .'

He hesitated, but not for long. 'I wonder if you'd

accompany me, allow me to take you. I'm on my own and so, it seems, are you. It would be pleasant to see it together.'

After his initial hesitation the words came out in a rush. While he waited for her answer, Chloe studied him. He spoke politely, seemed genuine. It wouldn't be the first time in her life she had been what her mother called 'picked up'. She was, after all, eighteen. Since the age of barely sixteen she had chosen to ignore her mother's warnings about what happened to girls who allowed themselves to be picked up by men, preferring to use her own judgement which, in fact, had not so far let her down, at least not badly. A few disappointments, but she had quickly let go of those, cut her losses, emerged unscathed.

Perhaps it was because she'd often said 'no', though she had not refused because of anything her mother had said, not because she herself had thought it wrong, but because most of the men who had made such propositions had not appealed to her. She was choosy; it was as simple as that.

This young man was different. She was attracted to him. Even in two short sentences he had sounded so unlike his Northern counterparts, better-spoken, more sophisticated. The thoughts went rapidly through her head as she reached the conclusion, not without regret, that she would refuse him. She would say 'no' simply because – and her mother's warnings didn't come into it – it was too soon for her to know about Brighton, about what the rules were, what was expected and where things led. In

Akersfield she would have known where she stood but Brighton was, as yet, foreign country.

Apart from which, an inner voice said, you are waiting for Josie!

'I'm sorry,' she said. 'I'm waiting for a friend.'

He shrugged, smiled.

'Too bad! But he's a lucky man!'

'I'm waiting for a girl friend,' Chloe said. 'She's a bit late.'

The words were hardly out of her mouth when Josie appeared, breathless and full of apologies.

'Good-evening, then, perhaps if I'm lucky, some other time,' the young man said – and walked away.

Josie stared after him.

'He's a bit of all right! Who is he, then?'

'I've no idea,' Chloe confessed. 'He wanted to take me to the Pier Theatre.'

'You should have kept him talking,' Josie said. 'He could have taken us both. He looked a bit of a toff to me.'

Josie was right, Chloe thought. He *had* looked – and sounded – a bit of a toff. She liked toffs!

'Let's get on the pier then,' she said.

They paid their money and went through the turnstile.

It took Chloe no more than half-a-dozen yards walking on the pier to imagine that she had left the land far behind her. It was not that she felt as if she was truly on a ship, sailing across the Channel to France, but rather that she was somehow in no-man's-land, in some sort of suspension between

Brighton, already left behind, and the deep sea ahead. The feeling was enhanced by the fact that when she looked down between the planks of the deck of the pier, what she saw, since the tide was now rushing in and would soon be full, was the sea below where she stood. She was truly, she thought, no longer on land. She was in a magic place where anything could happen.

'Let's walk to the very end,' Josie suggested. 'We can watch them fishing off the end of the pier.'

Privately, Chloe thought that to watch someone fishing was the only thing more boring than fishing itself, but on the other hand, with things as they were, nothing could be truly boring. There was expectancy, excitement even, in the air.

'If you like,' she said.

They set off at a good pace, their high heels clattering on the deck, occasionally and inconveniently catching in the spaces between the planks. They were not to reach the end of the pier uninterrupted; there were too many distractions. Slot machines, of which Josie must try every one, losing each time until her supply of pennies ran out.

'I don't care!' she said. 'I enjoy doing it! If I had three more pennies I daresay I could win it all back! I suppose I could change a shilling at the kiosk?'

'If you lose that,' Chloe pointed out, 'you won't have enough money to have your fortune told.'

They had agreed that it was what they wanted to do most of all, though not by Madame Binnie since psychology with advice on health and business was not what they were after.

'There's a gypsy a bit farther along,' Josie said. 'Madame Celestine. She tells fortunes from cards, or the crystal ball, or your hands. A friend of mine went to her and she told her she'd marry a rich man and have three children, two boys and a girl.'

'And has she?' Chloe enquired.

'Not yet,' Josie admitted. 'But she's sure she will. She had the crystal ball, which is the most expensive. Having your cards read is the cheapest.'

They went from the brightness of the evening into the amusement hall, a forest of machines and stalls for winning and losing money. By watching others roll pennies, turn wheels to race horses or guide football teams, endeavouring, without success, to throw rubber rings over coveted prizes, they enjoyed themselves for a full half-hour. They shared in the gains and losses, mostly the latter, of others without either of them parting with a single coin of their own.

'It's stuffy in here,' Chloe said eventually. 'Let's go outside.'

When they emerged from the gloom of the amusement hall into the brightness of the evening it was to see the sun, a fierce red ball, beginning to dip in the sky beyond the West Pier. The lights had come on along the promenade and the West Pier itself was outlined in fairy lights.

'What's the West Pier like?' Chloe asked Josie.

'A bit posh,' Josie said. 'Not as much fun as the Palace Pier.'

If it's posh, then there'll be a better class of people on it, Chloe thought. Toffs. Not that she was a snob, not at all, but people of a higher class were more interesting.

'If we're going to have our fortunes told we'd better get on with it,' she said. 'I more or less promised I wouldn't be late back on my first evening off.'

They strolled back to the fortune-teller's booth.

'You can go in first,' Chloe said to Josie.

Josie disappeared into the darkness of the booth while Chloe hovered outside, passing the time in reading glowing testimonials from crowned heads of distant countries to Madame Celestine's gifts of clairvoyance. She was reading a letter when the same voice which had spoken to her earlier in the evening said, 'Hello! So we meet again!'

She jumped sky-high this time. It was as if the aura surrounding Madame Celestine's booth had somehow summoned him up out of the ether.

'Oh!' she said. 'You startled me!'

'I'm sorry about that,' he said. 'I didn't mean to. What have you done with your friend?'

'She's in there,' Chloe informed him. 'She's having her fortune told.'

'And are you going to do the same?'

'I said I would. I know it's silly, but it might be fun.'

As Chloe spoke, Madame Celestine drew back the curtain a few inches and Josie emerged. The fortune-teller took a swift look outside and dropped the curtain again immediately. Josie stood there with a flushed face and glowing eyes.

'It was *wonderful*!' she said. 'You'll never believe what she told me!'

'I'll say good-night,' the young man said, and walked away once again. Josie was too enthralled to notice him.

Chloe went into the booth, breathed in the heavily-scented air, and took the chair indicated by the pointing figure of the clairvoyant. It was on the opposite side of a small table, covered with red and gold brocade, behind which the fortune-teller sat in a majestic pose.

'Nice weather we're having.' Her voice was husky.

'Very nice indeed,' Chloe agreed.

'The crystal is half-a-crown, palms one-and-sixpence for both, cards a shilling. I advise the crystal. It's been very clear to me all day.'

Nevertheless, Chloe thought, I'll have the palms. Half-a-crown is a lot of money, and how could it make the future any different?

'Please yourself,' Madame Celestine said.

She took Chloe's hands in her own, which though old and tobacco stained were surprisingly smooth and silky to the touch. She peered at Chloe's hands, back and front, then held them palms upwards, concentrating.

'You don't come from around here,' she said at last. 'You're from distant parts. Am I right?'

Bradford, she thought, or somewhere near. She'd done the Bowling Tide Fair at Bradford quite often before the war. She never forgot accents.

'You're right,' Chloe said.

'It's all here in the hands,' Madame Celestine said. 'The hands don't lie.'

She lifted Chloe's hands closer to her own face, peered intently at her palms.

'You've come to this place for a purpose,' she said. 'You have something in mind. I can't say what, but keep pursuing it and you'll get there in the end.'

They all came to Brighton for a purpose. They came from all points of the compass, drawn to its bright lights like moths to a candle. She saw them all the time, bright and hopeful, or sometimes nervous and apprehensive; all wondering what the future would bring.

'There's a young man here. Tall, slim. He's taken a fancy to you, but take care.'

That was good advice to anyone. She hadn't recognized the young man in the brief glimpse she'd had. He wasn't a regular on the pier. She knew all the regulars, women and men who walked on the pier every day. When she was short of customers she sat outside and watched and got on with her knitting. Even though the war was over she still went on knitting balaclava helmets.

'Is there anything you'd like to ask me?' she offered.

Chloe thought for a minute.

'Will I marry well?'

Madame Celestine studied each of Chloe's hands again, in turn.

'Without a doubt!' she said. 'Perhaps more than once.'

There *was* no doubt about it. With a face and a figure like that – and there was more to it than face and figure, for the girl had a sparkle and an intelligence about her – she'd be snapped up in no time.

'But don't rush it,' she said.

It was the advice she had always given to her own daughters, usually in vain.

When Chloe emerged from the booth the sun had dipped down to the horizon and there was a fresh, cool breeze blowing off the sea.

'I'm freezing,' Josie complained. 'I think it's time we left.'

But when they passed the open air dance floor, with couples dancing a quickstep, it was too much for them.

'Let's dance together, seeing we've no partners,' Josie suggested.

They had not gone once around the floor before two men broke them apart.

'We can't have two pretty ladies like you dancing together!' one of them said.

After that it was a waltz, then a slow foxtrot, then another quickstep. Chloe's partner spoke very little, he was there to dance and he did that expertly. It suited Chloe down to the ground. She loved to dance and was good at it, but she didn't particularly want to talk to him. What little he had said had been quite boring.

When the music stopped she glanced at her watch.

'Great Heavens! It's after ten! I must fly!'

She found Josie near by, grabbed her by the arm and together they rushed off the pier. At the entrance they parted company. Chloe crossed the road and began to walk quickly towards Sussex Square. To her mind it was not the least bit late, but it was her first evening out, ten o'clock had been specifically mentioned, and there was no point in blotting her copybook.

John Portman sat back in the taxi as it turned the corner from the Steine and went along the coast road towards home. It had been a long day, but a satisfactory one. He had made some useful contacts and he had, he hoped, left a good impression where it mattered most. Early on in his parliamentary career he had realized that it was not only what you did but also what you were *seen* to do. You had to be noticed. It was no use hiding your light under a bushel. And today he reckoned he *had* been noticed.

It was when the cab was passing Royal Crescent that he looked out of the window, idly, and saw Chloe, in the light of the street lamp, hurrying along. Although he had not previously noticed the way she walked, he did so now. Even hurrying, she walked gracefully, confidently, with her head held high as though the world was hers.

'Stop!' he ordered the driver. 'The young lady we've just passed – we can give her a lift.'

The driver stopped the cab and waited for Chloe to catch up. John Portman opened the door and called out to her.

'Chloe! What are you doing here? Jump in!'

'Oh, Mr Portman, thank you so much,' Chloe

said. 'I was with my friend and she wasn't well. I couldn't leave her though I knew I was late. I hope Mrs Portman will understand!'

'I'm sure she will,' John Portman said. 'Of course you had to look after your friend!'

6

Moira Portman, descending the stairs, heard the sound of the taxicab drawing up, and stopping. She ran down the last few stairs and went at once to open the door. She was always so happy to welcome John home. Would I be so eager to do so if he returned at precisely the same time every evening, if our lives together were predictable, dependable? she asked herself. Yes, I would, she decided. I would never tire of the sameness if John was part of it.

When she opened the door John, latchkey in hand, stood there in the shaft of light from the hallway and behind him stood Chloe. Moira experienced a small stab of surprise, mingled with something she could not have named, but it was almost immediately gone. John, followed by Chloe, stepped into the hall and kissed his wife. Chloe stood aside, waiting to see how the land lay.

'I spied Chloe walking along the road,' John said.

'I'm sorry I'm late!' Chloe broke in quickly. 'Josie wasn't well.'

'So Chloe looked after her,' John said.

'How unfortunate,' Moira said. 'I hope it didn't spoil your evening?'

'Not really,' Chloe said truthfully. She hoped she wouldn't be asked for details, symptoms. She had given no thought to how and why Josie might have come over queer.

'Poor Robert hasn't been well,' Moira said. 'He was sick in bed. Not long ago. I had to change his pyjamas *and* the sheets.'

Then thank goodness I was late, Chloe congratulated herself.

'Poor little lamb!' she said.

'He's all right now. He's fast asleep. But look in on him when you go up.'

'Of course!' Chloe said. 'I'll go to bed now. Will it be all right if I make myself a hot drink and take it up with me?'

'Certainly,' Moira replied. 'And you mustn't feel you need to ask something like that, Chloe. You can take it for granted.'

'Then I'll say good-night, Mrs Portman, Mr Portman.'

Minutes later, having deposited a cup of milk, two thick slices of bread and jam and a piece of Madeira cake in her room, she went next door to look at the children. Both were fast asleep. In the glow from the nightlight Robert looked pale, his eyelids faintly tinged with blue. Even in sleep he had a look of anxiety. Poor kid! She was sorry he had been sick but mighty glad that she had not been there. She hoped he wasn't sickening for something nasty.

Janet had flung aside most of her bedclothes, as if she had struggled to the last. Now, in sleep, she had a rosy glow about her. Her lips were pressed together and slightly upturned at the corners in a smile of satisfaction, as if she had got her way about something. For an instant there was something vaguely familiar to Chloe in the child's expression, and then she recognized what it was. She might well have been looking at a younger edition of herself.

She pulled up the bedclothes around Janet's shoulders, then went back to her own room.

'How was your mother?' John asked politely, not looking up from the letter he was reading. He did not like letters to do with his job to be sent to his home address, the House of Commons was the place for them, but somehow people got hold of his home address and there was usually something waiting here for him at the end of the day. He habitually read them before he went to bed; his secretary – his shared secretary – would deal with them at the House the next day.

He always asked after his mother-in-law when she had paid a visit though the truth was that he did not care two hoots how she was and he suspected Moira knew it. Lady Stansfield was a snob and a bore. It was true that, as Moira sometimes reminded him, she had worked her fingers to the bone right through the war, and had never shown the slightest fear however many guns were fired or bombs went off around her, but that, he reckoned, was because she was by nature bossy, she liked a finger in every pie, and the war had given her endless opportunities for commanding, ordering and interfering.

'She was well,' Moira answered.

She knew that he couldn't care less, that he would be secretly pleased he had not arrived home before her mother had left, but he was always a polite man.

'I don't think she totally approved of Chloe,' she said. 'She finds it difficult to accept that anyone from what she thinks of as the lower orders shouldn't immediately be at her beck and call, even when she's not in her own home. And of course she was appalled that Chloe should eat with us. Chloe, at any rate at the table, behaved rather better than my mother.'

'I don't know how you've managed to grow up so unlike your mother,' John said. 'But I thank God you have.' He put aside the last of the letters. 'That's enough for today. One more drink and I'm for bed!'

Moira rose to her feet and poured him a measure of whisky from the decanter.

'How did you come to give Chloe a lift home?' she asked.

'I told you, my love. She was walking along the road, running almost. I recognized her.'

'In the dark?'

'It wasn't dark, not all that dark. We're not still floundering about in the blackout. We've got street lamps!'

Moira smiled at him.

'I know! We've had them back for years. I just

hated the blackout so much, I keep on remembering it!'

He was about to say, but didn't, that he had immediately recognized Chloe's shape, the way she held herself, the way she moved. He had not needed to see her face. He had not known himself until that moment, and then in the cab, that he had been so aware of her.

The next morning Robert seemed as good as new. He sat at the table and ate his cornflakes with what was, for him, surprising gusto. Too often he had to be persuaded to eat.

Perhaps he'd got overtired yesterday, his mother thought, regarding him fondly. She would warn Chloe about that. Robert had never had Janet's energy or stamina, though he didn't lack the will or desire to do things. He needed an eye kept on him.

'It seems another lovely day,' Chloe said. 'I wonder if we might be able to go on the beach today?'

'I want to go on the beach,' Robert said.

'So do I.' Janet had decided that she would speak when she wanted something, though she would take no part in general conversation.

'*You* can't go on the beach,' Robert said. '*You'll* be at school.'

Janet glared at him.

'Not this afternoon I won't silly!'

'I think this afternoon would be a good time,' Moira said. 'The tide will be right.'

'I want to go somewhere this morning.' Robert's

voice was, for him, unusually demanding. His mother looked at him in surprise, and not a little pleasure.

'Then I daresay Chloe will take you somewhere when she's finished her chores,' she said.

'I want to go in the gardens,' Robert said. 'I want to play with Peter!'

'You're full of wants this morning, old man,' John Portman said. 'And who is Peter?'

Chloe explained.

'I see. Then if your friend Josie isn't recovered she might not be there with Peter.'

'I expect she will be if she can,' Chloe said. 'She's very conscientious.'

She doubted if it was true, but it sounded good. But where do all these arrangements fit in with *my* free time, she wondered. She couldn't have the evening again because, it had been explained to her, it being Friday Mr Portman would be home early, perhaps soon after lunch, and he and his wife had seats for the Theatre Royal in the evening.

'It will be a great treat,' Mrs Portman had said to Chloe. 'We don't often get the chance.'

I won't push it, Chloe thought, but if there were occasions when she couldn't take what time was due to her she would note it down, save it up. That was fair enough. Mrs Portman could not possibly have any objections, and when she had enough time saved up she would do something really exciting, like going to London. She longed to go to London.

'But there's your free time to think of,' Moira

Portman said now. 'We'll have to think where you can fit it in today. Unfortunately I couldn't do the beach trip because Eddie's too young and it's not suitable.'

'Oh, please don't worry, Mrs Portman,' Chloe begged. 'It doesn't matter in the least!'

'That's very kind,' Mrs Portman said.

'Not at all! Of course if you insist, I'll save it up and take it another time – when it's convenient.'

'Oh! Oh yes, what a good idea!'

The journey to school was once again a silent one. 'I'm not sure that I shall go to the beach with someone who can't speak,' Chloe threatened.

When she had delivered Janet to the school – since she was to take Robert out later in the morning he had stayed at home – Chloe decided not to hurry back. Who was to say she had not taken a wrong turning and got lost in the unfamiliar territory? With that in mind she took a right turn after leaving the school, down a road which clearly led to the seafront. At the bottom she crossed the road to the promenade and leaned on the railings, watching the sea come in, the waves breaking on the pebbles with a clattering sound, which turned to a sucking noise as each wave receded. The sight and the sounds, the regular rhythm of it, were hypnotizing. She lost count of time, her thoughts caught up in all that she had done in the last few days, all that she *would* do. A small dog which ran suddenly between her and the railings brought her back to reality. She began to run, ran all the way to Sussex Square and reached Blenheim House breathless.

'Chloe! Where . . . I thought . . .' Moira Portman, concerned rather than angry, looked for an explanation.

'I'm terribly sorry, Mrs Portman. I got lost!'

'Lost?'

'I know. It's stupid isn't it. I must have taken the wrong turning when I left the school. It was such a maze of streets . . . I quite lost my sense of direction.'

'I see!' She didn't exactly. How could anyone get lost between Eastern Road and Sussex Square? But I have to remember, Moira Portman told herself, that Chloe is an unsophisticated girl from the North of England.

'Well, you're back safe and sound,' she said.

'*You got lost?*' Mrs Wilkins said when Mrs Portman had left the kitchen. Her voice was weighty with disbelief.

Chloe looked Mrs Wilkins straight in the face.

'I did indeed Mrs Wilkins.' And you can't prove I didn't, she thought. No-one could. 'I find Brighton quite confusing!'

'Confusing, do you?' Mrs Wilkins said. 'Now myself I'd have thought nothing would confuse you! I'd have thought you were far too smart!'

'Thanks for the compliment,' Chloe said.

Halfway through the morning – Chloe had finished her jobs and was seeing Robert through his milk and biscuits before taking him out – there was a ring at the back door.

'Who can *that* be?' Mrs Wilkins said. 'The milk's been, the grocer's been, it's not the day for the laundry. It can't be a visitor or they'd use the front . . .'

'If one of us answered we'd find out,' Chloe said.

'All in good time,' Mrs Wilkins grumbled. 'I like to know who'll be at the door before I open it. Same as if I get a letter. I never open it before I know who it's from.'

The bell rang again.

'Shall I answer it?' Chloe offered.

'I've always been the one to answer the back door when Mrs Portman wasn't in the kitchen. Except of course when Mrs Lawrence was here – she was the housekeeper.' Mrs Wilkins moved, without hurrying, down the short passage towards the door. As she left, Moira Portman came into the kitchen. Two minutes later Mrs Wilkins returned.

'It's someone looking for you,' she said to Chloe. 'She *says* her name's "Josie".'

'Oh Josie! Then it must *be* Josie,' Chloe said.

'Please ask her in, Mrs Wilkins,' Moira Portman said.

'If you say so, Madam. I don't ask anyone into anyone else's house without they say so. You can't be too careful since the war!' Mrs Wilkins said heavily. She did not approve of servants – which was what Chloe was, in spite of any ideas she might have to the contrary – having visitors in working hours. Her own brood had strict instructions not to seek out their mother at Blenheim House except in a grave emergency, like the house was on fire or one of them had broken a limb.

When she came back again she was followed by Josie, who held Peter by the hand.

'So you are Josie,' Mrs Portman said pleasantly. 'I hope you're feeling better?'

'Feeling better?'

Chloe, standing behind Moira Portman, nodded her head.

'Oh yes!' Josie said quickly. 'Yes I'm quite better now, thank you.' She hoped she wouldn't be asked what the trouble had been. She would be sure to get it wrong.

'And you're Peter?' Moira said to the little boy.

'*I* know Peter,' Robert spoke up. 'He's nearly four. He's my friend.'

'Good!' his mother said. 'Then perhaps one day soon Peter could come to tea with you. I'll telephone his mother.'

The little boy seemed nice enough. He was much bigger than Robert, sturdy and solid, healthy looking. And Josie seemed pleasant. It would be good for Chloe to have a friend, it would help her to settle.

'And now you're all going in the garden!' she said. 'Robert had better wear a jersey.'

In the garden the two boys ran at once to the far end, to the spot from which they had watched the cars on the previous day. Chloe and Josie followed at a leisurely pace until they reached the nearby bench. It was the only bench not occupied. The morning was fine and warm and presumably that, and the proximity of the weekend, had brought the residents out.

'I don't think Robert needs a jersey,' Josie said.

'I know,' Chloe agreed. 'His mother's over-anxious about him. And he was sick last night, before I got home.'

'Did you get into trouble for being late?'

'No. I said you'd not been well and I'd had to look after you,' Chloe said.

'Cheek! So that's why Mrs Portman asked me if I was better. She seems nice. Is she?'

'Quite nice,' Chloe admitted reluctantly. 'A bit well . . . not exciting. You'd wonder what *he* saw in her, because he's quite something. He's like Leslie Howard, fair and good-looking, and lovely manners.'

'Errol Flynn is the one I like best,' Josie said. 'Do you like him?'

'I prefer James Mason,' Chloe said. There was something about James Mason quite apart from his dark good looks: an air of mystery, hidden depths. He was powerful, and power was what excited her. He was a man not easily conquered except by a very special sort of woman, and when she watched his films Chloe felt she *was* that sort of woman.

'Shall we go on the pier again this evening?' Josie suggested.

'I can't,' Chloe said. 'They're going to the theatre.'

'That's a pity. I thought we might just meet up with that fellow who tacked onto you. Anyone could see he was attracted to you – and if he had a friend . . .'

'I hadn't given him a thought,' Chloe said.

It was not quite true. In bed last night before falling asleep she had thought over the entire evening on the pier; Madame Celestine with her predictions, two marriages. 'I can't say what you're pursuing but you'll get there in the end.' She had remembered the young man as she lay in bed. She had found him attractive, but today she could hardly remember what he looked like.

'Well, I can't go,' she repeated.

'What about this afternoon? It's quite fun in the afternoon. Not as good as the evening, of course, but all right. We could take the boys. They'd enjoy it.'

'I've promised to take Robert *and* Janet on the beach this afternoon. I can't get out of it.'

Nor did she want to. She was looking forward to the beach, to lying in the sun browning her legs. If she could get a deep enough tan she could go without stockings.

'You should get a whole day off every week,' Josie said. 'If you were one of those high-and-mighty nannies in a grey uniform with a felt hat, you'd have it.'

'But would I want to wear that uniform – would you? Think of how you and me would look, dressed up like that!' They fell to giggling at the prospect.

'I reckon men like girls in uniform,' Josie said. 'Anyway, you should get a whole day off every week. I always get Sunday.'

And what would I do with Sundays? Chloe asked herself. Nowhere to go. No shops open, no dances. It would be different when she had made other friends, but she wouldn't want to spend all her Sundays with Josie nor, come to that, too much of her free time on any day of the week. Josie was all right: she was jolly, she was probably quite kind, but Chloe suspected that her aims in life and Josie's were quite different. She doubted that Josie, in spite of her stated desire to get married, had much thought in mind other than having a good time, and that in the present.

Chloe knew already, she thought she had probably always known, that to her marriage was not the be-all and end-all. There were other things in life. Of course if marriage brought with it those other things, which she had not yet totally defined in her mind, then that was another matter.

'Well anyway,' Josie said, 'we'll see you on the beach at three o'clock.'

'Does Peter's mother let you take him wherever you choose?' Chloe asked.

'Mrs Waleski doesn't mind where we go just as long as we're out of the house. And to tell you the truth I'm glad to get out. She practises on the piano all day long. Awful stuff! She never plays a nice tune you could sing or dance to.'

'I can't stay here long,' Chloe said after a while. 'It seems that little Madam Janet finishes school at lunchtime every Friday, so we have to go and collect her.'

The two little boys were reluctant to be parted from each other, and from their absorbing game of watching the cars, but the promise that they could meet up again in the afternoon softened the blow and Robert obediently left with Chloe.

'I would really rather stay,' he said, quite politely.

'Don't worry! We'll be going soon,' Josie told him.

Mrs Wilkins was just about to leave when Chloe and Robert arrived with Janet.

'Remember,' Mrs Wilkins said in a threatening

tone, 'I leave an hour earlier tomorrow morning. Saturday is Mr Wilkins's half-day and Sunday is the Lord's day. I like to give them both their due.'

She rolled up her pinafore and packed it into the brown paper carrier bag which accompanied her on every visit to Blenheim House. The bag was always bulging, though what else it contained apart from a tin of home-made furniture polish which Mrs Wilkins brought with her, preferring it to anything her employer could offer, was not known, since she delved into it in secret.

'So mind you keep your rooms tidy,' she said to the children. 'I don't want to come in on Monday morning with the place looking like a Council tip!'

'I expect you know what the Council tip looks like,' Janet said, breaking her vow of silence again, 'because that's where Mr Wilkins works, isn't it?'

'It is indeed. And let me tell you it's quite often tidier than your bedroom!'

She picked up her carrier bag and left, giving the door a hearty slam behind her.

'Mrs Wilkins is a very loud lady, but I'm not frightened of her,' Robert said bravely. 'She's really quite kind. She gives me sweets.'

'They rot your teeth,' Janet said. 'All your teeth will fall out and you'll not be able to eat and you'll get thinner and thinner and thinner . . .'

'I won't, because I'll have false teeth, like old Mr Simpkins. I shall have a gold tooth – or even two!'

'If the two of you don't eat up your lunch,' Chloe warned, 'there'll be no going on the beach!'

After lunch they packed a large striped beach bag with the children's swimming costumes, rubber bathing shoes because the beach was so pebbly, a ball, three apples and some biscuits. The children would carry their buckets and spades.

'Robert doesn't like changing into his swimming things on the beach,' Janet said. 'But I don't mind.' She gave Chloe a calculating look. 'What will you do?' she asked.

'Wait and see!'

In fact, she had put her swimming costume on under her dress, though she had yet to decide whether she would reveal it. She would see how the land lay, not to mention how cold the water was.

'Don't let Robert go in the sea without the strictest supervision,' Mrs Portman said anxiously. 'The waves can be very strong. And see that he wears his sun hat. The air is so clear here, especially by the water, which makes the sun more powerful.' She would be happier, on this first occasion, to be going with them, just to see how Chloe coped, but it was not possible. There was no way she would take Edward, nor yet leave him.

'Don't stay in the sun too long,' she said as they left the house. 'Try to find some shade if you can.'

They crossed to the garden and walked down towards the bottom of the slope, Robert skipping and jumping with excitement all the way.

'We're going through the tunnel!' he chanted. 'We're going through the tunnel!'

'No we're not, silly!' Janet contradicted. 'We're still in the garden!'

For a moment, Robert looked crestfallen, and then he recovered himself.

'But we're *going* to go through the tunnel and I have to show Chloe where it is because it's hidden!'

Chloe would not spoil his fun by telling him that she already knew where the entrance was. Josie had pointed it out to her earlier in the day. In any case it was overgrown and well hidden so it was not difficult to pretend she couldn't find it and to let Robert have the pleasure of leading her to it.

It was not at all what she had expected. She had thought it would be narrow, dark, a bit creepy. It was none of those things. It was surprisingly light, and quite roomy.

'I'm a train!' Robert announced, and began to puff-puff and choo-choo and emit a surprisingly shrill whistle. Chloe had never heard Robert so noisy, and every *choo* he made was amplified by the echo in the tunnel. He broke off being a train to speak to Chloe.

'If you shout, it will shout back at you!'

'Hello there!' Chloe called out – and back came the echo. 'Watch out for the train!' she shouted.

When they reached the end of the tunnel she unlocked the door and they went out and there they were, having travelled under the coast road, on a terrace overlooking the beach.

'It's a magic tunnel,' Robert said.

It was one of those afternoons in May which tantalize and make promises for the future by offering weather more suitable to late June, or even July. The morning's breeze had veered round and now blew from the south, gentle, caressing, but moderating the heat to exactly the right degree. It was perfection, Chloe thought, lying face down, luxuriating in the sun's heat on her legs and on her back.

She had quickly shed her dress and anointed herself with a mixture of olive oil and vinegar, a concoction, though a bit sharp to the smell, guaranteed to brown the skin in the shortest possible time. Now, in her swimsuit, she welcomed the sun on every part of her body. She and Josie had worked out a system of taking turns whereby they either closely watched all three children or totally abrogated their responsibilities and surrendered to the sun. Chloe could, if she cared to listen, hear their cries of pleasure as they gambolled about at the edge of the water. At the moment, however, she did not care to listen. She closed her eyes and thought she might well fall asleep.

Moira heard the key in the lock, and the next minute John was in the room.

'Darling! I didn't hear the cab!'

'You wouldn't. I walked.'

'You walked? All the way from the station?'

'All the way! It's such a beautiful day and I don't get enough exercise.'

He dropped his briefcase on to the nearest chair. He'd brought a load of work home but he wouldn't even look at it today. It had been a busy week and he was tired out. It was a fair stretch from the station and he'd walked it on impulse.

'Where are the children?'

'Eddie's asleep, but he's due to waken any minute. Chloe has taken Janet and Robert to the beach. I wish . . .' she hesitated.

'What?'

'I wanted to go with them. I was a bit worried about Chloe taking them, only I couldn't leave Eddie.'

'But isn't that what Chloe's here for? Why were you so worried?'

'Because we've only known her a day or two. Taking the children into the gardens, looking after them in the house, is one thing, but how do we know she'll watch them closely on the beach? The sea can be dangerous. And then there's the sun. It's the first *really* hot day we've had. You know how Robert burns. Perhaps I shouldn't have let them go on the beach at all!'

'Hey! Calm down!' John said. 'I'm sure they'll be OK. She's not an idiot. But now that I'm here why don't you go down and see for yourself?'

'Because Eddie will waken any minute and he'll be desperate to be fed.'

As if on cue a loud wail came from upstairs.

'You see?' Moira said. 'But you could go. I wish you would. Only don't make it look as though you're spying, don't say I'm worried.'

'Of course I'll go. And I'll be tactful.'

'Slip your trunks on under your trousers,' Moira said. 'Then you can take the children into the water if you want to. You'd enjoy it too.'

To his surprise, and though he had planned to put his feet up and do absolutely nothing, he found that once he had left the house he was no longer tired. There was a spring in his step as he went through the tunnel, looking forward to joining the party on the beach.

Chloe wakened from her brief sleep, wondered for a moment where she was, then felt the warm sun on her back and remembered. She stretched, yawned, got to her feet and made her way to where she could see the children at the water's edge. The tide had hardly risen at all, so she couldn't have slept long. Neither the children nor Josie, who was standing ankle deep in the water, saw Chloe approaching and for a moment she stopped to watch them. They were having a good time, splashing and shouting. Even Janet was joining in.

Oh, but this is wonderful! she thought. This is a wonderful place to be! She stretched her hands in an arc above her head, holding her body taut, taking deep breaths of the balmy air.

John Portman had seen the children from the terrace above the beach, but not until he had run down the steps and was making his way across the pebbles did he see Chloe.

He stood absolutely still. For a moment, as he watched her, silhouetted against the sea and the sky, with her hands raised above her head and her hair blowing back from her face in the slight breeze, she was suddenly the only person in the world. Every inch of her beautiful figure was outlined; the high, round breasts, the curve of her hips and abdomen, her long, slender legs, the feminine slope of her shoulders. His mind registered that she was wearing a tight, black swimsuit, but in fact as he looked at her she seemed to him totally naked. The sight of her took the breath from his body. He was rooted to the spot and couldn't move.

The children, pausing in their game, looked up and spied him, and called out.

'Daddy! Daddy!'

Chloe broke her stillness, lowered her arms, swivelled around and saw him. He walked towards them, the pebbles crunching under his feet. As he neared her his eyes met Chloe's. He could hardly look away from her even though his children were clamouring around him and he noticed another child and a teenage girl who seemed to be of the party. He saw only Chloe and she, he could tell, saw only him.

Afterwards, when he thought about it, which he did a thousand times, he realized that it had only been seconds, though at the time it had seemed world without end.

It broke up; she looked away first, and then he turned to his children, swinging Robert into his arms.

Chloe introduced him to Josie, and Robert presented his friend Peter.

'I've heard about you,' John told him.

'Josie, will you watch the children while I swim out a little way?' Chloe said. 'I'd like to get into deeper water, just for a minute.'

She swam away quickly. She was a strong swimmer,

John noted, breasting the waves with no difficulty. At one point she turned her head and looked back at him, then continued to swim forward.

He stripped down to his bathing trunks and plunged into the sea, furiously pursuing her. When Chloe saw him following she slowed down until he caught up with her. Then she turned towards him and he held out his arms. Their bodies, weightless in the water, clung together as if magnetized. No word was spoken, or needed to be.

A few minutes later, their hands stretching out from time to time to touch each other, they swam back to the shore.

7

Janet stood on the beach at the edge of the sea, waving her arms, waiting impatiently for her father to come out of the water. As he waded towards her, Chloe following behind, she called out to him.

'Daddy, do be quick! I want to go to the rock pools!'

'*I* want to go to the rock pools,' Robert echoed.

'And so you shall!'

As he reached the children John's voice sounded normal in his ears, hearty even, yet how could it be since nothing was normal any more? In a few short minutes the world had changed, turned upside down. The sea had taken hold of him, bewitched him – he would gladly have stayed in that sea forever, drowned in it with Chloe in his arms, and now it had cast him back on a shore which was not the same shore he had left such a short time ago. Everything was new, everything sharper. The water sparkled, the sun shone more brightly, warming the air. The pebbles on the beach were full of colour and his children's voices came to him sharp and clear. Chloe came out of the water and stood quite still a yard or two away from him. He was as conscious of her as when she had been in his arms in the water, as if every breath she took was his breath also, as if her heartbeats were his heartbeats.

'If we're going along to the rock pools,' Chloe said to the children, 'pick up your things and take them with you. If we leave anything behind the sea will come and take it away.' Her voice was quite steady.

'And we'll have to be quick about it if we want to spend time at the pools before the tide covers them,' John added.

Between them, Josie and Peter included, they picked up their belongings from the beach and began to move eastward towards the rocky area. Chloe had never known a seashore where there were rock pools. Her family's seaside holidays had been spent at Blackpool, with its boasted miles of golden sands, or at Morecambe with its wide bay. The high, white cliffs of this Channel coast, with shingle beaches where she would have expected sand, and rocks strewn about like giants' playthings, was new to her. On that first evening's walk when she had looked down on the area they were now approaching, she had thought how intriguing it looked, a place to be explored.

But not now. At this moment what she wanted was to explore her own feelings about which, unusually for her, she was not at all sure. It was fortunate, though, that she was able to hide her feelings when she wanted to; unless she willed it no-one could know what she was thinking. It was one of the things about her which irritated her mother most, that whereas her other children showed their emotions, joy or sorrow, anger or pain, Chloe could, when she so chose, remain an ice-maiden.

She did not feel like an ice-maiden now. She was not sure how she felt, walking along the seashore with John Portman only a yard or two from her side, not touching, not speaking to each other, hiding what they might have said behind everyday conversation with the children.

There were pools all around them now, small and large. The children scrambled over barnacle-encrusted rocks, peering first into one pool then another.

John paused.

'This looks a good spot. Shall we stop here?'

'It's better if you choose one pool and keep looking into it,' Josie advised.

'That's right,' John agreed. 'And choose one which has lots of crannies, holes in the rock where creatures can hide. Then concentrate hard, keep looking, because you don't see everything at once.'

'Here's a good one, over here!' Janet called out.

They moved across to where she was kneeling on the ground, gazing intently into a pool about three feet square.

'Look! There's a crab!' she said.

'Where? Where?' Robert cried. 'I can't see it!' He knelt down and Chloe knelt beside him.

'I see it!' Chloe said. 'There it is!' As she pointed a finger at the crab it scuttled away.

Was that what she wanted? she asked herself. Did she want to scuttle away, to hide in a crevice? No, she did not. She was not a person who ran away and hid herself, nor was she, she reminded herself, a person who lost her head. She had always prided herself on keeping control of her feelings, but it was different now. The trouble was she didn't quite know what her feelings were. It had happened too suddenly.

'Kneel down, Daddy,' Robert urged. 'You can see better.'

John knelt in the only space left around the pool, between Robert and Chloe. He did not want to be so close to her, it was too tempting, and yet at the same time he wanted it more than anything in the world. He could feel heat from her sun-warmed body and smell the sea on her skin. When he moved, leaning forward to see better into the pool, his arm touched hers and the shock swept through him. He remained still, waited for her to move away, but she didn't do so. She stayed exactly as she was, neither drawing away nor leaning closer; almost, he thought, as if she was unaware of him.

She was not unaware. She had felt his bare flesh against hers almost as if it were a burn. The fact was, she didn't know what to do, whether to lean closer to acknowledge it, or to draw away. She didn't even know whether he was aware of the contact, and for that reason she chose to remain still. She was not ready to make a statement either way.

A sudden movement from Robert dislodged her. He leaned forward, lurching perilously over the pool, and was immediately pulled back by his father.

'Steady on old boy, you'll fall in!'

The moment was over. Had it actually happened? John asked himself. But of course it had, as had those moments in the sea, and it needed no words to confirm that.

Janet jumped to her feet and stretched herself.

'I'm bored! I don't want to look at silly old crabs. I want to go on Volk's railway!'

Chloe had been told about the small railway which ran along the beach from Black Rock to the Palace Pier, but was yet to experience it, though apparently not today.

'We don't have time Princess,' John said. 'We must go home. Mummy will be wondering what's become of us.'

Not until the small group around the pool had been broken up by Robert almost falling in the water and Janet leaping to her feet had Moira come into his mind, but now that she had done so it was as if she was standing right there beside him, powerfully present.

'No she won't!' Janet contradicted. 'If Mummy was here she'd let us go on the railway.'

His daughter's stubbornness made up John's mind. Suddenly he wanted to be back in his own home, with Moira and the baby. Everything would be different there. They would all of them, Moira, children, Chloe and himself, fall into their own places. Am I running away? he asked himself. Perhaps he was, and wasn't that better than running full pelt in the wrong direction? He did not ask himself what Chloe felt.

'Well Mummy's not here,' he said. 'And I've said no and I mean it! So that's all. Ten minutes more, then gather your things together.'

Chloe heard the change in his voice. He did not look at her, concentrating entirely on the children. What now? she wondered.

They walked back, a straggly group, through the tunnel and up through the garden where, at the gate, Josie and Peter left them to go their own way. John, key in hand, walked up the path to his front door, Chloe and the children behind him. With one part of him he wanted to be on the other side of that door, safe where he belonged, but with Chloe only a step behind him he knew nothing would be as it had been, predictable, uncomplicated. What had happened, had happened.

Moira was in the hall when they entered, the baby in her arms and a smile of welcome on her face.

'I saw you crossing the road,' she said. 'Did you enjoy yourselves?'

'I saw a crab!' Robert called. 'I *almost* caught it. It *almost* bit my finger!'

'How exciting!' Moira said. 'And what about you, Janet?'

'*I* wanted to go on Volk's railway but Daddy wouldn't let me!' Janet grumbled. 'I never get to do what *I* want to do!'

'What nonsense, Janet,' Moira said lightly. 'Of course you do. And you can go on the railway another day. Chloe will take you.'

'I want to go with Daddy,' Janet persisted.

'Did you bathe?' Moira asked her husband. 'Did you manage a swim?'

'A short one,' John answered.

'Good! Did you enjoy it?'

Enjoy? John asked himself. It was not the word to describe the intensity of those few seconds. He had felt as if struck by lightning, and how did one describe that?

'Yes, I enjoyed it,' he replied.

'Chloe can swim!' Robert said. 'She can swim ever so fast.'

'Really?' Moira turned towards Chloe. 'Are you a good swimmer?'

'I am now. I learnt at school. We went to Akersfield swimming baths every Tuesday afternoon.'

She had hated it, hated everything about it: undressing in the small cubicle she was obliged to share with Mavis Pritchard who, when she stripped naked, had a funny smell. Mavis had a deep interest in her own body and in Chloe's, every week comparing and contrasting their rates of development. 'When will we have tits?' she said with longing. 'I'll bet I have them before you!'

'I don't care if you do,' Chloe had said. 'I *will* have them! Everybody does.'

'Only women,' Mavis said. 'Men don't.' She had screamed with laughter at the thought of men with tits.

Chloe had hated swimming lessons because she was no good at it, miming a stylish breast-stroke with her arms while hopping through the shallow end with one foot on the bottom. Then one day, by what seemed no less than a miracle, she had found herself swimming and had made at once for the deep end. From that day on she went in at the deep end. She would never forget that wonderful sense of freedom, any more than she would forget the smell of Mavis Pritchard.

'Well now, I suggest Chloe takes you upstairs,' Moira said to the children. 'Then we'll have tea.'

'I wanted to have Peter to tea,' Robert said.

'And so you shall, another day,' his mother promised him. 'Today we have Daddy. That's a very special treat, isn't it?'

Robert looked undecided.

'It isn't that I don't *like* you, Daddy,' he explained. 'It's that Peter's my friend.'

'I understand,' John said.

Moira moved away down the hall. Chloe began to climb the stairs with the children. John watched her until she was out of sight around the curve of the staircase. He wanted to go after her, he wanted her never to be out of his sight. He stood for a minute, then followed his wife into the kitchen.

'I'll make a cup of tea,' Moira said, filling the kettle, taking mugs down from their hooks on the wall. 'My mother thinks drinking tea from mugs in the kitchen is really going to the dogs. About all the time she spent in here was when she came to give orders. What a different world!'

'What? I'm sorry, I didn't catch . . .'

'You're not listening, darling,' Moira said indulgently. 'You're miles away. In Westminster I expect.

It would do you good to get your mind off work for a few hours.'

My mind is not on my work, John thought. The House was as far away as the moon. At this moment he wanted to be wherever Chloe was, which was probably in the children's bathroom. Could he find a reason for going up there? In the meantime he wanted to talk about her, wanted her name to be brought into the conversation, wanted to say her name out loud.

'Is Chloe a good swimmer?' Moira asked, as if on cue.

'Chloe?' He was surprised at how nonchalant, almost disinterested, he sounded as he said her name. 'I'm not sure. Possibly.'

'You weren't there when she swam? Then how could she leave the children?'

'Oh yes, I was there,' he recalled. 'Her friend Josie was there also. There was no problem about the children. Yes, she looked a good swimmer. Strong.'

In his mind he saw her again, striking out from shore, turning her head to look back at him over her shoulder, like a mermaid enticing a sailor to his doom. Doom, though, was emphatically what it was not. As he had plunged into the sea he had come alive, every stroke taking him towards her strengthening his feelings, so that taking her in his arms the moment he reached her had been inevitable. It was meant to happen. There had been nothing at all between them until the moment he had seen her standing on the beach.

'That could be useful,' Moira said. 'Perhaps she could teach Robert to swim? I don't have the opportunity with the baby so young, and you don't have time.' She poured boiling water into the teapot, stirred it, left it to strengthen.

It was not just that she didn't have much opportunity, she thought, she was always tired. Shall I ever be full of energy again? she asked herself.

'I daresay she could,' John said. 'She gets on well with Robert, though less so with Janet.'

'True. Though she knows how to handle Janet. In fact even after so short a time I don't know what I'd do without Chloe. I do hope she stays. We must do all we can to help her to settle.'

The children's voices – bickering – heralded their entry into the kitchen, Chloe behind them.

'You're telling lies!' Robert said. 'Mummy, Janet's telling lies. She says I'll never be able to swim because I'm afraid. It's not true!'

'It is!' Janet said.

'It's not! I can swim already – a little bit!'

'No you can't! That's just pretend swimming.' Janet, who had at an early age taken to swimming like a duck to water, was full of scorn.

'*I* used to swim like Robert,' Chloe said. 'One foot touching the bottom.'

'So there you are, Robert!' his mother said. 'And now Chloe's a very good swimmer! Or so Daddy says.' She smiled at Chloe.

What had he said? Chloe wondered. She looked at him then, finding his eyes on her, at once looked away again.

'I wondered if you might be able to teach Robert to swim?' Moira said. 'Especially now that the weather's getting warmer.'

'Of course,' Chloe replied.

'I think you might give the children baked beans for tea,' Moira said. 'It's what they really like, which is obliging of them because it's available – and nutritious, so we're told. John, shall you and I take our tea into the garden? There's still some sun!'

Chloe made the toast, heated the beans. I could sit down and eat the whole lot myself, she thought as she served them. Swimming always made her hungry and, she was interested to note, emotion – for in spite of her calm demeanour, inside she was awash with emotion – had not impaired her appetite. She sneaked a forkful of the children's beans and allowed herself a whole slice of toast.

'Can we go into the garden?' Robert asked.

'When you've finished your tea. For a little while.'

'And can I go on the swing? Will you push me?'

'I expect so,' Chloe said.

When they had eaten she cleared away the tea things, then went with the children into the garden. John and Moira sat on wicker chairs, away from the greengage tree, trying to catch what they could of the sun. In the afternoon, because of the height of the house which fronted to the west, the garden at the back soon became shady. Robert made straight for the swing.

'Push me, Chloe!' he demanded.

He liked to pretend that he wished to be pushed

hard and high, but it was not true. On the first occasion when Chloe had pushed him high she had heard his sharp intake of breath and his stifled cry as he swung into the air. When he'd got down he'd been as white as a sheet. She had quickly learnt just how high to go without frightening him, while at the same time not giving away his nervousness to anyone who might be watching, especially to Janet.

As she stood behind the swing Chloe faced John Portman, sitting with his wife a few yards away. They were both reading, Moira a book, John, head bent over his newspaper. Chloe, as she gently pushed Robert, felt able for the first time since they had been on the beach to look at John.

He was a handsome man, there was no doubt about that, but she knew that it was not his appearance which attracted her. It was something else. She already knew that what spoke to her in a man was the feeling – it had almost to be a certainty – that he was going somewhere, the recognition of his ambition and his power. She had not known John Portman long, but she had sensed these qualities in him. It was these attributes which were an aphrodisiac to her. She would not, she told herself, ever lose her head over lesser things. She would not allow herself to be infatuated. Infatuation spelled the end of reason.

John looked up from his newspaper and caught her eye. It was not that he had suddenly become aware of her. He had been aware of her every minute, every second. Now, he looked at her and found her looking directly at him.

Over the distance which separated them, over his

wife's head bent over her book, over Robert swinging through the air, they looked at each other.

'I want you,' his eyes said. 'With every bit of me, I want you!'

'I want you,' Chloe's eyes said. 'I want you!'

And then, almost immediately, she was not sure. What did it mean, apart from this urge in her body, which was new to her? In spite of what people thought about her, in spite of what her mother sometimes feared, she had not yet given herself to any man. She was still a virgin. She had wondered what it might be like. What would it be like with John Portman? she asked herself. But more important, where would it take her?

With a wisdom well beyond her eighteen years and far ahead of John Portman's she recognized in that moment that, however things went, she must keep a cool head. She didn't want to lose her job, she wasn't yet ready to move on, and she was not in a position to call the tune.

'Chloe! You're not pushing me!'

Robert's voice interrupted her thoughts. The spell was broken. She looked away from John.

'I'm sorry, Robert!'

Moira glanced up from her book.

'Just five minutes more, Robert, then it's time for your bath. Janet too!'

There was no need to ask where Janet was. Sounds from the house said that she was doing her piano practice, the only thing she did without being driven to it. The notes of 'Für Elise', hesitantly but not incompetently played, drifted back into the garden.

'In any case, it's getting chilly. The sun's gone,' Moira said. 'We don't want you catching cold.' She closed her book, rose to her feet, and went into the house.

Chloe slowed down the swing, then stopped it. Robert slid off the seat and ran into the house after his mother. John rose, and stood still, waiting for Chloe to move towards him, which she had to do to go into the house. When she was about to pass him he touched her hand and stopped her.

'Chloe! I have to talk to you!'

He had known when their eyes met as she pushed Robert on the swing that something had to be said. He had no idea what it was, he was far too confused for that, but it was impossible not to break this silence.

Chloe gave a barely perceptible nod and drew her hand away quickly. They were probably visible from the kitchen window. But side by side with her caution a tingle of excitement went through her. Now it was up to him. What would happen? She went into the house and he followed after her.

It came as no surprise to Chloe when later, as she was seeing to the children, John came into their bathroom. She was bending over the bath when she heard his footsteps. He stood there without speaking until, in the end, she raised her head. When he looked at her she felt the blood rise to her face. She was disconcerted by this sudden rush of emotion. She had been determined to remain completely in charge of herself, to be friendly, but to keep cool inside, and now suddenly she was nothing of the kind and she was not sure how to behave.

John saw her flushed face, her shining dark eyes, the way the steamy atmosphere had caused her hair to curl over her forehead. It was exactly the way he had seen her on that very first evening and he realized that what he felt now had had its beginnings then. He had to speak to her, to say something; he couldn't go on like this. He had to see her alone, yet whichever way he moved she was always with other people. He wanted, desperately, to take her away from them all, to have her to himself.

'Daddy! Daddy!' Robert cried. 'Are you going to read to us?'

Chloe stood up.

'Stay where you are,' she commanded the children. 'I'm going to fetch another towel. I seem to be one short.'

The linen cupboard was on the landing. She went out of the bathroom and started to rummage in the cupboard. Exactly as she had intended, John followed her. He came up behind her at the cupboard and put his hands on her shoulders. His touch sent a shiver through her, so strong that she thought he must feel it.

'I've got to talk to you,' he said urgently. 'I've got to see you alone! When? Where?'

'Tomorrow evening,' Chloe said quickly. 'Here!'

'Here?'

'Mrs Portman is going to a painting class.'

He remembered now. Moira had been asked to judge the paintings of the evening class pupils at the Art College. She had wanted him to go with her. 'It would give them a treat,' she'd said. 'A real live MP.'

'Let me off,' he'd said. 'You know it's not my line. Besides, it's a Saturday evening. You also know I like Saturday evenings free. I thought you did.'

'I do,' she'd said. 'I promised ages ago and I didn't realize it was a Saturday.'

'Yes,' he said to Chloe. 'Tomorrow then.'

As she made to pass him he took her in his arms, turned her around and kissed her, very gently, on the lips.

8

When Chloe came downstairs next morning, accompanied by Robert and Janet, John Portman had already left the house. It came as no surprise to her. At supper the previous evening what little conversation there was had centred around plans for next Saturday when John was due to make his monthly visit to his constituency.

'I'm so sorry I can't go with you, darling,' Moira said. 'It seems ages since I was there, but feeding the baby makes it impossible. I do hope they understand.'

'Of course they do.'

'Give them all my greetings. I shall make it for the summer garden party. Eddie will be weaned by then.'

She would be glad of that. She had enjoyed feeding her babies and wouldn't have done otherwise, but with Eddie, although it soothed her, she felt both tired and trapped. There were days when she longed to get away from the demanding routine, to be free not to have to watch the clock, to be able to leave the house and not think about what time she must be back.

'You know I would *like* to go!'

'I've told you, Moira, I understand! *They* understand.'

She looked up in surprise at the terseness of her husband's tone. It was unlike him.

'Are you all right? You're not worried about tomorrow, are you?'

'Why should I be worried?' John asked. 'It's the routine monthly thing with the party; meeting the committee, seeing some of my constituents, answering questions. They're nice people. What's to worry about?'

'And lunch with Sir Godfrey?'

'As you say. Lunch with the High Sheriff, which will be fun.'

He was looking forward to lunching with Sir Godfrey Milton in his impressive mansion, but without any trepidation. He had met him more than once. Sir Godfrey was an able, affable man, influential in the country. Also, even more important, he was a personal friend of the PM with whom he had been at school. Indeed it was Sir Godfrey who had introduced him to Winston, and the great man's beloved country home was quite close to John's constituency. All that could do no harm, no harm at all.

Yet even as the thought came he knew that he would gladly forego today's occasion just to stay at home and be where Chloe was. He did not want to be away from her even for an hour. As he looked across the table at her, steadily eating, not saying anything, he ached with longing. What was he going to do? How could he resolve all this?

Moira had turned to Chloe.

'Perhaps you might prefer to take your free time in the morning, tomorrow?'

'Thank you,' Chloe answered. 'I'd like that. I'd like to look at the shops in Brighton.'

Chloe was not entirely sorry now, on this Saturday morning, that John was not there for breakfast. She would not know what to say to him. She had felt uncomfortable in his presence at the dinner table, aware that his eyes were too often on her but thankful that Mrs Portman seemed not to notice. In the moments before she had fallen asleep – surprisingly few in spite of the happenings of the day – she had wondered what he would say to her when they were alone together; what she should say to him.

When she walked into the kitchen with the children Moira was not there, though Mrs Wilkins was, noisily washing the previous night's dishes.

'Where's Mummy?' Robert cried.

'She's not gone far,' Mrs Wilkins said. 'She's upstairs with the baby. I daresay she'll be down in a minute.'

'You're an early bird this morning, Mrs Wilkins,' Chloe remarked.

'It's the early bird gets the worm!' Mrs Wilkins answered.

'What worm?' Robert asked. 'I don't *really* want a worm.'

'You can cut worms into pieces and all the pieces wriggle!' Janet said with satisfaction.

'And a nasty thing for a well-brought up young lady to do!' Mrs Wilkins said. 'Anyway, I told you, I get here earlier than usual on a Saturday so I can be home with the dinner on the table when Mr Wilkins gets back. Saturday is his half-day.'

Chloe served the children and herself with breakfast. She wanted it to be over quickly so that she could escape to Brighton. Perversely, Robert dawdled, pushing his cereal around the dish, not even pretending to eat; and just as perversely Janet, having finished hers, demanded a second helping.

'Right!' said Chloe. 'Now let's see who can finish first!'

'Why?' Janet demanded.

'Well, we don't want to be here all morning, do we?' Chloe said.

'*Someone* doesn't!' Mrs Wilkins said.

'Quite right!' Chloe confessed. 'I don't want to waste time. In fact, I have some time off and I'm going into Brighton.'

'Can I go with you?' Robert asked quickly.

'Not this time. Another time, perhaps.'

'We *never* get to go to Brighton,' Janet complained.

'Well, one day I'll take you on the pier,' Chloe promised. 'If Mummy agrees.'

'If Mummy agrees what?' Moira enquired, walking into the room, holding a handful of letters.

'To let us go on the pier,' Robert said.

'I've said I will some other time, if you permit it,' Chloe said. 'But not today.'

'Quite right!' Moira said. 'There's a letter for you.' She handed Chloe a square, white envelope. Chloe immediately recognized Marilyn's round, childish handwriting. It was nice to receive a letter at any time, but not so exciting from Marilyn. She wondered what it would be like to have a letter from John Portman, but of course why would she, living in the same house?

'It's from my sister,' she said.

'How nice!' Moira said absently, sorting through her own envelopes, amongst which she saw one in her mother's strong, elegantly-sloped handwriting. She picked up a knife from the table and slit it open, with some trepidation since her mother did not usually write about anything pleasant and in any case was more likely to telephone.

'If you've finished, Chloe, don't wait,' she said. 'I'll see to the children. But be back in time for lunch. Twelve-thirty.'

'Thank you,' Chloe said. 'I will. Is there anything I can get you in Brighton?'

'There is in fact. I need some skeins of embroidery cotton. I'll give you the shade numbers. Vokin's or Hannington's will have it.' She had been embroidering a tablecloth for what seemed like years. It was time she made an effort and finished it. But who wanted embroidered tablecloths these days, except perhaps her mother, who had drawers full of them.

'Vokin's?' Chloe queried.

'You can't miss either Vokin's or Hannington's,' Moira said. 'They're almost next door to each other, at the bottom end of the town. Department stores.' She was reading her mother's letter, and frowning.

> . . . I think you are making a big mistake in treating this girl, pleasant though she may be, as family. Who knows where it may lead, and then how will you get out of it? And I am taking the trouble to write to you since you appear not to take seriously what I say . . .

Impatiently, Moira screwed the sheet of paper into a ball and flung it into the waste paper basket. She would not even bother to reply.

'Come along then,' she said to the children. 'If you're quick about it we can go to the shop and buy the sweet rations while Mrs Wilkins keeps an eye on Eddie.' She turned to Mrs Wilkins. 'I don't think he'll waken.'

'No matter if he does,' Mrs Wilkins said. 'I know how to look after a baby. I've had enough experience with my brood, Mrs Portman.'

'So you have,' Moira agreed.

When her employer and the children had left the house, Mrs Wilkins cleared the breakfast table then turned her attention to tidying the rest of the kitchen. When she came to the waste paper basket she picked out the crumpled letter, smoothed it, and began to read. She could be forgiven, she thought, because she had scarcely ever had a letter herself, and anyway if it was all that private Mrs Portman would have torn it into shreds, or burned it.

As she read it she nodded with satisfaction. She concurred exactly with Lady Stansfield's opinion. It was amazing how often she found herself agreeing with Lady Stansfield, not that the lady would ever seek her views. It was *not* right to treat that little madam as if she was one of the family, let her sit at the table, join in the conversation and all that. There's something about her that I don't quite trust, Mrs Wilkins thought, though what it was she couldn't say. But she's no worse for watching, she concluded.

She crumpled up the letter again and put it in the bag with the waste paper. All through the war they had saved every scrap of paper and now she couldn't get out of the habit, though goodness knew what they did with it, or ever had. You saved all sorts of things; tin cans, silver paper, bits of old metal, thinking they were going to be made into Spitfires or bombers or battleships, but you never knew the end of the story.

Chloe walked to Brighton, on the seaward side of the road. It was a fine morning, with the sun shining and just enough breeze to whip up the waves. Walking briskly it took her no more than fifteen minutes to reach the large square in the town. So this was the Old Steine! It was hemmed in on every side by elegant buildings and the centre was laid out with formal gardens, mature trees in fresh spring green foliage, and an elaborate fountain. There was nothing like this in Akersfield. She had glimpsed it before, on that first day when she had been driven in a taxi, but then she had been too nervous, too apprehensive, to take anything in.

She was no longer nervous. It had taken her no time at all to settle and already she felt surprisingly at home. Most things were to her liking, and where they were not quite so she had every confidence that she could change them.

She was, though, since yesterday afternoon, apprehensive. She was apprehensive about John Portman and when she thought about it, as she did now, crossing the Steine, there was a light but real physical turbulence in her body, a churning in her stomach. And that, she reasoned, was because she was not sure what he wanted of her or even what she wanted of him. She desired – she faced the fact squarely – whatever was on offer. She wanted the adventure but, until there was something else in sight, and as yet there wasn't, she would not compromise her job. Nor did she know what she was prepared to give. What I would really like, she acknowledged to herself, is to eat my cake and have it. And one day she would.

And now I shall stop thinking about him, she decided. I shall concentrate on my shopping. She had always been able to keep her feelings under control and only since yesterday had she felt that control slipping. But she would not let it. She turned her mind to her sister's letter.

Poor Marilyn! She sounded so fed up and unhappy. 'Nothing ever happens here,' she had written. 'School is boring. I wish I was in Brighton. You are the lucky one.'

I'll send her a picture postcard, Chloe thought. A funny one – and perhaps a present. She could well imagine how Marilyn was feeling but there was little she could do about it. Not yet fourteen years old, her sister had more than another year to go at school. And what came after that? A job in an office perhaps, or in a shop?

Following where her feet took her, Chloe found herself outside Hannington's. It looked rather grand and she felt nervous about entering. But why should I? she asked herself. My money is as good as anyone else's! She was particularly pleased, therefore, to find exactly the embroidery cottons Mrs Portman had asked for because, paying for her purchase, she felt the equal of anyone there, free to wander around the store and appraise everything, though without buying anything more because it all seemed well beyond her purse. Though it won't always be, she promised herself. One day I shall come here and buy whatever takes my fancy: dresses, shoes, hats, lingerie, perfume.

Leaving the store by a side entrance, walking a few yards, she found herself in the Lanes, a maze of narrow alleyways lined with restaurants, galleries, and shops of every kind. Outside one restaurant tables and chairs were set in the sun, with people sitting there, drinking coffee, eating cakes. Never in her life, except in films, had she seen anything like this. Everyone knew that abroad they thought nothing of eating in the street, it was quite usual, but never had she expected to see such a thing in England. She knew at once that this she must experience! It would be something to write and tell Marilyn about it, though unfortunately that would only make the poor child even more disconsolate.

Greatly daring, she took a seat at an empty table and waited to be served, but not for long. A young man in black trousers and an immaculate white shirt was quickly at her side.

'Madam?'

'Oh! Oh, coffee please.'

'And a pastry?'

'A pastry. Oh, yes please!' She eyed the dish on the next table. 'I'd like a chocolate éclair, please!'

'I will bring you a selection,' he said.

When the selection came it simply brought another difficulty. How was she to choose between meringue, cream sponge, strawberry jam tart, iced shortbread and the chocolate éclair, not to mention two other sugary confections which were totally new to her? Nevertheless, she thought, I will stick with my first choice. Spurning the tiny fork by the side of her plate she picked up the éclair and bit deep into it. The generous filling of whipped cream oozed out at both sides and spread to the corners of her mouth. It was truly wonderful; she closed her eyes in ecstasy.

'We meet again!' a voice said.

She looked up, startled, her mouth still full of chocolate éclair, straight into the eyes of the young man who had spoken to her on the pier. She swallowed hastily.

'May I join you?' he asked.

'Oh! Oh, yes, please do!' Quickly, and hopefully unobtrusively, she wiped her mouth. Why did she feel so flustered, as if she'd been caught in some surreptitious, ill-bred act?

'You do remember me?' he asked as he sat down. 'Though come to think, why should you?'

'Oh, but I do!' Chloe assured him. 'You were on the pier.' She remembered, most clearly of all, his charming voice. And now, as a look of pleasure crossed his face because she had recalled him, she remembered his smile.

'You were waiting for your friend,' he reminded her. 'I wanted to take you to the Pier Theatre but because of that I couldn't.'

The waiter came.

'Coffee, please!' the young man said. 'And I'll probably have one of these delicious-looking pastries.'

'And the next time I saw you, your friend was having her fortune told. Did you have yours done?'

'As a matter of fact, I did,' Chloe admitted.

'And was it good?'

Chloe thought back to what Madame Celestine had said. 'There's a young man here, tall and slim. He's taken a fancy to you.'

'Oh, just the usual stuff!' she said.

'By the way,' he said, 'I'm Simon Collins. And you are . . .?'

'Chloe Branksome.'

'Chloe. It suits you.' It was different and so was she. And it was not just her looks; scores of girls in Brighton were beautiful but there was more to her than that. She had a radiance, and when she looked at you it was with eyes alight with intelligence, almost awesome, as though she could immediately sum you up. He had thought about her briefly after he had left the pier but he had not expected to see her again. Brighton was full of people who came and went.

'Do you mind if I say something?' he asked.

Chloe raised her eyebrows.

'I don't think so. It depends.'

'I just want to say that you have a smudge of chocolate on your chin. Quite becoming, in fact, but I thought you might like to know.'

She took her handkerchief and rubbed at her chin.

'That's better! So when may I take you to the theatre – or wherever else you'd like to go?'

'But I don't know you,' Chloe said.

She demurred, partly for the sake of it, she didn't want to seem too easy, partly because a large part of her mind was on John Portman. She needed to know where that would lead her.

'You didn't a few minutes ago, but you do now,' Simon said. 'Or do you only accept introductions made by a third party? And if that's the case how would we get any further?'

He was right of course, and his manner of speaking, light and friendly, made none of it seem too serious. She didn't want to let him go, not yet, and there was no reason why she should.

'It needn't be the theatre,' Simon said. 'We could meet for a drink, or a coffee, get to know each other better, then you could judge whether I'm a fit person to sit beside in the stalls!'

'Very well,' Chloe agreed. What harm could it do?

And if she changed her mind, or something John Portman said changed it for her, then she could just not turn up.

'Wonderful! Not tomorrow, because Sundays I visit my mother – unless, of course, you like to come with me?'

'Oh no!' Chloe was emphatic. In Akersfield, once you visited the parents you were as good as engaged.

'Then Monday evening, by the pier, half-past seven?'

Chloe nodded agreement. There was no telling whether she could be free on Monday evening, but she'd work that one out.

'I'm sorry, I have to go now!' Simon said. 'I'm meeting a friend. 'Til Monday, then!'

Male or female friend? Chloe wondered watching him walk away. She imagined him with a wide circle of friends of both sexes, all equally well-spoken and sophisticated.

She drained her coffee cup, and when she asked the waiter for the bill discovered that Simon had already paid it. Resuming her tour of the Lanes she thought that in the whole of her life she had never seen as many displays of jewellery – diamonds, emeralds, rubies – or antiques, or beautiful clothes, as she did now. She had decided to buy a small gift to cheer up Marilyn, but everything here was beyond her price, though one day, she promised herself, I *will* shop here.

Reluctantly leaving the area, she found her way back to the seafront. Outside a small shop she studied a rack of picture postcards then decided that they were all too cheeky for her young sister. Moreover, her mother would die of shame if such vulgarity was delivered by the postman. In the end she settled on a view of the Palace Pier. Then, inside the dark shop, made more than ever like Aladdin's cave by its floor-to-ceiling display of souvenirs and gifts, she found just the thing for Marilyn: a small model of Brighton Pavilion in shiny metal. By the time she emerged from the shop, blinking against the strong sunshine, it was noon. She would have to turn her steps for Sussex Square if she were not to be late.

John Portman leaned back in the corner seat of his first-class carriage, his head resting against the rectangle of white linen so kindly provided by the authorities for their more affluent passengers. It had been a good day. There had actually been one or two new faces, younger ones at that, among the party faithful. Something always welcome. And his luncheon at Sir Godfrey's table, accompanied by a glass or two of fine claret and a Havana cigar to follow, had been excellent.

There had been no other guests, which suited John well. He had been the full focus of Sir Godfrey's attention and the baronet (for such he was, and an inheritor of an old title, not one of your jumped-up knights honoured for selling ice-cream) had been in expansive form. His not inconsiderable charm had been lavished on John alone.

'You're doing a grand job, John-boy,' he'd said.

'The party's pleased with you, I can tell you that, in confidence of course. You'll go places! You'll not always be sitting on the back benches. Just keep your nose clean and there's no telling where you'll end up! Believe you me!'

And John did believe him. Hadn't Sir Godfrey always been a man of his word? To the insistent rhythm of the train as it all but flew over the rails, behind his heavy eyelids John saw the green leather-covered seats of the House, saw the Great Man himself give a nod of welcome as the newest member of his Government slid into place on the front bench. What portfolio he carried was vague, but that didn't matter.

And then the rhythm of the train changed abruptly as it sped over points and John was jerked out of his reverie. He opened his eyes and looked out of the window. They had left behind the leafy landscape of Surrey. Now they were in Sussex, with its high green downs, bare of trees, cropped short by sheep. And with the sight of Sussex returned the thought of home which, since he had left early this morning, had seldom been out of his mind until his meeting with Sir Godfrey had taken over.

It was not thoughts of Moira or his children which occupied him. It was Chloe's face which superimposed itself on the green hills, her name which the sound of the train's wheels on the rails echoed incessantly. 'Chloe-Chloe-Chloe'.

He longed to see her. He consulted his watch and calculated how long it would be before he could do so. Yet what would the outcome be? The hours spent in his constituency, and then the meeting with Sir Godfrey, the latter's hints – more than hints perhaps – of a bright future, had confirmed yet again the rightness for him of the career he had chosen. To serve as a Member of Parliament was the only job he had ever wanted. He could not imagine life without it. Yet nor could he now imagine a life without Chloe.

Chloe had spent most of the afternoon with the children in the Sussex Square garden – all three of them this time, since she had taken Eddie in his pram while Mrs Portman stole an hour or two to work at some sketches.

'I shall be glad when I can find the time to start painting again,' she said to Chloe. 'But in the meantime it's wonderful if I can do some drawing. I hope you're happy here, Chloe. Already I don't know what I'd do without you!'

'I'm very happy,' Chloe said.

It was true, yet not quite true. Life was filling out, but underneath the excitement there was confusion. Still, never mind, she would sort it out!

In the garden she met Josie with Peter. She told her about Simon Collins, though not about John Portman. That she would never do.

'You lucky devil!' Josie said. 'Nothing like that ever happens to me.'

'I don't believe *that*!' Chloe said. She had already marked Josie down as a girl who would have dozens of boyfriends, if only because she was not all that choosy.

'So shall you go to the theatre with him when he asks you again – which he certainly will?' Josie asked.

'I might,' Chloe said. 'I'll have to think about it.'

'I wouldn't think twice if it was me. I could see he was keen on you from the way he looked. And as I said at the time, he's a toff. You can always tell.'

After tea, which was late because Moira had said there was no need to hurry back and the children were happy enough where they were, Chloe saw to Janet and Robert while Moira dealt with Eddie. When they were all settled, Moira looked at her watch.

'I thought my husband would have been home by now,' she said. 'He's not usually so late. But I'll have to go. I need to be there before the public arrives because I've not yet seen all the paintings. Anyway, he won't want much supper because he'll have had a huge lunch. I've laid out some salads and there's soup in the pan, so will you be an angel and see to him as well as to yourself?'

'I will,' Chloe promised.

John was late because when he left the train he made his way to the station bar and ordered a drink. He longed to be home, and yet he couldn't face it because he was no nearer to deciding what to do. After two whiskies he knew that he must give up Chloe because there was no way he could hurt his wife and children. He would say nothing to Chloe, act as though nothing had happened. The very act of doing and saying nothing would make his decision clear to her.

After a third drink, to underline his resolve, he knew that he couldn't treat her thus. It was cruel. He would tell her, face to face, what he had decided, that nothing could possibly come of the affair – which after all was not yet an affair.

He walked out of the station and took the first taxi.

Chloe checked on the children. All three were asleep. It was all the fresh air, she thought. Whatever it was, she was glad of it. It had been a long day and, whichever way she looked at it, all of it leading to this evening.

As she descended the stairs she heard John's key in the door, and caught her breath. She was trembling with excitement, with anticipation. What would he say? What would he do? She had never felt like this before.

Halfway down the stairs she halted as he came in at the door. For a moment they stood still, looking at each other, then without a word she ran down the stairs. He opened his arms wide and without hesitation she ran into them.

9

Standing in the hall they clung together, as closely as if they were lovers who, having been separated, had searched the world and at last had found each other; as if the longing in them had grown over an age, neither of them remembering that it was little more than twenty-four hours old.

John's lips fastened on Chloe's in a kiss the like of which she had never known before; a man's kiss, not a boy's. It swept through her, consumed her. She wanted to respond, to respond more and more and more, with a fervour she had not realized was in her. She wanted to give and give until there was nothing left of her. While he held her body close to his, his hands moving over her back, she raised her arms, caressed the nape of his neck, ran her fingers through the thickness of his hair.

Nothing was said – there was no need for it – until, eventually, when the first kiss ended, he said her name.

'Chloe!'

'John!'

She whispered his name as if it was the first time in the world it had been uttered, as if it was her own invention.

He let go of her briefly, then took her hand in his and led her across the hall and into the sitting-room, pulling her down beside him on the sofa, taking her in his arms again. And now his hands were everywhere, moving over every curve of her body, his lips buried in her neck. Then he raised his head and looked at her, his fingers gently stroking the contours of her face as if he was newly discovering it, smoothing her unruly hair back from her brow.

'My God, you are so beautiful, Chloe! You are unbelievable!' He looked at her in wonderment.

None of this is believable, Chloe thought. It was not what she had envisaged, though she didn't know what she *had* envisaged. Certainly nothing as sudden and overwhelming as this, this feeling of having been thrown into a deep pool, a whirlpool, in which she might drown, and indeed might willingly drown.

Then almost at once she knew she must not drown. However seductive, however inviting the water was, she must not let herself be sucked under, not let the water cover her, so that when John bent his head to find her lips again she lightly pushed him away, and when he used his strength to hold her more closely she used hers to escape from his embrace.

He looked at her in surprise.

'What is it? What's wrong, my love?'

She sat up.

'This is!' She could hardly find her voice.

'I thought you . . .'

He broke off and tried once more to take her in his arms, but she pushed him away again and moved to the far end of the long sofa.

'It's not right!' Chloe said. Then as he made a move towards her, 'No, please don't!' She was still not sure, remembering the passion which had surged through her body only moments before, that if he touched her she could resist him, however much her head told her she must.

'I know it's wrong,' John said quietly. 'We both know that. And I take the blame. But you don't know how irresistible you are.'

He and I don't mean the same thing by the word 'wrong', Chloe thought. He meant that he had a wife and children whereas until this moment she had not given a thought to Moira Portman, out at her Art Exhibition, or to the three children sound asleep upstairs, nor was it of the greatest importance now that she had thought of them. It was up to people to guard their own marriages. What is important, she thought, is that it's wrong for me.

She was, she admitted to herself, deeply attracted to John Portman. The strength of her feelings was something she had never before experienced. Perhaps this was love? In other circumstances she knew she would have held back nothing from him, and for her the circumstances were not to do with his marriage. It was, simply, that there was no future in it.

But that's wrong, she told herself. It *is* to do with his marriage. It's to do with the fact that *my* future, at any rate for a while, is tied firmly to Moira Portman and her children.

'So what are we to do?' John asked. 'Am I to give you up the minute I've found you? I've told you, my darling, you're irresistible. How can I live in the same house as you and treat you like . . . like . . .'

'Like a mother's help,' Chloe said.

'Exactly!'

This was not turning out as he had meant it to, not as he had decided during his sojourn in the station bar. There, in the end, he had planned it so smoothly. Hadn't he decided that to be fair to Chloe he would acknowledge something of his feelings for her, while at the same time telling her that nothing could come of it? And hadn't he resolved that for his part he would stick to his wife and family and concentrate on his career? It had seemed the right choice, and a simple one – even if not easy.

It was the path he had resolved to tread and his resolve had been firm, but it had been made in the absence of Chloe. The moment he had walked in through his front door and seen her standing there his resolve had vanished. At once, what he wanted most in the world was to possess her. He was overpowered by his feelings. Nothing else mattered.

'Though that's what I am,' Chloe reminded him. 'A mother's help. Mrs Portman's help.'

Just suppose, she thought, if he really couldn't bear to keep me at a distance – would he then persuade his wife to let me go? That way, I'd lose everything. I'd lose him and I'd lose my job. No, it was not to be contemplated. There must be other ways.

She looked at him, appeal in her dark eyes.

'Couldn't we be . . . friends?' she ventured. 'Good

friends, the very closest? I'd do anything for you, but I must be loyal to Mrs Portman and the children. I'm very fond of the children.'

'I would always want us to be friends,' John said. 'I'm not sure . . .'

He was saved from voicing his doubts by the telephone, loud and demanding. As he picked up the receiver Chloe jumped to her feet to leave the room. John put out a hand to stop her.

'Don't go!' he said. 'I don't suppose it's anything important.'

Chloe sat down again, and waited.

It was, as it happened, more important than John could have expected or even hoped for.

'Mr John Portman?' the voice asked. 'Sir Godfrey Milton would like to speak to you. I'll put you through.'

What can Sir Godfrey want with me on a Saturday evening? John asked himself in the seconds before the baronet's voice boomed into the room.

'You're wondering why I'm phoning you on Saturday night! I hope I haven't disturbed you?'

'Not at all, Sir Godfrey,' John assured him. 'Is there something I can do?'

'Well, yes and no,' Sir Godfrey answered. 'My wife's just reminded me that I'm in Brighton next week. A short conference I can't get out of. I thought I might just pop along and see you and your lady wife, if that's convenient.'

'But of course, Sir Godfrey. And you must come to dinner if you can spare the time!'

'Thank you. Delighted! Will Tuesday be all right?'

'Certainly!' John said. It wasn't. Next Tuesday was likely to be a busy day in the House but he wasn't going to turn down Sir Godfrey.

'Good! I'm staying at the Grand. I'll phone you!'

'I wonder what Sir Godfrey really wants?' John said as he put the receiver down. 'He's never proposed to visit before.' And I wonder what Moira will say when I tell her I've asked him to dinner, he asked himself.

'Is Sir Godfrey an important man?' Chloe said. 'He sounds it.'

'I expect you could hear every word,' John replied. 'Yes, he is rather. He's an influential man.'

No other voice, unless it had been that of the PM himself, which was venturing into Cloud Cuckoo Land, could without putting it into words, have reminded John more sharply where his priorities lay.

He crossed back to Chloe, took her hand in his, looked down at her.

'I think perhaps you are right, my dear,' he said thoughtfully. 'You are wiser than I am. I appreciate what you say about Moira and the children and there's no way either she or I would want you to leave this house. But you and I can be the closest of friends.'

He pulled her to her feet and kissed her gently on the lips.

'I shall like that,' Chloe said. 'I shall like that very much!'

There was a sudden cry, a distress cry, from upstairs.

'Robert!' Chloe said. 'He's having a bad dream. I'll go to him.'

She left the room and ran upstairs.

Robert was sitting up in bed, his face flushed, hair tousled and damp from sleep, his eyes frightened. Chloe sat on the edge of the bed and put her arms around him, holding him close.

'What is it, love?' she said. 'Was it a nasty dream?'

He clung to her without speaking.

'Tell me,' she suggested.

'She was chasing me. This big lady. I couldn't run away because my legs wouldn't move.'

'Well you're safe now,' Chloe said. 'It was just a horrid dream. I'm here now and there's nothing to be afraid of. I'll give you a drink of water then you can go back to sleep until morning.'

He sipped the water and lay back against the pillow.

'Will you stay?' he asked.

'Of course. I'll stay until you fall asleep,' Chloe promised.

Robert breathed a sigh of relief.

'Tell me a story,' he demanded.

'Very well,' Chloe said. 'But quietly, because we mustn't waken Janet.' Janet showed no sign of waking. She was curled up in a ball, as still and quiet as a mouse. 'Close your eyes and listen and when you fall asleep you won't have any more horrid dreams.'

'Begin "once upon a time",' Robert said.

'Once upon a time,' Chloe said, 'there was a little

girl who lived in a house a long, long way away from Brighton . . .'

'What was her name?'

'Her name was . . . Chloe.'

'That's your name,' Robert said sleepily.

'So it is. Shall I go on with the story?' Chloe answered.

'Yes. Please.'

'She lived with her mother and father and her big brother and baby sister. Sometimes they all went to visit her grandmother who lived in the country, and Chloe liked that. There was a river and the children played at the edge where the water was shallow . . .'

Robert's breathing slowed; his hand, in hers, went limp. Chloe allowed her voice to trail away and began to let go of his hand, but at once he clutched at hers again.

'And then what happened?' he asked.

'All sorts of things. She went to school, which she didn't like because she wanted to stay at home with her baby sister whom she liked better than anyone else in the world. Better than her mother or her father or her brother.'

'And then?'

'And then she grew up and left home and went to live at the seaside . . .'

'And what happened to her?'

His words came out slowly, with an effort, but there was no need to answer. Robert's hand slipped from hers, his head lolled sideways on the pillow. He was fast asleep.

What *did* happen to her? Chloe wondered. What *will* happen to her? Anything could, anything might. She felt alive at the prospect, tingling with a mixture of excitement, of apprehension, and caution. Though not, she thought, with fear. She was not the least bit afraid, she had the situation in hand.

She tucked the bedclothes around Robert's shoulders. He was a nice little boy but she had not intended to let herself grow fond of him and now she was beginning to do so. She tip-toed out of the bedroom and, walking along the landing, heard the front door open and Mrs Portman come into the house.

Chloe hesitated. She was not sure that she wanted to go downstairs and face Mrs Portman at this moment or, more to the point, Moira and John Portman together, but it would look strange not to do so, especially since she had been tending to Robert. She went into her own room to waste a minute or two; sat at the dressing-table and looked at herself in the mirror. 'Irresistible' John had said. Was it true? She appraised herself, trying to cool her thoughts, trying to gather the courage to go downstairs and act as though nothing had happened. She supposed she did look all right. She looked into her own dark eyes and wondered if others could read what was in them, what went on behind them. Was she an open book? She hoped not.

And I hate my hair, she thought. It's so unruly. She had read somewhere or other that in the near future you would be able to get curly hair straightened, the reverse of a perm. She looked forward to that.

She stood up, smoothed down her dress and went

downstairs. When she walked into the sitting-room Moira Portman was sitting side by side with her husband on the sofa. They both looked up.

'He's all right,' Chloe said. 'He'd had a bad dream but I took his mind off it and he's fast asleep again.'

'Thank you, Chloe,' Moira said. 'You are so good with him. I would have come up but I didn't want to disturb him again.'

Moira was looking rather pleased with herself. I reckon John's been telling her about Sir Godfrey's call, Chloe thought.

'My husband's just told me that we're to have Sir Godfrey Milton to dinner on Tuesday,' Moira said, on cue. 'I suppose it's quite an honour, really. He's an important man – High Sheriff and all that. But he's elderly and I daresay he'll be boring. You know how it is. The two men will talk politics all the time.'

'He'd not appreciate being called elderly, darling!' John said. 'He's on the right side of sixty.'

'I'm sure that's terribly ancient to Chloe,' Moira said. 'So I wondered,' she said, turning to Chloe, 'if you'd rather take your free evening on Tuesday. I know we arranged Monday but it can easily be changed if you'd prefer it.'

What you mean, Chloe thought swiftly, is that broad-minded though you are, it doesn't quite extend to seating your employee at the same table as your really posh friends!

'Well,' she said with suitable hesitation, 'the trouble is that I've already arranged to meet someone on

Monday evening, and I don't know how to get in touch with my friend to change it. I'm sorry!'

John Portman raised his eyebrows and Chloe watched a frown flit across his face; but it was not, she was sure, anything to do with changing the dates, much more that she was meeting a man of whom he had heard nothing until now. Anyway, I'd quite like to meet Sir Godfrey, she decided. She had never met anyone with a title. Sir Godfrey sounded as though he might be fun.

'Oh well!' Moira said. 'We'll sort something out, I'm sure. But I wouldn't want you to be bored, Chloe.'

'Please don't worry about me, Mrs Portman,' Chloe said brightly. 'I'm sure I won't be bored. And now I think I'll go up, and if Robert should have another bad dream, I'll see to him.'

She realized that she did not want to stay in the room, watching the Portmans side by side on the sofa. She was not yet used to this; she might give herself away. Or even more likely, John might.

And so he did, and would have done to anyone who might have been facing him as Chloe was. He looked directly at her and, in his eyes, she saw all that had been in his embrace a short time ago. For no more than a second she returned his gaze before looking away.

'Thank you, Chloe,' Moira said. 'Sleep well.'

'That's a pity,' she said to her husband when Chloe had left the room. 'I did want everything to be just so for Sir Godfrey.'

'It'll be all right,' John said. 'If he wants to talk

business after dinner I'll take him into my study. Anyway, he might quite like Chloe.'

'Oh, I daresay he will,' Moira agreed. 'Most men like a pretty face.'

He looked at her sharply, but she was smiling.

'And most wives know that,' she added. 'They put up with it because they know in the end it doesn't mean anything.'

'Would you?' John asked. 'I mean, put up with it.'

Moira laughed.

'Oh, I don't even think about it darling! They might fall for you, all these pretty girls – and why wouldn't they – but it's not the kind of thing you would do. Old Faithful, that's what you are! My dear old faithful!' She gave him an affectionate peck on the cheek.

How wrong you are, John thought. He felt a twinge of resentment. Until the telephone had rung, faithfulness had had no part in him; all he had known had been his desire for Chloe. Nor had it been the thought of his wife and family, much though he cared for them of course, and always would, which had brought him back to his senses. No, it was the hint of promise, in Sir Godfrey's voice, which had turned him back on to the right path. It was ambition, he recognized that, but what was wrong with that? It was not just selfish ambition. He wanted, didn't he, to do what was right for his party, for his constituents, for his country – and at the same time for his wife and children, and now for Chloe. He was not sure how it might affect Chloe, but there was no way he could leave her out of his life.

And why, he asked himself, should I not do all these things, include all these people? Of course he should, and could! He would, in the best possible way, be all things to all men. His heart swelled with optimism and pride.

'Old Faithful!' he said good-humouredly. 'You make me sound like a horse!' Am I so predictable? he asked himself. He knew he was not.

'A very nice horse!' Moira said.

He was no longer listening. Already his thoughts were back with Chloe. He wanted to bring her into the conversation, hear himself say her name out loud, as if in doing so he had summoned her into his presence.

'Chloe dealt with Robert very well,' he said.

'Indeed she did,' Moira admitted. 'She seems really to have taken to him, and he to her.'

'We must make sure she settles down,' John said. 'Make sure she likes it here. Perhaps we should arrange one or two little trips – with the children of course? Make her feel one of the family.'

'It's a nice idea,' Moira agreed. 'Though when do you have time to spare for little trips? It's ages since we went out together, as a family.'

'You're right,' John said. 'But we must. Now that the summer's here we should drive out somewhere, take a picnic on to the Downs.'

'I'm all for it,' Moira said. 'Though it will be easier when Eddie's a bit older.'

She was aware that the time spent on the baby

kept her too much away from the other children, but it couldn't be helped. He'd been a weak baby and was only now beginning to catch up. They were a family almost split apart, she with the baby, John busy and frequently absent, Robert and Janet in the middle, though thankfully now with Chloe.

'Yes,' she said. 'It would be nice to do more things together. And I don't think we need worry about Chloe settling. She seems quick to make friends. I wonder who the young man is on Monday evening?'

'She didn't say it was a man.'

'All the same, I think it is,' Moira said. 'If it had been Josie, she'd have known how to get in touch.'

John had had the same thought. He had felt a sharp stab of jealousy when Chloe had mentioned the meeting and he felt it again now.

'I hope he's all right,' he said doubtfully. 'We *are* responsible, in a way.'

'We can't choose her friends for her. She *is* eighteen,' Moira pointed out.

On Monday evening there was, for Chloe, the question of what to wear. The day had been fine, and moderately warm, but since it was still only May it might well turn chilly later when the sun went down.

She opened her wardrobe and studied the contents – which took no time at all because there was nothing, absolutely nothing, which fitted the occasion. In the end she chose a full skirt in floral cotton, topped by a cream blouse, short-sleeved and definitely not warm enough, though there was no way she would wear her only coat, a serviceable tweed. It would have to be the dreaded cardigan though she had already realized that cardigans, however beautifully knitted, were not *de rigueur* in Brighton. She would, however, tie it around the strap of her handbag, casually, as if it didn't belong to her. She was pleased she had had her way over her white shoes, which her mother had said were not only tarty but would ruin her feet. If her social life was to take off she must, she absolutely must, buy some new clothes.

How lovely she looks, Moira thought as she watched Chloe leave the house, treading so lightly in her pretty shoes, her skirt twirling around her slim legs. She hoped the young man she was setting off to meet was a decent sort who would not take advantage of her inexperience.

Once on the seafront Chloe walked slowly towards the pier. How awful if she were to arrive before Simon. On the other hand, if she was late would he wait for her? There was no need to worry. As she drew near to the pier she saw him standing at the entrance. He wore light grey slacks and a navy blazer but anyone could tell that, however casual, his clothes were well tailored and his hair, though ruffled by the off-shore breeze, was expensively cut. She was within a few yards of him before he saw her, and when he did he stepped forward to meet her, taking both her hands briefly in his.

'How nice to see you!' he said. 'What would you like to do first? Shall we walk on the pier –

or perhaps along the seafront towards Hove? The choice is yours!'

'Along the seafront. I haven't been any farther than the Palace Pier.'

Perhaps, she thought, they might go on the West Pier which thrust out into the sea not far ahead, looking more fragile, more elegant and ethereal than the robust Palace Pier.

'Then that's what we'll do.'

They set off at a moderate pace. There was no need to hurry. It was a beautiful evening, the sun no more than halfway down the sky, the sea so smooth that the fishing boats cast reflections in the water, the promenade pleasantly populated, not too crowded. As they sauntered towards the West Pier Chloe turned her gaze away from the sea and surveyed the buildings on the other side of the road. Small shops, selling sticks of rock, flashy fake jewellery, souvenirs, were hemmed in between large, imposing hotels. When they came to the great white edifice of the Grand Hotel, rising up like a many-tiered wedding cake, set back in a curve from the main road and fronted by a terrace where people were sitting at tables in the early evening sun, Chloe stopped dead.

'Oh! It's beautiful! It's like . . . it's like . . .' Words failed her.

Simon looked at her, at her shining eyes, her mouth half-open with surprise, then took her elbow.

'Let's cross the road. Let's take a closer look.'

He guided her through the traffic to the opposite pavement, then without pause, and without a word of explanation, he marched her up the wide front steps, into the entrance hall, said a few words to the commissionaire, and they were at once shown to a small table on the terrace.

Chloe looked around, wide-eyed with astonishment. Could this be true? Could it be really happening to her, the former Dora Branksome? Such a short time ago she had been stuck in Akersfield where nothing ever happened, and now here she was on the terrace of the Grand Hotel in Brighton! How could it all have happened so quickly? Was she awake or was she dreaming?

'What would you like to drink?' Simon's words broke into her thoughts.

'Oh! Oh, I don't really mind. Whatever you think.'

How stupid of me, she thought. How terribly, boringly unsophisticated. I ought to know exactly what to ask for but I don't. She glanced quickly at the drinks on nearby tables: short glasses, tall glasses – she had no idea what.

'Oh, anything!' she said lightly. 'You choose! What's everyone else drinking?'

'Cocktails. Or gin or whisky. But *we* don't have to. You perhaps don't like cocktails and I'm not fussy anyway.'

Her confident manner did not fool him in the least. She was nervous, and it was that very nervousness, her fear of saying or doing the wrong thing, yet covering it with an air of sophistication, which had drawn him to her when they had had coffee in the Square, and did so again now. She was like a small, bright child, trying to be a grown-up lady. He wanted to please her, to protect her.

'I don't, actually!'

She spoke as someone who had run the whole gamut of cocktails, found them wanting and given them up.

'Then why don't we both have a nice cold fruit juice?' Simon suggested.

'Can we?' Chloe said. 'In a place like this?'

'In a place like this,' Simon said, smiling, 'we can have whatever we choose to order. We can have a glass of water!' Though it would probably cost as much as a gin-and-tonic, he thought.

'Oh I don't want water!' Chloe said firmly. 'Water rots your boots, as my mother always says!'

Damn! she thought, why do I say these stupid things my mother always said?

'A fruit juice would be nice,' she said graciously. 'Pineapple.' It sounded more exotic than orange. Perhaps she would have a cocktail later when she felt more settled.

The pineapple juice came in tall glasses, ice cubes in the bottom, a sliver of fruit floating on the top. It was quite the best fruit juice she had tasted in her entire life.

'Happy days!' Simon said, raising his glass.

'Happy days!'

As she sipped her drink, Chloe looked around her. Everyone was so smart, so chic; some people were in evening dress, which in Akersfield was reserved strictly for the first night of the annual Conversazione and for the Civic Ball. Suddenly she felt out of place, dowdy.

'If I'd had the slightest idea we were coming here,' she said, 'I'd have worn something more suitable.' It was a black lie because she didn't possess anything the least bit suitable.

Simon gave her a long look before he replied. She felt her colour rising under his scrutiny.

'You are exactly right as you are,' he said at last. 'I wouldn't change a thing.'

He meant it – and he couldn't understand why. She was without doubt beautiful, but he knew a dozen beautiful girls. She was amusing, though mostly when she didn't mean to be. He doubted that she was well-educated or intellectual; her world, he was sure, was not that of literature and the Arts. When she forgot herself – he had discovered – she spoke with a North-Country accent, not musical to his ears. She was intelligent, oh she was that all right. Her face was alight with intelligence. Yet it was not even that which attracted him so strongly. So what was it? He didn't know. He didn't care. All he knew was that his feelings for her were as strong and as deep as they were sudden. He, who had flitted pleasurably from girl to girl without, to the despair of his mother, ever settling, had unaccountably come to a halt before Chloe. And she was not what he had envisaged or expected.

How extremely polite he was, Chloe thought. How well-mannered! Of course she had been complimented before, but never in such surroundings as these and never in such a wonderful speaking voice. She could have listened to him forever.

They finished their drinks and Simon called the waiter to order more. This time, in a rush of confidence, Chloe chose a cocktail, which came in a small, fancy glass with a cherry on top. She sipped it cautiously. It tasted horrible, like a foul medicine she had once been prescribed for a nasty chest cold, but not for the world would she say so. She swallowed bravely, managing to smile. After all, this was living!

She leaned back in her chair and imagined herself in a beautiful gown, emerald green satin, and at once felt like a film star – Vivien Leigh, perhaps? – so that it was rather a pity that the sun began to dip quite rapidly and a breeze sprang up and she realized at once that what she wanted most in the world was her cardigan. Involuntarily, she shivered.

'Oh dear!' Simon said. 'You're feeling cold. We must move! I can't have you taking a chill. In any case everyone seems to be going in to dinner and I don't think we'd like it here. *You* would be all right but I'm not suitably dressed, so why don't we leave and why don't you put on that pretty cardigan?'

With alacrity Chloe untied the cardigan from her handbag and slipped her arms into its soft comfort.

'I know a small place in Kemp Town where they do a good meal,' Simon said. 'Shall we try that?'

'Oh yes!' Chloe agreed. 'I'm as hungry as a man on horseback, in spite of all the nuts and things

I've eaten! But I mustn't be too late home. Mr and Mrs Portman might worry.'

'I'll make sure you're not,' Simon promised. 'Kemp Town is no distance from Sussex Square.'

He paid the bill and left, Chloe noticed, a substantial tip. Either he was well off or generous or, hopefully, both. As they descended the steps both piers were visible, lit for their whole lengths and seeming to be joined together by the continuous string of lights between them. She had seen lights before, hadn't she been to the Blackpool Illuminations? But these were prettier, more delicate. More refined, she thought with satisfaction. Oh, this was a lovely place!

Simon took her arm and they set out at a brisk pace, so that by the time they reached Kemp Town she was warm again. At first sight the restaurant was disappointing, *quite* unlike the Grand Hotel. Its frontage was no more than the width of the door, plus the one window, the latter draped in dark red, semi-transparent curtains through which the lights shone dimly. Stepping inside they sat at a bare-topped table, oak, laid with plain cutlery and white napkins. A waiter, dressed in navy bell-bottomed trousers and a navy-and-white striped jersey, brought them the menu.

'The thing they do best here is fish,' Simon said, 'hence the name. So what shall we have?'

'You choose,' Chloe said quickly. Her mother, not from lack of money, was an unadventurous cook, so that fish for the Branksomes meant fried haddock or fish pie, always on a Friday. Apart, of course, from fish and chips wrapped in the Akersfield Courier and eaten in the street by Chloe and her friends. But her mother was right, it was common, and no way to be referred to at the present moment.

'Do you like sole?' Simon enquired.

'Oh yes!' Chloe said with enthusiasm.

He gave the order and when the waiter had left them he said, 'Now tell me about yourself.' He wanted to know everything about all the years she had been alive until he had spotted her standing by the entrance to the pier.

'There's not much to tell,' Chloe said.

It was true. Her previous life had been totally uninteresting. It was only now that she was beginning to live. What in the world could she say that would interest him?

'Tell me what you do in Sussex Square,' Simon prompted her.

'Well . . .' She hesitated. 'I'm a sort of companion to a lady, Moira Portman. I do anything, really,' she said vaguely. '*Not* housework of course. Nothing like that. I live with the family, help a little with the children – they're dears! John Portman is a Member of Parliament. Perhaps you've heard of him?'

Simon shook his head, smiling.

'Really? Mrs Portman's mother is Lady Stansfield. I had tea with her the other day.'

'Ah!' Simon said. 'I *think* my mother knows Lady Stansfield. I think I've heard her mentioned. I'm not sure I've ever met her.'

'She was quite well-known in the war,' Chloe said. 'Quite important, I believe.' And that was about the limit of any good Lady Stansfield would be to her, though she had been a bit useful.

'Then that's how she and my mother would have known each other,' Simon said. 'The Red Cross, the WVS and suchlike. I was away at school most of the time, and I spent holidays with my grandmother in Surrey. Brighton was rather a dangerous place. So where were you?'

Chloe was saved from confessing to Akersfield Mixed Infants by the arrival of the fish; grilled, golden and succulent, with generous wedges of lemon.

She watched with fascination while the waiter skilfully removed the fillets of fish from the bone, then following Simon's example she squeezed lemon juice over the sole, savouring the delicate smell which rose to her nostrils. She was mighty hungry.

'In the war my mother used to say she'd give her back teeth for a lemon or two,' she observed – then at once thought what a vulgar way of putting it, but Simon seemed not to notice.

'And after that what did you do?' Anything, she thought, rather than have him ask about her drab life.

'I did what every young man had to do then,' Simon said. 'I did my two years' National Service. I hated every minute of it! A boring waste of time!'

Nevertheless, Chloe thought, he must have looked wonderful in uniform. She could easily imagine it.

'When I came out of the army,' he said, 'my parents took it for granted I'd study law, like my father and all the Collinses, but I wasn't having any.' He sighed. 'I'm afraid I was a great disappointment to my parents, which was why I left home. My grandfather had left me a bit of money so I was able to rent a very small flat in the Old Steine, which is where I live now.'

A man of independent means, Chloe thought. She had never known a young man of independent means.

'I don't know why I'm saying all this. Am I boring you?' he asked anxiously.

'Not in the least,' Chloe said truthfully. 'And are you still no longer friendly with your parents?' But that couldn't be, because he'd talked of taking her to meet his mother.

'Oh no, not at all! They live in Rottingdean and we're on good terms.'

How very sophisticated, Chloe thought, to live so close, yet separate from one's parents. How suave! It could never happen in Akersfield. If she'd stayed in Akersfield she'd have been with her mother until the day she married or died, whichever came first.

'Not that they approve of what I do,' Simon added.

'What do you do?'

'I'm a writer. Really just a freelance journalist at the moment – the local paper, magazines and so on. It ekes out my income.'

It must eke it out pretty well, Chloe reckoned. This restaurant, for instance, was expensive, she had seen the prices on the menu.

'But I'm writing a novel,' he said. 'That's what I want to be. A novelist. It's the only thing I'd ever want to be! That's my future. I'm sure of it!'

It was something he had never told anyone, an ambition secretly cherished, kept from the cold light of day lest the talent he believed he had should fade and wither; but not for one moment did it occur to him to hide it from this girl sitting opposite him, her hair, her face, glowing in the soft lamplight. He could tell her anything: his hopes, his dreams, anything.

'And I paint a bit,' he added.

A journalist! A novelist! A painter! She had never met even one such creature, let alone three rolled into one. And he was clearly not starving in a garret.

'How enormously interesting!' she said wide-eyed.

'And that's enough about me,' he said.

He wanted to know about her, and he would. Now that he had found her there was no way he would let her go.

For a few moments they ate in silence, Chloe thankful that he was not asking her more about herself. If she was to see him again she must sort out in her mind what she could say to him.

'Is your fish all right?' he asked. 'Don't feel you have to finish it if you don't want to. They're rather large portions.'

'And I have a small appetite,' Chloe said modestly. Now that *was* a lie! Reluctantly, she put down her knife and fork, leaving food on her plate, which her mother had always said was a sign of refinement and good breeding.

'Could you eat some pudding?' Simon asked.

Could a duck swim, Chloe thought as she rather sadly shook her head.

'Then perhaps we should go,' he said reluctantly. 'I don't want to, but I don't want you to be in trouble for staying out too late, otherwise I mightn't be allowed to see you again and I shouldn't like that.'

When they reached the door it was raining heavily. Simon turned back and asked for a taxi to be ordered.

'I can't have you getting wet and catching cold,' he said as he helped her into the cab. 'I've told you, I want to see you again. I *must* see you again.'

'That would be nice,' Chloe said truthfully.

'When?'

She paused, and considered.

'Well, tomorrow we have Sir Godfrey. Wednesday . . . I'm sure there's something on Wednesday.' There wasn't. The week stretched ahead, a blank sheet, but no-one need know that.

'Thursday?' he suggested. 'Or Friday?'

'Thursday,' Chloe said. 'In case we go to London at the weekend.'

When the taxi drew up at the door of Blenheim House, Simon alighted and helped her out. She had wondered if he would attempt to kiss her in the taxi but he was right, it was a very short ride and moreover he was clearly a gentleman. But there, in the light from the street lamp, he raised her hand and kissed her fingers, while John Portman watched him from the window.

10

Standing on the pavement, Simon watched Chloe as she walked away from him, treading the short path to the door of Blenheim House.

He wanted to call after her, to take hold of her and to persuade her to spend just another hour with him, to walk, to talk, to go back with him to his flat – anything so that he did not have to part company with her, for he could scarcely bear to let her go.

It was a sensation new to him. He had never felt like this before and he was not sure why it was so. Yes, she was bright, she was beautiful, she was funny, but she was also naive, she was gauche. She was, in spite of the air of confidence which he had known in the first few minutes to be assumed for his benefit, unsophisticated, lacking in knowledge of a world which was new to her. He wanted to take her in his arms and show her all those things she didn't yet know, and teach her. Yet at the same time he did not want her to change.

As it was, he watched her until she reached the

door of the house and then he turned away, stepped into the cab, and was driven off.

Chloe raised her finger to the bell-push and hardly had she done so before the door was opened by John Portman. His tight-lipped expression did not quite hide the eagerness in his eyes. She noticed both.

'I was just about to ring,' she said. 'I'm not late, am I?'

'No,' he admitted. 'I saw you arrive.'

She recognized the sharpness of jealousy in his voice. So he had seen Simon kiss her hand. She was rather pleased about that.

Damn her, she looked so lovely standing there, John thought. There was colour in her cheeks and brightness in her eyes. He hated the thought that this young man, whom he had glimpsed so briefly, had caused this air of excitement in her. He wanted to show her what a kiss could be – and it would not be a polite brushing of his lips on her fingers.

Moira Portman called out from the sitting-room.

'Come in here before you go up, Chloe! Come and tell us about your evening!'

Chloe's look questioned John.

'Please do!' he said.

He wanted, and did not want, to hear about it, but most of all he desired her just to be there, just a little longer. She had been in his thoughts all evening. Where was she? What was she doing?

He stood aside to let her pass. Moira Portman, sitting on the sofa, put down her book and looked up as Chloe paused for a moment, framed in the doorway. How pretty she looks, how alive, Moira thought. I must paint her, I really must.

'Come and sit down for a minute,' she said. 'Did you enjoy yourself?' It hardly needed asking. The girl was bathed in enjoyment.

'Oh yes, Mrs Portman!' Chloe said. 'I had a lovely time!'

'What did you do?'

'Well first of all we walked a little way along the seafront, and then we had cocktails at the Grand Hotel . . .'

'The Grand Hotel?'

'On the terrace. Simon is obviously well-known there. I could tell that.' Perhaps that wasn't *strictly* true, but then it might well be. The waiters had been most attentive.

'Cocktails?' Moira sounded doubtful.

'I only drank one,' Chloe assured her. 'I've never really cared for cocktails! Simon did think we might have dinner at the Grand but in the end he decided on somewhere quieter. We went to a place called Fishers.'

Moira looked across at John, who was standing with his back to the mantlepiece.

'Oh, but we know Fishers, don't we John? It's rather nice!' And the young man has good if somewhat expensive taste she thought.

'We had Dover sole,' Chloe said. 'I'm *very* fond of Dover sole.'

'And do you know anything about this young man? This what's-his-name?' John's interruption was brusque.

'Oh yes!' Chloe said brightly. 'He told me all about himself. Simon Collins is his name. He has a flat in Brighton, in the Old Steine. His parents live in Rottingdean, I gather they're quite well known. I think his mother is a friend of Lady Stansfield.'

'Good gracious, what a small world!' Moira exclaimed. She would ask her mother at the first opportunity what she knew of the Collins family. 'And what does he do?'

'He's a man of independent means, though he's also a journalist, *and* a novelist.'

'Oh really?' Moira said. 'I wonder what he's written. I might have read something.'

'*And* he's also a painter,' Chloe added. 'He wants to paint my portrait one day.' He had not actually said that but she was sure he would.

'As a matter of fact, so do I,' Moira said. 'As soon as I have the time. Will you sit for me?'

'Certainly. I'd like to,' Chloe agreed.

John Portman broke in.

'Well I hope you will give my wife preference over this . . . Simon Collins, did you say? A writer? I can't say I've ever heard of him.'

'But of course I will. It will be an honour to be painted by Mrs Portman.'

Though there is no reason, Chloe thought, why I should not sit for both of them. And would I be in an exhibition? She had once visited an exhibition in Akersfield Art Gallery with a party from school. There had been a portrait of the current Lady Mayoress, plump and plain in a low-cut evening dress showing her elderly bosom. They had all laughed their socks off at it. My portrait would *not* be like that, she concluded.

What would she wear? Red would be striking but black, quite plain, with a single strand of pearls might be better. And the neckline, with better reason than that of the Lady Mayoress, cut quite low. Who knew, she might well be discovered by some film producer.

'Well, I must say you seem to have had quite an evening!' Moira said, breaking into Chloe's dream. 'So do you plan to see him again?'

'I do actually, on Thursday, if that's all right with you. I knew you wanted me to be here tomorrow and I wasn't sure about Wednesday.'

Moira opened her mouth to say something but John broke in.

'You should be very careful,' he said sharply. 'You really don't know anything about this man except what he's told you.'

'He did offer to take me to meet his mother,' Chloe said. And that at least was true. 'But I will be careful, I promise.'

'I'm sure you will,' Moira said. 'Look in on the children on your way to bed.'

'Of course!'

She tip-toed into the bedroom. Both Janet and Robert were peacefully asleep. Really, she thought, children are quite attractive when they're asleep.

'Well,' Moira said to her husband, 'that seems to have gone off nicely. I'm glad she enjoyed herself. He seems a suitable person.'

'How can we possibly know that?' John snapped.

'He could be an absolute blackguard. We know nothing about him and she's very young.'

'She's eighteen, and sensible,' Moira said. 'In some ways even old for her years. I don't think you need worry, John. I'm sure she can look after herself.'

But what he had in mind was the memory of Simon raising Chloe's hand to his lips, the look of pure pleasure on her face as he did so, her shining eyes when he met her at the door. For a minute he hated Simon Collins, who was young, attractive, seemingly well-off and, above all, unattached.

Chloe tip-toed out of the children's bedroom, leaving the night light burning in case Robert should waken. He could not bear the dark. Back in her own room she undressed slowly, eyeing her reflection in the long wardrobe mirror. Down to her knickers and brassière, she paused. What a strange piece of work her brassière was: two circles of material close-stitched, round and round until they were as stiff as a board, then reaching a well-defined point at the centre of each cup, looking for all the world like two inverted ice-cream cornets fashioned from plaster of Paris. She had objected from the beginning to wearing a brassière of any kind. 'I don't need it!' she'd said. Her mother had been firm – as firm as the contraption itself.

'You might think that now,' she'd warned. 'But just wait until you're forty! Do you want to be all saggy?'

Still looking in the mirror, Chloe unharnessed herself from the brassière and let it drop to the floor.

She eyed her bosom critically. Saggy she was *not*, but nor was she the shape into which the garment on the floor had moulded her. No, she was altogether softer, rounder, more curvaceous, her nipples standing out firm and dark against the pale flesh.

Was it possible – the thought came to her suddenly – that Mrs Portman, or even Simon, might wish to paint her in the nude? Artists often did. They thought nothing of it. Supposing, just supposing, they wanted to paint her *altogether* in the nude.

She wriggled out of her knickers and let them fall around her ankles before she looked at herself again. Well, she thought, she looked a lot better than some of the naked ladies she had seen portrayed. At least she had a flat stomach and no rolls of fat. She breathed in deeply, held herself taut, until her abdomen was almost concave.

But would she allow such a thing? She wasn't sure. Though if it was for the sake of Art, then why not? Great art needed a subject as well as a painter.

But, and regrettably, portrayed as a nude she would not be named – Miss Chloe Branksome – as she would be in a clothed portrait. Perhaps just 'Chloe'? She saw the people, smartly dressed, crowding around the painting in the exhibition hall. 'Who *is* this beautiful Chloe?' they were asking. Well, if anyone influential wanted to know she was sure they would find out. She would be discovered.

She took one last appraising look at herself, then released her indrawn breath and taut muscles and turned away and picked up her nightdress from the bed.

And there was another thing! No way would she continue to wear this kind of nightdress, high neck demurely collared, made from winceyette, white with a patter of small pink rosebuds. It was truly awful, truly Dora Branksome of Akersfield!

She fell asleep within minutes of insinuating herself between the sheets and dreamed of Simon and John Portman, both clad like the man in the portrait of 'The Laughing Cavalier' which had hung in the school hall, engaged in a sword fight over who should take possession of her conical brassière. In the end they chopped it in two with their swords and took half each.

On Tuesday morning she wakened as fresh as a daisy and resolved, in the first five minutes, that she would use some of her savings, in her two hours off, to buy a new dress for the evening's occasion.

Mrs Portman, anxious and nervous about what she should cook for Sir Godfrey Milton's dinner, seemed reluctant to let her take her two hours.

'I'll go straight after lunch,' Chloe promised. 'When Robert takes his nap. I'll be back in time to collect Janet from school. I wouldn't want to disgrace you by not being well enough dressed for your important guest.'

'Very well then,' Moira Portman said. The girl was so excited she hadn't the heart to tell her that it didn't matter, Sir Godfrey wouldn't notice. 'And perhaps you'll help me when you get back? I could show you how to lay the table.'

'I'd be glad to do that,' Chloe agreed. It was, after

all, something which would come in useful when, as she surely would, she had her own beautiful dining-room.

She found exactly what she wanted in Brighton, in a small shop in a side street, though she caught her breath at the figure on the price tag. It was more than she had ever paid for a dress in her life.

'Try it on,' the assistant encouraged. 'You've nothing to lose just trying it on.'

She was wrong. From the moment Chloe pulled it over her head, looked at her reflection in the mirror, she lost all sense of whether she could afford it or not. The soft, cream silky material enhanced the creaminess of her skin. The neckline cut low, but not low enough to be immodest, showed off her neck and bosom. Cape sleeves fell softly over her upper arms and, as a finishing touch, the wide gold belt above the full skirt cinched in her small waist. She had to have it. There was no point in looking any further.

'It's you!' the assistant enthused. 'It's exactly you! You look beautiful!'

'I'll take it!' Chloe said.

'You'll never regret it!'

'You're back in good time!' Moira Portman said. 'Robert is still asleep.'

'I knew you didn't want me to linger,' Chloe said virtuously. The truth was that, after having bought the dress, and a length of cream velvet ribbon for a headband, she had hurried home to avoid the temptation of also buying new shoes. That was impossible, she would have to make do with what she had though, she consoled herself, they would mostly be sitting at the table and her feet would be hidden.

When Chloe fetched Janet from school Moira Portman said to the children, 'Now you must amuse yourselves for a little while. I am going to show Chloe how to lay the table.'

She did this by laying one place setting at the head of the table: the best silver from the huge canteen, two crystal wine glasses – 'The smaller one for white, the larger for red,' she explained. The snow-white damask napkin, the Wedgwood dinner service.

'Lay the other three places exactly like this,' she instructed. 'My husband at the head of the table, Sir Godfrey on his right, me on his left. I suppose you had better sit on Sir Godfrey's other side.'

She was not sure that Chloe eating with them every evening had been the best idea. There must be a happy medium. But it was too late now, they had gone beyond the point of no return. Oh well, she was sure the girl would behave quite well.

Chloe laid the remaining places slowly, and with precision, then stood back to admire her handiwork. Mrs Portman came in and added silver cruets and a shallow bowl of purple, velvety pansies from the garden.

'It's all quite beautiful!' Chloe said.

'Not bad,' Mrs Portman conceded. 'My mother would be pleased to see her best Wedgwood being used.' Perhaps she should have invited her mother but Chloe's presence at the table would have made that awkward.

'Now you'll just have nice time to see the children to bed and get changed. Thank goodness Edward went off so quickly and let's hope he sleeps through the evening.' She hoped, too, that John would be home any minute. She still had a few things to see to in the kitchen, and then to change, slap on a bit of make-up. She was pleased to have Sir Godfrey to dinner, especially for John's sake. They should start to do such things more often but it wasn't easy.

She heard John's key in the door as she went into the kitchen.

'I'm home!' he called. 'Where is everybody?'

'I'm in the kitchen,' she said. 'Chloe's just taken the children up.'

She smiled as she heard him race up the stairs. He was always so eager to see the children. If she hadn't felt exactly the same way about them she could have been jealous.

Taking the stairs two at a time, John's thoughts were not on the children. It was Chloe he wanted to see. All day long he'd thought about her. In the Chamber, at Prime Minister's Question Time, instead of the rows of faces of the Opposition he had seen her face. Slumped in his seat, he had heard nothing of the cut and thrust of Mr Speaker; even the PM's rumbling wit, which sent a ripple of amusement around the Tory benches, was lost on him. All he heard was Chloe's soft, clear North-Country voice. And in the train, all the way to Brighton, the wheels against the track had beaten out her name. Chloe! Chloe! Chloe!

She was emerging from the bathroom, hand-in-hand with a shining clean Robert, Janet trailing behind, when John reached her. He greeted the children perfunctorily, but his eyes were on Chloe and when she met his hungry look the colour deepened in her face. He wanted to touch her, wanted it desperately, but Janet's sharp gaze was fixed on him and with an effort he resisted the temptation.

'I'm just seeing the children to bed,' Chloe said unnecessarily. 'Come along, you two. Sharp's the word or we won't have time for a story!'

'Daddy can read to us!' Janet decided.

'Not tonight, Princess,' John said. 'I have to get changed. Mummy and Daddy are having a guest for dinner.'

'I know,' Janet said. 'He's called Sir Milton . . .'

'Sir Godfrey.'

'I want to see him.'

'You can't,' John said. 'Now off you go with Chloe, and don't give any trouble or I'll be very cross!'

It was the wrong thing to say, Chloe thought. It was exactly the thing which would make Janet play up all the more.

'But if you're good – very, *very* good,' John said, 'you shall have a reward.'

'What will it be?' Janet asked.

'We'll discuss it in the morning. Only if you've been good.'

'Will I get a reward?' Robert asked anxiously.

'Of course you will!' John promised.

With the thought of their father's promise the children were, for once, quick into bed. Chloe read them two stories at breakneck speed, then said, 'I must go now. I have things to do. Close your eyes and go to sleep quickly and we'll see what the morning brings!'

She had less than twenty minutes now to bathe, put on her new dress, do her hair and put on some make-up. She would have liked a leisurely hour to get ready for such an occasion. She had heard John go downstairs while she was reading to the children.

Fifteen minutes later the doorbell rang, and from the sounds which floated up the two flights of stairs she knew that Sir Godfrey had arrived and was being welcomed. She should have been down there, not to welcome him at the door, that was not her place, but somewhere in the background. It couldn't be helped. She just wasn't ready. She had spent too much time looking at herself in the dress, which looked even better than it had in the shop. She fastened the velvet ribbon around her head and was pleased with the result. It accentuated her hairline and showed up her widow's peak. A touch of lipstick, not too much, she thought, a drop or two of perfume – Lily of the Valley – and I'm ready. She watched herself in the mirror and she gave one last twirl before leaving her room.

Quietly, she opened the door to the children's room. It would please Mrs Portman if she could report that they were asleep. Janet was, but Robert, at the sound of the door, opened his eyes.

'You look like a princess in a story book,' he said sleepily.

She blew him a kiss, and left.

At the top of the main flight of stairs she took a deep breath, rested her hand lightly on the banister rail and, without the slightest hurry, head held high, descended. It would have been nice, she thought, if they had still been gathered in the hall as she came down the stairs, but she could hear them – Sir Godfrey had a deep, booming voice – in the sitting-room.

She paused outside the door. Should she knock? No, not really, especially as the door was slightly ajar. She was, after all, to eat with them. There was no need to act like a servant. She took a deep breath, and walked in.

The Portmans were deep in conversation with their guest. Chloe stood near the door, quietly waiting. Suddenly, Moira Portman looked up, and the two men followed her gaze. For a second or two, though it seemed longer to Chloe, there was complete silence and then the two men leapt to their feet, their eyes on Chloe, who stood quite still. Moira Portman was the first to break the silence.

'Chloe! Do come in. Let me introduce you. Sir Godfrey, this is Chloe, who helps me with the children.'

How incredibly lovely the girl looked, Moira thought. No wonder Sir Godfrey seemed struck dumb, momentarily deprived of speech and movement, but when Chloe smiled at him he recovered himself and stepped forward, his hand outstretched to take hers.

He is the spitting image of Horace Butterfield, Labour Mayor of Akersfield, Chloe thought. Short-ish, fattish, pink-faced, balding a little at the front, which at least gave him some semblance of a noble forehead. She was deeply disappointed. She had expected something quite different.

Mr Butterfield, in addition to being physically no great shakes, had been a silly old lecher. He had passed all too often through the office of the Borough Surveyor, always pausing to place a hot hand on Chloe's shoulder or run a finger down her back. But she knew how to deal with the Butterfields of this world, even though this version, as he greeted her, had a much more pleasant voice than his Akersfield counterpart. He was also better dressed; well-cut dark suit, gleaming white shirt, silk tie, gold cufflinks.

She is a corker and no mistake, Sir Godfrey thought, holding on to Chloe's hand fractionally longer than was necessary. Portman hadn't said a dickie bird about her – keeping her to himself no doubt.

Finally letting go of Chloe's hand he turned towards his host but John Portman, still rooted to the spot, was clearly seeing nothing except the vision of loveliness which was Chloe. His eyes were filled with longing, in fact with downright lust, Sir Godfrey thought. And who could blame him? If he thought he had a chance he'd be in there himself. He just hoped it was not obvious to the wife – a nice little woman whom he'd always liked, the best of wives for a rising young politician.

Moira's voice came through to John as if from a far distance and something in her tone told him that this was not the first time she had made the remark.

'Perhaps Chloe would like a small glass of sherry!' Should she be offering the girl sherry? Was she used to it?

'A very small one,' Chloe said.

'Sensible! Very sensible!' Sir Godfrey said, holding out his empty glass as John picked up the decanter. 'A good sherry. Very dry, the way I like it.'

'We have my mother to thank for it,' Moira said. 'She left us a good cellar when we moved in here.'

So that was it, Sir Godfrey thought. A wealthy mother. He had rather wondered at the elegance of the house and its furnishings for a backbench MP.

John handed Chloe her sherry without ever taking his eyes off her. She could see that his hand, which held the glass, was trembling. When she met his eyes as he gave her the glass, when she saw the longing in them, a sensation like a fierce flame leapt through her from top to toe, leaving her weak and shaken. It could only be compared to the feelings she had had when they had stood so close together in the sea. Whatever else, she must show nothing of it to the others. She wished John would stop gazing at her. She took the glass from him with a hand trembling scarcely less than his, and sipped at the pale gold liquid.

It was quite horrible! It was worse than the red

wine on that first night. Yet Sir Godfrey had praised it. Clearly, she had things to learn on what she hoped was the way up. Repressing a shudder, she sipped it again then set the glass down on a small table where she might conveniently forget its existence and hope no-one would notice.

'Shall we go into dinner?' Moira Portman said eventually.

Chloe sent up a swift prayer of thanks. She was beginning to think they would never eat and she was starving.

Seated next to Sir Godfrey at the table she wondered for the first minute or two what she should say to him. Was she, for instance, supposed to speak when she was spoken to? She need not have worried. At the same time as eating his way through the meal – it was delicious – which his hostess had cooked for him, Sir Godfrey kept up an effortless flow of conversation calculated to include everyone at the table. He spoke of politics not at all, for which Chloe was truly thankful since she knew nothing. They touched on general subjects: the weather, the prospects for cricket, the Royal family (always with approval – they did a good job) – the latest in films. It hardly mattered that Chloe had little to say; it was not noticeable. In any case she was happy to listen, to learn what an occasion like this demanded.

Most of the conversation fell on Sir Godfrey and on Moira Portman. John was quieter than usual and for too much of the time his gaze rested on Chloe, as though she was the only person in the room. Whenever she met his eye – and though she tried not to do so she could not help it, she was as powerless as a pin against a magnet – her bones turned to jelly. She hoped the other two had not noticed John's behaviour, though if they had they gave no sign of it.

Presently Sir Godfrey turned to Chloe.

'And how do you like living in Brighton? Is it as good as living in the North?'

'Much better!' Chloe said firmly. 'I like it very much.'

'And whereabouts in the North did you live?'

'In Akersfield,' Chloe admitted. If only she could have said 'Harrogate' or even 'Scarborough' she would have felt better, but how could anyone boast about Akersfield?

'Ah yes! Akersfield,' Sir Godfrey nodded. He sought for something to say about Akersfield. 'Wool, isn't it?'

'Yes.' 'Wool' was all strangers ever found to say.

'And have you been anywhere else in this part of the country? Have you been to London?'

'I came through London on my way to Brighton,' Chloe said. Her voice brightened, she looked up at Sir Godfrey with a sweet smile on her face. 'London is the one place I want to see! I *long* to go there!'

'I'm sure you will!' Sir Godfrey said. How nice it would be to show this young, innocent and beautiful girl from the wild north the sights and sounds of London! Reluctantly, he put the thought from him, and at the same moment John Portman sprang suddenly to life.

'I'm sure you will, too,' he insisted. 'And soon. From Brighton, nothing is easier!'

He would take her himself. Nothing could be more natural than that, as he went most days, she should at least travel with him, and indeed that he should take her to the House, show her how the Mother of Parliaments worked, give her lunch and then . . .

He drew a line across his thoughts. It was enough for the moment to think that he would have her for the whole day to himself.

This time Chloe allowed herself not only to catch his eye, but to give him a long look. She read the invitation in his eyes, and her own replied, 'Yes! Oh yes, I will!'

'The problem is,' Moira said, 'that with the children it's so difficult to do, except of course when we go to stay in the flat, which of course we shall do some time.'

Chloe looked again at John. 'I want to go now,' her expression said. 'And not with the children.'

John understood her immediately. The communication between them was uncanny. It needed no words. He nodded almost imperceptibly. So you shall, he thought, so you shall.

'Shall we have coffee at the table, or in the sitting-room?' Moira asked. 'What do you think?'

'Well if you'll excuse us,' Sir Godfrey said, 'there are one or two things I need to discuss with John. Tedious, I know, but it has to be done!'

John was jerked away from his vision of a trip to London. So what could it be? What did Sir Godfrey have to say?

'If you wouldn't mind, darling,' he said to Moira, 'Sir Godfrey and I will have our coffee in my study.'

There was nothing definite in anything Sir Godfrey had to say to John in the next half-hour, no firm promises, which was disappointing, but perhaps to be expected.

'The PM has his eye on you,' Sir Godfrey said. 'You've made a favourable impression!'

Well, that was something, John thought.

'This girl of yours, this Chloe,' Sir Godfrey continued. 'She's a corker isn't she? Where did you find her?'

'I didn't. My wife did,' John said.

Sir Godfrey nodded.

'Well, my boy,' he said. 'Keep it clean. Don't get entangled.'

'I never . . .' John began, but Sir Godfrey hardly heard the interruption.

'The party can't do with any breath of scandal. Everything's too unsettled since the war. Family values wanted, and all that. I'm not saying,' he added kindly, 'man to man, that a fellow can't have his fun, but I make it a rule never to play on my own ground. Play away! You get my drift?'

'Quite!' John said. 'Oh, quite!'

Nevertheless, he thought, I will have my day in London with Chloe. Just one, perfect day. All the Sir Godfrey Miltons in the world shan't stop me!

11

The week between Sir Godfrey's visit and the following Tuesday, the date which had been fixed for Chloe to go to London, was passed, at least by her, in thinking about it and planning for it. Nothing else entered her mind. She would have preferred to go sooner but that was apparently impossible for John. 'Believe me,' he said to Chloe on one of their rare snatched moments together, 'I don't want to wait, but needs must. I have so many meetings in the next few days that I wouldn't be able to spend any time with you.'

The whole purpose was, for him, to be with Chloe, away from everyone else, away from the constraints of his home. He wanted her entirely to himself if only for a few hours, but his desire, strong though it was, must remain hidden, bottled up inside. It could not be expressed even to Chloe, for he rarely saw her alone.

Chloe's thoughts, though she wanted to be with John and was excited at the prospect of having him to herself, at least for part of the time, were centred for the most part on London. The very name was magic to her, its streets were paved with gold. For the rest of that week and over the weekend she willingly sacrificed every hour of free time due to her, foregoing her daily two hours, working longer than called upon so that on the following Tuesday she would be as free as air and time would not matter. And every night she prayed that the children would not go down with measles, chickenpox or any other dread disease which would mean she must stay with them.

Only on one evening, after she had put the children to bed, did she leave the house, and that on Monday to keep her promise to meet Simon. This time, at his suggestion, they were to meet at the bottom of Lewes Crescent. He was there when she arrived. They crossed the road, walked down on to one of the terraces and sat on a bench.

'I'm here to tell you I can't spend much time with you,' Chloe said. 'Something's cropped up and I have to get back.'

'Oh no!' Simon said. He was clearly disappointed. 'I thought we might have a meal together – and I have something interesting to tell you! Why can't you stay?'

'Tell me your news first,' Chloe said.

He was only too ready to do so.

'It's marvellous! I had a letter from the Features editor of *John Bull* magazine – do you know *John Bull*?'

'I know of it,' Chloe said cautiously. There was no need to say it was a journal her mother wouldn't have in the house since she didn't like its politics.

'It's very good. I sent a suggestion for a series of articles on the Cinque Ports, it was ages ago, I thought they just weren't going to answer, then this morning came a letter from the Features editor. He's definitely interested and he wants to discuss it with me – would you believe, tomorrow? Short notice, but who cares.'

'Why, that's wonderful!' Chloe said. She would have to find out what the Cinque Ports were.

'It is, actually. If I'm successful it could be my big break. I've never quite got in on the national scene.' His voice was alive with excitement.

'And excuse my ignorance, but what *are* the Cinque Ports?'

Simon looked surprised.

'Why, they're towns along the Kent and Sussex coasts. They were given special privileges by Edward the Confessor in return for defending that part of the Channel coast. There were five at first – hence the name – then Winchelsea and Rye were added. There's a lot of interesting stuff to be written about them.'

'I see!' Chloe said.

She didn't quite. If they'd been going so long, hadn't it all been written? Hadn't *all* history been written? But not for anything would she dampen Simon's enthusiasm. She was truly pleased for him.

'Are you sure we can't have a meal? Just a quick one?' Simon persisted. 'Why not?'

'I'm also unexpectedly going to London tomorrow. I've been given the day off and I'm to travel up as far as Victoria with Mr Portman.' The unexpected bit was not quite true, but no matter.

'Oh, what a shame,' Simon said. 'I mean, what a shame that we can't spend the day together.' There was nothing he would have liked better than to show her the sights, watch her face as she saw everything for the very first time.

'But why does that stop you having a meal now?' he asked.

'Because I have a hundred things to do,' Chloe said.

'Like what?' Simon asked.

'Oh, I have to wash my hair and iron a blouse, do my nails, have a face pack . . .'

'A face pack?' He sounded amused.

'Josie got it for me from Boots. She said it did wonders for her. It got rid of her blackheads double quick!'

Simon laughed out loud.

'But you don't have blackheads. Your skin is flawless!'

'Thank you,' Chloe said. 'But just in case.' There was nothing she wouldn't do to reach the acme of perfection for the following day.

They walked along the high point of the beach where the tide, going out, had left the pebbles shining wet. How much more interesting, Chloe thought, than Blackpool's miles of flat, golden sand.

'Well then, another time,' Simon said.

'I'd like that,' Chloe said. She meant it. This was to be her first real visit to London but it would certainly not be her last.

'Then can I see you later in the week and you can tell me all about it?'

'Oh yes!' Chloe agreed.

She rose early the next day, saw to the children, chivvied them through breakfast. Mrs Wilkins arrived and was deputed, despite her disapproval, to take Janet to school so that Chloe was ready when the taxi arrived to take John to the station. It made sense, Moira had suggested to John, that though Chloe's trip to London was not in any way bound up with him, they should make the journey together and that when they reached Victoria station he would see her on her way.

Chloe had made a list of all the places and happenings she wanted to see: Buckingham Palace, the Zoo, St Paul's Cathedral, the Changing of the Guard, the Tower of London, Trafalgar Square. And all the large stores in Oxford Street.

Moira laughed when Chloe read out the list. 'It will take months to get through that lot!' she said.

She stood in the doorway with Robert and waved them off as they got into the taxi. Robert's lower lip trembled as he watched them go.

The Brighton Belle was waiting on the platform. It was quite different from any train Chloe had ever had the good fortune to travel in, distinguished by its colour, by the fact that every carriage bore its name on the side and, most of all, that hovering near the door of each carriage an attendant, in his ultra smart Pullman uniform, waited to assist his passengers. She tripped along the platform by John's side until he reached his usual first-class carriage and she swelled with pride when the attendant, a young man with sleeked down red hair, greeted John by name.

'Good morning, Mr Portman! A nice morning.' Then he turned to Chloe and smiled at her.

'Good morning, Madam!'

This was not the MP's wife. He had seen her on occasion and though she was quite nice, this one was in another class for looks. It would be a pleasure to pay her special attention.

'Good morning!' Chloe replied.

Not quite the accent of the MP and his lady wife, the attendant decided. He studied accents. But she wouldn't need it, she had other attributes. He climbed into the carriage after them and watched her, watched the way she walked, with a slight sway of the hips, as she followed John Portman along to his usual seat.

'I'm sure you'd like to sit by the window,' John said, standing aside to let Chloe pass.

She found herself seated opposite a man rather older than John, grey-haired and smartly dressed in a pin-striped suit. He smiled at her and directed an enquiring glance at John Portman.

'Miss Chloe Branksome,' John said briefly. 'Mr Lewis Corson,' he told Chloe. He added no further explanations. He had read the questions in the other man's eyes and decided, out of cussedness, to say nothing more.

'How do you do!' Chloe said brightly. 'This is a lovely train!'

She realized as soon as the words were out of her

mouth that she had given away her lack of experience, her unsophistication. But it was too late now and it didn't really matter.

'It's a good train,' Lewis Corson agreed. 'It gets to Victoria in just sixty minutes, giving us nice time to have breakfast.'

She had had breakfast with the children, but not much, and there was no way she would miss having a second one in such circumstances. The table was beautifully laid with gleaming cutlery on a linen tablecloth, and a pink-shaded lamp.

'I always travel up on the Pullman,' John said to her. 'I can't always make it back.' He handed her the menu. 'What will you have?'

She studied the menu carefully, her appetite sharpening with every word she read. She wondered what she ought to choose. This was the second time lately she had been given a menu and asked to choose. She rather liked it. The thought brought Simon into her mind. She hoped he was having as good a time as she was. The attendant came for their order but that was no help to her since John simply said, 'My usual!'

'And you, Madam?' the attendant asked, pencil hovering over the pad.

'Oh!' Oh well, here goes, she thought.

'I'll have bacon, eggs, fried bread, sausages, tomato – and toast and marmalade.'

'Thank you, Madam!' Where would she put it all in that slender body? 'And cereal?'

'No, thank you,' Chloe said in the voice of one who had only the smallest appetite.

'Coffee or tea?'

Coffee for breakfast was undoubtedly more sophisticated but really she preferred tea, strong and sweet.

'Coffee, of course,' she said.

'And I'll have kippers,' Mr Corson said. 'They do good kippers,' he informed Chloe. 'I hope you don't object to the smell?'

'Not at all,' Chloe said. She had toyed with the idea of kippers herself but there was the question of what one did about the bones when travelling first class on the Brighton Belle.

She saw very little of the landscape between Brighton and London as the train rushed through at however many miles an hour. She was vaguely aware, when from time to time she raised her eyes from the delights of her breakfast, of green fields and trees, of stations at which the Belle never stopped, but passed through so quickly that they seemed no more than toytown places on a child's train set, such as she remembered Maurice having in the attic playroom.

She was aware also of the close proximity of John Portman. When the train took a curve at high speed he was thrown against her. For the sake of Corson he made an apology and moved away so that he was not visibly touching her but, hidden by the table, the length of his thigh and leg remained closely pressed against hers. Nothing was said and no look was exchanged between Chloe and John, but every nerve in her body was alive to his body.

As for John, he leaned back his head and closed his eyes, shutting out the world. It was usually around this point in the journey that Corson was apt to embark upon his summing up of the Stock Market, which at the best of times had limited interest for John. All he wanted to think about now, all he wanted to experience, was Chloe. His emotions were those of a raw adolescent, in love for the first time. He admitted it, and could not help it. He slid his hand under the table, contacted hers, and for a few moments locked her fingers in his. She made no move away from him.

When the Belle slid to a halt on the platform at Victoria the young attendant positioned himself at the door so that he was able to hold Chloe's hand lightly as she stepped down. She smiled her thanks.

'You've made a hit there, young lady!' Mr Corson said as they walked along the platform.

John shot him a baleful look.

'Silly fool!' he said as Corson left them, exiting by a side entrance.

His hand under her elbow, he steered Chloe across the concourse and out to the front of the station where they joined the short queue for taxis.

'I sometimes walk from Victoria to the House,' he said. 'Especially if there's a long queue for cabs.' But now it was beginning to drizzle and Chloe, who had decided early on that this day of all days would be fine, dry and sunny, had not even contemplated bringing an umbrella.

When they reached the House of Commons it pleased her that the policeman on duty clearly recognized John and waved them through without glancing at his pass, though he gave Chloe more than a glance.

'They're splendid fellows,' John said. 'They recognize all the regulars and they're always helpful.'

Afterwards, when she came to think about it, and perhaps because later happenings filled her mind to the exclusion of almost everything else which occurred that day, Chloe's impressions of the House of Commons were – not so much hazy, for certain things stood out in clear pictures – but confused.

John led her through a busy lobby, thronged with people, mostly men but a few women, secretaries perhaps because they looked efficient and businesslike and carried papers and files. Everyone was talking, mostly in loud voices which they took no trouble to subdue but, on the contrary, contrived to outdo each other. The accents were cultured but one or two Welsh voices came through and once, as she passed him, Chloe thought she identified an Akersfield accent. Messengers and doorkeepers in their distinctive dress bustled around; uniformed policemen hovered.

'We'll go to my office first,' John said. 'I'll dump my briefcase, let my secretary know I'm here.'

Chloe was disappointed by the office. It was small, with two desks and two indifferent looking chairs crammed in, a high window with no view, a coat stand in a corner. She had expected important people, which she was sure John was, to have imposing leather-topped desks and deep armchairs.

'We have to share offices,' John explained as he rang for his secretary. 'I share with a member from

Yorkshire. I don't know where he is at the moment but we're each of us glad to get the office to ourselves from time to time.'

His secretary, a plain but pleasant-looking bespectacled woman of fifty or so, came into the room carrying a pile of post which she placed in the in-tray before turning to look at Chloe.

'This is Miss Chloe Branksome, a friend,' John said. 'Chloe, Mrs Carpenter. I'm going to show Chloe around,' he said to his secretary, 'and then we'll have lunch. Is there anything I should see right away?'

'A couple of letters on top,' Mrs Carpenter said. 'The rest can wait.'

He had introduced the girl as a friend, but surely she was Mrs Portman's new mother's help? She remembered him mentioning her, using the name 'Chloe'. Oh well, not her business, even if the girl did look as unlike a mother's help as was possible. All sorts of things went on in this place. She was part of none of the shenanigans. She did her job and at the end of the day went home to her elderly mother in Richmond.

John scribbled a few notes on the urgent letters, then said, 'There! You can deal with those!'

Chloe was far from disappointed by the rest of the House. It was all she had expected it to be, and more: elegant chambers with lofty, decorated ceilings, panelled galleries, sumptuous carpets, long corridors, libraries, splendid windows; dark shining wood with the patina of many generations of polishing and more elegant leather-upholstered chairs and benches than she could have expected to see in a lifetime. By the time John had shown her all this her legs ached and, in spite of the breakfast on the train, she was hungry.

'We'll eat early,' John said, leading the way to the dining-room. 'It can get very crowded later on.'

The menu was surprisingly ordinary, mostly familiar dishes, for which she was thankful: meat and vegetables, steak pie, fish, steamed puddings. Men's food.

'Nursery food, actually,' John said. 'It goes down well.'

Chloe chose leek-and-potato soup followed by roast beef and Yorkshire pudding. There was nothing wrong with the beef except that it was too pink, though she knew that this was the way one was supposed to prefer it, but the Yorkshire pudding couldn't hold a candle to her mother's, or come to that to any she had tasted in Akersfield. You had to hold your breath over her mother's pudding for fear you blew it off the plate. This was heavy and solid, but John seemed not to notice.

In fact it occurred to Chloe that he was eating his meal without tasting any of it. He seemed preoccupied by whatever was on his mind. She wondered what his thoughts were. Affairs of State perhaps? But when she looked across at him at a moment when he lifted his eyes from his plate, and looked into hers, she knew it was nothing of the kind. It was all there in his face; longing, hunger – but not for food. A shiver went through her as she returned his look.

And then she saw his face change. It was clear

he had seen someone approaching, and when she heard the voice behind her she caught her breath. Though she had heard it on only one occasion there was no mistaking those mellifluous tones, that high-class accent. It was the man on the train from Akersfield.

'Hello there!' he said. 'Long time, no see. I've been away.'

He had moved closer and was now standing between John and Chloe. He recognized her at once, but contained his surprise. He had, in fact, forgotten her, and he knew by the wary look on her face that she remembered him but was not about to acknowledge him. He studied her for a fraction longer than was necessary before turning to John.

'How is Moira?' he asked smoothly. 'And the children? I haven't seen them lately.'

'They're well, all of them.'

'Jolly good! I must pop down and see you all one day soon.' He looked towards Chloe with a question on his face which had to be answered.

'This is Chloe Branksome,' John said. 'She's helping Moira with the children, except that she's having today off to visit the big city.'

So she got the job after all. Charles was not surprised.

'And you're showing her how we run the country?' He smiled at Chloe. 'And are you enjoying it?'

'I like it very much.'

He wasn't going to give her away, thank the Lord. Not, Chloe thought, that she'd done anything really wrong, of course. It was just that she hadn't mentioned him.

'And what do you like especially?' Charles enquired.

Chloe looked him full in the face.

'I like meals on trains!'

'We had breakfast on the Belle,' John explained.

'Good for you! Well, I'll leave you both to it. Enjoy your day. Give my love to Moira and the children.'

'I will,' John promised. 'You really must get down to see us!'

'Oh, I will!'

He wondered exactly what was going on. He had seen John Portman's face as he'd approached the table, before John had been aware of him. But the girl, he reckoned, was a match for his friend any day of the week. It was nothing to do with him but it might be quite amusing, and as far as this place went it was par for the course.

'Sorry for the interruption,' John said to Chloe.

'Not at all! I thought he was quite nice.'

John pulled a face.

'Smooth! Very smooth. So what would you like to do next? I daresay you've seen enough of this place.'

He knew exactly what he wanted to do. It had filled his mind over the entire mealtime but he was not sure how swiftly he could come to it. He dreaded making the wrong move.

'Well,' Chloe said thoughtfully. 'I'd rather like to see Buckingham Palace. If you would tell me the way . . .'

'I can do better than that,' he said eagerly. 'It's not far. A few minutes in a taxi. I can take you there.'

'That would be wonderful!' Chloe said. She knew it was not far. She had a tourist map of London, which she had bought in Brighton, in her handbag. His reply was exactly what she had hoped for.

'In fact,' John said, 'my flat's quite close to here, behind Westminster Cathedral. There's something I want to pick up from there. Would you mind if I did that, then I'll take you on to the Palace?'

He held his breath – but how could she say 'no'?

'I wouldn't mind at all,' Chloe said. She hadn't known where the flat was, but she knew it was close to the House because he had explained to her about the Division bell and how he had to turn up to vote within a few minutes of its ringing, which was why so many Members had flats in Westminster.

They walked to the flat, along Victoria Street, as John had said, to a narrow street behind the Cathedral. The flat was in a tall, red-brick building with a smart entrance hall, but less smart as they climbed the stairs to the second floor.

'Here we are!' John said, turning his key in the lock.

He stood back to let her enter, closed the door behind them, then without moving another step he took her in his arms. She raised her own arms and put them around his neck, pulling his head down so that his lips were fastened on hers. He held her so tightly that she could scarcely breathe and his lips were so hard on hers that she felt her mouth bruised by his, but the pain was the pleasure and the pleasure was in the pain and nothing else moved or breathed or lived or counted.

In the end he relaxed his hold, but only long enough to take her hand and drag her through a sitting-room which she scarcely saw, and through a doorway on the far side which led into a bedroom. No word was spoken but fleetingly she thought, this is *their* bedroom, his and Moira's. It didn't matter.

He pushed her down on to the bed and then, but gently now, containing himself, he started to undress her, and as he did so he murmured endearments, words such as no-one had ever said to her before, words she had never heard. One by one he unfastened the buttons of her blouse and she could feel his fingers trembling against her as he did so. When he fumbled with her brassière she helped him with the clasp, and when it came off she flung it to the floor. Then he smothered her breasts in kisses and in all her life she had never known, could never have imagined, the sensations which raced through her.

He unzipped her skirt and pulled it off, and then the rest of her garments until she was naked, lying on her back, John looking down at her in wonderment.

'You are indescribably beautiful,' he whispered.

'My turn now,' she said.

She raised herself up, pushed him down on to his back and knelt beside him. Then one by one she took off his garments, flinging each one to the floor as she did so, until he too was naked.

She ran her fingers across his chest and around the curve of his hips, and in a moment he was on top of her again, and they were together, and she knew – there was nothing she needed to be told – what it was all about. And as he took her, and she surrendered her virginity to him, she knew that this was what she had been born for, that this was the culmination of her life so far, and that the act of sex was beyond all imagination wondrous, glorious, magnificent. She was made for it.

When he opened his eyes and looked at her he was staggered by the radiance in her face.

When it happened the second time it was, incredibly, better. Then he ran a bath for her, and when she stepped out of it he gently dried her. When he had finished she did the same for him. She had, until today, never seen a man's living, breathing body, only statues in cold marble. She had not known it could be so beautiful.

'You'll have to get back,' he said when they were both dressed. 'I'll walk with you to Buckingham Palace and then point you towards St James's Park, which is quite near and will give you one other thing to look at.'

And talk about, she realized he meant. How could she go back to Brighton and say she had seen nothing more than the House of Commons and Buckingham Palace?

'After that,' John said, 'you need only take the underground to Victoria. Only one stop, so you can't get lost.'

It was awful, he thought, how plans for deception came so easily and smoothly and with little or no niggling of his conscience.

'I should go back to the House,' he told her, 'and put in some work. I'll ring home from there but you can warn Moira I might be late.'

Before they left the flat he held her in his arms again in a long, lingering embrace. Then he pushed her away, but gently.

'We must go. At once!'

They walked to Buckingham Palace and stood there in front of it hand in hand, careless of who might see them. It was all too soon, too recent to take care, and they told themselves that London, in the summer, was full of strangers anyway.

'Wouldn't it be wonderful if the Queen was to come out on the balcony, or drive out through the gates?' Chloe said. 'Or the children. I'd like to see the children.'

'She's at home,' John said. 'You can see the standard flying. I always look for it. But I must go, my love, and so must you.' She looked up at him. He gave her a loving kiss on the cheek, and then reluctantly left her.

Simon, having taken the opportunity to do a few errands after leaving his interview with the Features editor – an interview which had gone well, he had had a firm offer to do the articles – leaned forward and looked out of the window as the cab passed Buckingham Palace. He always did. His journalist's instincts told him you never knew where a story might be found, and if it was found in the proximity of a royal palace, so much the better.

What he saw, in the short space of time it took the

cab to pass, was Chloe. There was no mistaking her. She was holding a man's hand and raising her face to his kiss. He saw her; she saw nothing and no-one except the man. Simon, trying to recall him later, had no impression whatsoever of the man. It had all been too quick and he was concentrating on Chloe.

John had told Chloe how to get to St James's Park and there she walked around, sat on a seat, watched the ducks. In spite of the fact that there were so many people around, it was peaceful. She would be able to say with truth to Mrs Portman that she could have stayed there for hours, except that she would imply that she *had*.

It was the first time she had been on the underground but, except for being horrified by the crush of bodies, it passed off without incident, and since almost everyone jumped out of the train at Victoria she was able to move with the crowd.

When she reached Blenheim House the children were already in bed.

'Did you have a good day?' Moira enquired.

'Wonderful! One of the best days of my life!' And that was certainly true.

'Then come into the sitting-room and tell me all about it,' Moira invited.

How excited, how invigorated the girl looked. She must, very soon now, begin to paint her portrait.

Chloe did not in the least want to talk to Moira about her day, even less to be questioned about it. All she wanted was to go to bed and to relive it in her mind. And supposing John returned while she was still with his wife and they had to face Moira together? Supposing she said the wrong thing, gave herself away?

She was saved from that when Moira answered the telephone.

'John,' she said. 'There's a Division. He'll be too late to get home. He'll stay at the flat. You must see the flat one day, Chloe!'

12

When Chloe awoke next morning, even before she opened her eyes, she knew that the world had somehow changed, and for a moment she did not know why. But only for a moment. Within seconds memory returned and she was with John Portman in London, every recollection sharp and clear: the House of Commons, Buckingham Palace, the flat in Westminster. Most of all the flat.

He would be waking there now, as she was waking here in Brighton – or was he still asleep? She wondered what he looked like when he was asleep. Sprawled on his back? Curled up on his side? His hair tousled, his chin and jaws needing a shave? What would it be like to lie by his side all night, to feel his weight against her, to waken beside him in the morning? Would she ever know that? Was it possible?

Inevitably her thoughts turned to Moira, to whom waking beside John was commonplace, probably never even considered. As quickly as she could, Chloe pushed away the thought of Moira. This was not the time for it, she would not let her intrude. Naturally she did not want to hurt Moira nor, for that matter, did she wish to jeopardize her own job, but then the cards were stacked in Moira's favour. She was the wife, wasn't she? She was in possession.

Chloe turned over in bed and with the movement resolutely changed the direction of her thoughts, something she had always been able to do when the wish was strong enough, until she was once again with John. She clasped her arms around herself as if they were John's arms, embracing her. She closed her eyes and remembered his kisses. She would like to go back to sleep, to dream of him, but the sun streaming in at the window on to her face and the sound of the early traffic on the road was too intrusive. There was to be no more sleep.

She got out of bed, stretched, yawned, went to the bathroom and took a long, leisurely bath. How considerate of the children not, for once, to waken early, she thought. What a wonderful respite from the usual morning rush and bustle. She was already dressed for the day before she heard Robert calling her name, and almost at the same time she heard the baby crying on the floor below. She went in to attend to the children and presently the three of them went downstairs.

She had wondered, though only briefly, how she might feel on meeting Moira this morning. Would it be awkward? Would she be embarrassed? In the event it was nothing of the kind, it was to all appearances exactly like any other morning. They both smiled, greeted each other pleasantly.

'I had a remarkably good night's sleep for once,' Moira said. 'Eddie slept right through. I hope you did after your tiring day in London?'

'I did, thank you,' Chloe said. 'And I awoke quite early.'

'It's going to be a beautiful day,' Moira remarked. She poured the tea, handed a cup to Chloe.

'Then can we go on the beach?' Janet begged. 'I want to go on the beach!'

'I don't see why not, darling,' Moira said.

She turned to Chloe.

'For some reason or other school finishes earlier this afternoon. You and Robert could pick up Janet and go straight down to the beach. What do you think?'

'I want to go to the beach!' Robert cried.

'I think it's a good idea,' Chloe agreed. 'We could go to the rock pools again if you'd like that.' And perhaps, she thought, if John were to arrive home early he would come down to find them as he had on that previous occasion.

Robert was all enthusiasm. So was Janet, but not for the world would she show it. She maintained a bored silence, eyes cast down but ears wide open so as not to miss anything.

'So we'll settle for that,' Moira said. 'Then I wonder. . . would it be possible for me to make a start on your portrait? Just for an hour, say. A preliminary sketch. I'm very keen to get on with it.'

She was more than keen. She was fired with enthusiasm for the project and she knew she must capture this enthusiasm and put it to use before it melted away, became absorbed into the daily round of domesticity which was what her life seemed to consist of. She had made attempts before but they had come to nothing. This time she was truly hopeful, partly because she was inspired by Chloe as the subject of a portrait – not for a long time had she felt so drawn to anything – but partly, also, because the circumstances were easier. The model she wanted was right here in her own home, no elaborate arrangements, no juggling with times and places were needed. Everything and everyone was to hand.

'I'd like that, if it suits you,' Chloe said. She was well pleased.

'I have a fancy to paint you in the garden,' Moira said. 'There's a wicker chair – you know the one, with the high back – I think it might do very well. And it couldn't be a better time of year for the garden itself.'

'What will I do?' Robert asked.

'Well, you could play with your toys,' his mother said. 'Just for an hour!'

'In fact,' Chloe said, 'I know what you could do, if you wanted to. You could make a picture of me also. You could use your coloured crayons.'

'Why, that's a brilliant idea!' Moira said. 'You like drawing. I'll pin a big, clean sheet of paper on your board.'

'I will, I will!' He was full of enthusiasm.

'What would you like me to wear?' Chloe asked Moira. No chance of an emerald green satin evening gown, and obviously no thought of a portrait in the nude, though she was glad about that. The sun was warm but there was a stiffish south-west breeze coming off the sea. Who would want to be painted covered in goose pimples? Also – the thought came into her mind suddenly, and she could not have put into words why it did, she did not wish Moira to look at her undressed.

Moira thought for a minute.

'It doesn't matter a great deal,' she said. 'Almost anything would be all right. But I did like you in the dress you wore when Sir Godfrey came to dinner.'

The conversation was taking place over breakfast, Janet dawdling so as to set off late for school, Mrs Wilkins darting about like an angry bluebottle, and with no more apparent purpose, between kitchen and scullery, every inch of her body, every loudly indrawn breath, heavy with disapproval, though only in the scullery did her opinions issue in words, addressed to the cat.

'Mummy, what does "goings on" mean?' Janet asked innocently.

'What? Never mind that,' Moira said. 'Get down from the table, wash your hands, and get off to school. Shall we say ten o'clock?' she asked Chloe. 'That will give you time to get back from school and change into your dress.'

'I *would* have had my hair done,' Chloe said.

'Oh no! I wouldn't want that. As loose as possible, your hair. Untidy, even.'

'Shouldn't I wear my velvet headband?' Chloe suggested. She had particularly liked the effect of the headband.

'Yes, I think so,' Moira said. 'It suited you, of course. But I want something not too formal. And no make-up. Except perhaps . . .' She studied Chloe critically. 'Yes. Lipstick. As bright as you like!'

Already she envisaged the finished painting. It would sing with colour; the soft gold of the wicker chair, the red of the early climbing roses on the fence behind, the fresh green of the grass, not yet parched and browned as it would be later in the summer, and most of all the colours of Chloe herself: the darkness of her hair, the deep blue of her eyes, the delicate flush of her skin. The fact that the dress was cream would only enhance every other colour. Humming a song, she went into the garden, where Eddie was already in his pram, and began to set up the scene. Not for a long time had she felt so excited.

Returning from school, Chloe was met at the door by an anxious Robert.

'Chloe, Chloe, I can't find my crayons! Mummy won't listen to me. She says she's too busy!'

'I'll help you,' Chloe said. 'Think where you had them last and that's where we'll look.'

'I don't know!' he cried anxiously.

'Then we'll start in the kitchen. You probably sat at the table there.'

They were easily found, at the back of the dresser.

'But if you'd put them away in their proper place, in your own cupboard, you'd have found them at once,' Chloe pointed out.

'I'm glad to hear you say that!' Mrs Wilkins said. 'Surprised, though! There's a proper place for everything – people as well as things. As the hymn says:

> The rich man in his castle,
> The poor man at his gate,
> He made them high and lowly
> And ordered their estate.'

The words rolled off her tongue.

'And that's what I believe. And there are those who'd do well to take notice. Hob-nobbing with one's betters is not the thing. That's what I always say!'

'I'm sure you're right, Mrs Wilkins,' Chloe said sweetly. 'I'll just go up and change.' Nothing Mrs Wilkins could come up with would upset her this morning.

She slipped quickly into the cream dress then studied herself in the mirror. It *was* a beautiful dress and it was not too conceited of her to decide that, yes, she looked good in it. It was a statement of fact. She would look much better if she re-arranged her hair but Moira Portman was the artist, and artists saw things differently. How would what she now saw in the mirror come out in the portrait? Come to think of it, she had not to her knowledge seen one of Moira's paintings, nothing in Blenheim House had been pointed out to her as such. Supposing she's a very modern artist, Chloe thought, and paints me with two noses and one eye in the middle of my forehead. But she didn't look that sort of painter.

'I'm just about ready,' Moira called out as Chloe went into the garden. 'I had a canvas prepared, I always do. Sit in the chair as seems most comfortable to you. Relax, and we'll see what happens.'

Chloe sat down, leaned her head against the high back, laid her arms along the curved arms of the chair.

Moira caught her breath. The girl was a natural. It was a perfect position without looking in the least posed.

'Wonderful!' she said. 'Can you stay exactly like that for a second?'

She scrutinized Chloe carefully, stepped forward and, finger under her chin, turned her head slightly to the left, changed the position of a hand so that the fingers splayed out over the end of the chair arm.

'I think that's it!' she said. 'Are you comfortable? If you are I'm going to mark the position so that you know how to get back to it. But you've got to be comfortable or it won't work.'

'I'm perfectly comfortable,' Chloe said truthfully.

'Can you pretend you're looking at someone sitting slightly to your left and forward from you? He, or she – it doesn't matter which – is returning your look. He's sitting slightly taller than you so that your head is tilted just a little. Yes! Yes, that's it! You've got it!'

She is looking at a young man, Moira thought. A boyfriend. It was there in the way her lips curved in a slight smile, in the look in her eyes. Perhaps this was how she looked at Simon Collins.

I am looking at John, Chloe thought. His was the only man's face she saw, or wanted to see, on this morning, in his garden.

Without looking directly at her she became aware that Moira's attention was concentrated on her. From the corner of her eye she could see the intensity of the other woman's gaze and for a second or two she was uncomfortable. Could Moira Portman see into her mind? But that was nonsense, wasn't it?

She need not have worried. No thought of husband, children, or anyone else in the world intruded upon Moira. All she saw, through narrowed eyes, was what was immediately in front of her: the light and shade, the colours, the planes and angles, and so great was her rush of confidence that she decided not to bother with preliminary sketches. She picked up her brush, a broad one, and began at once to paint. She worked fast, almost desperate to get everything down on canvas, as if what was in front of her might vanish into the air.

All was quiet in the garden. The baby slept; Robert sat at his toy easel, crayon in hand, unconsciously mimicking his mother's movements; Chloe thought about John. All that broke the silence was the raucous cry of gulls flying overhead, and the faint hum of traffic from the coast road, but the group in the garden heard none of that.

Presently – no-one had measured the passing of time – Moira stepped back from her easel, put down her brush and let out a great sigh. I have done well, she thought. Far better than she had dared hope.

'Let's have a ten-minute break!' she said. 'You've been wonderful, Chloe. So professional! You might have been doing it all your life!'

Chloe stood up and stretched herself. An artist's

model! What a wonderful way to earn a living and why had it never occurred to her before? But who would have wanted an artist's model in Akersfield?

'May I have a peep?' she asked.

Moira hesitated.

'I'd much rather you didn't. In any case you'd be disappointed at this stage. Wait until we've had a few more sittings.'

Moira went into the house, asked Mrs Wilkins to make a jug of orange squash for the three of them and bring it out. 'As soon as you can,' she said. 'I want to get as much as possible done before the baby wakens.'

Mrs Wilkins brought out the tray of drinks and banged it down on the table so that the glasses rattled. She poured for Mrs Portman and Robert, but not for Chloe. If the girl thought she was going to be waited on she had another think coming. Dolling up in fancy dress in the middle of the morning! It would serve her right if she got grass stains on it and they never came out.

The moment they had drunk the orange squash Chloe went back to the chair, Moira positioned her exactly as she had been before, down to the last detail, then took up her brush. She was more relaxed now, even more confident that all would go well.

'I've taken a risk, painting you in the garden,' she said to Chloe. 'The conditions are never the same half-an-hour together. The light changes all the time. But it seemed so right and I'm sure it's going to be. We must try to start at the same time each morning and pray it won't rain too often.'

It was, Chloe thought, as good a way of spending a morning as she could think of. She was sorry when the baby began to cry and Moira said, 'That's all for today! I'm quite pleased, really. And in spite of what I said you may look now. But bear in mind that this is only the beginning. The finished portrait will be much better.'

Chloe stood beside Moira and looked at the painting. It was astounding that on this flat, blank canvas a morning's work had brought a whole scene to life, and she herself in the middle of it, instantly recognizable.

'It's wonderful! It looks finished to me,' she said.

Moira laughed. 'Just you wait!' she said. But she *had* caught the girl already. She had captured the strange combination of youth and naivety, sensuality and worldliness, and the hint of hardness in the limpid eyes, of tenacity in the cupid's bow of her mouth. She had not been aware of this mixture of qualities until they had flowed, so to speak, from her brush on to the canvas.

'Look at mine!' Robert cried. 'You haven't looked at mine!'

Standing on either side of him, Chloe and Moira surveyed Robert's drawing.

Two circular eyes, one higher than the other, were almost hidden beneath a bush of curly, twirly hair which Robert had chosen to do in bright green. The nose was a straight line, more or less in the centre of the face, and the mouth a gash, with every tooth, top and bottom, carefully delineated as little squares, both mouth and teeth in bright red.

'Now that,' Chloe said, 'is what I call a really modern portrait!'

In the afternoon, Chloe and Robert collected Janet from school and they walked down to the beach.

'I've brought your swimming costume,' Chloe said. 'You can change out of your school uniform.'

'And I've brought my fishing net because I might catch something,' Robert said. 'I might catch a little crab and I can take it home in my bucket and have it for a pet.'

'It will die if you put it in your bucket,' Janet said.

'No it won't! I'll put lots of water in.'

'It will still die,' Janet said lugubriously. 'And you'll have killed it. You'll be a murderer! It'll come back and haunt you. It'll nip you with its claws just as you are falling asleep!'

She advanced on him, screwing her hands into claws. He backed away from her, his face pale.

'It won't! It won't! You're telling lies! Chloe, tell her it won't!'

'Of course it won't,' Chloe said firmly. 'Janet is just being silly. You mustn't let her frighten you. But if you catch a crab it might be kinder to put it back in the pool. I expect it will have brothers and sisters there, maybe a mother and father. You wouldn't want to take it away from its family, would you?'

'No,' Robert agreed. 'But I could come back to see it, couldn't I?'

'Of course! Any time. That's a promise!'

'It might even get to know me,' Robert said. He was quite happy again now.

'This looks a good place to sit,' Chloe said.

There was a fair-sized pool nearby, and two or three smaller ones. More important, she recognized it as the spot where she had been with the children on that previous occasion when John had been with them. If he *should* arrive home early, if he *should* decide to join them, he would know where to look. She put her bags down, took out Janet's swimming costume and offered to help her to change – an offer which was refused.

'Then I shall sit just here,' she said, 'and keep an eye on you both. Don't go any farther than that pool there.' She pointed to a pool less than a dozen yards away. 'And call me if you find anything exciting.'

She wriggled around until she had more or less made a hollow for herself on the shingle, took out her book and began to read. The words swam together. There was no way she could concentrate because her mind was on yesterday and she gave herself up to re-living every detail. She was therefore not pleased to hear someone speaking to her.

'They're nice, your children!'

She looked up and saw a woman looking down at her. She was tall, or she seemed so from Chloe's position on the ground, with straight, mouse-brown hair and a dress and cardigan of much the same drab colour.

'Thank you,' Chloe replied. 'They're not my children. I look after them.'

'I've seen you here before,' the woman said. 'I thought it was your husband you were with. And there was another young lady, with a little boy.'

'My friend Josie,' Chloe said. 'She's on holiday.'

Without waiting to be invited, the woman sat down on the pebbles a yard or two away from Chloe. Drat! Chloe thought. Company was the last thing she wanted, and now the woman would probably want to talk, to ask more questions and expect answers. It wasn't as if there wasn't plenty of room elsewhere, the beach was far from crowded. To her surprise, however, the woman said very little. She just sat there, making a remark from time to time. Chloe felt no compunction in returning to her book.

'What are they called, the children?' the woman asked presently.

'What? Oh – Janet and Robert!'

'Nice names. If I had a little boy I'd call him Daniel. Daniel is nice, don't you think?'

'Very nice.'

The woman got to her feet and wandered across to where Janet and Robert were on their knees, peering into a pool. Chloe watched her as she spoke to the children, peering into the pool with them. Then she stood up and walked away, quite briskly, and was lost to sight.

Chloe now also rose to her feet and went to the children. Robert was kneeling at the edge of the biggest pool, eagerly leaning over, his face almost touching the water. Janet, at Chloe's approach, had wandered away to another pool.

'Don't go *quite* so close to the edge,' Chloe advised

Robert. 'If you tip over and fall in and get wet through we'll have to go home. Have you seen something interesting?'

'All sorts of things. There's a very special crab. He's sort of reddish. I'm making friends with him.'

'Good! So what did the lady say to you?'

'The lady? Oh, she just said "Are you having a good time, Robert?" And I said yes because I am. She knew my name. Do you think a lot of people know my name?'

'I daresay they do.'

'She was a very nice lady.'

'Yes, she was,' Chloe agreed. 'Well, if you're all right I'll go back and read a bit more of my book. You'll be careful, won't you?'

He didn't answer. He was already peering into the water again. Chloe returned to her place on the shingle, this time lying flat on her back to soak up the sun. When it grew too bright for her she laid the opened book over her eyes. She longed to allow herself to fall asleep but she knew she must not. Then, in a little while, on the very edge of sleep – or had she indeed been asleep and was now waking – she became aware of someone standing over her, she was conscious of being looked down upon, though she had not, and presumably because she had dropped off, heard footsteps across the shingle.

It must be John! Who else would stand and look at her, not speaking?

Already, before she had become aware of him, he had been looking down at her, avidly, as if seeing her for the first time. And in a way it was the first time because yesterday had been a new beginning. In spite of the conflict in his emotions, which still raged in him, his feelings had not so much changed as deepened. This was the woman he wanted. He had known that for certain yesterday and not for a moment since then had the feeling left him, nor would it ever. And, no matter what the obstacles, she was the woman he would one day have.

While he continued to look down at her Chloe, finally waking, pulled the book away from her eyes, then sat up.

'Simon! It's you! I didn't expect . . .'

She faltered, trying to keep the disappointment out of her voice, but he noted it and in view of what he had seen yesterday he was not surprised. She had expected to see that other man – or had she just been dreaming pleasant dreams about him which he had interrupted?

'How did you know I was here?' Chloe asked.

'I didn't. I took a chance. It's a fine afternoon, you'd mentioned how much the children enjoyed the rock pools – and I was lucky! Where are the children? In fact, *which* are they? I don't know them, do I?'

She pointed them out. Robert was still gazing into the pool though now he was lying flat on his stomach. At least that made him less likely to fall in! Janet had moved to another pool and was talking to a girl a little taller than herself.

'How did you get on yesterday?' Chloe asked.

There was a pause. He was at a loss for words because what he wanted to say couldn't be said.

'Who was he?' he wanted to ask. 'Why have you never mentioned him? What is he to you?' And if he did ask there might be a simple explanation which would solve everything. An old friend. A cousin. 'Someone I've known all my life.' But it was no good, it didn't fit. He had seen the expression on her face as she had looked at him.

'What did the editor say?' she prompted.

'He was pleased.' He spoke in a level tone.

'And?'

'He commissioned one article. If it goes well, then he'll consider a series.'

'Why, Simon, that's wonderful! You must be delighted!'

'I am. Naturally!'

Chloe gave him a curious look. There was something not quite right here.

'Then why don't you sound delighted?'

He pulled himself together.

'I'm sorry! Of course I'm pleased, who wouldn't be. It's a foot in the door, a great chance on an important publication. Of course I'm delighted.'

'Well, I'm thrilled for you,' Chloe said.

'And you?' He forced himself to ask the question. 'What sort of a day did you have?'

'Oh, a very nice day!' What a tame way to describe the most wonderful day of her life. But somehow she wanted to keep yesterday to herself, she wanted to hug it in secret.

'What did you do? Where did you go?' He realized he was pushing her towards the questions uppermost in his mind, but he couldn't help himself.

'I walked a lot,' Chloe said. 'I walked to Buckingham Palace, and in St James's Park.'

'I' she said. Not 'we'. She was not going to tell him of her own accord.

'I thought Buckingham Palace was beautiful,' she said. 'The guards and everything. I didn't see the Queen, though. She was at home, but I didn't see her. I would have liked to.'

Sharp in his mind he saw again what he had observed from the taxi yesterday; every detail of it: her face uplifted, alight with joy; the loving kiss. He could not contain himself another second.

'I doubt if you'd have seen her if she'd been close enough to fall over!'

It was the sudden harshness of his voice rather than the words which startled Chloe; the total contrast to his usual calm, polite way of speaking.

'What do you mean?'

'I saw you. I was in a taxi. And at the moment I saw you if the Queen had ridden by leading a regiment of guards, you wouldn't have seen her! You were occupied!'

She felt the blood rush to her face and panic rise in her. Then almost as quickly she realized that Simon had never met John Portman, had told her he didn't know him. That was all that mattered.

'So who was he?' Simon demanded.

Her dismay turned to anger.

'What has that to do with you!'

'I don't give a damn about him! I didn't even see him. But I saw you. What's he to you?' They were both on their feet now, facing each other.

Robert, by the pool, heard their raised voices and ran towards Chloe, but neither she nor Simon heeded him.

'Mind your own business!' Chloe stormed.

'I thought we were friends,' he said.

'And so we are. But I don't belong to you and I won't be bossed. I left Akersfield because I was sick of being bossed. I came here to live my own life!'

'In that case,' Simon said coldly, 'I'll leave you to it.'

He turned and strode swiftly away.

'Do that!' Chloe shouted after him. 'Do just that!'

She watched him as he crossed the beach and climbed the steps to the road. She hadn't wanted to quarrel with him, she was sorry it had happened, but it was his fault, and in any case the feeling uppermost in her mind was that her affair with John was safe.

Robert moved closer to her and took her hand in his.

'He's a nasty man to shout at you,' he said.

'He's not really nasty,' Chloe said. 'He's just cross about something. Anyway, it's time we went home.'

John had still not returned home when Chloe went to bed that night.

'Who would be married to an MP?' said Moira, switching off the lights as she also went upstairs to bed.

Chloe lay awake longer than usual, waiting for the sound of John's return, and, while she lay awake, thinking also about Simon. She was sorry they had quarrelled, but he had no business to question her as he had, and what explanation could she have given him?

Looking back on the day she thought that the best bit of it had been when Moira was painting her portrait. Really, she quite liked Moira. It was a pity that things were as they were.

She fell asleep, but not for long. An hour or so later she was woken by cries from the children's bedroom. Robert was having one of his bad dreams. She went into him, sat on his bed and soothed him, and he quickly went back to sleep again, but by now Chloe was fully awake. There was only one thing for it, she would go downstairs and make herself a hot drink.

Walking through the hall she saw a chink of light under the sitting-room door. Clearly, Moira had not switched off one of the lamps. She pushed the door open and went in. John was leaning back on the sofa, a glass of whisky in his hand. She came in quietly, and startled him, so that he sat bolt upright and spilt a little of the whisky.

'Chloe! What . . .?'

She was equally startled, hardly knew what to say, but before she could utter a word he had put down his glass, moved towards her, and she was in his arms. He held her close, kissed her long and lovingly, then held her away from him and looked at her. Only then did she realize that she was in her nightdress, she had not stopped to put on a dressing-gown.

'I didn't know you were here,' she said. 'I came down for some hot milk. Robert woke me.'

'I didn't hear him. I must have fallen asleep. I came in late and poured myself a nightcap.'

He took her in his arms again, then pulled her down on to the sofa. For a few minutes there was no-one in the world but the two of them, and then in the room above the baby stirred, and began to cry. Chloe pulled away from John.

'I must go back to bed!' she said.

He pulled her back.

'I don't want you to go!'

'I must!'

She turned away and tip-toed up the stairs. The baby was still crying and as she passed Moira's room she heard her get out of bed to attend to him. The wood floor of the landing creaked, as it always did, and Moira called out.

'Is that you, John?'

Chloe continued up the second flight of stairs and reached the safety of her own bedroom. This was not what she wanted, not what she had envisaged. To make love to John, to her employer's husband, in the flat in London, which had seemed to have no connection with life in Brighton, was one thing. For it to happen here, in the familiar surroundings of his home, with his wife and children under the same roof, was different. She was not sure she could cope with this.

13

When Chloe went downstairs with the children next morning John was already at the breakfast table. He looked up as she entered, and their eyes met, but there was nothing to be said except 'Good morning, Chloe!' 'Good morning Mr Portman!'

She had lain awake, her thoughts spinning, her body, aroused by his embrace, aching for his, until she had heard him come up the stairs and go into his wife's room, heard their muted voices, though nothing of what was said – the house was too solidly built for that – and then, quite quickly, the cessation of the baby's crying. She closed her mind to what might be happening next in the room below hers, tossed and turned and decided there could be little sleep for her that night, then miraculously fell asleep almost before the thought had passed through her mind.

Now, Janet, when prevailed upon, gave her father a cool kiss; Robert hugged him with enthusiasm then, changing his tone, stood back and rebuked him.

'You didn't come home yesterday, Daddy!'

'Yes I did,' John said. 'But I was quite late and you were asleep.'

Being so late at the House he had thought of staying a second night at the flat, but the desire to see Chloe again was too strong and he had caught the late Pullman from Victoria, arriving in Brighton, because of a delay on the line, well after midnight. Too late after all, he thought, bowling along the almost deserted coast road in a taxi, to see her now. She would be in bed. He conjured up every excuse he could find for going to her bedroom, but nothing would do. It was, therefore, incredibly wonderful when she walked into the sitting-room, her hair tousled from sleep, her white, rather childish, cotton nightdress unbuttoned at the neck. When she came into his arms he was on fire for her, and when his baby son cried out, shattering the moment, he could have found it in his heart to hate him as, at that moment, he hated anything in the world which came between himself and Chloe.

She had been right of course to break away. He knew that now. It could not happen under his own roof. But when she came into the room and took her place at the breakfast table he knew also that his longing had not diminished. Even in the company of his wife and children he could not quell it.

'And I'm sorry to say,' Moira announced, 'Daddy won't be home tomorrow, or for the next few days.'

Chloe, helping herself to cornflakes, looked up quickly.

'That's right,' John said. 'I have to go to Paris.'

He was speaking as if to the children but Chloe knew that he was addressing her. 'I have to go on what's called a trade delegation. All rather sudden, because someone fell ill. I shall be away three nights.'

'*I* want to go to Paris,' Janet said.

'I know, Princess,' her father said. 'And one day I'll take you, but not this time.' He looked from Janet to Chloe, and Chloe knew what was in his mind.

'I would like to go to Paris,' she said. 'I've never been abroad.'

She could imagine, at the moment, nothing more delightful, more wonderful, than going to Paris. The crowds, the boats on the river, the night life, the shops, the Paris fashions! And to see it all on John's arm! Would it ever happen? She could only hope!

'It's a good chance for you, darling,' Moira said to her husband. 'Of course one wouldn't have wanted Clive Bentley to be stricken by appendicitis, but I'm pleased you were thought of in his place.'

'And so am I,' John acknowledged. 'I don't want to be away from home but it's part of the job.' Indeed, he hoped it would be one of many tasks to which he would fall heir. Every step, if properly accomplished, was a step up. He couldn't deny his gratification at being chosen. But he wanted, he quite desperately wanted, to see Chloe alone.

His feelings were in a turmoil, and every single person around the table was part of that turmoil. He had never felt like this before, never in his life. He loved his wife – of course he loved her, she was the best of wives. They had had seven happy years together, not a cloud in the sky. Naturally it was no longer quite as it had been in the beginning, how could it be? They had grown used to each other, the excitement had gone, but he could honestly say that he had not looked at another woman until Chloe had walked into his life. And now, though one part of him was troubled, there was a part of him which felt many years younger, alive, excited, renewed. How could he deny it?

'Hurry up with your breakfast or you'll be late for school,' Chloe said to Janet.

'It's bad-mannered to eat fast,' Janet said in righteous tones. 'And it gives you indigestion!'

With deliberate slowness she ate the rest of her cornflakes, drank her milky tea in tiny sips.

'Then that's one thing you'll never suffer from,' Chloe said.

'I have to go to the bathroom,' Janet announced when she had eaten the very last cornflake, drunk the last drop of tea.

'Then don't be long. And I'll follow you up. I need a clean handkerchief,' Chloe said.

As Janet rose from the table, so did she, at the same time looking across at John. When she had left the room he followed her, going slowly up the stairs until, seeing Janet go into the bathroom and close the door, he quickly caught up with Chloe.

'I've got to talk to you!' he said.

'How can you?' Chloe asked him. 'There's no time.'

'I'll telephone you later today. What time?'

'Mrs Portman feeds the baby at two o'clock. She hates answering the phone when she's doing that.'

'Then that's when I'll call you. Be sure to pick up the phone.'

'I will.'

He put his arms around her, pulled her close, but the sound of the cistern flushing in the bathroom heralded Janet's reappearance. He kissed her swiftly on the lips, then ran down the stairs.

'Do hurry!' Chloe said to Janet. 'We shall be late again.'

Robert was waiting in the hall.

'Can I go with you to school?'

'I'm afraid not,' Chloe answered. 'We're going to have to rush all the way. But I'll be back soon. Janet, get your things together. *At once!*'

Moira, walking through the hall on her way upstairs, raised her eyebrows at the sharpness of Chloe's command. It was unlike the girl to lose her cool, that was one of the good things about her, but Janet could try the patience of a saint.

'And as soon as you get back,' Moira said, 'come straight into the garden. We'll start again on the portrait.' It was going to be another fine day, like yesterday. Hopefully the light wouldn't have changed too much.

Walking back from delivering Janet to school – they had arrived there less than a minute before the bell rang – Chloe thought about John. What would he say when he telephoned? What *was* there to say? He had said he wanted to talk to her, but what about? There was no getting away from the fact that they could never be alone together unless it was somewhere other than at Blenheim House.

She had realized that last night, at the moment the baby cried and, even more, when Moira had called out as she passed the door. It was all too tricky. The instant she was found out she would lose her job, be sent packing with no reference.

Supposing, she thought, this should happen? Supposing she couldn't get another job in Brighton? And, the most awful thought of all, what if she had to go back to Akersfield? It was too horrific to contemplate, yet such was her present mood that she contemplated it in all its dreadful detail and decided that she could never allow it to happen.

It was wonderful to be in love, exciting and marvellous, and the prospect of danger, of discovery, added a certain something, a touch of magic. And she *was* in love with John, there was no doubt about it, and he even more so with her. It was as she'd seen it in a hundred films – the way always strewn with difficulties until the very last moment, but all coming right in the end.

But she must keep her feet on the ground. John must sort it out, he must think of something. Since Blenheim House was out of bounds they would have to meet elsewhere. Perhaps she could go to London again? Perhaps Moira might take herself off on holiday? Perhaps, even, she herself might have a few days, somewhere where John would visit her, stay with her? A nice hotel like the Grand, though there was no way *she* could pay for it. Her imagination took flight, she saw nothing of the streets through which she walked. She was on another plane. If any of the impracticalities of the situation arose she ignored them, lightly brushing them aside.

Love, she thought as she turned the corner into Sussex Square, love will find a way!

She walked straight through the house and into the garden, speaking pleasantly to Mrs Wilkins as she passed her, but receiving no reply.

Moira was setting up her palette – yellows, blues, reds – the primary colours. Although it was to be a garden subject there was no question of cool colours. In Moira's eyes Chloe was not a cool subject. She was far too vibrant, giving life and colour to everything around her.

'Sit yourself down,' she said. 'And relax. I shan't be a minute!'

'What can I do?' Robert demanded.

'You can do another drawing of Chloe,' Moira offered him. 'Or a model of Chloe in plasticine.'

'I've *done* Chloe!' he complained. 'I did her yesterday.'

'Then play with your Dinky cars,' his mother suggested. 'Mrs Wilkins will get them out for you if you ask her nicely.'

He trotted off into the house and came back a few minutes later with Mrs Wilkins in tow, carrying a full box of miniature cars, trucks, vans.

'There you are, love,' she said, walking deliberately between Moira and Chloe, banging the box on the ground. 'Not that you wouldn't be better going for a nice walk on a day like this, and if I hadn't far too much to do I'd take you myself!'

'Make yourself comfortable,' Moira said to Chloe. 'Try to relax!'

'Some of us don't have time to know the meaning of the word!' Mrs Wilkins said.

Moira ignored her; she found it the best way. While she squeezed the colours out on to the palette in great blobs she chatted to Chloe. It was good, she had always thought, for the sitter to have something to think about other than the fact that she was being painted.

'And how is your young man?' she enquired.

'My young man?'

'Well then, your friend. Simon Collins.'

'He was very cross!' Robert said, breaking off his surprisingly realistic sound of a racing car at full throttle. 'He shouted at Chloe!'

Moira looked enquiringly at Chloe.

'He was upset about something,' Chloe said. 'It was a misunderstanding.'

She had been so full of John that Simon had almost been forgotten, but now the thought of their quarrel came back with full force and she was surprisingly saddened by it. She liked Simon. She had enjoyed every minute she had spent in his company, until yesterday that was. Now she feared she had lost him. She doubted that he would come back to her. Why had she let fly at him like that? Yet how could she explain to him, then or ever, what he had seen outside Buckingham Palace?

Moira, studying Chloe minutely, saw the sudden change in her; the drooping of her shoulders, the way her dark blue eyes clouded over until they were almost black. She stopped painting. This was not what she wanted. It never ceased to amaze her, though she knew it was partly because she observed so acutely, how the subject's feelings showed themselves not only in the body, the slackening or tightening of muscles, the appearance of lines on the face, but even more in colours, the colour of the eyes, of the skin, the colour of vibrations given off. To say that Chloe was suddenly in a blue mood was no exaggeration, and it was not the fresh blue of the clear summer sky behind her but a darkening, grey-blue, a muddy blue. No, it was not a colour she wanted in this portrait.

'I'm sorry to hear that,' she said. 'I've never met him but from what you said he sounded a nice man.'

'He *is* a nice man,' Chloe said.

'Then let's hope it will soon sort itself out!'

'How can it?' Chloe asked herself. 'I might never see him again. And if I did, what could I say?' Of course John was the most important person in her life, there was no doubt of that, but she didn't have so many friends that she could afford to lose one. Let's face it, she thought, I don't have any other friends.

And Simon could give her things which John could not. Simon could take her places, show her the town, buy her meals. Everything was open between them. John could do none of that. Moreover, and it *was* a complication, she was getting quite fond of Moira, something she had never expected to happen, never wanted to happen. It would be so much easier if her employer was horrid. Not that she would allow

Moira's niceness to make any real difference. She didn't want to hurt her, but what Moira didn't know couldn't hurt her, could it? Ignorance was truly bliss and both she and John would contrive to keep Moira in ignorance, and therefore happy. And the wife, Chloe reminded herself yet again, had all the advantages.

That settled, she turned her thoughts back to Simon.

She is fidgety, Moira thought. No way is she relaxed. She laid down her paintbrush.

'I don't know! It's not going nearly as well as it did yesterday. I can't think what's the matter with me,' she said, taking the blame though there was nothing wrong with her, she was as happy as a lark on the wing.

'Let's have a break,' she suggested. 'I'll ask Mrs Wilkins to make us some coffee.'

'So can we go on the beach now?' Robert asked hopefully.

'Not this morning,' Moira said. 'When we've had our coffee I shall go back to my painting.' Make a fresh start, she thought, hope that Chloe's mood would have passed. She hoped also that Chloe's friendship with Simon Collins wasn't going to complicate their lives. The girl was in love, you could tell by looking at her, and young love could do some funny things. There was a lot to be said for being older, settled in life.

'And we can't go on the beach this afternoon,' Chloe said. 'I have to go into Brighton.'

She didn't have to go, but it was her free time

and she wasn't going to give it up. Anyway, there was always something to do in Brighton though naturally she would wait until after John had made his phone call.

When they had drunk their coffee Chloe went back to her pose and Moira to her easel. It still wasn't the same, Moira thought. There was something missing in Chloe today. She was sitting quite still and the position was right, but the spark wasn't there, it wasn't going to work. For the rest of the morning she would leave the face, concentrate on the background and, hopefully, return to Chloe tomorrow.

Mrs Wilkins came into the garden, unsmiling, tight-lipped.

'I've done my work,' she said. 'A fair day's work for a fair day's pay. And now I'm going off.'

She sounds like a firework, Chloe thought. For that matter she looked like one, as if she could explode with a loud bang and a shower of sparks.

'Thank you, Mrs Wilkins,' Moira said. 'See you tomorrow.'

When Mrs Wilkins had left by the back gate, her whole body stiff with disapproval, Moira said, 'I think we'll call it a day. And since you'll be out this afternoon it would be nice if you'd take Robert for a little walk now while I get lunch. I expect he'd like a change of scene.'

'We'll go down to the bottom of the gardens and watch the cars,' Chloe said. 'He enjoys that.'

'I wish Peter was here,' Robert said as they walked down the garden to his favourite seat.

'You miss him, don't you?' Chloe said.

In fact, though they were not bosom pals and never would be, she was rather missing Josie. There was so much going on that she would have liked someone to talk to. On the other hand, how much could she tell her? Nothing about John, nor did she want to talk about her quarrel with Simon. It boiled down to the day in London, with the best bits left out.

'When are they coming back?' Robert asked.

'Not long now. Are you going to tell me the names of the cars?'

After lunch she said to Moira: 'I won't leave until you've fed the baby – so you won't have the trouble of answering the telephone or the doorbell.'

'Thank you,' Moira said. 'That's thoughtful of you.'

While Moira was upstairs with the baby Chloe sat close to the telephone ready to snatch up the receiver the minute it rang. It was a quarter to two, but he might ring early, she wouldn't move anywhere.

She watched the hands of the long-case clock which stood in the corner of the room as they crawled towards the hour. It had an audible tick which was surely much slower than it ought to be? When, finally, its silvery chimes announced the hour she moved even closer to the telephone, hovering over it, waiting for the first ring.

When the clock chimed the quarter she was still waiting. What could have happened? Every possible thought came into her mind. He was ill, he had had an accident; the Prime Minister had summoned him. Or – but it was not something she wanted to believe, couldn't bring herself to believe, he had simply forgotten her.

As the half-hour chimed Moira walked into the room, the baby in her arms.

'Thank you for waiting, Chloe,' she said pleasantly. 'He was very slow today, bless him. I'm not sure that he was all that hungry. Anyway, off you go!'

There was nothing for it but to go, Chloe realized. She was reluctant to leave the telephone, but there was no point in staying. If it rang now, though she was sure it wouldn't because they had been precise about the time, then Moira would answer it.

She walked into Brighton, seeing very little of what went on around her. With every step she wondered where he was, why he hadn't telephoned. When she reached the Aquarium she crossed the road and turned the corner into the Old Steine, why she was not sure except that she might go up North Street and look at the shops. She felt aimless, not quite sure what she wanted to do – if anything. It was in this mood that she halted, trying to make up her mind, and when she looked up she realized that she was standing at the door of the building in which Simon had his flat. She had never visited him there but once, when they were walking through the Old Steine, he had pointed it out to her.

She realized, suddenly, that what she would really like most of all at this moment was for the door to open and Simon to walk out and see her there. And when he saw her for his eyes to light up and his face to stretch in his rather lop-sided smile.

She could not understand why she wanted to see Simon. He had been quite horrid to her yesterday. And I was to him, she acknowledged, but then he had asked for it. He'd had no right to say what he had said. So why would the sight of him be so comforting? It was John, not Simon, who had entirely filled her thoughts as she'd walked along the road from Sussex Square. It was John who had let her down, not kept his promise. Well, either he had let her down or something awful had happened to him. She was not sure which was worse. Of course she could never tell Simon about John, but she had the feeling that if that solid front door, with its column of bell-pushes and names of the occupants of the flats were to open and Simon were to appear, then everything would be better. She would apologize to him, after he had apologized to her, and all would be well, they would be friends again. He might take her out to supper, and since John was going to be in Paris for a few days that would cheer her up.

She stared hard at the door, more or less wishing it to open, but it remained obstinately closed. Should she ring his bell? She decided she couldn't, it would be a step too far. She shrugged her shoulders and continued on her way. She would go to Vokin's or Hannington's and she'd buy something: a scarf, stockings, even a blouse if one took her fancy. Spending money was always a solace.

Simon read what he had so far written, which was very little. He had thought when he'd suggested it that the Cinque Ports was a most interesting subject, plenty to be said about them. Now it seemed as dry as dust. Who wanted to know? But he had promised the article within a week and if he failed to deliver he might never get the chance again.

The trouble was, his mind was full of Chloe and it was difficult to concentrate on anything else. He had behaved stupidly yesterday, he had no right to question her as he had. And what did it matter that she had been so intimately engaged with this man? There was no doubt a simple, reasonable explanation. When the thought 'Why didn't she give it?' came into his mind he pushed it aside, then stood up and went across to the window.

His room was on the fourth floor, from which he had a bird's eye view of the Old Steine gardens, beautiful now with trees in their early summer green. Another month and the leaves would have darkened, the foliage thickened. Trees in high summer were not nearly as attractive as in the spring or autumn, or even in the winter, bare-branched, their whole intricate shape, every twig etched against the sky.

People were walking along the pavements, cars and trolley-buses moving along the road. Except for a few hours in the middle of the night the Steine was never deserted, never quiet, though up here the noise did not reach him and everything down there was miniaturized; model cars, toy people.

Far below him a girl was walking away across the Square, through the gardens. She walked, he thought, like Chloe, head in the air, a spring in her step, striding eagerly, as if she had so much vitality that any minute she must break into a run. But then, he saw Chloe everywhere he looked.

He left the window and went back to his desk. Then he pushed his typewriter away and took up a sheet of paper and a pen. He knew what he must do next.

'My Dear Chloe' he wrote.

'I've made a shepherd's pie for supper,' Moira said. 'Well, more of a high tea really. I thought we'd eat with the children since my husband's not here, save making another meal later. Next to baked beans on toast shepherd's pie is their favourite meal.'

It was close to being Chloe's favourite meal, though she would not have admitted it. It was, she feared, rather a common taste which she hoped she would one day outgrow. In any case she was not sure she was hungry enough, even for shepherd's pie. The day had been full of disappointments, one after another, culminating in the fact that she had found exactly the blouse she wanted, in the right colour, but they had not had it in her size.

'John phoned,' Moira said. 'He seemed to think he'd promised to phone me at two o'clock, though I don't remember that. He'd been in a meeting he couldn't get out of and he thought I'd be worried, not hearing. Especially as he was just setting off for Paris.' She turned to the children. 'Your Daddy is a most considerate man!'

Chloe's heart lifted. He *hadn't* forgotten, he *was* all right. And of course the message was for her. Her appetite returned in a flash and she passed her plate for a second helping of pie.

The letter, delivered by first post on the following morning, was correctly addressed – 'Miss Chloe Branksome, Blenheim House, Sussex Square, Brighton' – but Chloe did not recognize the handwriting, which was firm, bold, upright; nor did the local postmark give her a clue as to the sender. She was reluctant, she was not sure why, to open it at the breakfast table in the presence of others and pushed it into her pocket until she should be alone. Moira gave her an enquiring look, which she ignored by turning to Robert and wiping the marmalade from his fingers. She could never understand why Robert, a clean and fastidious child, when he came into contact with jam or marmalade, was at once sticky up to the elbows.

Breakfast over, she made her excuses and went to her room, where she tore open the envelope which had been burning a hole in her pocket.

'My Dear Chloe' she read, then immediately turned the page and looked at the signature, 'Yours ever, Simon', before going back to the beginning.

I am writing to apologize for my rudeness to you yesterday. I had no right to speak to you in the way I did. I don't know what came over me except that I was jealous, which of course I have no business to be since you aren't accountable to me.

Please forgive me Chloe! I will be on the beach this afternoon and if you are there too I will know that you have indeed forgiven my mulish behaviour.

Yours ever . . .

She read it a second time, a smile curving her lips as she did so. Of course she would forgive him, especially since he had conceded, quite rightly, that it was all his fault. It gave her a warm feeling inside to know that she was to be friends with him again. She put the letter away in a drawer and then, after changing into her cream dress, went downstairs for the third sitting of her portrait.

Thank heaven she is back to normal, Moira thought as she set to work. Chloe was all sparkle again, her eyes bright and shining, her skin aglow.

In the afternoon Chloe, hand-in-hand with Robert, who with his free hand clutched his bucket and spade, went to collect Janet from school. In *her* free hand Chloe carried Janet's bucket since, though she wanted it because she had decided to collect seaweed, Janet would sooner die than be seen carrying a seaside bucket.

They cut through the shortest way to the beach. Chloe was looking forward to meeting Simon and was disappointed, as they approached the appointed spot, not to find him waiting.

'I'm glad he's not here,' Robert said firmly. 'He shouted at you! I don't like people who shout!'

'He won't today,' Chloe assured him. 'You'll find he's as nice as can be.'

'Will he buy us some ice-cream?' Janet asked.

'He might,' Chloe said.

'I shall like him,' Robert decided, 'if he doesn't shout and buys us ice-cream.'

The woman who had spoken to them yesterday was sitting close by what Chloe and the children had come to think of as their special place, reading. She raised her head from her book, smiled and waved as they sat down.

'There's the nice lady,' Robert said, waving back. 'I like her!'

They did not have long to wait before Chloe saw Simon striding towards them across the shingle. He was smiling, and when he reached them he took Chloe's hand in his and held it for a minute.

'Am I forgiven?' he asked.

'Of course!'

Janet stood four-square in front of him, regarding him gravely.

'Are you going to buy us ice-creams?' she demanded.

'I might well,' Simon said. 'I'm in a very good mood today. I'd do anything for anybody.'

'But not just yet,' Chloe said to the children. 'Off you go and play for a while and we'll have ice-creams later. Don't go far away.'

Robert went to his usual pool and Janet to hers, a little farther off. Simon sat down beside Chloe.

'I was terribly afraid you mightn't come,' he said. 'I don't know what I'd have done if you hadn't. Walked up to Blenheim House, I reckon. Rung the bell and demanded to see you!'

'Well, you didn't have to,' Chloe said comfortably.

They sat for a minute in companionable silence, watching the children. The woman with the book rose to her feet and began to move in their direction. When she reached them she paused.

'A beautiful day!' she observed. 'The children are enjoying themselves.' Then she moved on, walking towards the sea, stopping to greet Robert.

'I hadn't noticed it when she spoke yesterday, but she sounds foreign,' Chloe said.

'French,' Simon said.

'How do you know?'

'I can tell. There are quite a few French living in Brighton. After all, it's not that far away. Just across the other side of the water.'

And just the other side of the water, Chloe thought, perhaps not much farther than I can see, is John. She wondered what he was doing. Was he thinking of her or was he too busy?

But she was happy for the moment with Simon, though she hoped he would not refer again to the scene he had witnessed outside Buckingham Palace because she had not yet decided what she was going to say.

'Did you come to this beach when you were small?' she asked.

'Not to this one, not that I remember. We mostly went to Rottingdean beach. There are good rock pools there. We could go there one day if you like.'

'I would like,' Chloe said.

'I'd like to take you to meet my parents,' Simon said. 'You'd get on well with them.'

She was not so sure about that. She didn't answer. She raised her head to check on the children. Robert was by his usual pool, peering into its depths. Janet . . . Where was Janet?

'I can't see Janet!' she said. 'Where is she?'

She jumped to her feet, and Simon with her. She shaded her eyes with her hand and looked anxiously in every direction. Simon was the first to see her.

'There she is! There, paddling in the water!'

She was more than paddling. The water was up to her thighs and the tide was sweeping in fast. Without another word Simon began to run towards the sea and with less than a second's delay Chloe ran beside him. The sea was reaching Janet's waist now and even while Simon and Chloe were running a huge wave swept towards the shore and knocked the child off her feet. They saw her throw up her arms as she went down.

'Can she swim?' Simon gasped.

'Only a little. Not against that!'

Every yard now seemed liked a mile. It was Simon who plunged into the water first. Catching Janet in his arms he scooped her out of the sea, then he turned around and carried her towards the beach, the sea rolling behind him. Janet lay still in Simon's arms, for the moment too frightened to do otherwise. When they were back in their usual place he laid her gently on the shingle.

'She'll be all right,' he said. 'But I think we'd better get her home. I'll carry her. You collect Robert.'

Chloe looked over to the pool where Robert had been – but he was not there. Nor was there any sign of him, anywhere on the beach. Nor was his bucket to be seen.

14

Chloe looked at Simon in horror.

'I don't understand! He was here by the pool! We passed him as we ran down to the water. I'm sure we did.'

At the same time as she spoke she was looking everywhere.

'He can't be far away,' Simon said. 'There hasn't been time for him to wander far.'

'We must ask everyone if they've seen him,' Chloe said frantically. 'Someone must have!'

'Then one of us must stay here in case he comes back,' Simon said. 'Which I'm sure he will, any minute.'

'Janet can stay,' Chloe decided. 'Then you and I can go in different directions.' She turned to Janet. 'Don't move from here! Do *not* move! We won't be long. In the meantime it would be a good idea if you were to change out of your wet costume, put some clothes on. Will you be a good girl and do that?'

'I want to look for Robert,' Janet protested. 'Why can't I look for him?'

'Because someone must be here when he comes back. And don't either of you move away when he does. Stay right here.'

'What if the sea comes right up and goes over us?' Janet asked lugubriously. 'What if we're both drowned?'

'You won't be,' Chloe's voice was sharp. She was sick with worry. 'We'll be back with you – and Robert with us if he isn't with you – long before the sea reaches here. Just do as you're told and you'll be all right.'

There was no time to argue with an awkward child. Without further ado Chloe walked away, taking the opposite direction from Simon who had already set off. She approached everyone, children and adults, first those who were nearest, then fanning out in a wider circle.

'Have you seen a little boy – he's three years old, fair-haired, wearing red swimming trunks and a white sun hat. He was probably carrying a small seaside bucket.'

No-one had seen him, or if they had they had no recollection of it. One small child in swimming trunks was much like another.

'They're always wandering off. You need eyes in the back of your head!'

This was the usual answer from the adults. The children were all too busy following their own pursuits to have noticed anything. The general consensus was encouraging. 'He'll not have gone far! He'll find his way back. Children do!' No-one seemed unduly perturbed.

Chloe looked up and saw Simon approaching. When he saw her he shook his head. His face was full of concern.

'No luck! No-one's seen him.'

Chloe suddenly felt sick inside. All the encouraging opinions that this was just something children did and that he'd soon turn up of his own accord seemed empty and meaningless.

'What are we to do?' she cried. 'Where can he be?'

'Well we can be fairly certain he hasn't gone in the direction of the sea,' Simon said. 'You told me he doesn't particularly like it. He sticks to the pools.'

'He doesn't like it when the waves are strong, as they are at the moment. But supposing he saw us running down and followed us?'

'Then he'd have seen us coming back.'

Nevertheless they turned and faced the sea, scanning the beach. With the strength of the newly-sprung south-west wind behind it the tide had advanced rapidly, and now there was more sea than shingle and people were picking up their belongings and moving back. There was no sign whatever of Robert.

'We must get back to Janet,' Chloe said.

She had only the faintest hope that they would find Robert with her. When they reached Janet that hope was extinguished.

'I expect he went for an ice-cream. We were *promised* an ice-cream!' Janet glared accusingly at Simon.

Chloe and Simon looked at one another.

'We should have thought of that,' Chloe said.

'Though of course he wouldn't have had any money.'

'Nevertheless,' Simon said. 'Let's go to the ice-cream cart.'

'We must take everything with us,' Chloe said. 'The tide's coming in fast.'

They collected their belongings. A wave of deep anxiety swept over Chloe as she picked up Robert's trousers and shirt and put them in her holdall. They looked so small. And where was the little boy, the lovely little boy, who should be wearing them? Where was he in his red swimming trunks and his white cotton sun hat?

The ice-cream man was packing up for the day. He had had a busy time of it, made a fair profit, and now people were leaving the beach, running ahead of the tide, not stopping to buy ice-cream. The sea, in the summer months, would not reach his stand, but he must take away everything he could fit into his van or who knew how much would be pinched, never seen again?

'Excuse me!' Chloe said.

'I've sold out,' he said. 'I'm closed.' He had not sold out but he wasn't going to start again.

'I just wanted a word with you . . .' Chloe began. 'It's a lost child . . .'

He continued with his packing. He had no time to stand and talk.

'Children are always getting lost,' he said. 'Their parents should take better care of them.' He glared at Chloe and Simon.

'I'm sorry,' Chloe said. 'I don't know who else to

ask now. He's three years old and small for his age. Red trunks and a white hat. Please try to remember if you've seen him!'

There was anguish in her voice and when the man stopped his packing for a second and looked at her, her eyes were full of tears. He was not a hard man, just tired, with aching feet from standing on the pebbles all day. And she was a pretty little thing.

'*Please!*' she begged.

'It's a description fits a lot of 'em,' he said. 'I haven't had many small kids in the last twenty minutes. As you can see, everybody's leaving.' He paused, and thought.

'No,' he said in the end. 'I can't place him. There was one little lad might have fitted the bill, but it couldn't be him because he was with a woman and they knew each other. She bought him a cornet.'

'That's what I wanted,' Janet said loudly. No-one took any notice.

'Wait a minute,' Simon said. 'What did she look like? What was she wearing?'

'I've no idea. You don't spend time looking at people's outfits.'

'Then did you hear her speak?' Simon persisted. 'When she asked for the ice-cream? Is it possible she had a foreign accent?'

'How do I know? She only asked for a threepenny cornet. You get all sorts of accents. I don't take any notice as long as I know what they're asking for. I've told you all I know. I reckon she was his mother. You'll probably find *your* little nipper's made his way home.'

He turned his back, closed the last remaining tin of wafers, and began to take things up to his van, parked on the road nearby.

As she watched the ice-cream vendor walk away, his back bent as he climbed the last steep yards of the beach, and then the steps which led to the promenade, Chloe felt suddenly deserted. It was illogical. There was no reason why she should have vested such hope in him, but she had. And when he finally disappeared from view it was as if he was carrying the last of her hopes away with him. She turned to Simon and when he saw the look on her face he put an arm around her and drew her close.

'Come on!' he encouraged. 'We mustn't waste time. There are still places to look. Let's get on with it!'

'Where?' Chloe said. 'Oh, Simon, where can he be?'

'Well he's not on the beach, that's for sure.' It was deserted now. 'We can go home, see if that's what he's done . . .'

'No!' Chloe interrupted. 'I can't possibly turn up without him. I can't face it!'

'Then we'll walk along the seafront in the direction of Brighton,' Simon decided. 'The three of us together. We'll keep on the seaward side. I don't suppose he'd have crossed such a busy road.'

'He could be watching the cars,' Chloe said, clutching at straws. 'He loves to do that.'

'Take my hand,' Simon said to Janet.

She did as she was told. She was, by now, unusually subdued.

'He could have been swept out to sea,' she said in a sombre voice.

'Oh, I don't think so,' Simon said. 'There were lots of people down by the water. Someone would have seen him.'

But would they? Chloe asked herself. Could Janet be right?

'We'll walk along here – and quite quickly,' Simon said. 'And we'll all keep our eyes open. In fact . . .' He hesitated.

'What?' Chloe asked.

'I think, as well as looking for a small boy on his own we should look for one with a woman.'

'You don't think . . .?'

'Probably not.' But he had a nasty feeling about it. He didn't know Robert at all well but from what little he did know, and from what Chloe had said about him, he found it difficult to think of the child wandering off on his own. He had not seemed an adventurous type, quite the reverse. Timid, actually. In that case would he allow himself to be taken away by a virtual stranger? There were so many questions to which the answers were unclear.

As well as looking at everyone who passed by they halted people and asked questions. Especially, in Chloe's case, they stopped people who were accompanied by small children, it being her belief that they would be more sympathetic, readier to help.

It was true that they were sympathetic, but it came to nothing in the end. No-one had seen a child, accompanied or not, who might well be Robert.

It was as if the ground had opened and swallowed him up.

Eventually they reached the Palace Pier.

'Shall we look on the pier or not? What do you think?' Simon asked.

Chloe shook her head in confusion. How was she to know? Whatever route she chose it left some other route unexplored, and who could decide which was the right one?

'I don't think so,' she decided. 'I don't think Robert would go on the pier on his own. We just can't know what he'd do with someone else. He might not have a choice.'

She could hardly bear to think of the consequences, of what might have happened.

'Where would he be most likely to go on his own?' Simon asked.

'Always supposing he'd go anywhere on his own,' Chloe said. With every minute which passed she found that more difficult to believe. It was simply not in his nature.

'He'd go home,' Janet said.

Chloe and Simon stared at her. They were the first words she'd uttered for some time.

'I think you're right, Janet,' Simon said. He looked at Chloe. 'I think that's what we should do next.'

'How can I?' Chloe said. She felt desperate. 'How can I turn up on the doorstep and say "I've lost your son"? How can I face his mother, and Robert not with me?'

'All the same,' Simon said gently, 'it has to be done. We can't keep it from her and by now the sooner she knows the better. There's the chance, in any case, that home is where we'll find him. Someone might even have taken him home.'

'Do you think so?' Chloe said eagerly. 'I hadn't thought of that! Do you really think so?'

'It's possible,' he said. In his heart he did not think it was likely. His thoughts, by now, were not happy ones – but there was no point in saying this to Chloe.

'You're right,' she said. 'We'll go back. Please go with me, Simon!'

'Of course I will,' he said. 'I wouldn't dream of doing otherwise!'

Chloe had her key with her, but for some reason which she herself could not understand, when they reached Blenheim House she stood on the doorstep, rang the bell, and waited for Moira to answer, which she did promptly.

'Chloe!' Moira said, surprised. 'Did you forget your key?'

She stood aside to let them come into the house, not, for a few seconds, registering that Robert was not with them, or that Simon, a stranger to her, was. It was, in fact, the sheer fright on Chloe's face which alerted her.

'What is it?' she asked sharply. 'There's something wrong!' Then, 'Where's Robert?'

In the brief pause while Chloe struggled for an answer a torrent of words poured out of Moira.

'Where is he? He's had an accident, hasn't he? He's been run over! He's in hospital! He's . . .' She could not bring herself to say the word which hovered on her lips.

'No!' Simon broke in. 'No. Mrs Portman, none of those things!'

'Then what? What is it? WHERE IS HE?' She looked at Chloe. 'Why are you standing there saying nothing?'

'I'm sorry.' Chloe faltered. 'We thought . . . we hoped . . . he might be here.'

'Here? He was with you! What's happened?'

It was Simon who explained, gently, clearly, telling it as it had happened, all they knew.

'Oh, my God!'

Moira, white as a sheet, swayed – and clutched at the door frame for support.

'You should sit down,' Simon said. 'May we come in?'

Without waiting for an answer he took her by the arm and led her into the first room he came to, which was the sitting-room. Moira sank into the nearest chair.

'My Robert!' It was a cry of anguish. 'My little Robert! What are we to do?' She put the question to Simon and then seemed to realize that he was a stranger.

'And who are you?'

'Simon Collins. A friend of Chloe's.'

Moira turned savagely on Chloe.

'It's your fault! While you were concentrating on your friend you didn't watch my son, who was in your charge!'

'It wasn't quite like that,' Simon said. 'We were

both aware of Robert right up to the moment when we realized Janet was in trouble. We had to go to her but we weren't away more than a few minutes.'

'I was drowning!' Janet said dramatically. 'I went down twice. If you go down three times you drown!'

'She was by no means drowning,' Simon contradicted. 'But she needed help.'

'But where is he? Where is my Robert?' Moira demanded. 'Are you telling me he's been kidnapped? Is that what you're saying?'

'I'm not telling you that. He could well turn up here, at home, any minute. In the meantime I think it might be best to inform the police. Would you like me to do that for you?'

'Yes! Yes, please do!'

In all this time Chloe had not spoken.

'And you!' Moira said to her. 'You haven't said a word! You are responsible for this! My children were in your charge!'

Simon was speaking on the phone. He paused to listen, then turned to Moira.

'The police will be along in a few minutes.'

He was looking into the pool, watching two very small black fishes chasing each other through the water, in and out of the rocks. He didn't hear Chloe and Simon as they raced past him. He didn't see them, he had his back to them. In any case he was deeply interested in what was happening in the pool. It came as a surprise when he heard someone speaking to him, but he recognized the voice, quiet, gentle, but sounding a little different, though he was not sure why, from any other voice he knew.

'Would you like an ice-cream, Robert? It is rather hot, is it not?'

He looked up into the smiling face of the nice lady – which is what he called her, partly because she was, and partly because he didn't know her name. She had a kind smile: not a big one showing her teeth, not a laughing one, but a small, pleasant smile which just turned up the corners of her mouth. She had soft brown eyes which looked straight into his own, inviting him.

'That would be very nice,' he said. 'I *am* hot. But I'll have to ask Chloe.'

'She's just run down to the edge of the sea, with the gentleman,' the nice lady said. 'But it's all right. We'll be back in no time at all.'

She held out her hand and he took it, and with his other hand picked up his bucket.

'I'd better not leave it behind in case somebody takes it,' he said.

'Quite right!' she agreed.

They walked quickly up the beach to the ice-cream cart where she ordered a threepenny cornet.

'Aren't you going to have one?' Robert said.

'Not at the moment.' She turned her head to look at the stretch of beach behind them. 'I see that Chloe and the gentleman are not yet back. Why do we not walk a little while along the road while you eat your ice-cream?'

Well that would be quite nice, Robert thought, because then he could see the cars.

She relieved him of his bucket as they set off again, carrying it for him so that she could hold his free hand firmly in hers.

'This is very nice ice-cream,' Robert said between licks.

'Good!'

They were walking quite quickly when she turned suddenly to the right and crossed the road, away from the sea.

'Where are we going?' he asked.

'Just for a little walk,' she replied. They had turned up a side street which led still further away from the sea. 'A little exercise will do us both good.'

'I shall have to be back when Chloe comes back from the edge of the sea,' Robert said. 'She'll wonder where I am.'

'Oh, we will be back,' the nice lady reassured him. 'In any case it is all right. I told her I would take you for a little promenade while she and the gentleman looked to Janet.'

'His name is Simon,' Robert said.

'A very nice name. Robert is nicer, but Daniel is my favourite name for a little boy.'

'What's your name?' Robert asked.

'What do you think?'

'I don't know,' he said. 'I call you the nice lady.'

'I like that very much,' she said. 'You shall always call me the nice lady. It is better than an ordinary name, like Mary or Helen.'

'My Mummy's name is Moira,' he volunteered. 'And my Daddy's is John.'

'Very nice!'

They crossed the road again, made another right turn, and now they were in a much narrower street with tall houses on both sides. The ice-cream was almost finished. He turned the cornet around and, as Janet had taught him, neatly bit off the bottom end and sucked the remaining ice-cream through the hole. They were walking quite fast now. He couldn't quite keep up and every few yards he had to do a little run and skip. It was also quite hot, now that his ice-cream was finished.

'Shall we go back now?' he suggested.

'Well, we are almost at my house,' the nice lady said. 'You would like to see my house, I am sure. And we could have a drink of lemonade. We could both do with that.'

No sooner had she spoken than they turned into a gateway – the iron gate had been removed – and walked up a short path to the door. The nice lady inserted a key into the lock and the next minute they were in a narrow passage from which steep stairs ran up to the next floor.

'I live on the very top floor, two more flights,' the nice lady said. 'You'll like it up there!'

The police came quickly. Within fifteen minutes of Simon's telephone call Janet, sitting on the windowsill, saw the car draw up at the door.

'Two of them!' she said. 'A man and a lady!'

When the bell rang Simon went to answer it. He was glad of something to do. Moira was still distraught, pacing up and down the room looking out of the window as if she expected to see Robert walking up the Square; shouting at Chloe who sat on the edge of the sofa, shoulders bowed, her hands twisting in her lap. The look of desperate entreaty on her face when she looked up at Simon, her eyes dark and wide with horror, tugged at his heart. It was as if she was saying 'solve it! Take this responsibility from me!' There was nothing he could do.

When the police officers came into the room Moira ceased her pacing and faced them and Chloe turned her look of entreaty on the man and the woman in uniform.

'I'm Police Constable Deakin,' the man said. 'This is WPC Manners. Shall we sit down?'

'Sit down!' Moira cried. 'How can you sit down with my little boy missing? We should be out there, looking for him!'

'And so we will be,' Constable Deakin said. 'But I need to ask a few questions first. WPC Manners and I need to know the circumstances in which the little lad went missing, as precisely as possible. Also what he looks like, any clues you might have as to which direction he took. It will all help.'

'He went missing,' Moira said furiously, 'because this girl, who was employed to look after him, in whose charge he was, failed to do so!'

She shot a venomous look at Chloe. In her eyes this girl who, when she left the house such a short time ago, had been competent, trustworthy, caring of the children and almost a friend to her, was now someone quite different. She was criminally careless and negligent, her mind completely taken up with her young man. The anguish in Chloe's face had no effect whatever on Moira, immersed in her own anger and fear.

'It wasn't like that . . .' Simon began.

Constable Deakin held up a hand.

'Please! We're wasting valuable time!' He turned to Chloe. 'Since you were there from beginning to end, perhaps you'll tell us just what happened, as you saw it. All the details, everything you can remember. What was the very last thing you saw of the child, for instance?'

Hesitantly, Chloe began. She could hardly find her voice.

'I saw Robert leaning over the pool. It wasn't far from where we were sitting. He was immersed in whatever he was looking at. He was wearing his sun hat. He can't do with the sun on his head . . .'

At the thought of him standing there – she saw him so clearly in her mind's eye – her voice broke.

'And then?'

'Simon saw Janet in the water. She looked as if she might be in trouble . . .'

'I was drowning!' Janet interrupted.

'. . . We both ran as fast as we could down to the water's edge.'

She described the rest, until the moment when, on their return, they had realized that Robert was not by the pool where she had last seen him. Seeing Chloe's distress, now, the constable turned to Janet for a moment. He would ask her only one question. He didn't want to be accused by the mother of harassing the child, though it was his private opinion that the girl might enjoy it.

'And did you see your brother at all? When Mr Collins was carrying you back from the water perhaps?'

'No I didn't!' Janet was emphatic. 'I was being saved from drowning!'

'I'm glad you were saved,' Constable Deakin said politely before turning to Simon.

It was Simon who, describing the subsequent events, mentioned Robert's 'Nice lady'.

'Who was she? Who was this woman?' Moira demanded.

'We don't know,' Simon admitted. 'We've both of us seen her before, but only for a few minutes.'

'You should never have let Robert speak to a stranger!' Moira said angrily. 'You know it's not allowed.'

'I didn't,' Chloe said. 'It's just that occasionally she was near us on the beach and she'd pass the time of day.'

'Well there may be nothing in it,' Constable Deakin said. 'There's not a lot to go on as regards her. But if you and Mr Collins could both give me the best description you can . . .'

WPC Manners, who had been taking notes, looked up, waiting. Chloe spoke first.

'There's not much to describe,' she said. 'She was very ordinary. A cream-coloured dress and a beige cardigan, I think. She was pleasant, but there was nothing about her you'd particularly notice.'

'Except her voice,' Simon said quickly. 'I'm pretty sure she was French. She spoke English fluently, as if she'd lived here some time, but the way she formed her sentences wasn't quite English.'

'That's interesting,' Constable Deakin said. 'It could be helpful if we trace her and if she *is* involved.'

'What do you mean, *if* you trace her,' Moira demanded. 'You've got to trace her. She has my little boy!'

'We'll do our best, Mrs Portman, and I expect we will trace her. But it's likely she hadn't anything to do with the case. Just as likely your little lad wandered off into Brighton, lost his way, and even now someone has him by the hand and is bringing him home. Does he know his address, by the way?'

'He does.'

Constable Deakin sounded more optimistic than he felt – at least he hoped he did. Whether the woman was involved or not, his hopes of tracing her were not high. He knew how many people came down to Brighton in the summer, and how many took the fast train back to London. No sense in saying this at this point. And ever present in his mind was the fact that the child was only three and Brighton was not a place where he'd like his own three-year-old son to be wandering.

'Now I'd like a photograph of Robert,' he said. 'As recent as possible. We'll put out his description right away and we'll all be on the lookout.'

Moira took a silver-framed photograph from a side table. It showed Janet and Robert standing side by side in the garden, Robert wearing short beige trousers and a red jersey.

At the moment, WPC Manners thought, the child is wearing bathing trunks and a sun hat. It was early summer and the evenings could be chilly. She hated child cases, there was so little you could do to comfort the parents. Also, she herself, as well as knowing what could and did happen, had a too-vivid imagination.

'It was taken only at Easter,' Moira said. 'By my husband. He's in Paris. Oh, why does he have to be in Paris!'

'Would you like him to come back – though of course, as I've said, as likely as not there's no need. Your son could be home long before your husband. But if you'd like him informed,' the constable said, 'I'm sure that could be arranged.'

Moira bit her lip, frowned with indecision.

'I do so want him here, but he has important meetings in Paris. I wonder if it would be best to wait until tomorrow?'

'I think so, on the whole, Madam,' Constable Deakin said.

'What else can *we* do?' Simon asked.

'How can I do *anything*?' Moira said. 'How can I leave the baby?'

'There might be something Chloe and I could do,' Simon said. It would be a relief to do anything.

'Then if Mrs Portman has another photograph the two of you could make a more detailed search,' Constable Deakin said. 'Ask in the shops, in the amusement arcades, the Aquarium and so on. Anywhere and everywhere. Of course we shall be doing that also, but we're stretched for men, as always.'

'Mrs Portman, I'm not sure you should stay on your own with the baby,' WPC Manners broke in. 'Is there someone we could contact who would stay with you?'

'There's my mother,' Moira admitted. 'Lady Stansfield. She lives in Hove.' She was not at all sure she wanted her mother, but perhaps it would be best. 'Very well!'

'Would you like to telephone her while I make a cup of tea? You look as though you could do with one. Or would you rather I telephoned?'

'No. I'll do it,' Moira decided.

'Would you like some tea?' WPC Manners asked Simon and Chloe.

'I think not,' Simon said. 'That is, if Chloe agrees. If Mrs Portman can find us a photograph we could set off right away.'

When WPC Manners brought in the tea a few minutes later – Simon and Chloe had already left – Moira was just putting down the telephone.

'My mother will come at once,' she said.

The young woman looked at Constable Deakin. He nodded his head.

'Then I'll stay with you until she arrives,' she said.

15

The Nice Lady held Robert's hand in hers as they climbed the stairs. There were rather a lot of them. They got steeper as the two of them climbed, and Robert's legs were short. He stopped for a moment on a small, square landing.

'Only one more flight,' the lady said. 'I can carry you if you like. You are probably not very heavy.'

'No thank you,' Robert said politely. 'I'm quite all right!' Only babies were carried, and he was certainly not a baby. He would be four years old before long, and probably then he'd be much heavier. He hoped so.

At the top of the next flight they faced a door, painted white, with a gold-coloured knocker in the shape of a lion.

'So!' the lady said brightly. 'Here we are! Now you shall sit down and rest your legs while I get us both a glass of nice, cold lemonade.'

While she was in the kitchen getting the lemonade Robert sat on the sofa – it was fairly low but his feet still did not touch the floor – and looked around the room. It was a nice room, though not big, like at home. There were green curtains at the window and bookshelves which went from the floor to about the height of his head, and on top of the bookcases there were photographs and a vase of yellow flowers. Yellow was one of his favourite colours.

The lady came back into the room carrying a tray with two glasses of lemonade and a plate of biscuits. She handed Robert a glass, took one herself, and placed the biscuits on a small table.

'Drink first,' she said. 'I expect you are quite thirsty!'

He was. He took a long, long drink. It was the kind of lemonade he liked, not with slices of lemon floating in it and no bubbles, but white and sweet and very fizzy, full of bubbles so that it tickled his throat and the back of his nose in a most pleasant way. They did not have this kind of lemonade at home because his mother said it was not the real thing and it was not as good for you. All the same, he thought, draining the glass, it was what he liked best.

'You were thirsty,' the lady said. 'Would you like more? Or would you like a biscuit first? The biscuits are very good.' She held the plate out to him. There were two kinds of biscuit; one was pale yellow, round, with currants to make eyes and a strip of red cherry for a mouth; the others were small gingerbread men with heads, arms and legs. It was difficult to know which to choose.

'Why not have one first and another to follow,' the lady suggested. 'In the meantime I will bring more lemonade.'

He liked the gingerbread men best. You could eat an arm, then a leg, then another arm and the second leg; then the head and, last of all, the body.

'I think you enjoyed that,' the lady said when he had eaten the last crumb. 'I am so glad. I made them specially.'

'For me?' Robert asked.

'Yes. For you!'

'Oh! How did you know I was coming?

'I knew you would come one day. They keep well in the tin. You are like Daniel. He always liked the gingerbread men best and he ate them just the way you do.'

'Who is Daniel?' Robert enquired.

'My little boy,' she said.

'Where is he now? Will he be coming?'

Suddenly she looked very sad.

'No,' she said. 'He won't be coming. I lost him.'

'Oh!' Robert said. 'I'm sorry!' No wonder she looked sad, but it was rather careless, he thought, to lose your little boy. His mother would never do that, nor would Chloe.

As his mother and Chloe came into his mind he realized how much he wanted to see them. Besides, they would wonder where he was. They might even think they had lost him!

He handed back his empty glass.

'Thank you very much,' he said. 'I'd like to go now.'

'Oh surely not yet!' she said. 'You've only been here a few minutes!'

'I would like to go,' Robert repeated. 'My mother will wonder where I am. So will Chloe.'

'Don't worry about that,' the lady said. 'I shall telephone your mother immediately.'

She picked up the telephone and spoke at once.

'Robert is with me. He would like to stay a little longer. We are having such a good time!'

She waited no more than a second before putting down the receiver.

'There!' she said. 'Your mother said you may stay as long as you wish!'

'I could have said "hello" to her,' Robert said. He wanted to do that.

'In fact she was just going out,' the Nice Lady said. 'But it is perfectly all right for you to stay.'

'Will she come and fetch me?' he asked.

The lady thought for a minute. 'Why, yes! I expect she will. So you should stay here and enjoy yourself until she comes. She will know where to find you.'

'And she won't lose me, not like you lost your little boy!'

'No,' she said. 'Not like I lost my Daniel. Though I don't think it's fair that some mothers lose their little boys and others do not, especially when the other mothers have more than one child.'

Perhaps some mothers are more careful than others, Robert thought, though he didn't like to say so.

'Perhaps he'll come back,' he suggested.

'I don't think so,' she said. 'Not now.' She paused, then said, 'He was very like you. Would you like to see his photograph?'

She took a photograph from the top of the bookcase and sat beside Robert on the sofa while they looked at it together.

'He is very like you, don't you think?' the Nice Lady asked.

Robert had to agree. Daniel had the same fair hair, which clearly refused to lie down on the crown of his head and shot up in little sprouts, just as his did. He wore sandals and grey socks and was dressed in shorts and a jersey.

'Which reminds me,' the lady said, 'I must give you something warmer than your trunks to wear. And luckily I have drawers full of Daniel's clothes which are just your size!'

She jumped up and left the room, returning a minute or two later with underpants, socks, grey shorts and a yellow jersey.

'Here we are!' she said cheerfully. 'Now I will help you to dress.'

'Thank you, I can dress myself now,' Robert said. 'I couldn't when I was two but I can now.'

'But of course!' she said. 'I will leave you to it. In the meantime I shall make tea. I expect you like fish fingers and chips?'

'Oh I do, very much,' Robert agreed. 'But I don't think I'll have time to stay for tea. I expect Mummy will call for me quite soon, or it might be Chloe.'

'Are you very fond of Chloe?'

'Yes. I love Chloe,' Robert said. 'I love Mummy and Daddy and Chloe. And I love Eddie – he's the baby – and sometimes I love Janet, but not much.'

'And what does Chloe do?' the Nice Lady asked.

It would be good to have him talk, to keep him interested. She wanted him to have a good time.

'She looks after me. She looks after me in the day and if I have a nasty dream she comes and looks after me in the night. Mummy can't because she's always feeding the baby.'

'Well I think we might have time for tea before Chloe or your Mummy come for you,' the lady said. 'At any rate I'll make it. I know little boys are always hungry.'

Not long afterwards – she was very quick at the job – she brought in fish cakes and chips, bread-and-butter, tomato ketchup and small iced cakes. They sat up to the table and ate together. Robert was surprised and disappointed when, by the time they had finished their tea, no-one had come to collect him.

'Never mind,' the Nice Lady said. 'I will clear away and then I will bring you some toys to play with.'

What she brought was a large box of toy cars, some of them exactly like the ones he had at home, some in boxes which had never been opened.

'I hope you like cars?'

'Oh, I do!' Robert said. 'They're my favourite things!'

'They were Daniel's too. In fact I still buy them when I see new ones. That is why so many of them are in their boxes.'

'Can I take them out of the boxes?' Robert asked.

'Of course you can. You can do anything you like while you're with me, Robert. You and I are friends, are we not?'

He enjoyed playing with the cars. There was a wonderful tipper lorry and the Nice Lady gave him a box of dried peas so that he could load it up, run it across the room, then tip out the load. It was good fun, but after a while he grew tired. He longed for his mother or Chloe to come for him. Where were they? Why didn't they come?

He pushed the tipper lorry away from him, left the peas in a heap on the carpet.

'Why doesn't Mummy come? Why doesn't Chloe come?' His voice trembled and he felt his eyes fill with tears. 'Where are they?' he asked.

'Oh, I shouldn't think they'll be long now,' the Nice Lady said. 'You should not worry. And you have enjoyed yourself here, haven't you? We had the lemonade, and a good tea, and now the cars.'

'Thank you. It was very nice. But I want to go home!' The tears spilled over and ran down his cheeks.

'Can't you telephone Mummy?' he pleaded.

'Well . . .' She hesitated, but not for long. 'Very well, I will do that. I expect there is a very good reason, so don't worry.'

She picked up the telephone and he watched her dial. He wondered how she knew the right number, but then grown-ups knew so many things it didn't surprise him. When she began to speak he moved closer to her.

'Robert says I'm to tell you he's had a lovely time but he's ready to come home now. What did you say? Well I'm sure he could. I would look after him . . .'

'Let me speak to her,' Robert urged. 'I want to speak to her!'

'One minute, Robert,' the Nice Lady said. Then she frowned, shook the telephone receiver, jiggled the hook. 'Oh dear,' she cried. 'We've been cut off! The line's gone quite dead!'

'What did she say? When is she coming?'

'What she said was that Chloe is out with her friend – what is his name?'

'Simon.'

'That's right. Simon. And that she cannot leave the baby because he is not well. She thought it would be a nice idea, and very helpful, if you were to stay here for the night and she would fetch you tomorrow, or Chloe would.'

'Can't you telephone again?' Robert begged. 'I want to talk to her.'

'I'm sorry, I can't,' the Nice Lady said. 'The line is quite dead. But you'll be all right here, I promise. You're very tired, I can see that, and I'm sure it's long past your bedtime. I'll get you some pyjamas and when you're tucked up in bed I will bring you a mug of cocoa. Then when you waken in the morning it will be tomorrow and you will see your Mummy!'

It seemed that he could do nothing else. Also, he was very, very tired.

She took him into the bedroom, gave him some blue-and-white pyjamas, then went away and came back with a mug of cocoa. He was already in bed.

'There you are, Daniel!' she said. 'Drink it up and you'll soon be fast asleep!'

'I'm not,' Robert said.

'Not what?'

'I'm not Daniel. You called me Daniel.'

'Did I? How silly of me! But it's because you are sleeping in Daniel's bed, wearing his pyjamas.'

When the Nice Lady had left Robert put his mug down on the bedside table, then lay down. She had very kindly left a small lamp switched on so that the room was not quite dark. He closed his eyes and wrapped his arms around himself as far as they would go. He would try not to cry but he did so terribly want to see his mother, and to be in his own bedroom, even if Janet *was* there. Tomorrow he would see them all, he would be home again.

She came into the bedroom ten minutes later. He was fast asleep, lying on his back, his head turned to one side against the pillow. It grieved her to see the tears drying on his cheeks, his eyelashes – dark in spite of his fair hair – still wet. She did so want him to be happy, and they could be, the two of them together. They would have a good life. She would never harm a hair on his head.

She drew up a chair and sat for a long time by the bedside, watching him as he slept. It was midnight before she went to her own room, and then she fell asleep, quickly and happily.

She didn't know how long she had been asleep – not long, she thought – when she was awakened by the screams. She ran at once to Robert. He was sitting upright, the bedclothes thrown off him. His face was flushed and his eyes too bright. She put her arms around him and his screams turned to sobbing.

'There, there!' she said. 'You are all right now. It was just a nasty dream!'

'They were coming after me!' he cried. 'They were chasing me!'

'There is no-one here now except me,' she assured him. 'You are quite safe.'

He was awake now, and recognized her, remembered where he was.

'I want my Mummy,' he sobbed. 'I want Chloe! You said they'd come.'

'And so they will, in the morning. It is not morning yet. I know, why don't you come into my bed and I will look after you? Then in the morning everything will be all right. You'll see!'

She took his hand quite firmly and led him to her bedroom. He went without protest. He was afraid to be in this strange room on his own.

There was no place they could think of to which Simon and Chloe did not go, did not show the photograph and ask questions. All along the seafront, from one amusement arcade to another, they queried stallholders, attendants, adults and children standing fixated in front of machines which offered them prizes, but seldom delivered. Very few were interested. They glanced at the photograph, shook their heads, and went back to the job in hand.

It was the same in the Aquarium, where the lighting was so dim that it was difficult to know how anyone would recognize even a familiar acquaintance. The waxworks offered no help, and along the seafront at the far side of the pier among the arches, even those who were sympathetic could offer no help.

'Shall we go on the pier?' Simon asked. 'What do you think?'

'He would have had to pay to go on the pier,' Chloe said. 'He had no money.'

'No he wouldn't. Not at his height. He could walk under the barrier unseen. I've done it myself when I was small enough.'

The pier yielded nothing. They walked back through the Old Steine and up St James's Street, where they called in every shop which was still open, though many were beginning to close. In the end they were close to Sussex Square; though they were not to know it they were passing the bottom of the street where Robert was at that moment playing with the cars. There was nothing left but to go back to the house.

When they reached Blenheim House it was Lady Stansfield who opened the door while Moira, the baby in her arms, stood behind her. One look at Chloe told them that there was no good news to be had.

'Well?' Lady Stansfield demanded.

Simon shook his head.

'We've been everywhere, everywhere we could think of. No-one offered the slightest clue. It seems as though small children go entirely unnoticed.'

Lady Stansfield rounded on Chloe.

'I hold you entirely to blame for this!' she stormed. 'You have been totally irresponsible and criminally careless! If I have my way, and I hope I do, you will be sent back to Yorkshire – or wherever you come from – by the very first train! I am not sure that you can't be prosecuted. You are not fit to be in charge of children and I never thought you were!'

Simon stepped closer to Chloe and put his arm around her shoulders. There was little point in saying anything to Lady Stansfield. She was incandescent with rage, in no state to listen to anyone.

They were still standing in the hall when the doorbell rang again. Lady Stansfield pushed past Simon and Chloe to answer it, and found Constable Deakin and WPC Manners on the doorstep.

'You've got news!' Moira cried.

'I'm afraid not,' Constable Deakin said. 'May we come in?' He nodded to Simon and Chloe. 'I hoped to find you all here.'

No-one knew what to say. Moira was ashen. Taking his cue from the atmosphere, the baby began to whimper.

'Could we move into the sitting-room?' Constable Deakin asked. 'There are just a few things . . .'

'And there are a few things I wish to say to you, Constable!' Lady Stansfield said sharply. She would like to know, to begin with, why a mere constable was apparently assigned to this case. Why not a much more senior person? But she would save the question until she had heard what he had to say.

They moved into the sitting-room. Moira jiggled the baby up and down in her arms, trying to pacify him but meeting with only partial success.

'For a start,' Lady Stansfield said, 'my daughter and I would like to know exactly what steps are being taken to find my grandson! We all know Brighton is full of crooks. Can we hope that you are questioning all of them?'

'We are contacting all – have already questioned some – who might be expected to have any information at all. But by no means are all crooks kidnappers, or in any way guilty of misdemeanours against children. Very few are, in fact.'

Constable Deakin spoke as patiently as he could. Amongst members of the public with whom he had to deal, the Lady Stansfields of the world were his worst nightmares. Any minute now she would threaten him with complaints to his superiors.

'I have to tell you,' she said as if on cue, 'I am not without influence in the community. I have friends in high places whom I shall not hesitate to involve. Your Chief Constable is a personal friend of mine!'

My Chief Constable, Deakin thought, must have more friends than the Queen. All the same he was sorry for the woman. Her bad manners, which he guessed were habitual, were almost certainly made worse by the depth of her anxiety. She was, after all, a grandmother, possibly a good and loving grandmother.

'If it is a question of money,' she said, 'if a ransom is involved, I will pay anything, *anything*, to get my grandson back. He is the dearest child in the world. Anyone who knows him will tell you that.'

It did not in the least surprise the constable that her eyes were brimming with tears or to see her take out a handkerchief and blow her nose vigorously.

'There's been no demand for a ransom,' he said.

'If that should happen I would let you know at once.'

If there were to be such a demand it would at least be some sort of communication. Anything was preferable to this empty silence, filled only by the imagination and a feeling of helplessness. His heart ached for everyone in this room, each concerned in his or her own way, but did none of them realize that he, too, was deeply worried, deeply fearful? He had children of his own.

'Then why are you here now?' Lady Stansfield asked. 'Why aren't you out there, looking for Robert?'

'Several people are looking for him,' Constable Deakin said. 'We're all on the alert, even if we're not directly assigned to the case. But I'm here because I guessed Mr Collins and Miss Branksome would be back. I want to hear what they have to report.'

'You'll find they have nothing,' Lady Stansfield said. 'And if it were not for that girl . . .' she could not bring herself to utter Chloe's name, '. . . none of this would have happened.'

'Children stray all the time,' the constable said mildly. 'Even when they're with the most vigilant and loving parents.' Or grandparents, he wanted to say, but didn't. 'It's impossible to watch them every second.'

He shot a compassionate glance at Chloe. She was paying dearly for whatever she had done, or failed to do; you could see that in every inch of her. And she was bound to get most of the blame. It was inevitable.

'Well she won't get a chance to do it again,' Lady Stansfield said. 'I've told my daughter, and she agrees with me, that the girl will have to go. The sooner the better!'

The constable looked at Moira.

'How could I ever trust her again?' Moira said in a quiet voice.

The words pierced Chloe. There was an area in her life where Moira would have been right not to trust her – she had betrayed her all right – but it was not so with Robert. She had cared for him, he had had her attention, and if Janet had not got herself into difficulties none of this would have happened. She felt devastated, she had not known until now how much she had grown to love Robert. Perhaps, she thought wildly, she was being punished for her wrongdoing?

'Then if you could just tell me how you fared, where you went,' Constable Deakin said to Simon and Chloe.

Simon did most of the talking. Chloe found it difficult to speak at all.

'We covered a great deal of ground,' he said finally, 'and in the end we got nowhere!'

'That's not quite true,' Constable Deakin said. 'At least you've eliminated some lines of enquiry. What I'd like you to do now is to come down to the station and look at some photographs, see if you can recognize anyone.'

'Of course!' Simon agreed. 'When?'

'This evening. As soon as you can.'

'And there's another thing,' Lady Stansfield broke

in. 'I think my son-in-law should be informed, and brought home as quickly as possible. I know my daughter is reluctant to alarm him unduly but I think his place is by his wife's side.'

Moira nodded. 'I would like him to be home,' she said.

However terrible it was, it would be better if John was here. She desperately wanted him.

'Then if you'll give me a few details I'll see to it,' Constable Deakin said.

Chloe was glad to leave the house to walk down to the police station with Simon. From the first moment she had gone back there, from the minute she had confessed that Robert was lost, everything had changed. She was unwelcome, unwanted, reviled even. She could cope with Lady Stansfield's anger, there had never been any love lost between them, but Moira's was hard to bear. Surely they knew that she also was devastated? And in addition she bore the weight of guilt.

She was apprehensive, too, about John's return. How would she face him? Whose side would he take? She could only suppose that it would be his wife's. Only Simon, she thought, could she rely upon. It would have been unbearable without him.

It was dark, and had turned cool, as the two of them walked through the streets.

'The darkness makes everything worse,' she said. 'Where is he? What's happening to him?' She asked the questions but could hardly bear to think of the answers.

At the police station they were shown several

albums of photographs. Not a single one bore any relation to what they remembered of the woman on the beach.

'I'm sorry!' Simon said.

'It's not your fault,' Constable Deakin said. 'It was worth a try.'

'What will you do now?'

'Continue our enquiries. Possibly do a house-to-house search, but just where to look is the problem. It seems likely that since you've seen this woman once or twice she could live locally. On the other hand she might be here on holiday. Anyway, thank you both.'

'I'll take you back,' Simon said to Chloe as they left. 'And I'll see you in the morning.'

When the morning came Chloe woke with a heavy heart. She had scarcely slept, and she dreaded the new day. When she went down, with Janet, to the kitchen Mrs Wilkins had already arrived. She said surprisingly little, but the look of condemnation and reproach which she turned on Chloe was more eloquent than any words.

'Any news?' Chloe asked. Of course there wasn't or she would have been told.

'No, poor lamb!'

'Where's Mummy?'

'She's taking breakfast with your grandmother in the dining-room – not that your mother can eat a bite, poor soul! I've laid your breakfast in there.'

But not mine, Chloe thought, and was glad of it.

The last thing she wanted was to be with Moira and Lady Stansfield.

'Mr Portman is on his way home,' Mrs Wilkins said. 'He'll be here in an hour or two, and what state he'll be in I dread to think. That man dotes on his children!'

An hour later John Portman burst into the house, calling his wife's name. Moira rushed into the hall, Janet by her side, Lady Stansfield behind them. Chloe, hearing his voice, walked slowly down the stairs. Standing halfway down she watched as John and Moira raced into each other's arms. Moira burst into tears. John held her close, stroking her hair, murmuring endearments.

'Oh John!' Moira said. 'Thank God you're back. Everything will be better now that *you're* here!'

'I came as quickly as I could,' he said.

It had been a nightmare journey, every minute like an hour, every second filled with anxiety, terror, remorse. His mind was in turmoil. It was a judgement, he had told himself. He had sinned, and he was being punished, cruelly punished.

In his anguish of mind, as he journeyed, he made a bargain with God. It was the kind of bargain he had made many times as a child – 'Let me have a bicycle for my birthday and I'll never lose my temper again!', 'Let it be fine for tomorrow's cricket and I'll do my maths homework every day!' The difference now was that he was desperate, the punishment was already on him, no price was too high to pay for salvation.

'Bring back my son,' he implored the God in

whom he had never more than half-believed, 'and I will never sin again!'

All this came out, with swift incoherence, as he held his wife in his arms. She made nothing of it, she scarcely heard the words.

'I swear I'll be the truest husband in the world,' he said.

'I know, my darling,' she soothed him. 'I know you will, you always have been!'

Their arms around each other, they moved into the sitting-room. Chloe watched them, watched Janet and her grandmother follow them, then turned, and went back upstairs to her room.

16

Even after she had taken Robert into her bed the Nice Lady slept very little for the rest of the night. For one thing there was a full moon which shone so brightly into the bedroom – she never drew the curtains – that everything there was discernible, including the small boy by her side. She spent a long time watching him. Though he never actually awoke his night was also disturbed. He jumped in his sleep, he murmured unintelligible words, his face was frequently contorted with anxiety, seldom in repose. She wondered what he was dreaming, poor little fellow, to make him so uneasy. At his age he should be tranquil.

But really she knew the answer. She faced the fact nothing she had done in the last few hours had settled him down, given him any peace of mind, though she had been kindness itself towards him. Hadn't she fed him and clothed him, given him toys to play with? Hadn't she dealt lovingly with him? She had so much love to give him if only he would take it.

She changed her position though still watching

him. She moved carefully, so as not to waken him, though with part of her she wanted to. She wanted to talk to him, hear him speak. He was so like Daniel. From the first moment she had seen him on the beach she had recognized his likeness to Daniel. She had loved Daniel – still did – from the moment he was born, though long before then his father had gone off – who knew where? – never to be seen again. That hadn't mattered. She and Daniel were totally happy together, they had never needed anyone else. He was her world and she was his. When he had caught a cold, which had turned into pneumonia so that within a week he had died, her world had fallen apart. There was nothing except darkness.

When she began to emerge from the darkness, though still into a twilight world, she knew for certain that the one thing she must have in life was another child, another Daniel, really, if anyone could be. She faced the fact that no man would want her – only Daniel's father ever had, and that for such a short time. Also, she was forty-two. She had watched several children over the last few months but none of them would do, until she saw Robert. It had seemed so easy, she was sure it would work. Now, as the night gave way to morning, the sky lightened and the gulls began their plaintive calls like souls in torment, she knew that that was not true.

Robert stirred again, turned on to his back and flung his arms wide. She kept perfectly still, hardly breathing. She no longer wanted him to wake up because now she knew that when he did she must let him go. She felt desolate. She asked herself all the questions which went around in her head so much of the time, but the answers were clearer than they had ever been. She must let him go.

When it grew lighter still she crept out of bed, washed and dressed herself, and laid the table. She would give him a good breakfast – Daniel had always enjoyed his food. It was while she was laying the table that Robert called out. She went into him at once; he was sitting up in bed, looking around the room, confused.

'It's all right,' she said. 'I'm here. Your mother said you could stay the night with me. Don't you remember?'

'I'd forgotten,' he said. 'But she *is* coming for me this morning, isn't she? She promised.'

'Oh yes,' the Nice Lady assured him. 'You will see your mother this morning. If she's not here by half-past eleven, then I'll take you home myself. Don't worry! Come and have your breakfast and then you can wash and dress. You must eat a good breakfast. I want you to tell your mother that you've been well looked after, don't I?'

She was pleased to see that he ate well – cereal, some scrambled eggs and toast fingers – and that he grew more cheerful.

'Now I'm going to find you the nicest clothes I can,' she told him. 'We don't want you going home looking like a rag bag, do we?'

She fetched him a pair of smart red shorts and a white shirt. When he had washed and dressed she said, 'Yes, you look very nice! Now I will just brush your hair.'

That was the hardest part, brushing his hair. It was so like Daniel's, the colour, the shine, the way it wouldn't lie down on the crown. She took a deep breath and willed herself not to cry.

'There!' she said when it was done. 'You can play with the cars until your Mummy comes.'

'Or Chloe,' Robert said.

'Or Chloe. And at half-past eleven, if they haven't been able to get here, because you see they might be quite busy, then I will take you. I did promise, and I will keep my promise.'

For Robert, though he played with the cars, the time crawled by. For the Nice Lady it raced, though at the same time she knew she could not have borne it to go more slowly in case, just in case, she should change her mind – which she knew she must not do.

At half-past eleven exactly she said, 'Now we'll put the cars away.'

'I have enjoyed playing with them,' Robert said politely. 'Thank you very much!'

'I know what,' she said suddenly, 'why don't you take the tipper lorry? It is your favourite, isn't it? A present from me!'

'Thank you very much!' Robert said. 'I really would like that. Could I have it in the box?'

'Of course!'

It seemed quite a long way back home. They went up and down a great many streets which Robert didn't remember seeing yesterday. In the end he recognized where they were – at the very top corner of Sussex Square. He wanted to shout with joy.

'Now tell me again where you live,' the Nice Lady said.

'Blenheim House, Sussex Square,' Robert said.

'And do you know how to find your way from here?'

'Oh yes!' he said.

She touched him on the shoulder, gave him a quick kiss on the cheek, then said, 'Off you go then! Tell your Mummy I looked after you!'

She watched him for a minute then, when she saw him break into a run, she turned and walked away.

John and Moira sat on the sofa, side by side, Lady Stansfield upright in the least comfortable armchair. Moira rose to her feet and crossed to the window, looked out into the Square.

'Come back here and sit down, darling,' John said.

She obeyed him, knowing that in another ten minutes or so she would be at the window again, looking out, always looking out, hoping that she would see Robert crossing the Square.

'We have to decide,' Lady Stansfield said. 'And we have to tell her. The sooner we do so, the better. She must go, and at once. The whole thing is her fault. If it were not for her irresponsibility darling Robert would be with us now. I thought you felt the same way, Moira.'

'I did. I do,' Moira said. 'I've already said I couldn't trust her again.' But it was not as simple for her as it was for her mother. When her mother had found a scapegoat, when her mother had decided whose fault it was and had punished someone, she would feel better. Nothing will make me feel better except seeing my son, Moira thought. She had no energy even to think of anything else.

'Then what are we waiting for?' Lady Stansfield demanded. 'Surely you agree with me, John?'

'I agree she must go,' John said. There were reasons his mother-in-law would never know, nor his wife, why he could not continue to live in the same house as Chloe. On that nightmare journey home, when every mile had felt like a hundred, he had made up his mind, made his bargain, and he would not go back on it. All the same, he would have liked to have spoken to Chloe. There had been no chance to do so and it looked as though there never would be. The moment her chores were over she had gone to her room and stayed there.

'Then what are we waiting for?' Lady Stansfield repeated.

'I don't suppose the police will want her to leave just yet,' John said. 'Nothing is settled. They might want her around.'

'Nevertheless, she should be told,' Lady Stansfield said. 'Instruct Mrs Wilkins to tell the girl to come downstairs at once!'

Moira capitulated. It was not difficult. She wanted Chloe to go, she wanted never to see her again. She also wanted her mother to go – she was weary of everyone except John – but there was little hope of that yet.

'Very well,' she said.

Lady Stansfield jumped to her feet and rang the

bell. Mrs Wilkins answered promptly. Though she was truly distressed by Robert's disappearance she had been disappointed that the police constable asked her so few questions and seemed to attach no importance to her answers. She felt that she had not really taken part. Perhaps now she was about to learn more.

'Mrs Wilkins, would you please ask Chloe to come down here?' Moira said.

'Certainly, Madam!' Mrs Wilkins said.

You're for it now, my girl, she thought as she climbed the stairs. And quite right too. Whose fault was all this anyway?

'I'll be down in a minute,' Chloe said. She would make no move while Mrs Wilkins stood in the doorway, waiting to escort her like a jailer. They looked at each other, neither moving. In the end it was Mrs Wilkins who gave way, retreating downstairs, muttering.

When Chloe entered the sitting-room three pairs of eyes fixed on her. She met John Portman's with a blank stare and ignored the others.

'Mr Portman has something to say to you,' Lady Stansfield said.

'Perhaps you would like to sit down?' John said. He looked and felt highly uncomfortable. He had no wish to be the spokesman, but his wife sat in a silence not to be broken, and there was no way he would allow his mother-in-law to have her say. That was a cruelty he was not prepared to inflict.

'I prefer to stand,' Chloe said.

'My wife and I have talked things over,' he said

quietly. He hardly knew how to put it into words. 'This is a terrible situation for all of us.'

'For which you must take a great deal of responsibility,' Lady Stansfield interrupted glaring at Chloe.

'Please allow me to finish,' John said sharply. 'In the circumstances . . .' He paused. How could he say this to Chloe? She looked so alone standing there, so vulnerable. But it had to be said, and in a way his mother-in-law was right. Chloe's part in all this could not be overlooked. She had been in charge of his son and now his son was missing. His own world had changed completely. He was consumed with guilt, of which Chloe was a part, and with repentance, with a need to pay for his wrongdoing. They must both pay.

'In the circumstances,' he continued, 'we do not think that you will wish to remain here. It would be . . . it would not work.'

Chloe looked directly at him. No-one spoke. Then she said, 'Is that what *you* want?' She did not regret the emphasis she laid on the word.

'Yes,' he said slowly. 'It's what I want.'

'And Mrs Portman?'

'Yes.' Moira's voice was almost inaudible. She did not even raise her head to look at Chloe.

'We will give you a month's wages in lieu of notice and you can feel free to go at any time the police agree to,' John said. 'Perhaps it might be best if you were to go back to Akersfield.'

'I will leave as soon as I can,' Chloe said. 'Whether I go back to Akersfield is for me to decide.'

'You will not find it easy to get another job in

Brighton,' Lady Stansfield said. 'All this is bound to come out in the papers.'

'My conscience is quite clear,' Chloe said. 'I grieve as much as you do. I would do anything to find Robert, but my conscience is clear.'

She was turning to leave when there was a loud knock at the front door, followed by a battery of knocks. She stood still. Moira jumped to her feet; Lady Stansfield gripped the arms of her chair. It was Mrs Wilkins, conveniently lurking in the hall, who reached the door first. As she opened it Robert rushed in.

'Mummy! Mummy!' he called. 'Where's Mummy!'

She was already in the hall. He was already in her arms, she sobbing as if her heart would break. Chloe stood close by, as did the others. She made no attempt to stop the tears which raced down her face. When at last his mother freed Robert, it was to Chloe he turned. He flung his arms around her and she took him into her embrace.

'So, Robert, you must tell us all about it,' Lady Stansfield said, twenty minutes later. He had been hugged and cosseted, given a glass of milk with two chocolate biscuits, and now sat on a small stool close by his mother's chair. Moira saw the look which came over his face at his grandmother's words.

'No!' she said firmly. 'Not now. When Robert wants to tell us, he will. He and I will have a chat when he's ready. For now it's just so wonderful to have him home.'

She swallowed hard. It was difficult to speak, difficult to keep her emotions under control, though she knew she must. For Robert's sake everything must be as normal as possible. She leaned forward and touched him, and saw him relax. She had said the right thing.

'We must let the police know,' John began.

Moira shot him a warning glance.

'Not yet, John!'

'But . . .'

'What does Daddy mean?' Robert asked.

'Nothing, darling. It's just that when we thought you were lost for a little while a kind policeman tried to find you. Presently we'll let him know you're home again. He'll be very pleased.'

She didn't want the police coming to the house at this moment, asking questions, upsetting Robert. It was necessary to go very carefully, let it come out a little at a time and at his pace. She knew the police would need to come, but hopefully not yet. Right now she wanted no-one there, just herself and Robert, not even John. She wished her mother would go home and wondered how she could persuade her to do so.

There was a ring at the doorbell. John went to answer it.

'I don't want to see anyone. Whoever it is, send them away!' Moira called after him.

He returned a moment later, Simon Collins with him. Simon's face was wreathed in smiles.

'This is wonderful!' he said. 'Quite wonderful! I came to ask if you had any news and if there was anything I could do. I'm delighted to see I'm not needed, so I won't intrude.' There were several questions he would have liked to ask but he sensed it wasn't the right time. 'But I'd like to see Chloe,' he added.

He noticed the slight hesitation before John Portman said, 'I'll go and get her.'

'Then I'll wait for her in the garden if I may.'

'I wonder if his mother knows he is entangled with a girl who is a domestic help, and an untrustworthy one at that?' Lady Stansfield said when Simon had left the room. 'His mother is a very nice woman. He comes from a good family. Perhaps she should be told?'

Moira said nothing. She was in her own cocoon of happiness, her son sitting only a yard away, her baby asleep upstairs, her daughter at school. Nothing else mattered. Later there would be questions to be asked and answered, but that she would do in her own way and in her own time.

John Portman knocked on the door of Chloe's bedroom. 'Chloe,' he called quietly. 'I have to talk to you.'

She opened the door.

'Are you here to tell me you've changed your mind?' Her voice was cool and steady, but inside she was on fire.

'No. That is, we haven't discussed it any further. In any case not in front of Robert.'

'Then there's nothing to be said.' She started to close the door but he stepped forward to prevent her.

'Please, Chloe! It's not as simple as that! We did wrong, you and I. We were punished. Oh, I blame myself. But I promised myself, I promised my wife that I'd be different!' This was not coming out as he wanted it to. He couldn't find the words.

'Does your wife know about us?' Chloe asked. 'Is that the real reason I'm being sent away?'

'No, she doesn't. But we know it can't go on. You and I can't live under the same roof!'

'Then your problems are solved. We won't be doing so, will we? And if it makes you feel better, don't blame yourself. No-one makes me do what I don't want to do, not even you. I misjudged you, that's all.'

Her tone was light, almost flippant, as if none of it was of any importance, and she saw that in speaking thus she had managed to hurt him. She would, she thought, have found pleasure in that, except that she was numb, and felt nothing.

'Now will you please go,' she said.

'I didn't want this to happen,' he said.

'Please go!'

'Very well. Simon Collins is waiting for you in the garden. And I have to ring the police. They might want to see you both.'

'Then you can tell them they'll have to make it quick. I'm likely to leave town!'

He would telephone the police from his study, he decided, going downstairs. And he'd do it now. They had to be told, but perhaps they'd agree to ask nothing of Robert for a while.

Chloe closed the door on him and sat down heavily

on the bed, her legs trembling, all the strength gone out of her body. She had thought, at the moment when Robert had run into her arms, been so delighted to see her, that everything might miraculously return to normal; not quickly, not easily, but it would. How could she be blamed forever? Surely she could be given a second chance? But John was using her. He was saving his own conscience at her expense. She wished she could hate him, despise him for it, but so far she couldn't. Not quite, not yet.

Simon, sitting in the garden, bathed in the sunshine, waited for Chloe. He had been there almost fifteen minutes, wondering what was keeping her, debating whether he should go back into the house and find out. From time to time he was conscious of Mrs Wilkins peering at him through the window. He had been surprised that Chloe had not been downstairs on his arrival, sharing in the rejoicing, but perhaps that was explained by Lady Stansfield's presence. The two of them did not get on. He wondered in what circumstances Robert had returned, and when.

At last Chloe came out of the house. He stood up to greet her as she walked towards him – and was immediately struck by her appearance. He had expected her to rush towards him, as full of joy as he was, treading on air at the turn of events. Instead she walked with no spring in her step, pale as a ghost, her face a mixture of pain and anger.

'Chloe!' he cried. 'Chloe, what is it? What's wrong?'

She tried to smile, she was pleased to see him,

but the smile wouldn't break through the stiffness of her face.

'Just that I've been sacked!' she said.

'Sacked? You mean . . .?'

'Dismissed, told to pack my bags and leave. Sacked!'

'I don't believe it,' Simon said. 'Why? What happened?'

'It seems I'm not to be trusted to look after children.' Her voice was bitter. 'Those were the words, among others.'

'I can't believe it,' Simon repeated.

He took her hands, drew her to the bench where they both sat down. 'Why this, when Robert's back, safe and sound? He is safe and sound, isn't he?'

'As far as I know he is. He's said next to nothing but he seemed all right. Thankful to be home, of course.'

'Then why?'

'I was given my marching orders before he returned. When he arrived I was in the middle of being told I would be given a month's salary in lieu of notice, and advised to go back to Akersfield.'

'That sounds like Lady Stansfield,' Simon said.

'It does, but it wasn't. It was Mr Portman himself.'

She could have borne it if Lady Stansfield had said it. She would hardly have listened to her. She could have tolerated it from Moira who was beside herself, hardly knowing what she was doing; but to hear it from John had been unbearable.

'But now that Robert's back he'll surely change his mind? They both will,' Simon said.

'No. I've already spoken with him. And in any case I wouldn't stay now, not at any price.'

'I don't understand John Portman,' Simon said. 'I don't know him, of course, but it seems strange.'

How can you understand him? Chloe thought. You don't know the half of it. She could hardly comprehend it herself. How could twenty-four hours and the disappearance and reappearance of one little boy change everything and everyone? No-one was the same as they had been this time yesterday – except Simon. She thanked God for Simon.

'What will you do?' Simon asked.

'I don't know,' she confessed. 'What sort of reference will I be given? Will I get another job? Lady Stansfield says it will all come out in the newspapers and I daresay she's right. I don't want to go back to Akersfield but perhaps I'll have to.'

'No!' Simon said firmly. 'You mustn't do that. We'll think of something. Perhaps . . . perhaps my mother could help. She's kind. She knows a lot of people. I've told you before, I want you to meet my mother.'

'We'll see,' Chloe said. She was by no means sure. 'I'm worried about Robert too. Will anyone explain to him why I've suddenly left? Whatever anyone else thinks I know Robert loves me.'

She could hardly bear to go on, and she was saved from having to do so by the appearance of John Portman.

'The police are here. They'd like to speak to you both.'

They followed John into his study. Constable Deakin introduced Detective Sergeant Greenwood.

'We meet in happier circumstances, Miss Branksome,' Constable Deakin said. 'You must be relieved.'

'I am,' Chloe said.

So why didn't she look it? the constable wondered. And nor did the young man. A tiff perhaps?

'We've been discussing with Mr Portman the matter of questioning Robert about where he's been,' Constable Deakin said. 'Naturally, we understand that Mrs Portman is worried about the boy being troubled with questions, but it's very important that we learn as much as we can . . .'

'And as quickly as we can,' Sergeant Greenwood put in. 'It's clear that he was taken away and we must find who did this. In the meantime I wonder if you, Miss Branksome, or you, Mr Collins, can recall anything else at all, especially about the woman on the beach? We shall have to question Robert in the end, but if either of you can give us any sort of lead . . . Something you might have forgotten up to now.'

'I can't!' Chloe said. 'I've thought and thought. The woman was so vague. She seemed so harmless.'

'And she was not,' John said sharply.

'It's not always easy to tell,' the sergeant said. 'And she might not be involved. But someone is.'

'Robert didn't say anything at all then in the

322

first few moments he was back?' Constable Deakin asked.

'No,' Chloe said. 'He hardly spoke. He just . . . clung to us. First his mother and then me.' She could still feel his small body in her embrace.

'Did anything strike you, Sir?' Constable Deakin asked Simon.

'I wasn't there,' Simon explained. 'I came along later. I hardly saw him, only for a minute.'

'What struck me,' Chloe said, 'was that he was wearing quite nice clothes, shorts and a shirt, though when we'd last seen him he was in his swimming trunks.'

'Well that tells us something, doesn't it?' the sergeant said. 'Whoever he was with must have had children's clothes, and of the right size, handy.'

'And there was something else,' Chloe said. 'He had a toy – a tipper lorry. It was in a box. Quite new it looked.'

Sergeant Greenwood turned to John Portman.

'You do realize, Mr Portman, how important it is that we ask your son a few questions. He hasn't been wandering around all night; someone took him, kept him, clothed him, gave him a present and presumably brought him back fairly close to his home. It's important that we find this person before she does it again with some other child.'

'I realize that of course. But my wife . . .'

'Perhaps if you were to put it to her as I've just said it to you she might see it differently.'

'I know what *I* would ask him,' Chloe interrupted.

'What?' Constable Deakin asked.

'I'd say "Did the Nice Lady give you the tipper lorry?" He called her the Nice Lady.'

'If we had the answer to that we'd be a step on the way,' Constable Deakin said to John Portman. 'Could you persuade your wife to ask that much?'

'I'll try,' John said. 'I'll do it now.'

Robert would tell *me*, Chloe thought. I know he'd tell me. But I'm not going to be allowed to ask him.

'We'll wait,' the sergeant said.

He was still puzzled by the young woman's demeanour. There was something here he couldn't put his finger on, indeed there was something not quite right about the three of them. He wondered what they were hiding from him.

'It's possible the little boy might confide in you,' he said to Chloe when John Portman had left the room. 'I daresay you were close to him, looking after him most of the time.'

'I was,' she replied, stony-faced. 'But I don't think I'm going to be allowed to talk to him.'

'Not talk to him? Why not? I understand his mother doesn't want him badgered, but I think you could be helpful.'

'I'm afraid I can't be,' Chloe said. 'You might as well know . . .' She paused. She hardly knew how to continue.

'Yes?'

'I've been dismissed. I've been asked to leave as soon as possible.'

'Dismissed?'

'Robert *was* in my charge,' she said. 'I failed him. It's my fault.' She was almost beginning to believe it.

'It's nothing of the kind,' Simon protested.

'I agree with Mr Collins,' Constable Deakin said. 'There isn't a person anywhere, in charge of children, who hasn't turned their back for a minute. And that's all it takes – as I'm sure Mr and Mrs Portman will agree when they've had time to think about it.'

There was another ring at the doorbell. They heard Mrs Wilkins go along the hall to answer it.

'When will you go?' Sergeant Greenwood asked Chloe. 'I'd like you to be around a little longer. What will you do?'

Mrs Wilkins came into the room and handed Chloe a telegram. She would have liked to stay to hear what was in it but she wasn't going to be allowed.

'Thank you, Mrs Wilkins,' Chloe said, not opening the telegram until Mrs Wilkins reluctantly left.

'Mother seriously ill,' she read. 'You are needed. Please come at once. Maurice.'

She read it a second time then handed it to Simon.

'From my brother,' she said. 'There's the answer to what I'll do.'

17

'I can't believe it,' Simon said.

The truth was he didn't want to believe it. As far as Chloe was concerned nothing was going right, and if it wasn't going right for her then it wasn't for him.

'You have to,' Chloe said. 'It's there in black and white.'

She wondered what else could go wrong. She had lost John, she had lost her job, and with it the home she had hoped would be hers for some time to come. Worst of all, she was about to lose Robert. She was surprised, because she had never meant to let herself get too fond of him, by how deeply this hurt her. And then she was immediately ashamed that these things, her own personal losses, and not her mother, were the first thoughts in her mind. But it was a fact and, after all, getting away from her mother had been one of her chief reasons for leaving Akersfield. Well, she wasn't getting away with it was she, though she recognized that her mother's illness – she wished Maurice had specified what it was, but that was Maurice to the life, too mean to spend money on a few extra words in a telegram – gave her a temporary escape from her present impossible situation. Temporary it must be, she had no thought of staying in Akersfield one day longer than need be.

'I shall have to go,' she said.

'I know,' Simon said. 'I realize that. But I must talk to you.'

He had to make sure she would return, and as quickly as possible, but how could he be sure of that when she had no job and no home to come back to? What prospects had she now in Brighton? He would gladly take care of her. He had known since the day they'd quarrelled that it was what he wanted above all else, but he also knew that she would not agree. She was not ready for it. There was a barrier between them which as yet he didn't understand, but instinct told him that if he tried to break it down too soon he risked losing her, and that was a gamble he was not prepared to take. But how could he say any of this in the presence of the policeman?

John Portman handed his wife a note. It was the only way he could think of asking her to come outside. He could not say what he had to say in front of Robert, she would not allow it and perhaps she was right. He didn't know.

Surprised, she took the piece of paper and read it. 'I have to speak with you alone. It concerns Robert and is important.' He stood before her, implacable, unmoving, until she finally rose to her feet.

'I'll be back in a minute, darling. Stay with

Grandma,' she said to Robert – and followed her husband out of the room. They walked to the far end of the hall, out of earshot.

'There's a Detective Sergeant with Constable Deakin, they want to ask Robert one or two quite simple questions. His answers might give a clue to where he's been and who took him. If we can find out that, then it's the first step to preventing the same thing happening to some other child.'

'I don't want Robert harassed,' Moira protested. 'I don't want him to be upset.'

'There's no reason why he should be. It's a small risk but it's one we have to take.'

'You're speaking like an MP,' Moira said. 'I'm thinking of our child.'

'I'm speaking like a parent,' John said. 'Any parent. Are you prepared to risk some other child, some other parents, going through this because you won't allow Robert to be asked a few questions?'

Moira was silent for several seconds, her face turned away from John, not wanting to look at him. In the end she turned to face him.

'Very well,' she said. 'Just tell them they must be very careful.'

'Oh, they will be. And at the same time your mother must keep quiet. If she doesn't I shan't hesitate in sending her out of the room.'

He went back to his study.

'My wife agrees,' he told them. 'She's not happy about it and she hopes – we both do – that you won't ask more than you need to. We don't want Robert upset.'

'Thank you,' the sergeant said. 'We'll be careful.' The trouble was that neither he nor anyone else knew just what would upset the child. He would have to take a chance.

'I'd like Miss Branksome to be there,' he said. 'She knows about the woman on the beach, we don't.'

'Very well,' John said. His mother-in-law would be furious but she'd have to put up with it.

'I'd like to wait for Chloe,' Simon said. 'Will it be all right if I wait here, or perhaps in the garden?'

'Wherever you like,' John agreed.

In the sitting-room Moira remained expressionless when Chloe entered with the others. Lady Stansfield gave her an unpleasant look, but said nothing. So Moira had warned her, John thought. Good!

The sergeant spoke generally, of something and nothing, for a minute or two, then he spoke directly to Robert, who was wheeling the tipper lorry along the floor.

'That's a very nice car,' he said. 'I haven't seen one like that before.'

'This is one of the kind policemen who looked for you when you were lost,' Moira said.

'I wasn't lost,' Robert said. 'Daniel was lost, but not me. And it's not a car, it's a tipper lorry.'

Sergeant Greenwood looked at Chloe, nodded almost imperceptibly.

'I haven't seen it before, either,' Chloe said gently. 'Did the Nice Lady give it to you? Or did Daniel?'

Robert answered without hesitation.

'Yes! Not Daniel though. She'd lost him. That's why she was a bit sad.'

There was complete silence in the room. The detective nodded at Chloe again. It was best, to his mind, that she asked the questions. He could sense the rapport between her and the child.

'That was kind of her,' Chloe said. 'Did she take you to her house?'

'Yes,' he said.

'That's interesting,' she said. 'I've never been there. Could you show me the way – if you were to go back, I mean?'

Robert shook his head vigorously.

'It was a long way. I don't want to go back again.' His voice was anxious.

'Well that's all right, you don't have to,' Chloe assured him. 'I expect she was quite kind to you, wasn't she? She seemed a kind lady.'

'She was very kind,' he said. 'She bought me an ice-cream cornet. We had a nice tea then she spoke to Mummy on the telephone.'

Moira looked up quickly, shook her head at Constable Deakin.

'But I don't want to go back,' Robert repeated. 'I didn't like going to bed.'

'You shan't go back,' Moira said. 'Not ever.'

'Is that the box for the tipper lorry?' Chloe asked. 'I've never seen one in a new box. May I look at it?'

He handed it to her.

'You can have a go with the lorry if you like,' he said kindly. 'It's best if you fill it with peas, then you can take it to the other end of the room and tip them out again.'

'Is that what you did?' Chloe asked. She was examining the box. On the underside there was a small, round label with the price written on it in ink. She handed it to the constable.

'Yes,' Robert said. 'Will you take me on the pier tomorrow?'

Her throat tightened. She swallowed hard.

'I would like to. I would like to very much, but I'm afraid I shan't be here. You see my mummy is very ill and I have to go all the way back to my home to see her.'

'I thought your home was here.'

She couldn't answer him.

'Will you be back the next day?'

He was clearly disappointed.

'I don't think so,' Chloe said. 'I shall have to see how she is. She might need me to look after her for a while. But I'll write to you. I'll send you a postcard.' Surely they would not forbid her to do that?

'Well there we are,' Moira said firmly. 'I expect Chloe has a lot to do if she's going away.' She didn't know what all this was about visiting her sick mother but as long as it convinced Robert then it was as good a tale as any. Later, perhaps tomorrow, she would ask Robert a few more questions, but in her own way and her own time. For the moment she judged he had had enough. And so had she.

'Let's go and see if Eddie is awake,' she said, taking Robert's hand.

When she had left the room Sergeant Greenwood spoke to John.

'So, at least we know who we're looking for,' he

said, 'except that we *don't* know either who she is or where she lives. It can't be far away, though. Robert is too small to have walked far.'

'Well, Sergeant,' Lady Stansfield said, speaking for the first time. 'I hope now you'll be able to solve this quickly. Whoever the woman is, she should be behind bars!'

'We'll do our best, Madam,' he replied. He turned to John. 'Do you think I might take this box with me?' He showed John the handwritten label. 'We just might be able to find out where it was bought, and when.'

When the police had departed Chloe, John and Lady Stansfield were left in the room together. I am not welcome, Chloe thought, nor had she any desire to be part of this uncomfortable triangle. John, in front of his mother-in-law, didn't know what to say to her and Lady Stansfield had nothing to say.

'If there's nothing you wish me to do,' Chloe said, 'I would like to telephone home for news of my mother.'

'By all means,' John said.

'After which I'll join Simon in the garden and when he leaves I'll start to pack.'

'If there's anything I can do . . .' John began.

'Of course there isn't!' Lady Stansfield interrupted. She would have liked to have ordered Chloe to see her young man off the premises, but since he was the son of a family she looked up to, revered almost, she forebore to do so. She was just pleased that since the girl was going back to where she came from Simon would soon be out of her clutches. And perhaps when Moira engaged someone else she would follow her mother's advice and go to a high-class, reputable agency. None of this would have happened if she'd done so in the first place.

Chloe telephoned her mother's house. There was no reply. Next she rang her brother's home, but with the same result. In the end she put down the receiver and went into the garden.

Simon jumped to his feet as Chloe came towards him.

'What happened?'

'The woman gave him the tipper lorry,' Chloe said. 'He told us one or two other things, but nothing which I thought sounded helpful, I mean to finding her.'

'Then there's nothing more you and I can do,' Simon said. 'And what's most important to me, now that Robert is safe and sound, is you going to Akersfield. Are you sure you have to?'

'Oh yes!' Chloe answered. 'I've tried to telephone but I couldn't get a reply. Anyway, it must be serious. My brother doesn't waste money on trivial matters. In any case I'm not wanted here, so where else would I go?'

'I could solve that,' Simon said, 'but I can see your mother must come first.'

'I shall go tomorrow, in the morning,' Chloe said. 'I'll telephone about trains and then I'll pack.'

'Don't telephone,' Simon said. 'I'll go with you to the station now. We'll find out more that way.' He wanted to keep her as long as he could, to spend what time there was with her.

'Very well,' Chloe agreed. 'I'll just tell them I'm going. I daresay they'll be pleased since they don't know what to do with me.'

Moira and Robert were back in the sitting-room. Chloe made her request.

'Of course you may,' Moira said. She *is* relieved, Chloe thought, and the thought was bitter.

'Can I go to the station with Chloe?' Robert asked.

'Not today, darling,' Moira said quickly.

'Then when can I go?'

'Some other time.'

They walked to the station, Simon because he wanted to prolong everything, Chloe because there was a certain balm in walking in the fresh air on a fine summer's day. She would miss this kind of weather in Akersfield – not, she quickly reminded herself, that she intended to stay there for long, and closing her mind firmly to what she would come back to.

They discovered that she would have to make an early start from Brighton if she was to reach Akersfield in reasonable time.

'I shall see you on to the train,' Simon said.

'There's no need,' Chloe told him. 'I can get a cab to the station.' Indeed, she thought, John would almost certainly order one. It was the least he could do.

'I don't mean at Brighton,' Simon said. 'I'm going to King's Cross with you.' For two pins he would go all the way to Akersfield, but she wouldn't want it, it wasn't the right occasion.

When they came out of the station Chloe said: 'There's one thing I want to do. I want to buy a present for Robert, a toy of some kind.'

'And I know the best toyshop,' Simon said. 'It's not far away.'

The choice was surprisingly wide. After the drab years of the war when it had been almost impossible to buy toys, the shop now looked like an Aladdin's cave, a riot of colour. In the end Chloe chose a glove puppet of a small, brown monkey, with soft fur, pink hands and appealing eyes.

'Robert will love it,' she said.

It was when they were walking towards the cash desk that they passed the display of model cars. Prominent at the front was the tipper lorry, and behind the unboxed cars the boxes were neatly piled up. Carefully, Chloe extracted one from the pyramid without upsetting the rest, and turned it over to find the small, round label with the price written in blue ink. She had known almost as she had put out her hand to touch the box that this was what she would find. A tingle of excitement went through her from top to toe.

'It's the same!' she said. 'It's exactly the same! She must have bought it here! Shall we ask some questions?'

'No,' Simon decided. 'We must leave that to the police, they're the experts. They'll find out more than we would.'

'Then shall we call in at the police station on the way back and tell them?'

'Certainly,' Simon agreed.

In the event, neither Constable Deakin nor Sergeant Greenwood were there, but the officer to whom they gave their information seemed to know everything about the case.

'That's very good,' he said. 'It will save us time looking everywhere. And time is important.' Privately he knew that that was the first shop Sergeant Greenwood would go to, had possibly already been, since it was the biggest and the best in the town, but knowing where it was sold was a long way from knowing to whom. Still, they'd acted quite properly.

Had he but known it, Sergeant Greenwood was at that moment in the shop, and had he been there only a little earlier he would have bumped into Simon and Chloe. He set eyes on the tipper lorry almost as soon as he entered – since he had a little boy himself he knew exactly where to look for model cars – and the box was in his hand and he found the price label. He waited until the short queue at the cash desk had dispersed before he went to speak to the cashier.

'I'm interested in this tipper lorry,' he said.

'Yes, Sir, it's very nice, isn't it? How old is the child you'd be buying it for?'

'I don't know that I am,' he said – though at the back of his mind he wondered if he might, with a birthday coming up. 'I'm interested in who might have bought one like it.' He showed her his identity card.

'Oh! Oh I don't know, I'm sure!'

'They'd have to come to you to pay for it?'

'Yes, of course. Unless . . .'

'Unless what?'

'Well you might be looking for someone who'd stolen it.'

'That's smart thinking on your part,' the sergeant said. 'I might well have been.'

The cashier blushed with pleasure at the compliment.

'I don't think that would be so in this case,' he said. 'No, I think it would have been paid for.'

'Well, we haven't had them in long,' the cashier said. 'It's a new model. But we have sold quite a few. We usually do with a new model. People collect them.'

'I see. And would you be able to tell just how many you'd sold?'

'Someone would,' she said. 'If they checked the original order, counted how many we had on the counter and how many were left in the stock room.'

'Well that could be very helpful.'

'Let's see! There was a man bought one this morning, early on . . .'

'No, it wouldn't have been today, nor yesterday. Before that.'

'It's quite difficult,' she said dubiously.

'You said they were a new model. When did they come in?'

'Last Friday,' the cashier said. 'But it's still difficult. You see, you don't always notice who buys something. In fact,' she confided, 'if you're busy you don't always look at the customer. You just check the price and take the money.'

'Naturally,' he said, 'when you're busy. But it *is* quite important. Perhaps I could have a word with the manager and see if he can check how many have been sold, then we'd have some idea what to look for. I shall tell him how helpful you've been.'

The manager was a short, fussy man, but affable. 'We like to help,' he said. 'Anything we can do! But it won't be easy. People come and go all the time, mostly strangers, not all that many regulars.'

'I understand,' Sergeant Greenwood said. 'But if you could check how many of this model have been sold since it came in last week it would narrow my search.'

'Well, yes, we can do that,' the manager said. 'If you would like to call in tomorrow morning . . .'

'I'd rather have the information today,' the sergeant interrupted. 'If you could put one of your staff on to it I'd be happy to wait. Time is important.'

'Something serious, eh?' The manager's mind ranged over assault, arson, murder – though it was not easy to associate any of them with the purchase of a small tipper lorry.

'Well let's just say it involves a child, and that's always serious,' Sergeant Greenwood said. 'More than that I can't tell you at the moment.'

'Quite!' the manager said. 'Mum's the word!' He beckoned to a sales assistant who was standing close by, unoccupied.

'Miss Atkinson, if you please!'

He gave her instructions and she went off to follow them. Meanwhile, the sergeant spent a pleasant fifteen minutes looking at toys.

'It seems we sold eight,' Miss Atkinson said, returning at the same time as the manager rejoined them. 'Including one which was sold this morning and another yesterday. Always supposing none of them were pinched.'

'Do you get a lot of pilfering?' Sergeant Greenwood asked.

'Unfortunately, yes,' the manager admitted. 'And not many prosecutions because it's difficult to catch people, especially in a holiday town. We keep an eye on the kids, of course. Would it be a child you're looking for?'

'Almost certainly a woman,' the sergeant said. 'I suppose in the case of a model car that narrows it down?'

'Not really,' Miss Atkinson intervened. 'Lots of women buy boys' toys – for their children and grandchildren.'

'Do you yourself sell any?' the sergeant asked.

'Not often. I sell more dolls and such like, but in any case I only work three days a week. Miss Rohmer – she's the one on the cash desk – is full time and she sees nearly everyone because they pay her.'

Except that she *doesn't* see them, the sergeant thought, because she doesn't always look. It was frustrating to know that the toy had been bought here, he had no doubt about that, and by one of only six people, and to have come to what seemed like a full stop.

'Then I'll have another word with Miss Rohmer, if I may. And thank you for your help, both of you.'

'Always pleased to further the course of justice!' the manager said.

Detective Sergeant Greenwood walked back to the cash desk.

'Well, Miss Rohmer,' he said, his voice full of encouragement, 'it seems we need bring only six people to mind, and I feel sure you can do that!'

She looked confused, worried.

'I really can't remember!'

He was going to get nothing out of her at the moment, especially as a short queue was forming in front of her.

'I'll tell you what,' he suggested. 'You give it some thought when you're at home this evening and I'll pop in in the morning and see you.'

'I shall be leaving in the morning,' Chloe said to Moira. 'Before breakfast.' She couldn't bear the thought of eating breakfast with them, everyone at the table, Mrs Wilkins hovering near. She would have a snack in the station buffet, if she felt like eating at all.

'Very well,' Moira answered. Her voice was softer now, more like her usual self. Chloe decided to take advantage of it.

'I would like to bath the children and put them to bed,' she said. It seemed as though Moira had taken over the children, was keeping them entirely to herself.

Lady Stansfield opened her mouth to speak.

'I really don't think . . .'

Moira interrupted. She wished her mother would

go home, leave them all in peace. There never was any peace around her.

'Of course! And I'm sorry to hear about your mother.'

'Thank you.' My mother, for once, thought Chloe, has timed everything beautifully.

She made the bath as special as she possibly could, whipping the soap through the warm water to make bubbles, adding a few drops of her own cologne to make it smell good. The children, even Janet, revelled in it. Chloe wanted it to last for a long, long time but in the end the water grew cold and, reluctantly, she helped them out. Janet, at once back to her usual independent self, set about drying herself, but Robert stood there while Chloe wrapped him in a warm towel and, holding him close, dried him with loving care.

'Why are you wiping your eyes?' Robert asked. 'Have you got soap in them?'

'I think that's what it is,' Chloe said, burying her face in the towel.

When they were tucked up in bed she read two whole books of Thomas, then she said, 'I've got a little present for each of you.' She gave Janet a small, pretty box with a gilt clasp, and to Robert she gave the glove puppet. 'Shall I show you how it works?' she asked. 'But you'll do it better than I can because it's made for smaller hands than mine.'

'I like monkeys especially,' Robert said. 'Anyway, I'm going to give you a present!'

He looked along the shelf where his soft toys sat in a long row. It was a difficult decision. 'I'll give you my rabbit!' he said in the end. 'You will look after him, won't you?'

'I'll treasure him,' Chloe said.

Chloe paused in the doorway of her room and looked around. It was as bare and impersonal as on the day she had first seen it, no sign that she had ever inhabited it, that she had been happy here.

She would go downstairs when she heard Simon's ring at the door, and not before. It should be any minute now. Her farewells had been said last night and she didn't want to go through them again. John, who had bidden her *bon voyage* in the presence of his wife and mother-in-law before she went to bed had, she knew, already left since he had an early meeting at the House. The rest of the family were at breakfast.

It was a relief to hear the doorbell. She picked up her case and went downstairs, and as she came into the hall so did Moira and Robert, the latter still in his pyjamas.

Chloe opened the door to Simon.

'I won't come in,' he said, taking her suitcase. 'The taxi is waiting.'

Moira held out her hand.

'I hope you have a good journey,' she said politely. 'I hope you find your mother improved.'

Robert tugged at Chloe's skirt and she knelt down and took him in her arms.

'Be a good boy,' she said. 'Look after Mr Monkey and I'll look after Mr Rabbit.'

'She's Mrs Rabbit,' Robert said. 'She's a lady!'

'Better still! Then I'll treat her like a lady! Goodbye Robert.'

She left the house as quickly as she could, not looking back. As the taxi rounded the corner of Lewes Crescent and gathered speed along the coast road she looked at the sea, the tide coming in now. Then she looked at the houses and hotels which lined the road on her right; tall, cream-painted, altogether elegant. When she'd first seen them they'd seemed like something in a fairy-tale or a film. Would she ever see them again? Simon, without breaking the silence, reached out and took her hand in his.

'It's the best place I've ever known,' Chloe said as they turned into the Old Steine. 'I feel as though I was born here. I would have stayed forever!'

On the train to Victoria little was said between them. Simon's head was full of things he wanted to say, but there was no point. She was inside a barrier he could not get through. They took a taxi to King's Cross, arriving, to the relief of both of them, not more than ten minutes before the train to Akersfield was due.

'I wish I was going with you,' Simon said miserably.

Chloe shook her head. 'You wouldn't like it. You belong to Brighton.' He wouldn't fit in in Akersfield.

I belong where you are, he wanted to say, but there was no time.

'If you don't jump off pretty quick,' Chloe said, 'you *will* be going with me!'

She watched him on the platform, waving, until

he was a speck in the distance and then not there at all. She lifted her suitcase down from the rack and unpacked a book, but it was no use, the words ran into each other, blurred.

She thought about her journey from Akersfield to King's Cross, full of high hopes, on fire with expectation she had been then. She remembered Charles Hendon, who had treated her like a lady, given her a meal, put her into a taxi. It was not long ago by the calendar but in a way, in the way she felt now, it was another lifetime.

18

The train left King's Cross exactly on time, quickly gathering speed through the dreary London suburbs. To Chloe, dumped in her corner seat, gazing without any real interest out of the window, the scene – dull, grey, misty and damp, the sun hidden behind low cloud – exactly matched her spirits. She would rather be anywhere in the world than where she was, going where she was heading for.

In Brighton, at about the same time, Detective Sergeant Greenwood was in the toyshop talking, with the permission of the manager, whose name turned out to be Arnold Spiller and who hovered nearby, to Miss Rohmer. He was not getting far with her.

'I'm sorry,' she said. 'The only one I really remember is a boy who came in with his mother to spend his birthday money. He couldn't decide between the tipper lorry and an MG car. So he decided on the car and then at the last minute, when I'd wrapped it up, he changed his mind and wanted the tipper lorry. It's funny how you remember the awkward ones, isn't it?'

'I suppose it is.' Exasperating was the word which sprang to the sergeant's lips. 'Do you just possibly,' he persisted, 'have anyone who comes in regularly for new models? A woman? Perhaps buying a present for her son?'

'Would she have her son with her?'

'No,' he said. 'At least not recently.'

Miss Rohmer turned away to deal with a customer. When she turned back to the sergeant there was a glimmer of light on her face.

'It just occurred to me,' she said. 'There *is* one lady. She does come in every so often to see if there's anything new – in the model cars, I mean.'

'Can you describe her? Does she come alone?'

'She's always alone,' Miss Rohmer said. 'I don't know about describing her. She's nothing special. Quite ordinary. She wears sort of fawn-beige clothes, not smart. Her hair's the same colour.'

'Blonde?'

'More mouse. It's not bright enough for blonde. She's not really bright at all.'

Every person who had spoken of the woman, if it was *the* woman, had described her in the same way: nondescript. Oddly enough, the sergeant thought, that did amount to a description. He felt a tingle of excitement.

'Miss Rohmer,' he said, 'I could kiss you!'

Miss Rohmer blushed crimson with pleasure.

'The one I'm thinking of doesn't look as though she could afford much, but she buys the models just the same, as long as they're new. They have to be new out.'

'Is there anything special about her voice?' the sergeant asked. 'Does she speak in any different sort of way?' He drew back in time from putting words into her mouth. There was a point at which she might well say anything to please him.

'She never says much. She just hands over the money.'

Sergeant Greenwood turned to the manager. 'We might just have a line here. It's very tentative but worth following. Tell me, are you expecting any new models in the next few days?'

'As a matter of fact,' the manager said, 'we are. There's a new double-decker bus.'

'And I see you advertise regularly in the *Argus*. Could you specifically mention the bus in your advertisement?'

'The advertisement's already gone in . . .'

'But as a regular customer I'm sure they'd let you drop another line in?'

'I expect they would, if I got it round quickly. The advertisement's due out the day after tomorrow.'

'Then could you also persuade the *Argus* to publish it tomorrow? You must be a pretty good customer. They'll do you a favour.'

'I don't see why not,' the manager said. 'I can try.'

'And if the lady does come in, and if Miss Rohmer even *thinks* she's the one, will you please ring 999 immediately. Break off serving her to do it, so that she won't leave. And then somehow detain her until the police arrive – I don't care how, but do it. Take her into your office, Mr Spiller – anything. The police will be here in no time at all if you make a 999 call, and they'll be aware of what it's about.'

'Naturally, I'll do anything I can to help,' the manager said.

He felt quite chuffed. He saw an imminent arrest, his name in the paper, his appearance in the witness box.

The train left London behind quite quickly. The sun came out and lit up broad acres of green fields. It penetrated the compartment where Chloe was sitting, brightened up the seaside poster on the wall, but did nothing to lighten Chloe's mood. Sun, rain, fog, snow – it was all one to her.

She tried to read – Simon had bought her a glossy magazine at the station bookstall – but without success. Over every page as she flipped from hairstyles to recipes, fashions to film reviews, agony letters to child care, other images imposed themselves. John Portman, guilty about her, guilty about his wife, guilty about everything; self-absorbed, dithering between weakness and strength, trying to make bargains with God. Moira, still badly shocked – you could see it in her eyes. Looking for someone to blame, and finding me, Chloe thought. Simon: a rock to lean against, a shoulder to cry on, a friend, strong and reliable – but not exciting.

Most of all it was Robert's image she saw. His every feature clear, the tears in his eyes as she had left, the feel of his small body as she had embraced him. And it was Robert she felt she had betrayed because she knew he would want her and she wouldn't be there, he would be sad and she couldn't comfort him.

She felt guilty also because among these images her mother had no part. Though she was the reason for this journey she had hardly impinged upon Chloe's consciousness. She was still, in her head and in her heart, in Brighton, though the train was by now firmly in Yorkshire, speeding towards Akersfield, Doncaster left behind and Wakefield fast approaching.

It was the change in the landscape which eventually caught her attention: slate-grey slag heaps like miniature mountains, high, smoking chimneys, a blackened church spire; even the green of the grass on the railway embankment was tinged with black. Oh yes, she was in the West Riding all right! She was back in the place she had expected hardly ever to see again, let alone within a few weeks.

But there was no need, she decided, to return with her tail between her legs. No-one knew what had happened in Brighton, nor would they. She was simply a dutiful daughter returning to see her mother in her hour of need.

They were running into Akersfield now. Dark, many-chimneyed buildings hemmed in the view on both sides. Only small patches of sky, though surprisingly blue, showed between them.

Maurice, accompanied by Marilyn, was waiting at the barrier. Chloe saw them at once, Maurice with his usual morose expression, Marilyn frantically waving. It was just like Maurice not to have bought platform tickets so that he could have met her as she stepped off the train and carried her luggage along the platform.

She gave up her ticket, wishing, not for the first time, that she had had the courage to buy a return, but that had seemed like tempting Providence too far. Also, she did not have money to burn.

Marilyn pushed in front of her brother and threw her arms around Chloe.

'Oh, Dora!' she cried. 'It's so wonderful to have you back!'

'Chloe.' And I'm not back, she thought. I'm simply visiting.

'What?'

'Chloe. I'm not Dora any more. I told you in my letter.'

'Oh, I forgot,' Marilyn said. After the first enthusiastic greeting she seemed nervous, distant.

Maurice took Chloe's suitcase. There was no kiss from him. It was not that he was entirely cold-hearted, just that he didn't go in for all that flummery, never would. Besides, he had other things on his mind.

'I've got the car outside,' he said. 'It was difficult to park. We'd best get on.'

'So how is Mother?' Chloe asked. 'Who's looking after her? Is she well enough to leave?'

Her questions met with an immediate silence, and then Marilyn burst into noisy tears. Maurice looked annoyed at his younger sister's behaviour. Tears were something you shed – and only if you were a woman or a child – in the right place at the right time, and the station car park was not that place.

'I'm sorry to have to tell you,' he said, 'that Mother's dead. She passed away late last night. She'd had a stroke – that's why I sent for you – then last night she had a second one and died soon after.'

They had reached the car. Marilyn climbed into the back seat and collapsed in a further flood of tears. Chloe got in beside her and took her in her arms. She could think of nothing to say, not a word. She was numb. Whether you liked her or not you did not expect your mother to die, not without warning. Mothers were meant always to be there. Why had it never crossed her mind for one moment that her mother might die? She would never have wanted that, however far apart from her she'd felt. She wanted her to be there, safe in Akersfield where she belonged.

'Why did you do it?' she wanted to shout. Then, as Marilyn's sobs grew more frantic she pushed her own thoughts away and held her sister closer. Marilyn's behaviour was the right one, the natural one. She would like to have reacted in the same way and was grieved and ashamed that she could not.

'There wasn't time to let you know,' Maurice said. 'Anyway, we knew you were coming today. I'm sorry to give you a shock.'

Chloe recognized that those few words were the nearest approach her brother could make to sympathy. He was the true son of his mother, unable to show his feelings. And I am not much better, Chloe thought. Marilyn has the emotion for all three of us.

'Baxter's are doing the funeral,' Maurice said.

351

'She's in their chapel of rest. Would you like to go on the way home?'

'No,' Chloe said. 'If you don't mind I'd rather wait a bit.'

'I'll take you later this evening,' Maurice said. 'In any case Lucy will have our tea ready for us.'

'How is Lucy?' Chloe asked politely.

'As well as can be expected. We've left the children with her mother.'

Had Lucy been ill, then, Chloe wondered, but forebore to ask. If it was so she'd get every detail from her sister-in-law soon enough. She was quite pleased that the children were not there. Two spoilt little brats, they were.

Royal Lodge was no more than fifteen minutes' drive from the station. What a pretentious name, Chloe thought as Maurice turned the car down tree-lined Mount Grove; but to her surprise the house looked good. It was a large, double-fronted semi, solidly built at the turn of the century of local stone which, like all the stone in Akersfield, was blackened by years of smoke from the mills. Nevertheless, it was handsome, with large windows and an imposing front door with stained glass panels. She wondered whether, in all the years she had lived here, she had ever really looked at it before.

Lucy had seen them turn into the drive and she opened the front door before they were out of the car. She stood on the top step, the expression on her thin face suitable to the occasion, a mixture of righteous sorrow and polite welcome, though Chloe knew for a fact that Lucy and her mother-in-law had never got on well for more than half a day at a time, and would not have lasted even that long had they not lived twenty miles apart.

'This is a sad day Dora, a sad homecoming for you,' Lucy said as Chloe and Marilyn mounted the steps.

'Chloe.'

'Pardon?'

'Chloe. I changed my name to Chloe. I'm not Dora any longer.'

Lucy looked at Chloe in affronted amazement. Dora had always been different . . . but this! And at such an unsuitable time!

'Can you do that? I mean . . . is it legal?'

'I've already done it. Whether it's legal or not hasn't come into it yet, but I wasn't going to go through life being called Dora!'

'Well I'm afraid you'll always be Dora to me. It's your given name, chosen by your dear father and mother, God rest their souls!' Lucy's voice was stiff with pious disapproval.

Nevertheless I won't answer to it, Chloe thought.

'Well, tea's all set in the dining-room,' Lucy said. 'I daresay you're hungry.'

It seemed a terrible thing, Chloe thought, with the news of her mother's death given her no more than a half-hour ago, but she was ravenous.

'I am rather,' she admitted. 'I'll just go and wash my hands.'

'That's right. I've put you in your old room, with Marilyn,' Lucy said. 'You'll be company for each other.'

Why, when there are at least two other bed-rooms empty, not to mention attics? Chloe asked herself. However, she would do something about that tomorrow.

The tea was sumptuous. This was one thing they knew how to do best in Yorkshire. Ham, salad, pickled beetroot, tomatoes, brown and white bread, currant teacakes, fruit cake, jam tarts.

'Ask no questions about rations,' Lucy said, 'and you'll get no lies!'

When tea was over Maurice said to Chloe, 'I'll take you down to the undertaker's now, if you like.'

'Yes!' Lucy said amiably. 'Off you go, the two of you. I'll stay behind, clear away and wash up. I don't mind!'

Lucy spoke, Chloe reckoned, as though they were setting off on a pleasure trip, leaving her to the chores. But then, she enjoyed her little martyrdoms, as long as they didn't go unnoticed, so why deprive her of them?

'I'm ready when you are, Maurice,' Chloe said.

It was not something she wanted to do but it was unthinkable that she should not visit her own mother in her coffin, especially as, when her mother had breathed her last, her elder daughter had not been at her bedside but had been, of all places, in Brighton. 'Enjoying herself' would be implicit, though not said.

Maurice, in a rare show of tact, waited in another room, allowing Chloe to see her mother on her own. It was an experience which brought her no comfort at all. The woman lying there seemed a stranger.

Her face was bruised, and still a little contorted, from the stroke. I wouldn't know her as my mother, Chloe thought. But then, she asked herself, physical appearance apart, how well did I ever know my mother? Perhaps to a certain extent when I was little, but not for many years. And wasn't it even more difficult to say farewell to a mother you'd never been close to than to one with whom you'd had deep bonds of love? She didn't know.

It was a silent journey back to the house. Once inside Maurice said, 'We'll have to have a talk. There's things to be settled, and if you're going back to Brighton straight after the funeral . . .'

'I might stay on a bit,' Chloe said. 'I'll have to see.' She didn't want to stay, but where was she to go?

'It'd be as well if you did,' Maurice said.

They joined Lucy and Marilyn, already waiting for them in what Mrs Branksome had always referred to as 'the front room', and had used only at special times. Chloe sat next to Marilyn on the sofa, Lucy in an armchair. Sitting on the best three-piece gave the occasion an air of formality and when Maurice took up his position, standing with his back to the empty fireplace, it was clear who was to be in charge.

'Well,' he began, 'like it or not, we'll have to get down to brass tacks!'

But he *will* like it, Chloe realized. Every minute of it!

'First of all there's Mother's will,' he said. 'And as her executor I am naturally apprised of the contents, and I don't see any reason why, in the circumstances, I shouldn't reveal those to the four of us here even

355

before the funeral. We're all of us concerned and there are matters we need to discuss and agree.'

'I'm sure we'll all agree with whatever you suggest, Maurice love,' Lucy said firmly. 'You are, after all, the eldest, and the only son, as well as being executor.'

'I hope you're right,' Maurice said. 'But you know what they say. Where there's a will there's a quarrel.'

'Oh, I don't think it will come to that,' Chloe said. 'I hadn't even given a thought to the will.'

It was quite true. What had happened in Brighton had driven everything else from her mind, and even now most of her thoughts were far from Akersfield.

'I won't read the actual words of the will – though naturally I have a copy, until after the funeral,' Maurice said. 'It wouldn't seem respectful. But I'll tell you the main provisions.'

Lucy sat upright in her chair. She knew no more of what was to come than did the others. Maurice took his duties as executor so seriously that he had given nothing away, probe him as she might.

'It's quite simple really,' Maurice said. 'Everything is divided equally between the three of us: Marilyn, Chloe and me. That means money in the bank and the building society, a few shares Father left, the insurance money and, of course, this house. There's a small bequest to Mrs Pitcher who, as you know, has cleaned for Mother for fifteen years; a bit to the church and then, of course, my expenses.'

What we all want to know, since the subject's been brought up, Chloe thought in the silence which followed, and what no-one will ask, is how much each is that?

'What about our children? Her grandchildren?' Lucy asked. 'What about George and Betty? Surely there's something for them?'

'She made no separate provision for them,' Maurice said. 'I did venture to mention it but her view was that there'd be other grandchildren to come and it wouldn't be fair to them if George and Betty were the only ones to benefit.'

'Well that's a strange idea,' Lucy objected. 'George and Betty are already here. She's had the pleasure of them!'

Or pain, Chloe thought.

'And another thing,' Lucy was in full spate now. 'I do think that as the eldest, as her only son, you might have come in for a special share, Maurice. After all, who looked after her, with one daughter too young and another at the far end of the country?'

'It never seemed to me that my mother needed anyone to look after her,' Chloe said mildly. 'She was always self-sufficient.'

Lucy glared at her. 'You can't know what your brother has done. You've not been here!'

'Anyway, there it is!' Maurice interposed. 'Whatever we think there's no point in frittering money away contesting it. We'd end up worse than doing just what the will says. We'll each have a few thousand pounds, plus a third share of the house.'

'How can we share the house?' Marilyn spoke for the first time. 'You can't chop a house into three pieces.'

'We'll have to sell it, of course,' Maurice said.

'Sell it!' Marilyn's voice rose to a scream. 'But I live here! It's my home! Where will I go? What will I do?'

'That's something which has to be sorted out,' Maurice said. 'There are one or two possibilities we'll have to discuss over the next day or two.'

He spoke with more calm than he felt. Marilyn was certainly the fly in the ointment. She and Lucy didn't hit it off at all, and yet he might have to offer her a home. The only bright side to that was that Marilyn would bring her money with her. It would be in trust, of course, until she was of age, but he felt sure that the law would allow a certain amount to be released. All in all, and money not-withstanding, and in view of Lucy's temperament, when it came to Marilyn he'd rather have her room than her company.

'What possibilities?' Marilyn demanded. She was near to tears. 'What do you mean?' She appealed to Chloe. 'Chloe, what's going to happen to me?'

'Marilyn, don't worry! We'll work it out!'

Chloe spoke with more conviction than she felt. Fond though she was of her sister, she was not ready to take responsibility for her. That was asking too much. All she wanted was to be away from Akersfield, as quickly as possible and preferably back in Brighton. And now that there was the prospect of some money – she had no idea how she would get at it before she was twenty-one, but there must be ways – she would be able to support herself until she found a job which would do so. Of course she would never stop missing Robert, nothing would change that, but it was wonderful how money *did* change things.

And Marilyn did not fit in with her picture of the future. I am too young to be responsible for someone else, she thought. I want my independence. I want my own life.

'You haven't answered me,' Marilyn cried. 'Not one of you has answered me!' She looked from one to another, her face anguished.

Chloe put an arm around her sister.

'I've told you, love. Don't worry! We'll work it out.'

'You don't think you'll be abandoned?' It was an attempt on Maurice's part to be jocular which did not come off.

'You'll always have a home with one or the other of us,' Lucy said. She was, for the moment, more moved than either her husband or Chloe by Marilyn's distress. After all, she was a mother and Marilyn was still a child, more or less. All the same, she didn't really want her as a permanent lodger. 'Perhaps you could spend six months with us and six months with Chloe?' she suggested brightly.

'You make me sound like a parcel,' Marilyn objected. 'Pack me up and post me on to the next one!'

'To be fair, I don't see how that would work,' Maurice said. 'Chloe has her job and it's a living-in job.'

Chloe fought with herself to keep silent. That was all she had to do. No-one would know. In the face of her sister's distress she could not quite do that.

'I've left my job,' she said.

Three pairs of eyes looked at her in astonishment.

'Why?' Maurice asked.

'It didn't work out.'

'Then you and me can live here, in this house!' Marilyn said eagerly. 'Oh, Chloe, that would be perfect!' She didn't ever want to live with Maurice and Lucy and she didn't care who knew it.

'You can't do that!' Lucy said quickly. 'This house has to be sold. You're surely not expecting Maurice to give up his share?'

'Don't worry,' Chloe said. 'I don't want to live here. I don't want to stay in Akersfield.'

'Then take me with you!' Marilyn begged. 'I'll live with you in Brighton. I'll live with you absolutely anywhere. *Please* Chloe!'

'Marilyn don't!' Chloe begged. 'I can't decide all this on the spur of the moment. It's too soon. Mother's not even buried. It's no more than a few hours since I learned she was dead. Just let's say that between us we'll look after you. Surely we can wait to discuss the rest until after the funeral.'

Marilyn, strangely, seemed appeased, as if she had found the perfect solution and everyone else would fall into line. She had shifted her burden on to her big sister.

'I know you'll look after me, Chloe,' she said. 'I trust you!'

'I'll make a cup of tea,' Lucy said. 'I'm sure we could all do with one.'

*　　*　　*

On the day of the funeral Chloe woke early, got out of bed quietly so as not to waken Marilyn – she had not, on second thoughts, insisted on moving into another bedroom, it seemed too unkind – and looked out of the window. The sky was a uniform grey, fine rain fell steadily. It was the kind of day the West Riding could, and did, so easily produce in the middle of a week of fine summer weather. It was also suitable weather for a funeral.

She would creep downstairs and make some tea. It would be good to have the house to herself if only for an hour. She had slept badly, as indeed she had every night since she'd arrived in Akersfield. Never in her life had her mind been so crowded with problems, all of them seemingly insoluble. Never had she felt so indecisive. It was not in her nature.

She poured the tea, cut herself a slice of bread and spread it with her mother's homemade marmalade. Sitting at the table in the oh-so-familiar kitchen she thought of Robert. How was he? Was he missing her as much as she was him? She thought of John Portman, who for such a short time had meant so much to her. Shouldn't common sense have told her that Moira would win in the end – though not in that awful way. But common sense hadn't come into it. She thought of her mother, about whom she felt an undefinable guilt. And this is the last time I shall eat her marmalade, she told herself gloomily, because it was the last jar in the cupboard. And like a ton weight there was Marilyn. She had made no decision about Marilyn, yet she knew she must, and soon.

And then there was Simon. Her thoughts about

Simon were the only ones which were not unhappy, the only ones on an even keel. She wished he were here. He would know what to do.

When she had finished her breakfast she went back upstairs, had a bath, and dressed for the funeral. She had no suitable clothes, but then she hadn't expected to need them and clothes rationing, now mercifully ended, had cured most people of rushing out to spend coupons on funeral black. Before she went downstairs again she woke Marilyn.

Lucy and Maurice were already in the kitchen, at the table.

'The postman's been,' Lucy said. 'There's a letter for you.'

Though she had had only one previous letter from him Chloe recognized Simon's writing and felt a wave of pleasure as she slit open the envelope. Lucy waited expectantly. She had noticed the Brighton postmark.

'It's from a friend,' Chloe said.

He had not seen Robert, or anyone at Blenheim House. He had not liked to call. Nor had he seen anything more of the police, though he expected he might when they had anything to report. 'I miss you very much,' he concluded. 'It would be nice if you were to telephone me. I'd like to know how you are.'

She replaced the letter in the envelope and put it in her pocket.

'Not bad news, I hope?' Lucy asked.

'Not at all,' Chloe said.

'The weather's clearing up,' Lucy observed.

Chloe looked out of the window. The rain had stopped and the sun was shining. 'I have to make a telephone call,' she said. The telephone was in the hall. She closed the kitchen door behind her.

19

She could hear the telephone ringing in Simon's flat. It went on and on. Why didn't he answer? And then, as she was about to hang up, he did.

'Simon Collins.'

'It's me,' Chloe said. 'I thought you must be out.'

'I went for a newspaper. I was just coming in. I ran up the stairs. I hoped it might be you. How are you? How's everything?'

'Not good. My mother died the day before I got here. The funeral's this morning.'

'Oh, Chloe! I'm so very sorry!' She sounded so bleak, so far away. He wanted to put his arms around her and comfort her. 'Is there anything at all I can do?' he asked.

'Not really. I just wish I could talk to you. I have a problem I don't know how to solve. In fact none of us knows how to solve it.'

'But you *can* talk to me,' Simon said. 'Right now. I'm here at the end of the phone. If you want me to I'll come up to Akersfield.'

'No,' she said. 'It wouldn't help at the moment. It's my sister.'

She told him about Marilyn.

'I don't know what to do,' she added. 'I don't feel able to take her on, yet she's assuming I will. She hates the thought of living with Maurice and Lucy and if you knew them you'd understand why. And the difficulty is, it's got to be sorted out quickly. She can't live alone – she's not yet sixteen – but I don't want to stay here.'

'It's a dilemma all right,' Simon agreed. 'But I don't think you should decide anything in a hurry.'

'Does that mean you think I *ought* to stay on with her for a while?' Chloe asked.

'Oh no!' Simon's reply was fast and certain. If Chloe stayed in Akersfield she might get used to it and he couldn't bear the thought that she might go out of his life. 'Why don't you bring Marilyn down here for a week or two?' he suggested. 'A little holiday. It might help you to see things more clearly. As soon after the funeral as you can.'

'Marilyn would just love that,' Chloe said. But where would we stay and how could I afford it? she asked herself. She had a month's wages in hand, and a few pounds in savings, but there was no telling when she'd need that money for herself. It wouldn't stretch far for the two of them. And who knew how long it would be before she received money from the will?

'Oh, we'd find somewhere!' Simon said. 'Leave it to me. There are plenty of boarding houses, or lodgings. And if you're thinking of the cost, then don't. I can easily lend you the money.'

'I wouldn't want that,' Chloe said firmly. 'I don't want to borrow money.' Though, she thought, he probably wouldn't miss it. He never seemed short. 'Anyway,' she said, 'I'd better go now. There are things to see to.'

'Then ring me after the funeral,' Simon said. 'Or tomorrow if that would be better for you. But I'm sure what I've suggested would work.'

Back in the kitchen Lucy looked pointedly at the clock.

'It's so much cheaper,' she said in a voice of sweet reason, 'if you make long-distance calls in the evening!'

'Thank you for telling me,' Chloe said, equally sweetly.

The funeral was sparsely attended. Elizabeth Branksome had been an only child and her parents were long since dead. A few dutiful members of the Mothers' Union were there, together with a neighbour or two, and an elderly cousin who left the minute the last words had been pronounced in order to catch her train back to Sheffield. Mr Ruskin, family solicitor and friend of the late Mr Branksome, returned to the house together with the neighbours, to take a glass of sherry and a few bites to eat – sausage rolls, potted meat sandwiches and sponge cake mostly. He lingered after the neighbours had left to discuss the will.

'It's all quite straightforward,' he said. 'When

you've had time to think about it you can tell me what you want to do about the shares – sell them or keep them.'

'When can we sell the house?' Maurice asked. 'We don't want to keep it any longer than we need. It has to be looked after, insurance paid and all that.'

You mean you want to lay hands on the money, Mr Ruskin thought.

'You can't sell it until the will is proved,' he said. 'Which shouldn't take long. But there's nothing to prevent you looking around for a suitable buyer in the meantime.'

Marilyn, already upset by the funeral, looked sick at the thought. Her whole life was being turned upside down. But then, she comforted herself, Chloe was there. She would leave it to Chloe. Chloe would look after her.

As, in Akersfield, Chloe was standing beside her mother's grave, holding Marilyn tightly by the hand, in Brighton Ethel York was leaving her flat in College Terrace, bound for the toyshop. She had seen the advertisement in last night's *Argus* and she would have set off there and then had it not been too late for the shop to be open. She had planned, therefore, to be away in good time this morning, but things had gone against her. Sleeping so badly at night meant that she woke late in the morning, and today had been worse than usual, but she had dressed hastily and not bothered with any breakfast. It would be terrible to find the double-decker bus sold out by the time she got there.

She had, in any case, been meaning for the last two days to visit the toyshop. Now that she had given the tipper lorry to Robert, Daniel's collection was not complete, and that she must put right. Not for one moment did she begrudge Robert the toy, but the fact that she had to replace it and then in addition buy the new double-decker was quite difficult. She was, as always, short of money. To buy both would take most of what she had.

There were scarcely any customers in the shop when she arrived. Having set up their counters earlier and flicked a feather duster over everything which needed it, the assistants were now standing idly around. Miss Rohmer watched Ethel York enter the shop and walk straight to the model cars – and recognized her at once as the lady who bought new models as they came out, the lady she had tried to describe to the police. She had not been far out in her description, she thought. She *was* beige, from top to toe. Even her face was a washed-out shade of beige. She was now picking up the double-decker bus, examining it with interest. Then she picked up one of the boxes to check the price, and frowned.

While not taking her eyes off the woman Miss Rohmer sidled over to where Miss Atkinson stood.

'Watch this customer for me,' she said. 'I'm sure she's the one! Don't let her out of your sight while I'm telling Mr Spiller!'

'Wonderful!' the manager said. 'I'll dial 999 at once! You go back to your post, Miss Rohmer, and I'll be with you in a jiffy!' He picked up the telephone and was dialling even as he spoke.

Miss Rohmer went back to the department, nodded to Miss Atkinson, then returned to her place at the cash desk. The woman put down the double-decker and picked up a tipper lorry. For a moment Miss Rohmer's thoughts wavered. Had she been wrong? The woman she'd had in mind had already bought the tipper lorry last week. That was one thing she did remember. How awful if the police walked in, as they must any minute now, and it was the wrong woman!

Ethel York took out her purse and counted the contents. There was no need to, she knew what she had and it was just enough to buy the two toys, with two shillings left over. There was no choice, of course. She had to have them. She picked up both models and advanced towards the cash desk and, at the same time and much to Miss Rohmer's relief, Mr Spiller walked towards them, stopping short while he pretended to examine a display of clockwork animals. There was no sign of the police.

'I'll take both of these,' Ethel York said.

She put them down on the desk while she opened her purse and took out the exact money.

Miss Rohmer shot an agonized glance at Mr Spiller. Do something! it said. If she took the money and handed over the goods the woman would be out of the shop in two minutes flat. How could she delay her? And where were the police?

'I'll just take the models out of the boxes, check that they're all right,' she said with a sudden flash of inspiration.

'Oh, I'm sure they will be,' the woman said.

369

Miss Rohmer nodded. 'I expect you're right. But it's a new rule. We had one slightly damaged the other day, new from its box would you believe? So now we have to check them.'

Hark at me, wittering on, she thought. She usually had nothing to say to customers unless they asked her a question. Now, as slowly as possible, she took the double-decker bus out of its box and examined it carefully, managing, in the process, to remove a small rubber tyre from one of the back wheels, dropping it to the floor.

'Would you believe it!' she said. 'There's a tyre missing! I'm very sorry. But what a good thing I checked. I'll get you another one, but first I'll look at the tipper lorry.'

Fumbling, as if she was the clumsiest shop assistant in Brighton, she began to take out the tipper lorry. Mr Spiller moved closer. What in the world was she doing? And where were the police? He could feel the drops of sweat gathering on his forehead.

'You were quite right, Mr Spiller, to have us check them, even if it does take up time,' Miss Rohmer said to him. 'This double-decker is short of a tyre!'

She looked up at the customer.

'Perhaps I'm mistaken, Madam, but didn't you buy a tipper lorry last week?'

'I did,' Ethel York agreed. 'I gave it away from my son's collection, so now I have to replace it.'

'I thought you did! I never forget a face!' Miss Rohmer lied.

Then, to her great relief – she was not sure how

much longer she could keep this up – she saw Detective Sergeant Greenwood, accompanied by another man, walk into the shop and head straight for the model cars.

Mr Spiller moved closer.

'Good-morning, Miss Rohmer!' Sergeant Greenwood said. 'Good-morning, Mr Spiller!'

He spoke next to Ethel York, standing there, wondering who these men were, interrupting in this fashion.

'Good-morning, Madam! I see you're interested in model cars.'

'Yes,' she said.

Who was he? Why had he barged into the middle of something which didn't concern him? But perhaps it did? Perhaps he was a salesman for the company which made them?

'The tipper lorry and the double-decker bus,' the sergeant said. 'I'd like to ask you a few questions about them.'

'Why don't we move into my office?' the manager suggested.

'A good idea,' the sergeant said.

Mr Spiller led the way, Sergeant Greenwood stepped aside to let the woman precede him.

Why am I doing this? she asked herself as she joined the small procession.

'Do you want me?' Miss Rohmer asked hopefully.

'I'm not sure,' Sergeant Greenwood said in a kindly voice. 'If we do I'll let you know.' She had been smart, very smart. He must remember to thank her.

In the office Mr Spiller pointed the woman to a chair, then took his place behind his desk. Offered a chair, Sergeant Greenwood declined it, preferring to stand beside the desk, facing the woman, his colleague behind him.

'I am Detective Sergeant Greenwood. This is Detective Constable Quickly.'

For a moment he wondered if they really had got the wrong woman. She looked totally confused, disbelieving, as if she could think of no reason for being there.

'And your name is?'

'Mrs York. Mrs Ethel York.' She *was* confused. What could they possibly want with her? She'd done nothing, simply come into the shop to buy a couple of toys. 'I don't understand . . .'

'Are you acquainted with a small boy, name of Robert? Robert Portman, Mrs York?'

The colour drained from her face. It had been beige, now it was a pale, liverish yellow.

She's the one, the sergeant thought.

'Do you know Robert Portman?' he repeated.

She nodded. Her voice wouldn't come.

'I see. And did you give him a tipper lorry?'

Her voice came back, no more than a whisper.

'Yes. He liked it so much I gave it to him. I was buying another one just now for my son's collection.'

'You have a little boy yourself?'

'No,' she said. 'I had. I lost him.'

'Your little boy died?'

She flinched at the word.

'It wasn't that I didn't look after him. The doctor said he'd been very well looked after. No-one could have done more, he said.'

'I'm sure that's true,' Sergeant Greenwood agreed. 'I'm sorry about your son. Daniel, was it?' He hated this. He hated what he would have to do but there was no escaping it.

'Yes, Daniel!' she said, brightening a little. 'Did you know him?'

'No. Where was Robert when you gave him the tipper lorry?'

'In my flat,' she said.

'You took him there?'

'He was on his own by the pool. I took him to buy him an ice-cream and then I thought he might like to go home with me.'

'And did you let anyone know he was with you? Did you keep him all night?'

'I didn't hurt him,' she said. She was beginning to sound afraid. 'I would never have hurt him. He was so like Daniel, you see. And the next morning I took him home – or quite close to his home. He liked me, you know. He said he did. He said he called me the Nice Lady.'

'I see that,' the sergeant said, 'but you do know, don't you, that what you did was very wrong? You abducted Robert and you kept him, I suspect against his will.'

'Abducted?' She queried the word as if she hardly knew what it meant. 'I didn't do anything like that. I would have given him a very good home. We'd have been happy.'

'Abducted,' Sergeant Greenwood said. 'It's a very serious charge. I'm afraid I have to arrest you and take you to the police station. Is there anyone you'd like me to inform as to your whereabouts?'

'What? Oh, no. I don't know anyone.'

She went quite quietly with them, bemused, not protesting. At the door of the shop she stopped.

'I haven't got the double-decker bus and the tipper lorry,' she said. 'I'd like to have them. I paid for them.'

Miss Rohmer, at a signal from Mr Spiller, brought them across and handed them to her. Ethel York clutched them to her breast as she was bundled into the police car.

'You're the one to let Blenheim House know,' Sergeant Greenwood said to Constable Deakin a little later in the day. 'You seem to have a rapport there and I've no more questions to ask them. I don't see they'll be wanted in the magistrate's court. It'll be put off to the Quarter Sessions without a doubt. We'll need the nanny and Simon Collins though. They can identify. You'd better let them know.'

'No time like the present,' Constable Deakin said. 'I'll go now.'

'I hate this case,' Sergeant Greenwood said fiercely. 'The woman's pathetic; as nutty as a fruit cake, but there isn't an ounce of malice in her. She'll not get bail because it's too big a risk. She'll be held in custody until Quarter Sessions and she'll hardly know why.'

'I doubt she'll be any trouble,' Constable Deakin said.

'I daresay not. But prison's not the place for her.'

Moira answered the door to Constable Deakin.

'Could I have a word?' he said. 'There's been a development.'

'Come in,' she said.

Aside from the fact that he reminded her of the episode, which she'd rather forget, but couldn't, she quite liked Constable Deakin. She listened closely while he told her what had happened.

'I'm glad she's been found,' Moira said. 'Children aren't safe with someone like that around.'

'I take your meaning,' Constable Deakin said. 'And of course she can't be left loose. But that aside, I daresay she's as harmless a woman as you'd ever come across. I reckon it was losing her own child that did it.'

'All the same,' Moira said, 'and sorry as I am about that, I'm glad she's out of the way.'

'Well there it is!' the constable said. 'I doubt you'll be needed, though you might be at the Quarter Sessions. However, Miss Branksome will be – and Mr Collins. They can both identify her. So if I could just have a word with Miss Branksome . . .'

She looked at him in surprise.

'Surely you knew? She's left? She's gone back North.'

'I didn't know,' Constable Deakin said. 'Oh, I did hear talk of it but I wasn't sure it would happen – and certainly not so quickly.'

'That was partly because her mother was ill,' Moira said. 'She was sent for.'

And it was even more because I sent her packing, she thought, and that I should never have done, not in the way I did. I judged her too quickly, too harshly. She had told herself in the last few days that she had acted under her mother's influence. Since her mother had returned home she had begun to see things differently. But she couldn't blame her mother entirely. She should have stood up to her. And John himself had wanted to see Chloe go. If he had pleaded for her to stay . . . but he hadn't.

'Your little boy must miss her,' Constable Deakin said. 'They seemed quite fond of each other.'

'He does,' Moira admitted. 'He seems very little touched by his night away from home, for which I'm thankful, but quite upset by Chloe's absence.'

'Well that's children for you,' the constable said. 'So would you have Miss Branksome's address? This was the only one she gave.'

Moira went to her desk and opened a drawer.

'Here it is!' she said.

While Constable Deakin was writing it down the door opened and Robert came in. His face brightened when he saw the policeman.

'Have you brought Chloe with you?' he asked.

'I'm afraid not,' he admitted. 'I'm just writing down her address so that I can write to her.'

'Will you ask her to come back?' Robert said.

'She might not be able to,' Constable Deakin said. 'Not if her mother's poorly.'

'Well will you tell her I want her to come back as soon as her mother's better?' Robert pleaded.

'I'll do what I can,' Constable Deakin promised.

He looked at Moira Portman. It was her place to deal with this, not his. 'She'll have to come back for a night or two in the near future,' he said.

'Perhaps we'll see her then.' Moira was hesitant. Perhaps she should write to her. In fact, she should apologize to her. But she couldn't have her back because John wouldn't agree. Robert's short disappearance had changed them all, not least her husband.

'Then I'll take my leave,' Constable Deakin said. 'And I'll keep you informed.'

His next call was on Simon Collins. He expressed his surprise that Chloe had left so quickly.

'Her mother was ill,' Simon said. 'Though that wasn't the only reason she left. She was kicked out, to put it bluntly.'

'I've gathered that.'

'Her mother died. The funeral was this morning,' Simon told him.

'I'm sorry to hear that. We'll still have to ask her to come back for a couple of days,' Constable Deakin said. 'It's a case of identification. She's our main source. She saw the woman two or three times, I understand.'

'Yes. I only saw her once. I remember her voice, though. I shall be speaking to Chloe on the telephone, possibly this evening. Shall I tell her what you've said?'

'Please do,' Constable Deakin said.

When the telephone rang Lucy dashed into the hall. She liked to be the one to answer it. She snatched up the receiver, listened, then replied in her best telephone voice.

'Certainly! Not at all! One moment please!'

'It's for you, Dora!' she called out. No way would she say 'Chloe'.

Chloe debated for a moment whether she would answer to 'Dora' but the lure of a telephone call was too strong. She hurried into the hall.

'Name of Simon Collins,' Lucy said. 'I must say, you're a dark horse. You didn't tell us you had a boy friend.' He had sounded ever so posh. Nice with it, though. Very polite.

'He's not a boy friend,' Chloe said, taking the telephone from her sister-in-law. 'He's just a friend.'

'He must be a good friend to ring you long distance,' Lucy said, hovering.

Chloe spoke into the phone.

'Can you hold on for a minute, Simon?'

Then she waited without speaking until Lucy took the hint, and left.

'Right!' she said to Simon.

'How are you? How was the funeral?'

'I suppose it was all right,' Chloe said. When was a funeral all right and when was it not? She didn't know. 'I'm no further with the other problem,' she added.

'Well, I've got news which might make a difference,' he told her. 'They've found the Nice Lady. She's been arrested.' He told her how it had happened. 'Her name's Ethel York. She lives in Kemp Town.

'The police will need both you and me,' he

continued. 'We both saw her on the beach. So you're going to have to come to Brighton, and fairly soon, as I understand it.'

'What will I do about Marilyn?' She was thinking out loud. She didn't expect Simon to solve what was, after all, her problem.

'As we said, you could bring her with you, make it a short holiday. Or you could leave her with Maurice temporarily. That way you'd give yourself time to think. I don't think you should make a final decision quickly.'

'Perhaps you're right,' Chloe said. 'I'll think about it. Have you heard anything from Blenheim House?'

'Constable Deakin went there with the news. He saw Mrs Portman and Robert.'

'How is Robert?' Chloe asked quickly.

'Apparently he seems remarkably unharmed by the episode, as far as anyone can tell. The main thing is that he's missing you. His mother admitted as much.'

'I miss him terribly,' Chloe said.

Would they let her see him when she went to Brighton? Surely Moira wouldn't be so cruel, either to Robert or to her, as to forbid it.

'I'm thinking I might write to Mrs Portman and ask her if I can see him when I come to Brighton. She can only say no, and perhaps she'll say yes,' she said to Simon.

That was exactly what she did when she had concluded her conversation with Simon. She sat at what had been her mother's desk. Why did my mother need a desk, she wondered? She hardly ever wrote to anyone. It was incredibly tidy, paper and envelopes stacked neatly in the pigeonholes, a book of stamps in a drawer, pens on a tray. Nothing at all out of place, no sign of use, as if its only function in life was to be a nice piece of furniture.

Pen in hand, she debated what to say. Short, polite and to the point was probably best.

Dear Mrs Portman,
As you probably know, I have to come to Brighton soon at the request of the police. I wonder if I might call and see Robert for a minute or two?
I am sorry to say my mother died before I reached Akersfield.

'I'm going out to the post,' she said to Marilyn.

'I'll do it for you,' Marilyn said eagerly. She would do everything she could to please Chloe, to show her that she would be easy to live with, that they'd get on together.

On the way to the post box she read the address on the letter. Was Chloe arranging for the two of them to go to Brighton? Was that what it was about? She longed to know. She longed for someone to tell her what was going to happen.

At Blenheim House on the same day Moira Portman sat down to write to Chloe. She owed her an apology and she could not go another day without making it. Nothing could change what had happened, and there was no going back on it, but at least she could say she was sorry. She looked at

Robert playing on the floor with his toys. Should she let him put his name on the letter? It was Chloe who had taught him how to write his name. But no, better not. It might seem to promise too much.

The two letters crossed in the post.

On the night before she received Moira's letter Chloe slept little, which was unusual for her, mostly she went out like a light and slept until the following morning. There was too much to think about and the next step would have to be taken quite soon. It sounded all very well to take Marilyn to Brighton for a short holiday, but it was not as simple as that. Knowing Marilyn, knowing Brighton, her sister would almost certainly get a taste for the place. She would not want to return, except on the promise of later being taken there permanently. And do I really want her? Chloe asked herself. Am I ready for that?

She knew in her heart that she was not. All the time she was growing up she had wanted her freedom, and then at last, through her own efforts, she had found it. She had had it for such a short time, but in those few weeks she had welcomed every experience like someone emerging from a stuffy room to take in great gulps of fresh air. She had earned money, she had travelled on her own, she had met people of what she considered as a much better class than her own. She had bought clothes, she had made friends. She had lost her virginity. Not everything had worked out, but on balance it had been good and she was confident that, on her own and independent in Brighton, it would be good again. She did not want this freedom snatched away from her. She was greedy for it. She knew she was selfish – she'd been told so often enough – but you had to look out for yourself or you'd get nowhere in life.

And how, she asked herself as she tossed and turned in the bed, would this fit in with taking on the responsibility of her sister? It wouldn't.

As if to make her plea, Marilyn moaned a little in her sleep. The sound pricked Chloe's conscience – and few things other than her sister could prick Chloe's conscience.

Tomorrow, she told herself, turning over yet again, burying her head in the pillow, she would definitely decide on the next step. Not necessarily the final step, but the next one.

20

After her sleepless night it seemed like an answer to a prayer when the post brought a letter from the Brighton police, telling her that her presence would shortly be required in Brighton. Would she, they requested, communicate with them.

She saw no reason to explain to Maurice and Lucy, or Marilyn, exactly why she was wanted. It was nothing to do with them.

'It's just that I slightly knew this woman they're holding on some charge or other,' she said.

'Do you mean they'll have an identity parade and you'll have to pick her out?' Marilyn asked. She had seen such things in films, it sounded quite exciting, the kind of thing that *would* happen in Brighton.

'Oh, no! Nothing like that,' Chloe said. After all, the woman had pleaded guilty. 'But I must go tomorrow.' No need to tell them, either, that she might have some say on the time, since the police had not set a specific date. The best thing was to take the opportunity, and go.

Marilyn perked up.

'And I can go with you!' she said.

Chloe shook her head.

'I'm afraid not, love. Not this time.'

'Why not?' Marilyn demanded. 'Why can't I?'

Because I want to go on my own, Chloe thought – but would not say so.

'Because I don't have time to arrange things. I don't even know where I'm going to stay. Most of all because you must get back to school tomorrow. You've had three days off already; you can't stay away any longer. I'm sure your exams start any day now, and that's important.'

'Exams aren't important,' Marilyn protested. 'I don't care about exams!'

Nor would I have, Chloe thought. She hadn't given them a thought, yet at the moment they seemed the very best reason why Marilyn should stay in Akersfield, at least for now.

Fortunately, Maurice backed her up.

'Chloe's right!' he said. 'You need to take your exams, probably stay on until the end of the school year. It's only six weeks. You can live with me and Lucy, and come here by train each day. It's quite easy.'

'I'm sick of everyone else deciding what's best for me!' Marilyn said furiously. 'I don't want to take the stupid exams! I don't want to stay on at school! Most of all, and you might as well know it, I don't want to stay with you and Lucy!'

'Thank you very much, Miss!' Lucy retorted. 'But for once you'll have to do as you're told. You're still only a child, you know!'

384

'I am *not* a child!' Marilyn cried. 'I'm almost sixteen. If I can't go to Brighton with Chloe, why can't she come back as quickly as possible and live with me here?'

'Don't be silly!' Maurice said. 'You know you can't live here, not for much longer. The minute the will's proved this house will be sold. It'll sell very quickly. Mount Grove houses are always in demand.'

'I can't come back at once from Brighton,' Chloe put in. 'If there's to be any hope of you joining me there I've got to find a job *and* a place to live.' Less and less did she want to be pinned down to anything. 'And *you* have to get some sort of qualifications so that *you* can find a job. I can't afford to keep you.'

Marilyn burst into noisy sobs.

'You don't care! None of you care about me! I'm homeless, and nobody wants me!'

She ran from the room and, in her flight, blinded by tears, she knocked over a small table which deposited its display of fine china knick-knacks in fragments on the floor.

'I hate you all!' Marilyn shouted as she slammed the door behind her with a force which shook the room and its occupants.

Lucy was the first to recover.

'Silly child!' she said. 'Of course she's not homeless, she has a home with us. But I'll not stand any nonsense.'

She began to pick up the broken china from the floor. Chloe felt a pang of guilt at Lucy's words, but she pushed it away. She knew what she had to do; her course was clear.

'What a pity!' Lucy said. 'All this lovely stuff! Your mother was particularly fond of this crinoline lady and now it's beyond repair!'

'I don't suppose that will worry my mother now, wherever she is,' Chloe said shortly. 'In any case, it was hideous.'

'As a matter of fact,' Lucy said icily, 'I gave it to her!'

'And if you say she loved it, I'm sure she did. Anyway, I must telephone Brighton.'

'If you wait until after six . . .'

'I'm not prepared to wait,' Chloe said. 'I presume Maurice will pay the telephone bill from Mother's estate, at which point he can deduct the call from my share *if* he so wishes!'

'Oh, stop it, the two of you,' Maurice said. 'Don't be so damned silly!'

'I'll be in Brighton at four o'clock,' Chloe said to Simon.

'And I'll be at the station to meet you,' Simon said. 'And don't worry, I'll find you somewhere to stay. Oh, Chloe, I'll be so pleased to see you!'

'As I will be to see you,' Chloe said. She would be even more pleased to see Brighton. It would be like going home – more so than Akersfield had ever been.

Before she went to bed that night Chloe packed her suitcase. She had brought everything she owned with her from Brighton to Akersfield, not knowing what the future held. Now she would take it all back again, determined that her future would be in

Brighton. What's more, she thought as she struggled to fasten the case, when I get my money I shall buy the leather suitcase I promised myself.

Marilyn, red-eyed and speaking to no-one except from absolute necessity, had left for school before Maurice got the car out to take Chloe to the station. Chloe was pleased about that. She could not bear the reproach in Marilyn's eyes every time they met hers. 'I'm not abandoning you forever,' she'd said at breakfast. 'I'm not going to Outer Mongolia, only to Brighton. I'll be in touch. I just have to see how things work out.' No way did she want Marilyn at the station, with the risk of another tumultuous outburst. Maurice could be relied upon to be unemotional.

'Look after yourself,' was all he said as he lifted her suitcase on to the train. They did not kiss – they had never kissed each other in their lives. 'I daresay you'll have to come back to sign a few things,' he said. 'I'll let you know.'

No need, Chloe thought. It can all be done by correspondence. In the end he could simply send her a cheque in the post.

It was an uneventful train journey, no Charles Hendon, no-one at all she was tempted to talk to though she did, greatly daring, take herself into the restaurant car – not first class – and found it less intimidating than she might once have done. At King's Cross she went further, and took a taxi to Victoria. When it drove up the Mall and around the Palace she was consumed by memories which were at one and the same time both exquisite and painful. What had happened on that day had been, without any doubt, the most wonderful experience of her life and she knew that, given the chance, she would repeat it.

At Brighton, Simon was waiting to meet her. He took her case from her, put it down, and took her in his arms, holding her as fiercely as if she had been away for years. To her surprise – because for the last hour, ever since she had glimpsed the Palace, her mind had been filled, and she had allowed it to be filled, with thoughts and images of John Portman – she found herself responding to Simon's embrace. When his lips fastened firmly on hers she returned the pressure and found herself thrown off-balance by the pleasure which coursed through her body.

Presently he let her go, holding her now at arm's length and looking at her.

'Oh Chloe!' he said. 'You look as lovely as ever! I've missed you so much!'

'It was only a few days,' she reminded him.

'It seemed like a year! Did you miss me?'

'Of course I did,' she replied.

She had missed him along with all the other things she liked about Brighton; the sea, the pier, the constant stream of people with bright eyes and a spring in their step. Probably because they're on holiday and the weather's good, Lucy had said when Chloe had tried to explain it to her.

'Did you find me somewhere to stay?' she asked Simon. 'Not too expensive, I hope.'

'I did,' he said. 'And really very cheap. In fact you're going to stay with my parents for a night or two.'

'Oh no!' Chloe was dismayed. 'I can't do that! I don't know them!'

'Well of course you don't, but you will. And they'll be pleased to have you. I've explained the circumstances, why you're here, that it's only for a night or two. They're looking forward to meeting you.'

'I thought you'd have found me a small hotel,' she said. 'Or a guest house.' She was not at all happy.

'This will be much better,' Simon assured her. 'And they won't eat you! Also, it will please me.'

'I would like to please you,' Chloe said.

She meant it. He had been good to her since the day she had met him. She supposed, really, that he was her best friend. Perhaps her only friend. She had never known a great need for friends.

'Very well, then!'

He picked up her heavy case as if it was packed with feathers. In the station forecourt they took a taxi. Being driven along the seafront on yet another sunny day – Brighton, Chloe thought, had more than its fair share of sunny days – everything looked as wonderful as ever, as if she had not been away at all. The pier was sparkling white, the sea, today a greenish-blue with the tips of the waves whipped into a white foam by the off-shore wind. The tide was in, close to full, so that those who would have been on the beach leaned against the railings on the promenade, watching it.

When the taxi passed by Lewes Crescent Chloe looked out eagerly, hoping against hope that she might somehow catch a glimpse of Robert, hoping that he might be kneeling on a seat in the garden, watching the cars. There was no sign of him.

Except for her short walk on that first evening she had not been more than a few yards east of Sussex Square. She was surprised by how much greener everything was, the cliff tops covered by short-cropped grass and, in places, the South Downs sweeping without visible interruption to meet the coast road.

When the road dipped towards Rottingdean the taxi turned away from the sea, into the High Street, and finally came to a stop outside a house which faced the village green.

Grace Collins was at the door to meet them before Simon had time to ring the bell. She had been intermittently looking out of the window, interested and curious – certainly looking forward but not entirely without apprehension – to meeting this girl who seemed to mean so much to Simon. He had had other girl friends, some she had met, some she hadn't, but there was a difference when he spoke about this one. She wished the girl was someone they knew, or whose parents they knew; someone from their own world, but she was aware that she mustn't prejudge the girl. In any case she had had a bad experience in Brighton and now she was coming almost straight from her mother's funeral. She would need a little kindness; allowances must be made.

Glimpsed briefly through the window as they got out of the taxi, paid the driver, walked to the door, Grace thought Chloe looked nervous. Extremely pretty, but nervous. She wondered if Simon should have brought her here to stay quite so quickly. When she opened the door to them she gave Chloe a reassuring smile.

Chloe saw a tall, slender woman in a dark green dress which, though unremarkable, was undoubtedly expensive. Her hair was reddish-brown slightly streaked with grey, her hazel eyes were bright with intelligence and, most comforting at this moment, she looked kind.

'Hello, Chloe! Do come in! You must be tired after your long journey,' Grace said.

The hall was narrow. Oriental rugs partly covered the parquet floor and the walls were hung – crowded actually – with water-colours.

'I'm going to take you straight up to your room,' Grace said. 'Take your time, there's no rush, but when you've unpacked and rested come down and we'll have a cup of tea. I expect you're ready for it.'

'Thank you,' Chloe said. She was even more ready for food. It wasn't all *that* long since she'd eaten but nervousness always made her hungry.

'Where's Father?' Simon asked as he carried the suitcase up the stairs.

'He had to see a client in Lewes,' Grace said. 'An elderly lady he always visits in her home. He won't be long.'

Mr Collins, Chloe knew, was a solicitor. That was all she did know. Simon had not talked a great deal about his parents except to say that he wanted her to meet them. And here she was.

She went downstairs quickly. Tea was, mercifully, ample, with sandwiches, scones, small cakes. She tried to restrain herself in a ladylike manner but fortunately Mrs Collins pressed food upon her.

'I have a few things I absolutely must see to in the garden,' Mrs Collins said when tea was over. 'Will you both excuse me? Join me there when you like.'

'We should let the police know you've arrived,' Simon said when his mother had gone.

'I told them I was coming today,' Chloe said.

'But they don't know where you're staying. I expect they'll see us fairly soon, as you have to go back.'

'As a matter of fact . . .' Chloe was hesitant.

'You're not worried about it, are you?'

'Oh no! What I'm trying to tell you – I didn't on the telephone because I wasn't sure, it was all done in a rush – the fact is, I'm not going back. Until further notice Marilyn is going to live with Maurice and Lucy.'

'Not going back? For how long?' Simon's face was one wide smile.

'Not at all. Not if I can help it. I thought . . .'

He didn't wait to hear what she thought. He picked her up by the waist and swung her around.

'That's wonderful! That's marvellous!'

'Will you put me down?' she said.

'But what will you do?' he asked. 'Not that I care, just as long as you're here.'

'I shall get a job. I don't know what. It doesn't much matter to begin with, as long as it supports me. And I shall have to get a furnished room, something quite cheap.'

'You could stay here. Ma wouldn't mind.'

Chloe shook her head.

'No,' she said firmly. 'I couldn't. It's kind of your mother to have me at all, but I must find a room tomorrow.'

'You know what I'd like,' Simon said. He was suddenly serious. 'I'd like you to stay with me. Chloe, I have something to say to you and I can't wait any longer. I love you, Chloe. I want to marry you. I want to marry you and look after you forever.'

She stared at him in astonishment. No words came.

'Don't look like that,' Simon said. 'You must have known. You must have guessed. I fell in love with you the first time I saw you. I didn't know where to look for you but I knew I'd find you. And then there you were, sitting outside the café, biting into a chocolate éclair, cream all around your mouth. I've never stopped thinking about you since.'

'I can't,' she said.

'Why can't you?' he demanded. 'You mightn't love me but you will! And you like me, don't you?'

She looked at him as if she was seeing him clearly for the first time.

'I think . . .' she said carefully, '. . . I think I *like* you more than anyone I've ever known. But it's not enough.' He did not turn her blood to water, make her head spin as John Portman had done. When he touched her she was not set on fire; she didn't lie awake at night thinking about him. She had never imagined herself lying naked in his arms as she had in John's – and surely *that* was love? Excitement, longing, passion.

'It would be enough to start with,' Simon said. 'The rest would come. I know it would.'

There was part of her which was tempted. A house, a husband – reasonably well off – a position in the world where no-one could look down on her. Were those the things she wanted? One day yes – but they came later, after the adventures not at the beginning.

'I can't!' she repeated. 'Not yet.'

'What do you mean, not yet? Does that mean that one day you will?'

She looked around the room, almost as though she was looking for a way of escape. It was a lovely room, comfortable, chintz-covered armchairs and sofas, bookshelves, small tables which looked as though they had been polished over half a lifetime, a Chinese rug in front of the fireplace. She supposed if she were to marry Simon she could have a room like this, except of course that hers would be much more up-to-date and fashionable.

'Is that what you mean?' Simon persisted.

'I'm not sure what I mean, except that I'm not ready.' At least she was sure about that. And when she saw the disappointment in Simon's face she was sorry, not that being sorry could change her mind.

'It's nothing to do with you,' she said, 'not really.'

'Then I shall ask you again,' Simon said. 'At regular intervals.' He was convinced he could change her mind.

'Tomorrow,' Chloe said, 'when I've reported to the police, I shall start to look for a job, and a place to live.'

'I'll go with you to the police station,' Simon offered. 'I'm staying here overnight. Afterwards I have two articles to finish, one of them commissioned. I'm doing quite well at the moment.'

'I'm also going to pluck up courage to ask if I can see Robert for a few minutes. Mrs Portman can only say no.'

'Then telephone from here,' Simon suggested. 'If she agrees, then I'll go with you. We can stop off on our way to Brighton.'

The telephone in Blenheim House was answered by John Portman. Chloe had not expected that, it was too early in the evening, and at the sound of his voice a wave of longing swept her from top to toe, so that for a few seconds she was unable to answer him.

'Hello!' he repeated. 'John Portman.'

'It's Chloe!'

'Chloe?' he sounded neither friendly nor unfriendly, just surprised. 'You're phoning from Yorkshire?'

'No, I'm back in Brighton.'

'I see!' He didn't see, Chloe thought. Or if he did he didn't sound pleased about it, simply neutral.

'Could I speak to Mrs Portman?'

'My wife. Yes, I'll get her.'

Did he have to say 'my wife'? Did he have to rub it in?

There was a short pause before Moira came to the telephone.

'Chloe? This is a surprise. I knew you would have to come for a visit, but I didn't think so soon.'

She sounds even more nervous than I feel, Chloe thought.

'I'm not on a visit,' she said. 'I'm back for good.'

'Oh! I didn't think . . .'

'I just wondered how Robert was?'

'He's . . . quite well, thank you.'

There was a pause, in which it seemed to Chloe that they had come to the end of their conversation and she had not asked if she might see Robert. Nor, she realized, did she have the courage to do so. The words wouldn't come.

'Would you like to see him?' Moira asked suddenly. 'I'm sure he'd love to see you.'

'Oh! Oh yes, I would!'

'Where are you?'

'I'm staying with Simon's parents in Rottingdean. We have to go to Brighton in the morning. Perhaps, if it suits you, we could call then?'

'That would be fine,' Moira said.

'Will it be all right if Simon comes with me?'

'Certainly!'

I must remember to tell my mother that Chloe is staying with Mr and Mrs Collins in Rottingdean, Moira thought. She'll be mortified.

John was not totally approving when Moira told him she had invited Chloe to see Robert.

'Is it wise?' he questioned. 'Isn't the whole episode best put behind us?'

'It isn't best for Robert. He needs to see Chloe, to know that everything's all right between them.' It would be good for her too. She had dealt badly with the situation and she needed to clear herself, to quieten her conscience in the best way she could.

'Well, don't get too involved,' John warned.

'I shan't be involved at all, only as far as what's best for Robert, and what decency and good manners demand towards Chloe.'

She wondered why John should be so cool. He had been as keen on Chloe as the rest of them. Before all this happened she could do no wrong. But above all else, she thought, John was a political animal. His mind was upon his job, his real life in the House of Commons, his aspirations, on his career, on his promotion. And he would, she was sure, and sooner rather than later, come by all he aspired to. She accepted, had for a long time now, that she and the children came second and anything else a poor third. Poor John, she thought. He doesn't allow himself to live in the real world.

There were times, in the night, when Simon, sleeping (or, rather, not sleeping) in his old room in Rottingdean wanted to cross the landing and walk into Chloe's room; to creep into her bed to waken her from her sleep, to take her in his arms and make love to her; to make love to her all night without end. She had no idea how she set him alight, just the sight of her, or the sound of her voice on the telephone. How long could he wait for her? He didn't know the answer to that, only that he couldn't take her here and now in his parents' house but that, equally, he would never give her up.

He fell asleep, but not before the early dawn crept

around the edges of the curtains and a blackbird began to sing on the lawn below. Two hours later he awoke, tired and unrefreshed. Chloe, on the other hand, slept well and awoke rested and renewed. Her first thought was that she was to see Robert, her second that today was the day she must find a job.

She had no idea at what, except that she would not be a mother's help and no way would she go into an office, thus throwing away with no more than one thought the skills which her parents had paid, handsomely they had reckoned, for her to acquire. There must and there would be other jobs to which she was suited: shop assistant, receptionist, telephonist, waitress, and so on. Waitress seemed the most likely. She counted up her attributes: reasonable appearance, marginally pleasant, good feet, clean fingernails. That should fill the bill.

She bathed and dressed then, looking out of her window, she saw Mrs Collins already at work in her garden at the back of the house. A little nervously she went downstairs and joined her.

'What a lovely garden!' she said.

'It *is* nice,' Mrs Collins agreed. 'And these high walls shelter it a little. This is a very windy place to live, which I suppose is why the house is named High Winds!'

'It's a beautiful house! Is it very old?'

'Well over a hundred years. And yes, it is beautiful. However, we shan't be living here a great deal longer, my husband and I, that is. We have a house in the south-west of France and when my husband retires, which he will in the autumn of next year, we intend to live there.'

'Oh! Won't you miss this house?' Chloe asked.

'Of course we will! But the climate where we're going will suit my husband so much better. He's inclined to be chesty.'

She was about to say 'this house will be Simon's' – and thought better of it. She didn't know this young woman at all well. She didn't seem like a gold digger, she seemed pleasant, but who could tell?

'Come inside,' she said, cleaning the soil from her trowel. 'We'll have some breakfast. Is Simon down?'

'I don't know,' Chloe said.

At breakfast, at which Simon appeared one minute before it was on the table and his father one minute after, they talked of the day's plans.

'We're going to Sussex Square,' Simon said. 'To see Robert.'

'I'm glad about that,' Mrs Collins said. She considered Chloe had been harshly treated and that the child, if he was half as fond of Chloe as Simon said he was, must be a confused little fellow.

'After that I'm going to look for a job and for rooms in Brighton,' Chloe informed her.

'Oh! I thought you were going back to Akersfield,' Mrs Collins said.

'No. I've decided to stay here,' Chloe said. 'I like Brighton and I'm sure I'll get a job and somewhere to live.' She quite liked, also, the thought of being near Simon though she wouldn't say so to his mother; it was too soon, she might read too much into it.

'Then I wish you luck,' Mrs Collins said. 'And if you're stuck for somewhere to sleep you can come here for a few nights.'

'Thank you. It's kind of you.' She wouldn't do that unless she had to. She wanted to be independent.

Standing on the doorstep of Blenheim House, waiting for Moira Portman to answer the bell, Chloe felt nervous. She was glad to have Simon with her. She couldn't help but recall her departure from the house, ostensibly to go to her mother but actually because she was being banished. And now she was to be allowed back, if only for one short visit.

On the other side of the door, stretching her hand out to open it and knowing who was there, Moira Portman was equally nervous. She had been unfair to Chloe, she wanted to make amends and she didn't know how. Last night she had discussed it all again with John.

'You can't turn the clock back,' he'd insisted. 'It's not possible!'

'Why not?' she'd asked.

'In any case,' he'd reminded her, ignoring her question, 'only a week or two and we'll be leaving for the summer holiday, and after that Robert goes to school. He won't need to be looked after all day. And the baby will be weaned, you won't be nearly so tied down.'

He had not taken Chloe into consideration at all, Moira thought as she opened the door to her.

'Good-morning!' she said. 'Do come in!'

'Thank you.' Chloe stepped into the hall, Simon following.

One word was enough to alert Robert. He flew like an arrow from a bow from the sitting-room into the hall, and rushed at Chloe, shouting her name.

'Chloe! Chloe! I knew you'd come back!'

He clung to her skirt. Chloe knelt down and drew him into her arms while Simon and Moira looked on.

'Let's move somewhere more comfortable,' Moira suggested. 'And in the meantime I'll ask Mrs Wilkins to conjure up some coffee.'

When Mrs Wilkins brought in the coffee she threw a baleful glance in Chloe's direction, but said nothing, except to herself. Sitting there, drinking coffee as if nothing had happened, she fumed. That one would get away with anything!

The conversation was as general as they could make it because there were so many subjects which, though uppermost in the minds of all three adults, could not be touched upon in Robert's presence. The Nice Lady, Robert's stay in her house, the police, were all taboo. In the end there was little left to talk about.

'Will you take me down the garden to watch the cars?' Robert asked Chloe. 'Simon can come as well,' he added kindly.

There was a moment's silence, in which Moira made up her mind.

'If you have time, Chloe,' she said. 'That would be very nice!'

'I'm sure we have,' Chloe said quickly, turning to Simon for confirmation.

'Half an hour,' Simon said. 'Then we have to go into Brighton.' He was not sure that this was a sensible move, but how could he say no when Chloe suddenly looked happier than she had for a long time?

Minutes later Moira watched as the trio, Robert clutching Chloe's hand, crossed from the house to the garden and began to walk towards the coast road. It would not be true to say that she saw Robert disappear from her sight without a qualm. Since the morning he had turned up at the door after his disappearance she had not let him out of her sight, though she knew that eventually she must, for his sake and her own. She knew also, as she watched them, that she had been wrong to say she could never trust Chloe again. She could trust her with her son's life.

She left the window and then, on an impulse, went up to her studio at the top of the house. She had not entered the room since the last time she had worked, in the garden, on Chloe's portrait. The painting stood there on the easel. Even as she walked in at the door its colour, its vibrancy, sang out to her. It was like nothing she had ever painted before. There had been at the time, there must have been to have achieved this result, a rapport between herself and the subject, and now that rapport was gone.

But the painting was there. It needed very little work to finish it, she thought. Indeed, too much work might spoil it, take away its spontaneity. And it was wrong that, in spite of her differences with the subject, this painting should languish in her attic studio.

Half an hour later Chloe and Simon returned Robert to Blenheim House.

'We won't come in,' Simon said. 'We do have to get to Brighton.'

'I had a lovely time,' Robert said. 'Can Chloe take me out again?'

'Of course she can,' Moira answered.

21

The visit to the police station was short.

'You'll probably be called for the Quarter Sessions,' Inspector Greenwood said. 'But that's a little way off. And since you're back in Brighton permanently, Miss Branksome, we'd like your address.'

'I don't know it yet,' Chloe admitted. 'I'm looking for rooms. I expect I'll be able to tell you in a day or two.'

'In the meantime you can contact her via me,' Simon said.

'What about Mrs York?' Chloe asked. 'What's happening to her?'

'We're waiting for medical reports,' the inspector said. 'Now *there's* a lady who needs help, but don't worry, one way or another we'll see she gets it. I don't suppose you've any news of the little boy?'

'In fact I've seen him only this morning,' Chloe said. 'He seems fine!'

'What do I do next?' she asked Simon as they left the police station. 'Do I look for a job or for a place to live? Which comes first?'

'Possibly a job,' Simon said. 'You heard what my mother said. You can always stay there for a while.'

'It's very kind of your mother but I wouldn't want to presume.'

In fact, pleasant though Simon's mother was, Chloe was a little in awe of her. She somehow felt that Mrs Collins could see into her mind and that she found her wanting, not quite the person she would have chosen for her son. As for Mr Collins, he was polite but remote. Chloe doubted that he cared for any visitors.

'I like to be independent,' she explained. 'Also, travelling to and from Rottingdean would cost money. I have to think about that. But I'll do as you suggest, get a job first and then a place to live. Who knows, I might manage both in one day!'

She felt lucky. The unexpected opportunity of taking Robert out, and Moira's attitude, had raised her spirits. Life might well be taking a turn for the better.

'I'll buy a newspaper,' she said. 'Study the situations vacant and the furnished rooms to let.'

'Also, there's a shop in St James's Street, round the corner from my flat, where they have cards in the window. I'll go with you,' Simon offered.

'No!' She was quite firm about it. It was something she had to do, wanted to do, on her own. 'You told me you had some writing to do. I'd much rather you got on with that.'

'Then come and have some lunch with me later,' Simon said. 'I can make omelettes.'

'Very well!'

They walked down to the Old Steine together, stopping to buy a newspaper, then parted company, Simon to his flat and Chloe to St James's Street where she walked into the first small café she came to, not so much to drink the coffee she ordered but to study the newspaper.

The café was busy, and larger than she had supposed from the outside since, like many other local properties it had a narrow frontage, but went a long way back – the depth of two rooms, joined by an arch, and beyond that a kitchen. From the front room a staircase rose with, across the bottom step, a large sign, 'CLOSED'. Chloe looked in vain for an empty table. In the end she paused before a table for two in the front window at which a woman sat alone, clearly nearing the end of a cup of coffee and a buttered bun.

'Excuse me!' Chloe said. 'Do you think I might share your table? I can't find a seat.'

'Certainly,' the woman said. 'I'm nearly finished.'

Chloe sat down. She was, as always, hungry. She would have a Bath bun with her coffee. She waited to give her order. And waited. And waited. She could see a waitress, elderly and slow-moving, clearing tables in the back room, but no-one came near the front.

'Do I have to go and give my order to someone?' she asked the woman opposite.

'Not really. She should come to you and I expect she will in the end. They're short-staffed. They usually have two waitresses but Rosie left. She got caught.'

'Caught?'

'A baby. If you'd seen Rosie you'd know it was an accident waiting to happen. The way she dressed, if you know what I mean. She was asking for it, wasn't she? Anyway, they say she's had a nice little boy, seven pounds twelve ounces, both doing well. And that's what makes the world go round, isn't it? Are you in a hurry?'

'I don't suppose so,' Chloe said. All the same she would like some service. She raised her hand, trying to catch the waitress's eye and this time, to her surprise, she was successful.

'Well done!' the woman opposite said as the waitress approached. 'And since she's here I reckon I'll have another cup of coffee. Are you on holiday?'

'No. I live here,' Chloe said. Well I will, she thought, when I've found somewhere to live.

'You don't sound like you come from round here,' the woman said.

There was another interminable wait for the coffee, during which time the woman, by a series of direct questions – how did you get to know, she always said, if you didn't ask – elicited that Chloe was in Brighton to stay but without either a roof over her head or a means of earning a living.

'Well I wouldn't want my daughter to be in a like predicament, not in Brighton,' the woman said. 'You'll have to watch out!'

'Oh, I will,' Chloe said. 'I've bought a newspaper. I'm going to see what it offers.'

The woman shook her head. 'Don't believe everything you read in the newspaper. Especially advertisements! They can be a pack of lies!'

In the end the coffee arrived. It was surprisingly good; hot and strong, and the buns fresh.

'Oh, they serve good quality,' the woman conceded. 'When it finally gets to you. I reckon you could do a job here, they must be desperate for another waitress. But perhaps that's not in your line? Perhaps you're more of an office type?' The girl looked a bit too smart for a waitress.

'On the contrary,' Chloe said, 'I hate offices! Do you really think they might want someone?'

'It stands to reason. If they don't do better than this people will get up and walk out. I nearly did myself. The owner will be in the kitchen. She does the food. Why don't you have a word with her?'

'I will!' Chloe said. 'I quite definitely will!' What was there to lose? But it was no use waiting for the waitress to take a message; she was lost to sight again. So I'll just walk through to the kitchen, Chloe decided.

The woman rose to her feet and picked up her shopping bags, festooned them around her person.

'Well I'm off,' she said. 'The very best of luck to you!'

Chloe set off in the direction of the kitchen. The tables were packed together and she had to pick her way between them. You had to be slim to work here, she thought, which the elderly waitress, who almost dropped her tray at the sight of Chloe about to enter the kitchen, certainly wasn't.

'You can't go . . .' the waitress began.

She was too late. Chloe was already on the other side of the door.

A middle-aged woman with grey hair and wearing a white overall stood at a table buttering buns. She looked up, startled, as Chloe gave a small cough to attract her attention.

'What . . .?'

'I wanted to congratulate you,' Chloe said pleasantly. 'I've just had a very nice cup of coffee and a delicious bun in your café. I don't know when I've tasted better.'

'Thank you,' the woman said. 'I don't often get bouquets!'

'The only thing is,' Chloe went on, 'you do seem to be very short-staffed. I wondered if I might be of help? At the moment it so happens I'm free. I've been taking a break. So if it would help at all . . .? I'm Chloe Branksome.'

The woman put down her knife and turned to face Chloe. Was she supposed to know who Chloe Branksome was? Was she an actress, what they called 'resting'. There were always plenty of those in Brighton. She racked her brains but nothing came.

'It's quite true that I need someone,' she admitted. 'Have you any experience as a waitress?'

'Well, not *as such*,' Chloe said. 'But it's a matter of common sense, really, don't you think?'

The woman smiled. She was quite attractive when she smiled, and somehow she looked less tired.

'Common sense, a polite manner, and good feet!' she said. 'It's no use if you have varicose veins!'

'Oh, but I don't!' Chloe said quickly. 'Whatever those are. I'm as strong as a horse!'

Shall I give her a try? the woman thought. A few days will sort out whether she's any good. And I can't go on like this . . .

'Then I think you've got yourself a job,' she said. 'But I'm too busy to discuss it now. Come back just before half-past six. I close then, we don't do an evening trade.'

'Thank you. I'll do that. Can I pay my bill – your waitress is very busy.'

'On the house!' the woman said, waving her away.

Chloe looked at her watch as she left the café. It was close to lunchtime – she had waited around so long – therefore she would go to Simon's flat, study the newspaper there and look for rooms after lunch. Crossing St James's Street she came across the shop with advertisements in the window, but there was nothing to suit her and the rents – when they were mentioned – were far too high. She might well have to settle for a bed-sitter with a gas ring in the corner. No matter, a bed-sitter would do perfectly well. At least she'd have it to herself, she'd be able to come and go as she pleased.

She had hardly taken her finger off the bell-push before she heard Simon running down the stairs, and then he was at the door, looking delighted to see her.

'I'm early,' Chloe apologized. 'Am I interrupting your work?'

'You're the most welcome interruption I could possibly think of!' he assured her.

The fact was that he, who could forget the whole world when he was writing, couldn't this morning concentrate for two minutes together. Chloe's face constantly came between him and the near-blank sheet of paper, and her voice, clear and soft with its slight but unmistakable Yorkshire accent, so unlike those around him in Brighton, or the cultured tones of his own family, took over from the writer's voice in his own head.

Chloe followed him up the stairs to his flat. They stepped from the landing into the living room, large and lofty, well-proportioned. A half-open door at the far side gave a glimpse of the kitchen and the closed door next to it, she presumed, must lead to the bedroom. Every piece of furniture in the living room, of which there were enough but not too many, appeared well-chosen and exactly right for the space it occupied, from the round table in the window to the large, mahogany desk against the far wall. The desk top was crowded with the tools of Simon's occupation, typewriter, pens, notebooks, paperclips, nor was the rest of the room particularly tidy. The cushions on the dark green velvet-covered sofa were heaped and crumpled, magazines and newspapers were strewn around. She approved of all that. Over-tidy places reminded her of her mother's front room in Akersfield. Fleetingly, she thought of Akersfield and wondered what Marilyn might be doing, then she quickly brought her thoughts back to where she was.

'I've found myself a job!' she announced. 'At least I think I have. I have to go back at half-past six for a proper interview.'

'That's wonderful!' Simon said. 'At least it is if it's what you actually want.'

Selfishly, and he knew he was being selfish, he didn't want her in any job which would distance her physically or, even more important, in her mind and thoughts from him. He had made up his mind about Chloe even before she went back to Akersfield, but in her absence his thoughts had clarified and strengthened. He wanted her. He wanted her all the time and for ever. But if he couldn't, as yet, have that, then he wanted her close in every other way as well as physically. He wanted to be in her thoughts, and she in his. He had never felt like this about any other woman.

'Come and sit down and tell me about it!'

He took her hand and pulled her gently down to sit close to him on the sofa. When she told him about the café his face creased in a slight frown.

'I know the one you mean,' he said. 'Isn't it called The Seashell?'

'That's the one!'

'Well,' he said doubtfully, 'I suppose it might be all right, though it's not the kind of place I imagined you working in.'

'You mean it's not posh?' Chloe was immediately on the defensive. 'It seemed quite respectable to me – and since I've no experience whatsoever they'd hardly take me on at the Grand Hotel, would they?'

'If they saw you through my eyes they'd take you on anywhere,' Simon teased. 'But Chloe, you don't have to settle for the first job that comes, or indeed any job at all. I can look after you. Why won't you let me?'

'And what would I do while you were writing?' she demanded. 'Sit here on the sofa with my knitting?' All the same, she thought, glancing around the room, noting now the water-colours on the wall, the expensive lamps, there were worse places. And when she'd had enough of sitting she could always go out shopping, or have her hair done. She would only have to cross the Old Steine to step into a world of shops and hairdressers.

'I wouldn't keep you prisoner,' Simon said. 'Even though I'd like to. You could go out whenever you wanted to!'

Then the teasing note left his voice and he was serious. 'Oh, Chloe! I do love you so very much! Can't you possibly say you love me?' His eyes searched her face for the response he longed for.

'I . . . I . . .'

While she was hesitating for the words, yet not knowing what those words were, he drew her towards him, into his arms, and stopped her mouth with his kiss. And to that there was no hesitation in her response. She opened her lips to his and gave herself up completely to the waves of feeling which flooded her body. She raised her arms and caressed the back of his neck, ran her fingers through his hair. She was aware that he was unfastening the buttons of her blouse and when he fumbled with them she moved to help him, shuddering as his hand found her breast.

Surely this must be love? Surely? There was nothing she would not do for him, or let him do to her. What were the exquisite tremors which swept through her, what was her delight in the closeness of their bodies, of his flesh against hers, if it was not love? How else to describe it?

When it was over, when they were, for the time being, satisfied, they lay quietly in each other's arms, gently stroking, caressing, until the passion began to flare in them again; and the second time it was better than ever. They had a sweet familiarity with each other. There was no rush. They knew, and explored, each other's bodies.

It was in the quiet moments afterwards that Chloe realized that John Portman was not, as she had believed until now, the only man in the world who could raise her to the heights. In fact, she thought – and the feeling gave her deep satisfaction – with Simon by her side, in Simon's arms, she had outgrown John Portman, left him behind. He had been transcended. She felt herself totally assured, comforted.

Simon did not. There was something he now had to face and he had no idea how it was to be done. He could ignore it, pretend it wasn't there, tell himself it didn't matter, as he had when they were in the midst of making love; but that wouldn't work in the end. It wouldn't go away.

'What time is it?' Chloe asked. She was deliciously sleepy.

'Half-past two.'

'Oh dear! Then I'll have to be up and doing if I'm to go looking for rooms!'

Simon rose to his feet, looked down at her as she lay on the sofa. Love-making had made her more beautiful than ever. There was a glow on her skin and in her dark eyes.

'I'm famished,' she said. 'I'm really hungry!' It seemed a lifetime since she had had a cup of coffee and a bun.

'I'll make the lunch,' Simon said.

She followed him into the tiny kitchen and watched as he cracked eggs into a bowl, grated cheese. The kitchen, unlike the living room, was as neat as a pin, totally tidy. Kitchen tools and gadgets hung in their proper groups from racks on the wall, pans gleamed, the sink was spotless.

'How do you keep it like this?' Chloe asked in amazement.

'I don't,' Simon said. 'Mrs Watson does. She comes in every morning and cleans. But I keep it tidy. I can't cook in a mess, and I like to cook.'

'I can hardly boil an egg,' Chloe confessed. 'In fact I can hardly boil water! As soon as we've eaten,' she added, 'I'm off to look for a room.'

Simon nodded.

'I'm sorry I can't go with you. I have to finish the article and get it in the post.' It was not totally true. It could wait another day.

'Don't worry,' Chloe said. 'I'm happy to go on my own. In fact I thought if I found a furnished room I might move straight in, tonight!'

'I doubt you'll be able to do that,' Simon said. 'You wouldn't be welcome in new digs – not respectable ones – with no luggage and no more than you stand up in.'

It was true, she thought. Who would take her with no belongings, not even a toothbrush?

'In any case you're expected in Rottingdean. You're staying with my mother. She's expecting you.' He gave the eggs in the bowl a final whisk and poured them into the pan.

Chloe's face flamed at the thought of Mrs Collins. Even from their short acquaintance she felt that Simon's mother, though kind enough, was all-wise and all-knowing. She will take one look at me, Chloe thought, and she'll know exactly what's happened.

'Very well,' she said. 'But I must find a place where I can move in tomorrow.'

She ate her omelette with relish, greedily, then picked up the newspaper and turned to the furnished rooms column. There were no more than two or three places which sounded reasonable.

'Where's Preston Park?' she asked. 'It's a nice name.'

'And a nice area. But if you're working in St James's Street it's a bus ride away.'

'Even so, I'll try it,' Chloe decided. 'The others just give telephone numbers. I'll have to ring them.'

'I'll give you directions,' Simon said. 'I know where places are.'

He wanted to go with her, he wanted to touch her, to hold on to her, never to let her go, but there was something he had to work out before he could be with her again. It was burning a hole in his mind.

Chloe telephoned. One was close to the railway station, one in Kemp Town, which Simon told her was near by, and then there was the Preston Park one which appealed to her.

'I'll come back here after my interview at The Seashell,' Chloe said.

Since it was the nearest she tried the house in Kemp Town first, but the room had already been let.

'Not more than ten minutes ago,' the woman said. 'I know you phoned, but I couldn't be sure you'd come. People don't always.'

Chloe liked the place in Preston Park. There was a tree-shaded garden where she would be able to sit, but there were three rooms – living room, bedroom and kitchen – and the rent was far too high. The one near to the station was a small, dark attic, chilly and smelling of damp even on the summer's day, with the shared bathroom on the floor below and the thunder of trains which shook the house every few minutes. It simply wouldn't do.

As she walked away she glanced up at the station clock. She would reach The Seashell only just in time for her interview and she badly wanted the job, in fact she had to have it if she was to pay for a room.

There was no problem about the job. In a very few moments everything was settled.

'I can't pay you a lot,' the woman said. 'But you can have your meals here and you might get a few tips. And if we have a really good week, then I'll pay you a little more.'

'When would you like me to start?' Chloe asked.

'The sooner the better. Why not tomorrow?'

'Tomorrow would be fine,' Chloe said, 'except that I might have to take a little time out because I have to look for a room. I don't suppose you know anywhere?'

'As a matter of fact, I do,' Mrs Evans said. 'There are the rooms upstairs. Two rooms and a bathroom. The people who had The Seashell before me lived over the shop. I use one of the rooms as a store room and I couldn't let that go. The other room I did open up once as extra café space but it wasn't worthwhile. So you could have a bed-sitter and a bathroom.'

'That would be wonderful!' Chloe said. She could hardly believe her luck.

'I'd only let it furnished,' Mrs Evans said. 'A month's notice either side. That way, if I needed it back, which I don't expect to, there'd be no difficulty.'

'It's not furnished now, is it?' Chloe asked. 'I need a room quickly.'

'No. But that's no problem. I have loads of stuff at home. I could have it ready for you by tomorrow night.'

There must be a snag, Chloe thought. This was all too easy. Perhaps it would be the cost?

'What would the rent be?' she enquired.

Mrs Evans mentioned a figure which was just within Chloe's means.

'That's settled then,' Mrs Evans said. 'You can move in tomorrow, about this time. It might not be completely furnished but you'll have the necessities and we can see to the rest at the weekend.'

It was twenty past seven when Chloe reached Simon's flat. When he opened the door to her she rushed into his arms, delighted to see him, so conscious of her new relationship with him which had been sealed earlier that day; pleased to be bringing the news of her job and her room.

His embrace was perfunctory, not what she expected, but his words explained that.

'It's almost half-past seven. Had you forgotten my mother's making supper for us?'

'Oh, Simon! I'm so sorry! I lost count of the time. I promise I won't be two ticks!'

She would, oh so gladly, have stayed here with him, not gone to Rottingdean. She didn't want to face Mrs Collins but, much more than that, she wanted Simon to make love to her again. She wanted the bliss and excitement of his body against hers.

They arrived late in Rottingdean, but not so late that anyone remarked upon it. There was a difference in Chloe, Mrs Collins thought. There was something in her manner which had not been there on the previous evening; a reticence, an unwillingness to meet her eye, a space between the two of them.

There was also, and this surprised Mrs Collins more, a gulf between herself and her son. He was holding something back and she thought she knew what that something was. My son is a grown man, Grace Collins told herself. However much I might disapprove of whatever it is, it is not my business. She hoped he would do nothing to hurt the girl. She was also relieved that her husband, unobservant and immersed in his own affairs, would not be aware of any of it. The evening passed, in fact, as any other evening might, except that they all went to bed a little earlier than usual.

For the second night in his parents' home Simon lay awake, thinking of Chloe. For the second night Chloe tossed and turned, longing for Simon to come to her, expecting him to do so. Eventually, sleep came to both of them, lying in their own beds.

The next morning the two of them left early.

At half-past eight Chloe reported to Mrs Evans at The Seashell. Later she was introduced to Edith, the fat waitress, who arrived fifteen minutes late, by which time Chloe had put out the cups and saucers, sugar basins and ashtrays.

'Pleased to meet you,' Edith said. 'It'll make sense if we split the job. I'll take the back part and you take the front.'

'How kind,' Chloe said. The front of the café was much nicer; more light, more air.

'Not really,' Edith said. 'There's twice as far to walk to the kitchen from the front, but you're younger than I am. By the way, we pool the tips, put them in the basin and share and share alike at the end of the week.'

'Do we get many tips?' Chloe asked hopefully.

'No we do not! They're mostly as mean as a Scotsman with no arms!'

The first to arrive were the breakfast people: strong tea, bacon sandwiches, sausages.

'Why don't they eat breakfast in their own homes?' Edith demanded.

Next came the shoppers – coffee and buttered buns, shopping bags just where you could fall over them – and later the visitors, day trippers in search of a light lunch: eggs on toast, beans on toast, tomatoes on toast – and sometimes a threepenny tip. After that there was a lull in which Chloe and Edith ate their own lunches, choosing whatever was left on the restricted menu. Then the afternoon tea brigade started.

At six o'clock Edith said to Chloe, 'You don't mind if I leave you to it, do you? There won't be many more in now and I could get an early bus. All you have to do is clear everything off the tables, wipe them down and stand the chairs on top so you can get to sweep the floor.'

She turned back as she was about to leave.

'Too bad, duck! I think you've got another customer!'

Chloe looked up and saw Simon. He was carrying a large cardboard box.

'That's all right, Edith. He's here to see me. He's a friend.'

Edith appraised him quite openly.

'Ooh! Very nice too! You've kept quiet about him, haven't you? He looks as though he's moving in!'

'You'll miss your bus, Edith,' Chloe prompted.

Simon stood aside to let Edith pass. He had come, as he had promised he would, to help Chloe get her room to rights and to bring her a few things until she had time to shop: a kettle, towels, sheets, a packet of tea, and so on.

'Do you want to take them up?' Chloe asked. 'It's the door on the right at the top of the stairs. Or would you rather wait here? I have a few things to do.'

'Such as?'

'Oh, nothing much! Finish clearing the tables, sweep the floor.'

She shouldn't be doing this, Simon thought. Cleaning tables, sweeping floors. He felt sure she had not been brought up to this sort of thing. But then, he asked himself, what did he really know about her? It was the question he had been asking himself over and over again in the last twenty-four hours, and the answer he came up with every time was that he knew nothing. Not only that, but he knew less than he had thought he knew. And yet, and no matter what, he was in love with her; deeply and passionately in love as he had never been before in his life. That, amidst all the confusion, was his one certainty.

'I'll go up,' he said. 'I'll be unpacking this lot.'

Two minutes later Mrs Evans emerged from the kitchen.

'I'm off home now. I still have a few things to collect for you – small stuff; tin-opener, bread knife, an extra pillow and so on.'

She had arranged for a single bed, a table, a rug or two, an armchair and sundry other pieces of furniture to be delivered earlier in the day by a local carrier. They were already in the room.

'I thought I heard a last-minute customer,' Mrs Evans said. 'Was I wrong?'

'Not quite. It was my friend, Simon. He's brought some bits and pieces and he's going to help me to put the place in order. I would have introduced you. I didn't realize you were leaving just yet.'

'No matter,' Mrs Evans said. 'I'll be back in less than an hour. I'll meet him then. Drop the latch behind me. I'll let myself back in.'

Simon unpacked the box, setting down the contents wherever he could find a space. The room was a jumble, everything piled just as the carrier had left it, but he was not in a mood to notice that. He hardly saw anything except for the vivid pictures in his own mind, and they grew and grew until his head felt near to bursting. He must have it out with her. They couldn't go on with this between them. He waited impatiently for Chloe to come up to the room, while at the same time dreading the sound of her footsteps on the uncarpeted stairs.

Chloe wiped down the last of the tables, stacked the chairs, took a final look around the café and in the kitchen for anything which was edible, just *in case* of mice. They weren't troubled by mice, Mrs Evans said, but it was an old building, you couldn't be too careful, and you could get into hot water with the authorities if there were mice in your café. Chloe thought she would die if one ever crossed her path and she devoutly hoped that should one decide to visit it would keep firmly to the ground floor!

Everything seemed to be in good order. What a nice day it had been, she thought as she started to climb the stairs! She was smiling happily as she opened the door to her room. *My room*, she thought. My very own! I can do what I like with it!

Simon was standing with his back to the unlit gas fire. Chloe opened her arms wide and rushed towards him. He raised his hands, palms facing her, in a gesture which pushed her away the moment before she touched him.

'No!' he cried. There was agony in his voice. 'No!'

Chloe stared at him.

'What is it? What's wrong?'

'There's something we have to talk about,' he said.

22

Chloe backed away from Simon as if he had, in fact, physically pushed her.

'I don't know what you mean!' she said. 'Simon, I don't understand!'

She was speaking the truth. Looking at his face, contorted with anger, his eyes filled with pain, she was at a loss. She winced at the harshness of his voice, at the words coming from his lips. Yesterday he had spoken of love, he had spilled over with endearments. What had changed since yesterday? What awful thing had she done?

'Please, Simon,' she begged. 'Please tell me what's wrong. I truly don't understand.'

He blurted it out, though it was not the way he had meant to do it, he had meant to be calm and rational, but it was impossible. He was sick with the pain of a jealousy which had been building up inside him, which he could now no longer control.

'You didn't tell me I wasn't your first lover! You didn't tell me you'd been with other men!'

Chloe felt herself go icy cold from head to foot,

and then, in quick succession, heat swept through her, she felt herself on fire, and with it came feelings of shame and anger, inextricably mixed.

'I didn't . . . I haven't . . .'

'Don't tell me you haven't!' Simon said bitterly. 'Don't make it worse by denying it! Did you think I wouldn't know the moment I made love to you? What sort of a fool do you think I am?'

She stared at him, dumbfounded. She couldn't believe that any of this was happening. She couldn't believe it was Simon, loving, caring Simon, saying these words. But it was. He was standing there, no more than a yard away from her, white-faced and miserable.

'I didn't think of any of those things,' Chloe said. 'I didn't think of anything beyond the moment. There was no question of deceiving you.'

It was perfectly true that in the act of their lovemaking she had thought of nothing other than the moment – what else would have been worth thinking about? John Portman had only come into her mind afterwards, and then only to be erased from her life forever. He no longer counted.

If I had thought of him beforehand, before Simon started to make love to me, would I have said anything, she asked herself? She knew she would not. It was also true that her ignorance was so real that she didn't know that a man would be able to tell she was not a virgin. The Branksome household was not one in which such things were ever discussed. As for school, reproduction was touched upon hurriedly by an embarrassed science mistress who dwelt largely on earthworms, frogs, fishes. Human beings were not in the syllabus.

'If you knew at once,' she said, 'why did you make love to me a second time? If I'm as bad as you think I am, how could you bear to?'

'I couldn't bear not to,' Simon said roughly. 'You were there. You were tempting. I couldn't have left you alone!'

'So you used me?'

'And you used me,' Simon said. 'You were not the innocent you pretended to be . . .'

'I didn't pretend *anything*!'

'. . . You had been with other men!'

'I had *not* been with other men!' She was screaming at him now. 'I went with one man on one occasion. It never happened again. He was an older man, I was flattered. I thought he loved me. I suppose I thought I loved him. Neither case was true. I didn't know what love was. I don't think you know, either.'

'Of course I do! I've never loved anyone as I have you.'

'But you don't trust me. You make up your mind about me without knowing anything of the circumstances.'

'Can't you see,' Simon demanded, 'that I just can't bear the thought of other men having you . . .'

'It was NOT OTHER MEN!'

Chloe shouted the words at him. She felt weak and trembling now, her only strength arising from her anger.

'Did I ask you who you'd been with before you met me?' she said. 'No, I did not. And

I shan't. It's in the past – and so is what I've told you!'

'Then tell me who he is! I'd feel better if I knew who he was, how you came to know him, what you felt for each other.'

'Then you'll have to put up with not feeling better,' she said. 'Because there's no way I'll tell you.'

Of one thing she was quite certain. She would never do anything which might possibly rebound on Moira Portman and her children. She had come so near to doing that in the past and only events had put it right. She would not do it now.

'It was the man I saw you with outside Buckingham Palace, wasn't it?' Simon said. He saw the two of them again in his mind's eye, looking at each other, oblivious of the world around them. 'Just tell me who he is, how you know him!'

'I will not!' Chloe said. 'I will do no such thing, either now or ever. I've told you, it's over and done with. I refuse to resurrect it in any way, not even by discussing it. It has nothing to do with you!'

They stood facing each other as if squaring up for a physical fight. If he would take me in his arms, Chloe thought desperately, we could resolve all this.

Instead Simon said, speaking now in cool, measured tones:

'It seems that whatever we had between us we've somehow lost. I think I'd better go.'

Chloe took a deep breath to steady herself. She would not show what those words had done to her.

'I think you'd better.'

She spoke with equal calm, then stood quite

still while he passed without touching her. She continued to stand there, rooted, as she heard him walk down the stairs and let himself out of the café door.

As the door banged behind him, as he walked out of her life, one thought came into her mind. What have I done? she asked herself. I love him! I do truly love him!

Two minutes later, footsteps on the stairs heralded the return of Mrs Evans. She knocked on the door and, in response to Chloe's invitation, went into the room.

'I've almost been knocked down by a young man leaving in a hurry,' she said. 'What was all that about?'

Chloe, who was still standing in the spot where Simon had left her, pulled herself together.

'Oh! Oh, that was Simon!'

'The boyfriend?' She looked around the room. It was in a total muddle. 'I thought he was here to help you to put everything to rights?'

'We quarrelled.'

Mrs Evans read the expression on Chloe's face. It said, 'Don't ask me more.'

'Ah! A lovers' tiff!' she said lightly. 'I'll give you a hand with this lot!'

They worked together quickly, and in near silence, making up the bed, placing the furniture, unpacking the bags Mrs Evans had brought.

'There!' Mrs Evans said in the end. 'It's all right for tonight. You can do the rest tomorrow. I'll get back to my mother now. I left her in bed, I hope she stays there! You don't know about my mother yet, but you will!'

When she had left Chloe undressed quickly, turned out the light and went to bed. All she wanted was to hide in the darkness, and for the day to end, but sounds drifted up from the street below; traffic, people shouting and laughing, and as so far there were no curtains at the window the light from a nearby street lamp picked out, in monochrome, everything in the room. She saw Simon standing there, accusing her, judging her. Why was it that out of all the time she had known him, and in those moments this evening when they had seemed so divided, so far apart, she had felt at the same time so tremendously close to him, had longed to be close?

Why, after not knowing what love was, what it was about, why it was known to others but not to her, had it finally come to her at the same moment that it had left her?

Not until long after the sounds in the street had ceased, the customers of the pubs and clubs had made their way home, not until the early hours of the morning when the street lights were switched off, leaving a merciful darkness, did she at last fall asleep.

When she awoke next morning, at first confused to find herself in a strange place surrounded by unfamiliar furniture, her first thought was of Simon. Could what she remembered possibly have happened? Yes, she thought, it had! And with it her life had changed. What should she do with it now?

She lay there, wondering. Perhaps she should never have left Akersfield? Perhaps she should go back? There would be money waiting for her there, she would be amongst her own sort of people. Perhaps she would never fit in in the South?

A shaft of sunlight came into the room, lighting it up, and with it her mood changed. Life, she decided, must go on as usual – though not as usual because it would be life without Simon. Very well. She must learn to do without him. Like John Portman, he was now in the past.

In the week which followed, her first week in her new job and her new home, Chloe did everything which was expected of her. She worked hard and efficiently, she was pleasant to customers, friendly with Edith, but she worked mechanically. She was like a clockwork machine which had been wound up with a key and functioned exactly as it was meant to function, rhythmically, smoothly, but with no feeling inside.

From starting work each morning and throughout the working day she refused to let her thoughts stray from the job in hand, except that, every time the café door opened, with its distinctive click of the old-fashioned latch which Mrs Evans insisted on keeping, she turned her head, raised her eyes from whatever she was doing, certain that it was Simon returning, coming back to make everything right between them.

It never was Simon. At the end of the first week she no longer turned her head. She knew now that he would not come.

On a Saturday morning some days later she made her bed, and tidied her room just enough for it to be reasonable to return to at the end of the day, when she would be in no mood for housework, and went downstairs.

Mrs Evans was already at work, baking the daily batches of scones – plain scones, cheese scones, fruit scones. Chloe sniffed the air appreciatively. The smell of baking was one of her nicer memories of home.

'My mother tried to teach me to make scones but I was a failure,' she said to Mrs Evans. 'They always turned out like hard biscuits!'

'I suppose,' Mrs Evans replied, removing a batch from the oven, golden brown, risen high, 'being a Yorkshirewoman and no good at baking was the reason you had to leave home? Do help yourself!'

She had asked Chloe nothing about her private life, nor had Chloe volunteered much. There had been no mention whatever of the handsome young man who had dashed past her – now a week or two ago – but Mrs Evans recognized unhappiness when she saw it and she missed the liveliness, the sparkle in Chloe's eyes which had been so apparent on the first two occasions she'd seen her. She did her work well, no-one could complain about that, but she was not the same girl.

Chloe got on well with Mrs Evans, who was a cheerful, though not over-talkative widow, no children, who ran her small business and went home at the end of each day to an invalid mother. She was also on amiable terms with her fellow-waitress, once she accepted that Edith would be late every morning, would leave early at the end of the day to catch her bus, and would move at a slightly-quicker-than-snail pace because of her feet and her veins.

'We should be busy today,' Mrs Evans remarked. 'A Saturday in summer, there'll be day-trippers.'

She would like not to have to work on Saturdays, to be able to spend time with her mother who spent so much of her days alone, but she was in the wrong trade for that. Every weekend she prayed for a fine Sunday so that, once she had done the books, she could push her mother out in the wheelchair for a breath of air.

Chloe had no plans of her own for the coming Sunday. Without Simon she was not interested in making plans. Nevertheless, she intended to telephone Moira Portman this evening to ask if she might take Robert out. Moira had, after all, hinted that this might be possible, so the sooner she held her to that half promise, the better.

Edith arrived, puffing and blowing, exactly as Chloe had laid up the last of the tables, Edith's as well as her own.

'My bus was late again!' Edith gasped. 'It's disgraceful! I ought to complain about it but I never have the time.'

It was interesting, Chloe thought, that the morning buses always ran late and the going home ones early.

Mrs Evans was right. It was a busy day. Breakfasts, coffees, lunches, teas – there was no let-up between them. Lunch was a sandwich on the hop with a cup of tea snatched in the kitchen. On the other hand, the till rang merrily all day long and there were more tips than usual beneath the plates, even a few silver sixpences. The Seashell was a nice little business, Chloe reckoned, especially if you owned it. And at the end of the day Mrs Evans gave her five shillings extra in her wages.

'Could I use the telephone?' Chloe asked. 'A short local call.'

'Of course!' Was she going to ring the young man?

Chloe spoke to Moira.

'Er . . . yes. I think so,' Moira said.

Chloe was not to know that Moira sounded hesitant because John was in the room and she knew he would not wholeheartedly approve. All the same, *she* would make the decision.

'Yes,' she affirmed. 'Why don't you come round about half-past two. Will Simon be with you?'

'Not this time,' Chloe said.

Moira put down the phone.

'Who was that?' John asked.

'Chloe. She wants to take Robert out tomorrow. I told her she could.'

John frowned. 'Was that wise?'

'I don't see why not.'

'We've made the break. Wouldn't it be better to leave it at that?'

He did not want Chloe back in their lives. It was a situation fraught with difficulties, danger even. How could he ever be sure quite what she would do? The affair was over, he had put it behind him, but had she?

434

He recognized now that what he had felt for Chloe had been infatuation: swift, strong, consuming like a fire while it lasted but by its nature, because it *was* infatuation, short-lived. It might, who knew, have lasted longer had not the awful happening brought him to his senses.

'No, it wouldn't be better to leave it at that!' Moira was adamant. 'I misjudged Chloe and I intend to make what small recompense I can. Anyway, quite apart from you and me it will be good for Robert to see Chloe from time to time.'

She couldn't understand John's attitude. He seemed so hard, so unforgiving. It wasn't like him.

The weather on Sunday was perfection: blue skies, sparkling sea, hot sun, with just enough gentle breeze coming off the sea to temper the heat. Chloe walked along the crowded seafront pavement towards Sussex Square, trying to tell herself how lucky she was to be back in Brighton, with a job, and a place to live, and now on her way to see Robert.

Moira Portman opened the door. Robert was standing behind her, his eyes bright with excitement.

'I'm all ready!' he cried. 'Where are we going?'

'He's been ready for hours,' Moira said. 'And I have a favour to ask. Could Janet also go with you? Well, it's her request really. She's so keen to go and she's promised she'll be good.'

'Of course, if she really wants to!'

'I do! I do!' Janet wriggled with excitement.

'Then we'll make a move,' Chloe said. 'Where

shall we go?' She asked the question of Robert. It was his day and would continue to be so.

'On the pier!' He had no hesitation. 'You promised before to take me on the pier!'

As they set off towards the seafront Robert slipped his hand into Chloe's, and in doing so at once gave her a warm feeling of pleasure. Perhaps for an hour or two this afternoon she could pretend that things were all right. And though she did not have Simon – she wondered what he was doing on this beautiful afternoon – at least she had freedom. No-one could tell her where she must go, what time she must be in, even put before her what she must eat. She knew now that she had never been cut out to be, more or less, a servant in someone else's house. She would never have lasted.

She didn't regret it. It had brought her to where she was now and she still had a small share in Robert. She squeezed his hand in hers as they crossed the road to the sea and he looked up at her and smiled.

Nothing marred the outing, not even Robert's temporary anxiety when he glimpsed the sea beneath them through the gaps between the floorboards.

'I don't *think* I can fall through,' he said. 'I think I'm too big now.' Nevertheless, he held on to Chloe's hand.

Chloe bought the children huge mounds of pink candy floss and then, because it made them thirsty, fizzy lemonade. Janet wanted to go on the ghost train but Robert did not, so they compromised and went on the Dodgem cars and after that on a roundabout.

When they passed the fortune-teller's booth Chloe saw Madame Celestine. Well, what she told me didn't come true, she thought; but on this lovely afternoon with the sun shining down on them and the children, even Janet, enjoying themselves, she refused to be downcast.

The afternoon had to come to an end. She delivered the children back to Blenheim House at five o'clock, as promised. Robert's short legs were tired so she piggy-backed him off the pier.

'I'm tired too,' Janet said. 'I'm so tired I think I might collapse! Why can't we go home on Volk's railway?'

'Why not?' Chloe said. 'That's exactly what we'll do!'

At the house, John Portman opened the door to them. He had not wished to do so but he had been given no alternative.

'My wife's upstairs in her studio,' he explained. 'She'd like you to go up.'

How strange, Chloe thought! If he'd opened the door to me only a few weeks ago my heart would have thudded twenty to the dozen, my stomach would have turned somersaults. Also, we would have looked into each other's eyes, but now he avoided looking at her and she didn't mind a bit because it allowed her to look at him and to marvel that she felt so differently. He was more or less the same as she had always known him. She noted that his stomach bulged a little over the top of his trousers and that he was older than she had once thought, but he was just as handsome, just as distinguished looking.

I *was* in love with him, she thought. Or I thought I was! Did love come and go so quickly, then? Was that how it had been with Simon?

She's certainly attractive, John thought as he watched her climbing the stairs. He could congratulate himself on his good taste, there was no denying it, but if in the future he decided to do something of the kind again – which of course he would *not*, he had every intention of remaining faithful to Moira – then he would take Sir Godfrey's advice and play away from home.

Moira was at her easel when Chloe went into the studio.

'I've been working on your portrait,' she said. 'Come and look at it.'

Chloe looked at it for a few seconds without speaking. She could hardly find the words.

'It's . . . it's absolutely lovely!' Chloe said. 'I don't mean *I* am. I mean it's such a lovely painting!'

'I'm pleased with it,' Moira admitted.

She was more than pleased. She knew it was the best thing she had ever done. 'There's a little bit more to do to it,' she said 'and I wondered . . . Do you think you could come and sit for me again, Chloe? Twice would do.'

'I'd like to,' Chloe said. 'The thing is, I've got a job. I work during the day.'

'Then could you come after work? The evenings are quite light.'

'Yes, I could do that,' Chloe agreed.

Chloe could hardly take her eyes off the painting.

'I do think it captures you,' Moira said. Yet there was something in it, a hidden something, she could not quite recognize in the Chloe she knew, nor could she paint it out.

'Is it for sale?' Chloe asked. 'Not that I could ever afford it!'

'It's not, actually. I want to submit it for the Summer Exhibition at the Royal Academy next year. Coronation year. In any case things have to be done to it even when I've finished the painting. The oils have to settle and until that happens it can't have its first coat of varnish. No, I can't let it out of my sight. And I can't promise that I'll sell it even in the end.'

That was a lovely afternoon, Chloe thought as she walked back. If only Simon had been there it would have been perfect. She would like him to see her portrait.

She had arranged to sit for Moira on the Monday evening, and again on the Tuesday. She would put nothing in the way of having her portrait painted. Just imagine seeing it hung in an exhibition in London, crowds of people looking at it! It would be the most exciting day of her life. No-one in Akersfield would believe it, of course! The only pity was that she was going to have to wait a year for it to happen.

All Monday evening she sat, until the ache in her back was as bad as toothache, and again on

439

Tuesday. Towards the end of Tuesday evening, the light was just beginning to fade, Moira put down her paintbrush.

'That's it!' she said. 'Come and look, Chloe. Tell me what you think.'

Chloe stretched herself, then stood before the easel. She gazed in stunned admiration. There she was, in her cream dress and her headband, looking so real that she could have stepped down from the canvas. How could anyone be so clever as to do this?

'It's wonderful! I don't know what else to say. It's just wonderful!'

'I'm happy with it,' Moira said with quiet satisfaction. 'I think it stands a chance.'

One morning, a few days later, when Chloe came downstairs, Mrs Evans handed her two letters. Both were postmarked 'Hebghyll'.

'From my brother and sister,' Chloe said. 'Maurice lives in Hebghyll and for the time being Marilyn lives with him.'

She opened Marilyn's letter first. Of the time she spent thinking about her family, which grew less and less, partly because she was busy, partly because her head was full of Simon, thoughts of Marilyn were uppermost. She had, in any case, never given much thought to Maurice and even less to Lucy, but Marilyn was different. Though she pushed the feeling away because it never occurred at a convenient time, she felt guilty about her sister; guilty because she had made no decision at all as to what was to be done about her. Marilyn's letter, therefore, came as quite a comfort.

> I am working really hard for my exams and Brian helps me with my homework. Sometimes we do it on the train because we travel to and from Akersfield together and sometimes I go to his house. His mother is nice. Brian is at Akersfield Boys' Grammar School. His mother says they will take me on holiday to the Isle of Man so I might not be able to come to Brighton just yet . . .

'Just listen to this,' she said, reading it out to Mrs Evans.

Mrs Evans laughed. 'Your little sister is clearly in love!'

'But she's only sixteen,' Chloe protested.

'It can hit you just as hard at sixteen. Surely you remember that?'

In fact I don't, Chloe thought. There had been no-one in Akersfield she would have dreamt of falling in love with.

'I wonder what Brian is like?' she said.

'Perhaps the other letter will tell you.'

There were two letters in Maurice's envelope, one from himself and one from Lucy.

'Incredible!' Chloe said. 'I've seldom had a letter from Maurice and never from Lucy.'

Maurice's – and the fact did not surprise her – was brief and businesslike. The will was going through probate as expected. It might be another six weeks. In the meantime there was a potential buyer for the house, very keen on it, so everyone hoped the will wouldn't take too long. There was likely to be more money than they'd expected because their mother had had shares from her parents which she'd never touched, and as luck would have it they'd greatly increased in value. Also, she'd been economical. (I can vouch for that, Chloe thought!) Marilyn seemed all right. He would be in touch when there was anything more to report.

Chloe unfolded Lucy's letter. It was written in violet ink on pale pink paper.

> Marilyn is working quite hard for her. She has this boyfriend and they live in each other's pockets. So sweet! He's quite nice, well-mannered, a bit spotty but he'll grow out of that. Marilyn's spots are a lot better. It must be the moorland air at Hebghyll. I expect you are having a wonderful time, living the life of Riley . . .

Chloe broke off reading. 'And listen to this,' she said to Mrs Evans.

> Of course Marilyn is expensive to keep – school uniform, new shoes, tennis racquet, pocket money. She has a hearty appetite and now she wants to go on holiday with Brian's family! We shall have to work out all these costs with the solicitor and see that we get a proper allowance.

'That is Lucy to a T,' Chloe told Mrs Evans. 'And knowing her she won't be the loser. But if she looks after Marilyn well I suppose that's fair enough.'

'At least Marilyn sounds happy,' Mrs Evans said. 'I don't think you need worry about her for the moment.'

I don't want to worry about Marilyn, and I won't, Chloe thought. She was pleased her sister was going through a happy patch and she wouldn't even think about how long it might last or what would happen when it was over. Tomorrow could take care of itself.

'Such a pity your mother had to miss Marilyn at this age,' Mrs Evans said. 'I wouldn't have liked to have been without my mother when I was growing up, or she without me.'

'I envy you your relationship with your mother,' Chloe said. 'Mine was never like that with my mother. She never wanted to let any of her children go, with the result that we couldn't wait to escape. Marilyn would have been the same in a year or two.'

Sometimes, when she thought about her mother, she regretted that things hadn't been better between them. It was too late now.

'Oh well!' she said, putting the letters in her pocket, 'I'd better get on with the work. I can't have Edith arriving and the tables not laid!'

23

Chloe looked around her room with satisfaction. Each week she added something to smarten it up, make it seem more homelike. This week it had been a big, squashy cushion in all the colours of the rainbow, last week a small, wood-framed mirror. She was saving up for a new bedcover which would make her bed look less like a bed and more like a sofa.

From under the bed she fished out the flat, lace-up shoes she wore all day in the café for comfort, but would not be seen dead in in the street. She put them on, gave a final glance at herself in the new mirror, and ran downstairs.

'Thank goodness you're here!' Mrs Evans called out from the kitchen.

It was an unusual greeting and the voice was not Mrs Evans's usual one, calm, quiet, with a note of humour in it. This voice was sharp and anxious.

Chloe hurried into the kitchen.

'I'm not late am I?' she asked.

'Of course not! It's my mother. I'm so worried about her.'

'I'm sorry! Is she worse?'

Mrs Evans shook her head. 'I don't know! She is and she isn't. Physically she's much the same – frail, trying to do too much – but she's not been her usual self for days now.'

'You haven't said anything.'

'I try not to. It's not easy to tell what my mother's usual self is, she's so up and down. But the last few days she's been mostly down.'

'I am sorry,' Chloe repeated.

She started to gather the things together to lay the tables. There was no time to stand and do nothing and, indeed, Mrs Evans herself did not break off from her baking – rolling and cutting out the scones, placing them on the trays to go in the oven.

'What does the doctor say?' Chloe enquired.

'Very little! There doesn't seem to be much he can do except give her pills, and sometimes they work and sometimes they don't. This morning they worked, so at least I've left her sleeping, but she's been up most of the night. At three in the morning she decided to turn out the kitchen cupboards, said Olive and Hilda would be arriving for breakfast and she wouldn't want them to see things so untidy, which they weren't of course. They never are.'

'Olive and Hilda?' Chloe had seldom heard Mrs Evans mention friends, especially ones who might arrive for breakfast.

'Figments of my mother's imagination, poor love! But there was nothing I could do to stop her, save using force, which I would never consider. And I couldn't leave her to it because she's not safe, climbing on step stools, lifting piles of crockery. So I'm worn out! And thank goodness, so is she!'

'Will she be all right? I mean when she wakes?'

Mrs Evans shook her head.

'I just don't know – which is why I said thank goodness you're here. As soon as this last batch of scones is in the oven I'd like to pop back home to make certain. Can you manage?'

'I'm sure we can,' Chloe assured her. 'Edith will be here soon. She can serve at the tables and I'll make toast or sandwiches – whatever's required, though I'm not sure about bacon and eggs!'

'Just say bacon's off the menu,' Mrs Evans said. 'Offer poached egg on toast. That's easy enough. And thank you very much indeed, Chloe.'

She was every bit as grateful as she sounded. Chloe had proved to be the best waitress she'd ever had, in spite of her inexperience. And really, Mrs Evans thought, she is much too bright for the job, she's capable of much more.

Edith was her usual fifteen minutes late, puffing and blowing.

'Would you believe it, the bus broke down!' she said.

Not really, Chloe thought.

'I haven't quite finished your tables,' she said. 'And now I have to go into the kitchen.' She explained the situation.

'Will we manage, just the two of us?' Edith queried.

'Of course we will – you out front, me in the

kitchen, though I'll pop out and help you whenever I get the chance.'

'Can you cook?' Edith sounded dubious.

'I'll soon find out, won't I? Except that I already know I can't bake scones!'

'Although I say it myself, I *can* bake a scone,' Edith said. 'My husband reckons I bake the lightest scones in Sussex!'

Mrs Evans, emerging from the kitchen, wearing her hat and carrying her handbag, overheard Edith.

'I don't think there'll be any need,' she said. 'I shan't be long, I just need to make sure Mother's settled. I think the scones will last out, but if not, Edith, you've found yourself a job!'

All went well. Chloe was not called upon to cook bacon nor, because Mrs Evans was soon back, having seen to her mother and prevailed on a neighbour to pop in and check on her from time to time, did Edith have to demonstrate she could bake a scone. However, this proved to be the first of many days on which Mrs Evans arrived at The Seashell weary from lack of sleep and had to slip home again.

I don't know what's going to happen, Chloe thought. Most days Mrs Evans looked terrible. Pale-faced, with dark shadows under her eyes – and she had certainly lost weight. 'I do really feel sorry for her,' Chloe said to Edith. 'We've got to help her all we can.'

'I don't see how I can do much more,' Edith said. 'I've got my husband to go home to. He likes his meal on the table. And then I've got the travelling. It's different for you. You live on the premises.'

Well, that was true. And as a matter of fact Chloe didn't mind the extra responsibilities which Mrs Evans's situation increasingly placed on her. She also enjoyed the extra money her employer insisted on paying her. It helped towards furnishing her room which, these days, she concentrated on with the determination of a bird furnishing a nest. She was well aware that she was building herself her own small fortress. She could shut herself in there at the end of the working day and no-one could invade her. It was all part of missing Simon and she didn't know why it had taken her like this, just that she missed him quite desperately.

She had not seen him at all, not once since he had stormed out of the café. It was extraordinary that this was so, she thought, since she lived and worked within five minutes' walk of his flat. When she looked out of the café window, as she purposely did many times in the day, she half-expected to see him walking by. She knew he did his shopping in St James's Street. She never did see him. It was as if he had vanished from the face of the earth, and the earth was a lesser place without him.

She took on more and more responsibilities. Mrs Evans tried to get in early each morning to do the baking, and if she couldn't then she baked what she could at home and brought it to the café a little later. On these occasions Chloe opened up, and since Mrs Evans seldom nowadays stayed on until closing time she also learnt how to deal with the till – cashing up at the end of the day, dropping the money into the night safe of the bank in St James's

Street. She became interested in the takings, pleased when they were up, trying to analyse why when they were down.

'Just don't get too involved,' Edith advised. She had no resentment about Chloe taking charge so often, just as long as she was left to go at her own steady pace.

'Why not?' Chloe questioned. 'I like being involved. It's much better than simply taking orders, serving tea and pastries – not that I mind that in the least, but I've discovered there's more to the job.'

She had by now mastered bacon and eggs, and the other breakfast dishes which were variations on that, and when driven to it by Mrs Evans's absence or Edith's disinclination to lend a hand she could even bake a scone, though never with the magic lightness of her employer.

The interesting thing was that, though she was working harder than she had ever worked in her life, harder than when she was looking after Robert and Janet, *far* harder than when she had worked for the Borough Surveyor in Akersfield, during working hours she was seldom tired. Each new interest seemed to generate fresh energy. Work was not the problem. The problem was the empty hours outside work.

Twice more in the last few weeks she had taken Robert out on a Sunday afternoon – once with Janet, once on his own because Janet had gone to a birthday party. He hadn't wanted to go anywhere special, just to hold Chloe's hand as they walked along the seafront towards Brighton, stopping to admire the smart coaches which had brought day-trippers in from all over the place and were now parked along Madeira Drive and up Duke's Mound, just opposite Sussex Square. And the trippers themselves, thronging the promenade and the beaches close to the Palace Pier as if they didn't want to go too far away from the coach which had brought them there. And then, closest to the pier, were the coaches waiting to take people for short drives: Eastbourne, Worthing, Mystery Tour – back in time for tea.

'Where do mystery tours go?' Robert had asked.

'That's the whole point,' Chloe replied. 'If we knew it wouldn't be a mystery!'

'Does the driver know?'

'He's the only person who does,' Chloe said.

'Can we go on a mystery tour?' Robert asked.

'Not today. But if your mother agrees we'll go another day,' Chloe promised.

When they'd reached the pier he had persuaded Chloe to stand for a while, watching the policeman in his white helmet directing the traffic.

'I'd like to do that when I'm older,' he'd said.

'They are the only policemen in the country who wear white helmets in the summer,' Chloe informed him.

'Then they must be very special,' Robert said.

Although they didn't venture on to the beach in Brighton – it was far too crowded – one afternoon they had been to a beach in Hove, which was quite different from the beach they knew at Black Rock and held no bad memories – not that Robert seemed to suffer at all from bad memories.

On neither of these occasions, while collecting and delivering Robert, had Chloe seen John Portman. Nor did she want to. She had discovered that she could take him or leave him, with scarcely a trace of emotion. It was Simon she wanted.

Two weeks later Chloe telephoned Moira Portman to ask if she might take out Robert again on the Sunday.

'I'm sorry,' Moira said. 'My mother's coming on Sunday and of course she'll expect the children to be here.'

And you don't need to tell me, Chloe thought but didn't say, Lady Stansfield would have a fit at the thought of me taking the children as far as the garden gate!

'After that,' Moira continued, 'we go on holiday. We've taken a house in Cornwall, so that should be fun!'

Which I might well have been sharing, Chloe realized, but aside from Robert her regret didn't go very deep. And when they returned from Cornwall it would be time for him to start school. School would change his life. New friends, new challenges; would there be room in it for her?

On the following morning Chloe was making an early start on the tables when Mrs Evans arrived, looking pale and drawn and altogether terrible.

'Leave that for the moment!' she said as she walked through to the kitchen. 'I have to talk to you!'

In the kitchen she made no move to start on

the baking. Instead she sat down – which in itself was a rare sight – and motioned to Chloe to do the same.

'If I don't sit down,' she said, 'I think I might fall down!'

Chloe said nothing. Mrs Evans had not brought her in here to tell her how tired she was. It was not her way. She waited, sensing there was much more to it than that.

'I have had the most horrendous weekend ever!' Mrs Evans said. 'I don't know who will go stark raving mad first, me or my mother! What I do know is that it can't go on and I'll have to give in!'

'You mean . . . she'll have to go into hospital?'

'No. They wouldn't have her in hospital, not the ordinary hospital, anyway. She's not curable.'

'You mean in a home, then?'

Mrs Evans shook her head.

'Not that either. I once went to see a friend's grandmother in an old people's home and I shan't ever forget it. This woman was suffering from dementia – which is the label the doctor has put on my mother's illness. My mother isn't as bad as this woman was but she will be, she will be! Unless she dies. And why would she die? She's strong and healthy. So that's how she will end up.'

'I'm dreadfully sorry,' Chloe said in the pause which followed. It seemed such an inept thing to say; quite useless.

'But not *where* she'll end up, I assure you! Do you know, this woman I went to see was kept locked in her room most of the time? She needed constant care and there weren't enough nurses to spare for that. It wasn't their fault. But I couldn't subject my mother to that. You see, all of my life until the last year or two my mother's been a lovely woman. She's been there whenever I've needed her, and that's been many times I can tell you – so how could I let her down now? Even if I didn't love her, which I do, dearly.'

'So what will you do?' Chloe asked.

'I've made my decision,' Mrs Evans said. 'It wasn't easy. I shall have to give up the business.'

Chloe stared at her, disbelieving.

'Give up the café? That's terrible!'

'I know. I don't want to. For a start it's my living. It was meant to keep me for the rest of my life, now I'll find it difficult to make ends meet. But my mother must have full-time care and I'm the one to give it. No-one else would take it on, nor should they have to. It's I who should do it.'

'Does that mean you're going to *sell* the business?'

In a flash, genuinely sorry for Mrs Evans though she was, Chloe saw all the consequences to herself. She would lose her job and, almost more important, her home. She had already lost Simon, would probably soon lose Robert, and now she would lose the security she realized had become important to her.

'Of course I shall try to sell it as a going concern,' Mrs Evans said. 'There must be a certain amount of goodwill in the place. But I might not be able to. I might just have to pack up the business and sell the lease.'

'I'm terribly sorry,' Chloe repeated. They seemed to be the only words she could think of to say.

'I had to tell you at once. I know what it might mean to you. If I can manage to sell it as a going concern you might be able to keep your job, but the upstairs rooms – who knows?'

'I might not even be able to keep the job,' Chloe said.

'Let's face it, that's true!' Mrs Evans agreed. 'And the same goes for Edith. I must tell her. I have to leave you both free to make your own plans. As for today, my neighbour's stepped in for two hours but I can't rely on her from now on. It's not something she wants to do. However . . .' She stood up and began to make a move. 'I'll make the scones and then I must go home. Will you be all right?'

'Of course! Don't worry!'

'You're a brick,' Mrs Evans said. 'I couldn't have carried on as long as I have but for you.'

This was the very first time in her life anyone had said anything like that to her, Chloe thought. To be fair, it was probably the first time it could have been said with any truth!

For a Monday it was unusually busy in the café. There were the usual regulars, plus visitors who had stayed over for a long weekend. Chloe was pleased it was busy, it gave her less time to think or to discuss the bad news with Edith. Edith had taken it hard, with the result that she concentrated even less on her work and moved at an even slower pace.

She came into the kitchen to order a pot of tea and baked beans on toast for two.

'I don't know what I'm going to do,' she said. 'I don't know how we'll make out. It's true my husband earns the bread and butter but unless I earn my bit here there's no jam on it!'

'I'm sure you'll find another job,' Chloe said. She was trying to console her. She didn't really think Edith would easily find another job. She was unprepossessing and slow of speech. She sometimes wondered why Mrs Evans had taken her on in the first place.

'If it was the beginning of the season you could be right,' Edith said. 'But a few more weeks and the season will be over. Out-of-work-waitresses will be a penny a dozen then!'

'It'll be the same for me,' Chloe pointed out. 'Except that I stand to lose my room as well.'

They could go on talking like this all day, and would, Chloe reckoned, if Edith had her way. She set the tray, put the piping hot beans on the toast, and hurried Edith out of the kitchen. 'Don't let it get cold!' she warned.

Mrs Evans rang just before closing time to say that on her way home she had called in at the estate agents and had put The Seashell Café on the market.

'There's no point in wasting time. Every day nearer to the end of the season means less likelihood of a customer. As the agent pointed out, people like to buy with the prospect of a profitable season right there in front of them. It stands to reason, doesn't it?'

It did, Chloe admitted.

She agreed to Edith leaving a quarter of an hour early. The mood she was in, she wasn't much good to anyone. 'If I'm late in the morning,' she said gloomily as she left, 'it'll be because I'm looking for a job!'

When the last customer had gone Chloe tidied and swept, then cashed up – at least the takings were reasonable – and locked the door behind her as she went across the road to bank the money. When she came back she took a last look around, then climbed the stairs to her room.

She looked around that, almost as if seeing it for the first time while wondering how long it would be before she was doing it for the last time. It was a good-sized, well-proportioned room and everything she had done to it since she'd moved in had added to its comfort and appearance. Since she'd discovered that if she walked up the street just as the flower stall was closing at the end of the day she could buy flowers cheaply, she'd never been without flowers in the blue glass vases she had found in a junk shop. Pink carnations filled them now, where they stood on the small table under the window.

Also, she had decided to replace the flowery, summer curtains which hung at the window now with something heavier. She had seen the exact material, crimson velveteen, in a store in North Street. They would give the place a very cosy look.

She would hate, she would just hate to have to leave this place. She desperately wanted someone to talk to, to confide her troubles and her fears. There was no-one. Mrs Evans had her own, and far worse, worries. Edith was a broken reed.

Above all she wanted Simon. Where was he? What

was he doing at this very moment? Did he ever give a single thought to her in return for the hundreds she spent on him? Supposing, just supposing, she were to walk down to the Steine, supposing that just as she was passing his door he came out, surely he would stop and speak to her? She had spent so much time in recent weeks missing him, longing to see him, that she had almost forgotten the subject of their quarrel, she had pushed it to the back of her mind. Deliberately, now, she brought it out, thought about it, tried to remember the details of what they had said to each other, and as she did so she realized that in refusing to tell she had made a decision she couldn't go back on. That would have to remain.

So if she took that walk, and if she bumped into Simon as he came out of the house, what could she tell him that would be any different?

I could tell him that I love him, she thought. It was something he had always wanted to hear and she had never been able to say, because she hadn't known it until the moment she'd heard him walk away. If he knew that she loved him, truly loved him, and no-one else, would it make a difference?

She took a cardigan from the hook behind the door – the evenings were turning a little colder – and went back downstairs and out into the street. She walked to the bottom of St James's Street, then turned left in the direction of Simon's flat. Outside his door she stood still, waiting, willing him to come out. In the end, defeated, she crossed the road and sat on a bench in the gardens. She was sure it was a bench he could see from his window if he should happen to look out.

She sat there until the sun began to go down and the sky over the sea was streaked with wide bands of crimson and orange and purple. She shivered, then stood up and began to walk back to The Seashell Café.

From her room – the café faced a narrow street which ran through from St James's Street to the coast road – she could catch a glimpse of the sea and the sky. She pulled up a chair and sat there in the window, watching the bands of red change to crimson and then to navy blue, the purple turn to grey, and then every colour was swallowed up in the darkness which merged sea and sky into one, rendered them invisible. The only light now on the inky darkness of the sea was that which was deflected from the brightness of the Palace Pier and from the street lamps. She switched on a light in her room, then drew the curtains together. She was glad to see the end of the day, though the ending had brought no solutions to all its problems.

She drank a cup of milk, then went to bed early, opening a book, trying to read, but the story was dull and after a few pages the print began to blur. She had thought that at this stage sleep would come, but it didn't. Another fifteen minutes and she was wide awake again, her head whirling with thoughts, mostly anxious ones.

If only, she thought, if only I had the money which is due to me then I could buy The Seashell. But in the first place, why would she want to do that? It wasn't a thing she'd ever thought of before, not the kind of ambition she'd ever had. On the other hand, it wasn't an outrageous idea and she had no other plans for the money. If The Seashell were hers she could build it up, change it, make it what she wanted it to be – and she knew she would have no shortage of ideas. And if and when she tired of it she could sell it, and then do something else. There was no doubt that a certain amount of money was an asset. With money you could achieve what hard work on its own could never do.

The rub was, would she be allowed to have the money due to her? She was almost certain she would not, not until she was twenty-one, not unless the solicitor knew some means by which he could release it to her. Surely it would be worthwhile asking him? Maurice would not approve, of course. She was quite certain of that. Twenty-one seemed an age away, certainly too late to buy The Seashell.

Inevitably, her thoughts returned to Simon. She *must* find a way – there must be a way – to meet with him, even if it was only to result in a final parting. Anything would be preferable to how it had ended. But how was she to do this?

The sky was lightening with the next day before she fell asleep, still not having solved anything at all.

24

When Chloe awoke next morning, almost as soon as she had opened her eyes the idea she had searched for yesterday, and through most of her wakeful night, came to her. It was as if, in the short time when she *had* slept, her mind had taken charge of her doubts and worries, had sorted them out and had now come up with a solution.

Well it *might* be a solution, she thought. It was worth considering, worth discussing with Mrs Evans, hearing what she thought about it. Whatever the outcome, it would only affect The Seashell situation. It would do nothing to assuage her unhappiness about Simon, except perhaps cause her to work harder and thus have less time to think about him. Last night the thought of Simon had loomed over everything. Sitting in the Steine Gardens she'd felt she couldn't bear not to see him and this morning, in spite of her new ideas about the café, the thought of Simon was like a lead weight in her heart.

But, she told herself as she dressed, I will deal with one thing at a time. She would do her best for the next few hours not to think about Simon. She would telephone Mrs Evans and tell her there was something she would like to discuss with her.

'As a matter of fact,' Mrs Evans said, 'I intend to come in for an hour or so this morning. My mother's had a good night and this looks like being one of her better days – though of course one can never tell. Anyway, all being well I'll be with you shortly! In the meantime, would you light the oven?'

She was as good as her word. Chloe, having made an early start, had everything ready in the café, though Edith had not yet put in an appearance when Mrs Evans walked in.

'I'm keen to hear what you have to say,' she began. 'In the circumstances any ideas are welcome. But since I don't have much time it will make sense if I knock up a few scones while I'm listening.'

'And in any case,' Chloe said, 'if customers come in I shall have to break off to serve them. Edith hasn't turned up!'

Mrs Evans, already in her apron, measuring flour from the bin, looked up.

'Oh! Do you know why? She's not ill, is she?'

'I shouldn't think so. Perhaps even more trouble with the buses?' She didn't think this was the time to tell Mrs Evans that Edith was probably already looking for another job.

'I'm afraid Edith isn't the best waitress in the whole of Brighton,' Mrs Evans said. 'And I daresay she knows it. I took her on because I was sorry for her. She was going through a bad patch. Her husband had lost his job – though he found another

461

one soon after she started here. Anyway, what about your ideas?'

'Well,' Chloe said, 'I know you've put the café up for sale, and I expect that's what you actually want to do. I can see why you would. I did wonder at one point whether I might be able to buy it from you, as a going concern. I have a fair amount of money to come from my mother. The trouble is, I don't think I'll be able to lay hands on it until I'm twenty-one.'

'And I can't wait for that,' Mrs Evans said.

'I know. I'm prepared to ask the solicitor if it can be done but I doubt if he'll say yes. So I thought of something else.'

'Yes?'

Mrs Evans turned out the scone dough on to the board and began, with the lightest possible touch, to roll it.

'I wondered . . .' Chloe took a deep breath. There was only one way to say it and that was straight out. 'Since you can't be here yourself, if you'd consider letting me manage the café for you?' She observed the startled look on Mrs Evans's face. 'Oh, I know I don't have much experience but by now I think I know quite a lot and I would . . .'

Mrs Evans broke in.

'I couldn't afford you, Chloe! It's not that I think you couldn't do it. You'd be better at it in some ways than I am. You're good with the customers whereas I'm more interested in the baking and the cooking. But no way could I afford to pay a manager as well as take out enough money for my own living expenses. It's a lovely idea but it won't work!'

She was disappointed and she couldn't help showing it. She didn't know quite what she'd hoped for, but this wasn't it.

'It could,' Chloe said. 'I wouldn't expect to be paid as a manager, not unless business boomed fantastically. I'd be content with my usual wages, plus a bonus in any month when profits were over a certain amount. We would fix the amount and the percentage of the bonus. Neither of us would lose from that arrangement.'

'And what would *you* get out of all this – except a bonus which might or might not happen?' Mrs Evans didn't see much possibility of them doing extra trade. It wasn't that kind of business. But Chloe had the optimism of the young.

'For a start I'd get to keep my job and my room,' Chloe said. 'I like both.'

Also, she thought, though she could see Mrs Evans didn't believe it, she was confident she would increase the trade, or at least keep it at a reasonable standard when the season ended. That way she would earn the bonuses.

'Also, I actually like the management side of the business, if you can call anything I've done management.'

'But there's the baking and the cooking,' Mrs Evans pointed out. 'Doesn't that mean we'd either have to get another waitress or a cook?'

'Well, I had an idea about that,' Chloe said, diffidently. 'But it's entirely up to you. You might not like it or be able to do it.'

'Well?'

Mrs Evans gave the scones a final brush-over with an egg and milk mixture, then put them in the oven.

'I thought . . . I don't mean to be presumptuous, but I thought that since you *are* confined to the house you might like to continue to do the baking – scones, cakes, bread rolls, buns – at home. It would mean having them delivered by taxi every day but that wouldn't cost much. It really depends on whether you'd have the time and whether you'd like it.'

With the scones in the oven and the kitchen filled with the smell of baking, Mrs Evans sat down.

'I would like it,' she said thoughtfully. 'I dread the idea of being at home every day with my only occupation being to look after my mother. And I expect I could find the time. I don't have to attend to her every minute, I just have to be there. And then there are times when she sleeps and I'm awake. Yes, I think I could do that! But that doesn't solve the problem of paying for another waitress.'

'I don't think we need another waitress,' Chloe said. 'Or certainly we won't when the season ends. In fact if Edith . . .' She hesitated.

Mrs Evans finished the sentence.

'If Edith pulled her weight it would make all the difference in the world! I know that. But I can't sack her!'

Then I earnestly pray, Chloe thought, that right at this moment Edith is being offered another job! She hadn't much hope.

'Edith would have to be told that under the new

464

arrangements we'd all have to work a little bit harder!'
she said.

Mrs Evans gave her a straight look.

'And who would tell her?'

Chloe gave back an equally straight look.

'I would! Because the other thing I have to say
is that if you decided to let me manage the café
I'd want a free hand. I don't think I'm likely to
do anything you'd disapprove of, but I would have
to be in charge.'

'Yes,' Mrs Evans said. 'You're quite right, you
would. And actually that's a part of the job I don't
like very much.'

I would change the menus, Chloe thought. I would
simplify everything, make everything more attractive.
I would look at expenses, try to cut them. Yes, she
would certainly make changes. But now was not the
time to say any of that.

'Well then,' Mrs Evans said, 'I must have a little
time to think about it and to do my sums. A few
hours will be enough. I wonder – could you come
to my house after you've closed today? We could
talk about it then.'

Mrs Evans stayed a few more moments until the
scones were ready. She took them out of the oven
and put them on the racks to cool before picking up
her handbag and leaving.

'See you later!' she said.

On the way out she all but bumped into a
morose-looking Edith on her way in.

'Sorry! Can't stop!' Mrs Evans said. She was in
no mood to listen to Edith's moans.

'She's in a hurry!' Edith said to Chloe.

'She has to get back to her mother. So what happened to you?'

'What do you mean, what happened to me?'

'It's half-past nine,' Chloe said. 'Buses again, was it?'

'As a matter of fact, no,' Edith said. 'Not that they were any better than usual! Actually, I went after a job. My next-door neighbour put me on to it. Waitress in Hove. Much handier for me!'

'Did you get it?' Chloe didn't need to ask. The expression on Edith's face gave the answer.

'No, I didn't! The same old story, they wanted someone younger.'

'I'm sorry,' Chloe said. It was the truth.

'I shall have to keep on looking,' Edith said, taking off her coat, putting on her frilly white apron. 'Come to that, so will you. We don't know when we'll be thrown out on our ears, do we?'

Chloe said nothing. She had no intention of telling Edith about her plans, not until she had had an answer from Mrs Evans. She thought the chances were fifty-fifty that Mrs Evans would take her up on it. If she doesn't, Chloe thought, then I too will have to start thinking about something else.

The customers began to trickle in and then as the morning went by the trade increased. As she buttered scones and toasted buns, and then as lunchtime came heated the soups, made sandwiches, poached eggs – and frequently took the meals to the customers herself when Edith was plodding her own sweet way, she thought about what she would do if Mrs Evans did agree. For a start, she thought, she would have more variety in the soups: different days, different soups. It took no more time to open a tin of Scotch broth or mushroom than the everlasting tomato and oxtail, which was all they ever served.

'Wouldn't it be a good idea to have something different?' she asked Edith as she put the soup plate down on the hatch. 'Don't you think the regulars might get fed up with the same thing every day?'

'Oh no!' Edith disagreed. 'They like what's familiar. And if they don't like it they can always go somewhere else!'

Precisely! Chloe thought. And what a way to look at it!

But through all the tasks and through all her thoughts, even when she was planning in her head what the new regime might be like, the thought of Simon never went away. When she went out into the café to serve a customer it was never without glancing out of the window in case he might be passing, and when from the kitchen she heard the opening of the front door she wanted to rush out to see if by chance he had walked in, looking for her.

She had to do something. She couldn't possibly go on like this, not knowing – or not facing the fact that it was over. One way or the other she wanted to hear the words said. It was true that he had walked out on her and therefore he should be the one to walk back, but she was beyond caring about the niceties. If it meant she had to make the first move then that was what she would do.

After the café lunches had finished came the

quietest time of the day, the lull before the customers came in for tea. It was the time at which she and Edith took their own meal, sitting at a table at the back of the café.

Chloe ate her toasted cheese quickly, hardly tasting it, then said:

'Edith, can you hold the fort for quarter of an hour? There's something I have to do upstairs.'

In her own room she took out paper and pen and began to write.

Dear Simon,
Once before when we quarrelled you wrote a letter to me, and then we made up. Now I'm writing to you.

You might not want to make it up but replying to this letter won't hold you to anything, I promise you. I would just like us to meet so that even if we are going to part we can do so amicably, not as enemies. Is that too much to ask?

If you agree, you could come to the café any day, except today, at closing time. Or we can meet anywhere else you say.

One thing I have to say, which I have never said before – Simon, I now know that I do truly love you. Whatever you think about me, I love you.

I hope you will answer this letter.

Without re-reading it, in case her courage failed her, she put it in the envelope, sealed the flap and ran downstairs.

'I'm just going to the post!' she called out.

It wasn't true. There was no way she would trust her letter to the post. She passed the pillar box and walked to the Steine and there she put the envelope through Simon's door. There was no way he could fail to get it.

Edith was still at her lunch, enjoying a piece of jam sponge, when Chloe returned.

'My word, you do look flushed!' she said. 'Not to mention out of breath!'

'It's quite warm out,' Chloe said. 'And I hurried back.'

'That shouldn't take your breath,' Edith said. 'A young thing like you. It's only two strides to the post.'

The truth was that Chloe was breathless and flushed – she could feel the heat in her face – at the enormity of what she had done. Or it seemed an enormity now, though at the time of writing the letter it had seemed the natural thing to do, the only thing to do. Should she, perhaps, have written it, read it, then torn it up, not delivered it? And now it had gone for good, there was no getting it back. She wondered if Simon was at home, if he had picked it up from the floor, if even at this moment he was reading it? Was he angry? Was he pleased? Would he tear it into pieces?

'There's a cup of tea in the pot,' Edith said. 'I don't know why, but you look as though you could do with it.' In fact the girl hadn't been herself all day. Half the time she'd seemed a hundred miles away, and for sure the cat had got her tongue!

'Thank you. That would be nice,' Chloe said.

It wouldn't really. A cup of tea wouldn't make the slightest difference to how she felt. The only thing which would, would be to hear from Simon.

There were no customers in the café. 'It's going to be a slack afternoon,' Edith said with satisfaction. 'That's because it's half day closing. I don't see why we shouldn't close when the other shops do!'

'Because we cater for visitors. In fact for anyone who wants a cup of tea. But if this were my business I'd close on Monday afternoon and open on Sundays. That's when you'd get the customers.'

'You'd lose me,' Edith said. 'My husband wouldn't hear of that. He likes his Sunday dinner and his bit of a kip afterwards. You think too much about work, and that's a fact!'

'Well just to prove you right,' Chloe said, 'as we're going to have a slack afternoon why don't we clear out a cupboard or two?'

'Not on your life!' Edith was deeply indignant. 'I'm a waitress! I wait on tables and that's all I do. Anyway, it's not up to you to decide about clearing out cupboards. That's Mrs Evans's decision – and if she's not here she can't make it, can she?'

Whatever capacity I end up in, Chloe thought, life won't be easy with Edith. She would never pull her weight.

'Well then, you stick to your serving and I'll do a cupboard,' she said.

'And what if they want something cooked?'

'Then I'll break off and cook it.'

She wanted to work. She wanted to be so busy that the time would fly until she had to go to Mrs Evans's.

And then she wanted it to fly beyond that until she heard from Simon.

Half an hour later – she had emptied a store cupboard and the contents were spread out on every available surface in the kitchen – her wish to be busy was granted. The café door opened and customers streamed in, filling every table in the front and some at the back.

'A coach trip!' Edith said. She was disgusted.

From then on there must have been several coach trips. They were kept busy until closing time and for at least fifteen minutes afterwards.

'I've missed my bus and no mistake,' Edith grumbled.

When the last customer had left, when Chloe had cleared away, cashed up, banked the money, she set off for Mrs Evans's house. Her employer lived twenty minutes' walk away from The Seashell, in the thickly populated hinterland of small streets which lay to the east, behind and parallel to the seafront, almost as far as Sussex Square. It was a tall, narrow house with a small front garden and steps up to the front door. Before Chloe had time to press the bell Mrs Evans opened the door to her.

'I saw you coming,' she explained. 'I thought I'd save you ringing because my mother's lying down, hopefully asleep. If she'd heard you she'd have been up again and it would have been very difficult for us to talk. She insists on joining in the conversation though she doesn't understand a word of it. Have you been busy in the café?'

While she was talking she led Chloe into a room which opened off the hall.

'The last part of the afternoon, yes. Very busy. Coach trips. But we managed all right, especially as they nearly all wanted afternoon tea, nothing cooked.'

'I've been thinking all day about what we discussed this morning,' Mrs Evans said. 'I think it's worth a try.'

She watched as Chloe's face lit up with a wide smile. What a charmer she is, Mrs Evans thought, and with such enthusiasm.

'Oh, I feel sure it will work!' Chloe said. 'I really look forward to trying.'

'There's just one thing . . .' Mrs Evans was hesitant. 'But it is quite important. I do think I ought to keep the business up for sale. In fact I've decided I must do so. It's in my best interest to sell it, though I know it won't be easy at this time of the year. I've had another word with the estate agent and he thinks it might well be next spring before I find a customer. So are you willing to take on the management on that condition, Chloe? It would mean that if prospective customers came to view you might have to show them around if I couldn't get away.'

'Very well,' Chloe agreed.

She was slightly disappointed, but who knew where any of them might be next spring? Who knew where she might want to be?

'I'm very pleased,' Mrs Evans said. 'So we'll get down to the details, shall we?'

Everything was arranged amicably; Chloe to take over the management of The Seashell, consulting with Mrs Evans should the need arise but otherwise free to decide on the day-to-day running as she thought best. Mrs Evans would do the baking and arrange for it to be delivered.

'And if that doesn't work out,' she said, 'we shall have to buy from a wholesaler.'

'Agreed,' Chloe said. 'Though we'll hope we don't have to. It would eat into the profits.'

It was important to keep up the profits, even to increase them. Mrs Evans must take her living from the café, as she did now; Chloe must have the incentive of bonuses since, for the present, she was willing to take on the extra work without an increase in her wages. Also, both women had agreed that before long something must be done about Edith. She couldn't be carried forever. She would have to go and her place be taken by someone younger and with an interest in the job.

'I hate the thought of having to sack Edith,' Mrs Evans said, 'though of course that unpleasant job will now fall to you!'

'I don't relish it,' Chloe confessed. 'But I'll do it if I have to. What I pray for is that she'll find another job first and that will solve it.' She had told Mrs Evans of Edith's intention to do just that.

'Then I'll come down the day after tomorrow and put Edith firmly in the picture about you.'

'Thank you,' Chloe said. 'She'll need to know.'

'And I'll inform all my suppliers that you have authority to place orders.'

'But I will need advice,' Chloe said. 'I'm sure there's a lot I don't know.'

'It's there for the asking,' Mrs Evans assured her. 'And I'm sure you'll soon learn the ropes.'

When she went to bed that night Mrs Evans thanked God – though these days she seldom thought of God – that from now on the unending struggle with balancing two sides of her life, giving neither side the skill or attention it merited, was over. Her mother, for however long was left to her, could have the attention she deserved. And indeed the care I want to give her, Mrs Evans thought. She would not begrudge one minute of it, night or day.

As for Chloe, she walked back home highly satisfied, her head filled with what new things she would do, and what she would no longer do. Back in her room she took out a notebook and began to make lists. 'Changes to be made'. 'Things to do'.

Nevertheless, when she finally went to bed and turned out the light it was of Simon she thought. In comparison with him nothing else mattered. Had he replied to her letter? Was his answer already in the post? If it was she would have it in the morning.

She heard the post come early and ran downstairs to collect it. There were two letters, one addressed in Maurice's angular handwriting, the other type-written, with an Akersfield postmark. Nothing from Simon.

She climbed slowly back upstairs, her disappointment so deep that she couldn't bring herself to open the two letters in her hand. Why had he not written? And then the happier thought struck her, and she clutched at it, he had not written because he was coming to see her in person. Wasn't it what she had suggested he should do, so why was she looking for a letter in the post? Comforted by the thought she opened the two letters, Maurice's first.

The probate of the will was finally through, he informed her. She would be hearing from Mr Ruskin directly. The customer for the house was still keen so there was nothing to prevent that sale going ahead. And in view of that they must empty the house – which was still exactly as their mother had left it – as quickly as possible. The house and its contents, he reminded her, had been left to the three of them.

As I understand it, you and Marilyn won't be able to touch any of the money arising from the will until you're twenty-one. As I said before, I shall try to get an allowance for Marilyn and I suppose it might be possible for you to do the same. Anyway, about the contents of the house . . .'

He added that if there were any items – furniture, personal possessions of their parents' and so on – which any of them would wish to have, he thought this would be all right.

He went on to write about Marilyn who, he reported, had decided to stay on at school and then try for Teacher Training College. She was influenced, he said, by the boyfriend, but he seemed a good influence and he and Lucy were not against it.

Chloe put down Maurice's letter and opened

the other one, which indeed proved to be from Mr Ruskin. It confirmed what Maurice had said, including the fact that she could not inherit her share of her mother's money until she came of age. There were things to be signed and settled and he wondered whether she might be coming to Akersfield. He hoped to hear from her and was hers truly, Herbert Ruskin.

The two letters raised queries in her mind. She was pleased to hear of Marilyn's plans and honest enough to recognize the benefits to herself. If this is what Marilyn wants to do, she thought, then it will save me a lot of trouble. As for the furniture and so on, she had never given a thought as to what she might want but, come to think of it, there was a small mahogany desk of her mother's which she had always admired and she would quite like some table silver, of which her mother had had a large supply.

She would have to think about whether she would go to Akersfield. If there was any chance of getting enough money to invest in The Seashell, she would go. If not, then not. The contents of both letters made that unlikely and it would be difficult to take time off just as she was about to start to manage the café.

She looked at the clock. It was time to go down and start work.

It was reasonably busy in the café that morning. At about half-past eleven Edith came into the kitchen.

'Two coffees, two scones with butter and jam, and there's a lady wants to see you. She asked for you by name.'

'Who is she?' Chloe asked.

'I don't know, do I? She didn't say and I didn't ask.'

'I'll be out in a minute, when I've done this order.'

Who could it be? She knew very few people in Brighton. The only person she could think of was Moira Portman and, as far as she knew, the Portmans had left for Cornwall.

She took off her apron, looked in the mirror to check her hair, and went out into the café. From a table by the door Mrs Collins raised her hand.

25

Chloe stopped dead. Why Mrs Collins? Perhaps there was a simple explanation. Simon's mother knew I worked here, Chloe thought. Didn't I stay in Rottingdean the night before I started this job? Perhaps she was in the area, realized she hadn't seen me for a little while, decided to pop in and say hello?

She didn't convince herself. It didn't fit with Mrs Collins. Chloe pulled herself together and walked towards her. It was just possible that Mrs Collins didn't know that she and Simon had parted, and if so she wasn't going to enlighten her.

'Good-morning, Mrs Collins!' Chloe said, smiling. 'How nice to see you! Can I get you a cup of coffee?'

'No thank you!' Grace Collins spoke hurriedly, then just as quickly she changed her mind. 'No, that's wrong! I'd appreciate a cup of coffee!' She was agitated, she who was usually so calm, so in control of herself.

Chloe signalled to Edith to bring coffee. Edith raised her eyebrows, but obeyed.

'It won't take a minute,' Chloe said. 'How are you?'

'I'm all right.' She waved away the question. 'It's Simon!'

'Simon? What is it, Mrs Collins? Please tell me!' There was no mistaking the anxiety in the other woman's voice. Chloe's skin pricked with apprehension.

'He was knocked down by a car in the Steine yesterday evening. He's badly injured . . . in the Royal Sussex.'

She said more, but after the words 'badly injured' Chloe heard nothing clearly. The room spun, as if cups and plates and scones were flying through the air. She grabbed at the table, slumped into the nearest chair, then bent her head on to the table to stop the dizziness.

'I'm sorry to give you such a shock,' Grace Collins said. It was not something she could have put tactfully even if she had had any strength left to search for the right words. She had spent the whole of yesterday evening, and the entire night, at Simon's bedside, waiting for him to regain consciousness, not sure that he ever would.

Chloe lifted her head, looked at Mrs Collins.

'Is he . . . Is he going to . . .'

'Going to die' were the words she couldn't bring herself to say.

'No. No he's not. He's conscious again, otherwise I wouldn't have left him. He wasn't very coherent.

When he came round he kept mentioning a letter. It was the ward sister who remembered there was a letter amongst the things they'd taken from his pockets . . .'

Edith interrupted them with the coffee. 'I brought a cup for you as well,' she said to Chloe. 'You look as though you could do with one!' She was avid to know what was happening but she would clearly have to wait.

'Then he said your name.' He had spoken so faintly, she had had to bend over him to catch it. 'I asked him, did he want to see you? Was that it? And he nodded.'

It had been such a brief, almost imperceptible nod, little more than a blink of the eyelids. He'd been in such pain – but the look in his eyes had given her the answer.

Mingled with her deep anxiety, for a second or two almost surpassing it, Chloe felt a great surge of happiness. He wanted to see her! In her mind that could mean only one thing, that whatever there was to forgive, he had forgiven her. Perhaps he had been on his way to see her when the accident happened?

'Did he . . . did he tell you what was in the letter?' She had to know where she stood with Mrs Collins.

'No. He couldn't do more than say your name – and hardly that. I think he was worried that the letter might be lost, and he wanted to see you.' She paused, then said: 'Chloe, may I ask you something?'

'Of course.'

'Simon hasn't been his usual self lately, and

we've seen nothing of you. Have the two of you quarrelled?'

'We had a . . . difference of opinion,' Chloe said guardedly.

'I do hope it's something that can be put right. I wouldn't want anything preying on his mind.'

'Nor would I,' Chloe said. 'And of course I'll go and see him.'

But when? She longed to go this very minute, to rush to him, but how could she? It would soon be lunchtime, the café was already filling up. Edith was doing her best – indeed she seemed to be moving rather faster than usual – but there was no way she could manage single-handed.

Mrs Collins looked around.

'You can't leave this minute,' she said. 'I can see that. But try not to worry. He'd been given an injection just before I left and he'd fallen asleep. He might still be sleeping. I shall go back now and if he's awake I'll tell him you're on your way.'

'I won't be a second longer than I can help,' Chloe promised. 'Mrs Evans will be here quite soon. I'll try to get away then.'

'Thank you, Chloe!'

'And please give him my love!'

Ten minutes after Mrs Collins had left Mrs Evans arrived. She walked into the kitchen and took one look at Chloe's white, anxious face.

'What's wrong?' she asked. 'Has something happened?'

Chloe explained.

'I'm desperate to go to him!' she said.

'Of course you are,' Mrs Evans agreed. 'And you must. No matter what! For the moment I've left my mother in the care of another neighbour, Mrs Dean, so I'll phone at once and ask her if she'll hang on a bit longer. And will you stay now just long enough for me to explain the new arrangements to Edith? It's what I came for and you must be here when I do it. It won't take more than a few minutes and then you're free to go to the hospital.'

Edith came into the kitchen and walked through to the scullery with a tray of dirty crockery. On her way back Mrs Evans put out a hand to halt her.

'Spare me a minute, please, Edith. There's something I want to say. It won't take long.'

Edith looked at her with suspicion.

'If it's about me being late, then you'll have to blame the buses. I can't do anything about that!'

'It's nothing to do with that,' Mrs Evans assured her. 'It's about the new arrangements I've made for The Seashell.'

What now? Edith thought. 'You're going to close down?' she said.

'No, I'm not! Quite the contrary! This is what we're going to do.'

She explained what had been discussed between herself and Chloe on the previous evening. While she told Edith the new plan for the baking and said that from now on Chloe would be in complete charge of the café, Chloe stood quietly by and watched Edith's face, though most of her thoughts were with Simon and of how soon she might see him.

'Well,' Edith said, with surprising graciousness, 'I

don't really *mind* Chloe being in charge, I've never been one for wanting to be boss (though don't let her think she can lord it over me! she thought privately). She's a bit young, but then I've noticed since the war that the world belongs to the young! Naturally you'll need extra staff. The two of us can't do everything.'

'You're coping very well at the moment,' Mrs Evans said. 'And it won't get busier. I really can't afford to engage extra staff just now.'

'Well I can't work any harder than I do,' Edith declared. 'Though of course I'll do my best as I'm sure anyone would admit I always do!' She had no wish to lose this job before there was another on the horizon, which she hoped would be as soon as possible.

Mrs Evans turned to Chloe.

'Is there anything you want to say?'

'Not really. I'm sure it will all work out. Edith and I get on well enough.'

'Right! Then you must get off to the hospital, Chloe.'

'*Hospital?*' Edith queried.

Chloe explained in one sentence. She was desperate to leave.

'And what am *I* to do while Chloe trots off to the hospital?' Edith demanded. 'I've only got one pair of hands – not to mention my feet!'

'Don't worry. I shall stay here until Chloe returns,' Mrs Evans said.

'Oh, but I don't just mean today!' Edith said. 'This sounds like a long job. I expect it'll mean visits every day.'

'I daresay it will,' Chloe acknowledged, 'though I hope to make them in the evenings. But . . .' She paused, and looked from Edith to Mrs Evans, speaking to both of them. 'If there's an emergency with Simon at any time of the day, if he really needs me, then I shall go, even if it means closing the café!'

'Don't worry about that now,' Mrs Evans said. 'We'll deal with that if it arises.'

At the hospital, when Chloe arrived at the ward to which she'd been directed, she was met by a nurse who informed her quite firmly that Mr Simon Collins was not allowed to have any visitors.

'But he's asked to see me,' Chloe explained. 'His mother came to tell me so only an hour ago.'

'Please wait a moment,' the nurse said. She went away, and when she returned a minute or two later she was accompanied by the staff nurse,

'Nurse Mailer is quite right,' the staff nurse said. 'Mr Collins is not allowed visitors.'

'But he's asked for me!' Chloe repeated.

'And you are . . .?'

'Chloe Branksome.'

'Oh! Chloe! Yes, of course you may see him, but only for a short time. He's quite unwell.'

She led the way and Chloe followed her along the corridor.

'Try not to be too upset by his appearance,' the nurse said. 'He has suffered a lot of injuries.'

She showed Chloe into a small, private room next to the main ward. Chloe halted just inside the doorway. Even the nurse's warning had not prepared her for the sight which met her eyes. Beneath his bandaged head Simon's face was black and blue, swollen and cut. His plastered leg was hoisted in a sling, there was a cradle over the lower part of his body, tubes and wires sprang from him at every point.

Mrs Collins was sitting beside the bed. When Chloe came into the room she stood up and turned towards her, taking her hands. Both women looked into the tear-filled eyes of the other.

'Thank you for coming so quickly,' Mrs Collins said. 'He was asleep when I got back. When he awoke I told him you'd soon be here. I'll leave you with him. I'll wait around somewhere and see you before you leave.'

Chloe stood quietly at Simon's bedside. Her whole body ached with compassion at the sight of his battered body, and with longing to do something for him. He lay totally inert, his eyes closed, only the slight twitching of his eyelids showing any movement. Gently, Chloe touched his hand and as she did so he opened his eyes and looked at her with instant recognition.

'Chloe!'

She was shocked by the weakness of his voice. He tried to smile but his lips were too swollen and stiff to allow it, though the smile which he could not manage with his lips showed in his eyes. She smiled back at him. In spite of everything, and incredibly considering the awfulness of it all, she knew that this was one of the happiest moments of her life. She had only to look at him to know that everything was all right between them. There would be things to talk about later, but everything was resolved here and now. She leaned over and kissed him, very gently so as not to hurt him.

'I came as quickly as I could,' she said. 'I know you got my letter. I meant what I said. I do love you very much. Perhaps I always did, but I wish I'd known sooner.'

She saw her answer in his eyes and then, in the next minute, the nurse came.

'I'm afraid your time's up, Miss Branksome,' she said. 'Mr Collins has to have an injection now, and after that he must get some sleep.'

Chloe stood up, leaned down and kissed Simon again.

'I'll be back this evening,' she promised.

'I'm sure you've done him good,' the nurse said when they'd left the room. 'He has a very long way to go but every little helps.'

'Thank you,' Chloe said. 'I'd like a word with Mrs Collins before I leave. Do you know where she is?'

'There's a little waiting room at the far end of this corridor,' the nurse said. 'She's in there.'

Mrs Collins told her the extent of Simon's injuries, which were legion.

'He'll get better. I know he will!' Chloe said.

She walked back to the restaurant worried and anxious, but deep beneath that she was confident and happy. She had believed exactly what she had said to Mrs Collins.

'You haven't been long,' Mrs Evans said. 'How is he?'

'I wasn't allowed to stay for more than a few minutes,' Chloe said. 'He's badly injured. Pelvis, head, leg, chest – and not yet out of danger. I'm going to see him again this evening, and indeed every evening.'

'Well, if you need to go during the day,' Mrs Evans said, 'let me know. I'll work something out.'

'Was everything all right here?' Chloe asked.

'Quite all right. Edith's a bit subdued. I think it's the threat of extra work. Anyway, now that you're back I'll go.'

Chloe's second visit of the day to the hospital was much like the first except that the initial shock was over, she had experienced that earlier. She didn't therefore have to guard herself against showing how horrified she was at the sight of Simon. She sat by his bed as long as she was allowed to, which was a little longer than in the afternoon. She stroked his hands, which had miraculously escaped injury, and spoke quietly to him about something and nothing. He was not able to speak to her but she knew by his eyes that he listened and understood.

'When will he be off the danger list?' she asked the nurse as she was leaving.

'Possibly as soon as tomorrow or the next day,' the nurse said. 'We can't tell for certain. But he's lucky to be alive!'

'Does anyone know what happened?'

The nurse shook her head.

'Not in any detail. I understand the driver of the car

has been questioned, but of course Mr Collins can't be. The doctor wouldn't allow it however much the police wanted to.'

Mention of the police brought the Nice Lady – she thought of her so rather than as Mrs York – into Chloe's mind as she walked away from the hospital. The Quarter Sessions must be almost due. Simon was out of that, but would she be called upon? With things as they were at the café it would be difficult to spend time in court. She thought she might call at the police station and see what she could find out.

Back in her room she made herself a sandwich, then wondered if she should write to Maurice and to Mr Ruskin. Perhaps she would leave it until she returned from hospital the following evening? The emotions of the day, as well as the physical activities, had left her exhausted. She would, she decided, go to bed and dream of what life would be like when Simon was once again restored to health.

Next morning, no sooner had Chloe set foot in the kitchen than the telephone rang. She caught her breath with fear as she sprang to answer it. Simon! It could only be the hospital, phoning her about Simon! Something terrible had happened in the night! Such was her state of panic that she didn't, at first, recognize Mrs Evans's voice.

'Hello!' Mrs Evans repeated. 'Is that you, Chloe?'

'Oh, yes! I'm sorry, Mrs Evans.'

'You sound out of breath. Are you all right?'

'Quite all right, thank you. I was a bit confused.' Her heart had stopped racing, was slowing down again.

'How was Simon last evening?'

'Holding his own. I'm going to ring the hospital in a few minutes. How is your mother?'

'The same,' Mrs Evans sounded weary. 'I was up with her very, very early, so when she'd calmed down I stayed up and did the baking. It'll be down to you quite soon. I've a good idea of what you need each day but if you want to change anything you must let me know.'

When Mrs Evans had rung off, and before she made a start on the day's chores, Chloe telephoned the hospital. The night sister was still on duty. There was no change in Mr Collins's condition, she said. He had had a reasonable night. She made no mention of the time she had spent sitting at his bedside in the early hours of the morning, holding his hand, so aware of his pain, willing him to live. When you were a night sister you saw the worst of everything.

'If you're still there when he wakens will you give him my love?' Chloe asked. 'Tell him I'll be in later in the day, but earlier if he needs me.'

She hung up. Then she sat down on the nearest chair, and prayed. She was not someone given to prayer, she had never had much faith in it. The last time she had prayed in earnest was when she was ten years old and had petitioned God for a bicycle. God had not answered. Perhaps, her mother had said, he'd simply said 'No' – but Chloe hadn't cared much for a God who said no.

She was not sure that He would answer now, but it was all she could think of to do. She would have liked to have begged the whole world to pray for

Simon but as far as she could see she would have to do it all herself.

Presently, she rose. There were the whole day's chores in front of her – the first day of her management – and time was passing. She also wanted to telephone Mrs Collins to see how she was, to ask if she had any further news, but it would have to wait a while. As it turned out it was Mrs Collins who phoned her, from the hospital, just before lunchtime.

'I don't want to alarm you,' she said. 'Nothing is any different, but I thought it might not be easy for you to catch me. In fact I've been here all morning. The doctor has decided to put off the surgery Simon needs on his leg until he's a little stronger. It's quite clear he's not well enough for it yet.'

'Thank you for letting me know,' Chloe said. 'Mrs Collins . . .' She hesitated. 'I prayed for Simon this morning. I prayed really hard. Does it do any good?'

'Who knows?' Mrs Collins said. 'I don't know – but I do it just the same. I do it all the time.'

It was a busy day in The Seashell. Nothing went wrong, everything went well, though Edith's stream of minor grumbles and rumbles would have pointed to the opposite. Still, she did what she had to do as well as she could and there were no major problems.

At the end of the day Chloe deposited the takings in the bank and set off to walk to the hospital. It was a twenty-minute walk away, a little further than, but in the same direction as Mrs Evans's house. Mrs Collins was in Simon's room when Chloe arrived, and once again vacated it so that Chloe could have him to herself.

'I would say he's fractionally better,' she told Chloe. 'The doctor seemed pleased with him. Who knows, perhaps tomorrow they'll be able to say he's out of danger?'

That night, when she was home again, feeling easier in her mind about Simon than she had been on the previous night, Chloe decided that she must reply to Maurice and to Mr Ruskin.

There is no way, she told Maurice, that I can come to Akersfield, not until Simon is much better – and I don't know when that will be. If Mr Ruskin wanted her to sign things, she said, he would have to send them to Brighton. 'As for the contents of the house,' she wrote, 'I can't remember what there is and in any case I don't want much. I don't have room for it.'

She mentioned the desk and the table silver and then, as an afterthought, said that she could do with some bedding. Sheets and blankets. She was pleased about Marilyn and she would write to her. She was writing to Mr Ruskin.

In her letter to Mr Ruskin she asked what the chances were of using some of her money to invest in a reputable business. Privately, she thought as she sealed the envelope, she had no hope that it would be allowed, but it was worth asking. In the event, he wrote back quite quickly with exactly the answer she had expected.

The days in the café, the visits to the hospital, settled into their routine. Each day Simon grew a little stronger, able to speak, able to eat more, then able to sit up.

She would never forget the first day he had spoken to her. She had seen his lips working, known that he was struggling, and had bent her head down so that his mouth was close to her ear.

'Chloe,' he said. 'I love you!'

It was scarcely audible, so weak, so unlike his normal voice; but it *was* audible, there was no mistaking what he had said.

'I love you too,' she replied. 'With all my heart!'

The surgery on his leg was successful, though the surgeon warned him that it would be a long time before he could walk without a limp.

'What does a limp matter?' Simon said. There were crutches to be mastered first, then two walking sticks, then one. A limp was nothing! It was almost the end of the road.

Early in December Edith gave in her notice. She had found a job in a café in Hove, much closer to her home. Chloe was delighted by the thought of her departure but tried not to show it.

'We shall now be able to get a *real* waitress,' she said to Mrs Evans. 'I shall start looking tomorrow.'

She was quickly successful. Within a few days she found Jeannie, a young Scots girl with some experience and full of Northern energy. She started the day after Edith left and proved herself a jewel from the start.

It was almost Christmas before Simon was allowed to leave hospital, and then not to his own flat but to his parents' home in Rottingdean, where he would have someone to care for him.

'We very much want you to spend Christmas with us, Chloe,' Mrs Collins said. 'We'd be most disappointed if you didn't.'

'Come as early as you can on Christmas Eve,' Simon said. 'Stay for as many days as you can.'

He would have liked her to have been there indefinitely. In the last few weeks in hospital they had had time to talk and all their differences had been resolved by the strength of their love.

'Mrs Evans is closing the café after lunch,' Chloe said. 'She says there'll be no-one around wanting cups of tea on Christmas Eve afternoon.'

'Then come here straight from work,' Mrs Collins suggested. 'Help me to trim the tree. I never do it before Christmas Eve, I don't like to anticipate Christmas.'

'I'd enjoy doing that,' Chloe said. 'I shall also want to call in at Blenheim House to leave presents for the children.'

She had seen Robert and Janet, had in fact taken them into Brighton to view the Christmas lights. Robert, she was pleased to discover, was enjoying his new school. Most of his conversation was about the new friends he had made.

'I'm glad Mrs York will be having a decent Christmas,' Simon said. 'At least as far as we know she will.'

At the Quarter Sessions – to which, because Mrs York had pleaded guilty, neither Simon nor Chloe had been summoned – because she had been held on remand for so long she was put on probation on condition that she continued the regular medical treatment which had been started while she was in prison. It had also been agreed that this could take place in London where she had friends who would keep an eye on her and a probation officer could be found who would have her in his care.

'I agree,' Chloe said. 'It somehow seems important for people to be happy at Christmas.'

It would be her first Christmas ever away from Akersfield. She was not sorry not to be there, she belonged now to Brighton, but she was pleased that everything was going well for her family in Yorkshire. It was strange how she somehow felt closer to them than she had when she'd lived with them.

By two o'clock on Christmas Eve the café was deserted, though when Mrs Evans looked out of the window St James's Street was thronged with last-minute shoppers. She had made a quick trip from home to wish her staff a Merry Christmas and to bring them presents; Christmas cakes decorated with snow scenes, every detail of which she had meticulously crafted and coloured: fir trees, sledges, tiny figures, skaters on a pond, a church, carol singers.

'There's no point in us staying,' she said. 'They're all far too busy to spend time in here. We might as well go home!'

And what will I go home to? she asked herself. Certainly not a merry Christmas! Yet there had been Christmases in the past when her mother had made it a magical time, and these were the occasions which she would remember this year, and of which she would remind her mother who, though she might not always remember her daughter's name, or what day of the week it was, could sometimes remember the past with great clarity.

Chloe, talking to Simon – they had so much to get to know about each other – remembered happy Christmases in the past, especially when she had been quite small.

'Of course that was before the war,' she told him. 'Lots of food, a stocking *and* a pillowcase bursting with presents on Christmas morning!'

In the war it had been different. Presents had been simpler, fewer, often home-made. Even the paper to wrap them in had been hard to come by.

'My mother explained,' Chloe said, 'that that was why, even when the war was over, she still made us unwrap our presents carefully so that she could iron the paper and save it for another time. Still,' she added, 'my parents did their best. If we went short of anything we weren't aware of it.'

But this Christmas, she thought, will be the best ever! How could it not be? After she had left The Seashell, carefully carrying the cake she had been given, she'd called at Blenheim House briefly, set eyes on the children and left their gifts. Now she was in the comfort and warmth of the house in Rottingdean. And since Christmas Day this year fell on a Saturday the café would not re-open until Tuesday.

'I have you under the same roof for three whole days, plus what's left of today!' Simon said happily.

He was still not totally strong, still couldn't move

without his crutches, but nothing mattered now that he was home and Chloe was with him.

On Boxing Day, after lunch, Mr and Mrs Collins set off for a walk over the Downs. 'I feel stuffed with food, and quite lethargic!' Grace Collins said. 'I must blow away the cobwebs!'

'Which we shall certainly do in this wind!' Mr Collins added. 'No wonder whoever built this house called it High Winds!' He was not at all sure he wanted this walk his wife was so set on.

'What would you like to do?' Simon asked when his parents had left.

'Nothing! Absolutely nothing!' Chloe replied.

'Then come and do it here,' Simon said. 'Sit beside me on the sofa.'

'Chloe,' he said after a while, 'I'm going to do something you asked me not to do again!'

'What's that?' she murmured. She was deliciously warm and deliciously comfortable.

'I'm asking you to marry me! Oh, Chloe, I love you so much!'

She sat up quickly, turned and looked at him, her shining eyes meeting his.

'Oh, Simon, I'm glad you didn't.'

'Didn't what?'

'Didn't keep your promise, I mean not to ask me. If you hadn't . . . well, I do truly think I might have asked you!'

'You mean you will?'

'Of course I will! I love you Simon, I'll marry you whenever you wish!'

He took her in his arms, kissed her long and deeply.

When at last he let her go he said: 'I'd like to marry you tomorrow, my darling! Surely you know that? But we'll be married when I can walk with one stick. I'm not going down the aisle on crutches, or even on two sticks. I want a hand free to hold yours!'

'I'd be happy to marry you on a stretcher,' Chloe said. 'I'd have married you in your hospital bed. But if you insist on making me wait until you can walk down the aisle, then you'd better start practising.'

Mr and Mrs Collins returned from their walk, he pinched and cold, the end of his nose red, his eyes watering; she rosy-cheeked and glowing. Mr Collins made straight for the fire, warmed his hands, then stood with his back to it.

'We have news for you!' Simon said, not even waiting for his mother to be seated. 'Chloe and I are going to be married!'

There was a moment's total silence, then Grace Collins shouted with joy.

'Wonderful! The very best news!' Her face was one huge smile.

She really means it, Chloe thought. She really is pleased!

'Are you surprised?' Simon asked his mother. 'Or had you guessed?'

'Not guessed. But hoped! Yes, certainly hoped!' Somehow she managed to embrace them both at the same time.

Mr Collins moved forward from his warm spot, shook hands formally with his son and gave Chloe a peck on the cheek.

'I'm very pleased!' he said. 'Chloe, you're most welcome to my family!'

'We must make plans!' Grace Collins enthused. 'When is it to be?'

'Before you go into all that,' her husband intervened, 'we must drink a toast!'

'It will be the moment I can walk with one stick,' Simon said. 'Who knows when? Certainly some time next year.'

'Coronation year!' Grace Collins said. 'And now your father and I have some news for *you* – not that it will come as a great surprise, we've talked about it often enough. We are finally going to live in France, permanently. Doctor Malcolm is quite firm, he says it would be better for your father not to spend another winter here. And you know how we love France.'

'So when?' Simon asked. 'Not before our wedding, I hope?'

'Of course not, silly! And not until after the Coronation.'

'You realize what this means, don't you?' Mr Collins added. 'It means that you and Chloe will have a place to live. This house will be yours.'

'It's too big for us anyway,' Grace Collins said. 'When Simon first moved out I thought I might turn it into a guest house, but I never got on with it.' Now, she thought hopefully, Simon and Chloe might fill it with children.

What will it be like, living here? Chloe wondered. Will I still work at the café, and if not, what shall I do with myself all day long? She wasn't worried.

Everything would sort itself out. She looked forward to the future with confidence.

'Nineteen-fifty-three is going to be a most exciting year!' Grace Collins said happily.

26

It was a day in June, nineteen-fifty-three. The new young queen had been crowned almost two weeks ago now but the shops and streets were still *en fête* and London, thronged with visitors from the four corners of the earth, throbbed with excitement.

It had been a slow journey from Victoria station because of the traffic, hold-ups all the way, but it had suited Chloe, who spent every second gazing out of the taxicab window at the passing scene. Given the choice she would have been out there in the thick of it but, though he was immeasurably improved, it would not have done for Simon. That was why they had not come to London on the day of the Coronation. Instead, Mr Collins had bought a television set in honour of the occasion, and the four of them had watched everything from the comfort of High Winds.

Chloe had given up her job at The Seashell only the week before. In the early spring of the year Mrs Evans's mother had died, quite suddenly, and peacefully. Within a week Mrs Evans was back in the café and had taken back her old job.

'In any case,' Chloe had told her, 'I shan't be able to stay on once I'm married. Simon will need me.'

Mrs Evans had agreed. 'I've been so glad to have you,' she'd said. 'I don't know what I would have done without you!'

Chloe thought fleetingly of The Seashell as she watched the Coronation on the flickering television screen. There were so many other things to think about, so much to look forward to.

'We are seeing far more than anyone in the crowds could possibly see,' Mr Collins had said with quiet satisfaction.

It was true, of course. How many of the people sitting in the stands outside Buckingham Palace, standing in the Mall, packed six deep all along the route, periscopes held high, waiting for the procession to pass, could see the crowning in the Abbey, as the Collinses and Chloe had from the comfort of their armchairs in Rottingdean?

All the same, Chloe had thought at the time but had not said, I would like to be there!

But today was even more exciting. It was, without a shadow of a doubt, the most exciting day of her life, and for that reason, as at last they turned into Piccadilly – she had had enough of crowds and slow-moving traffic – she wanted everything to speed up so that they could zoom ahead and reach their destination.

'If I were the Queen,' she said, 'someone would

wave a magic wand and the road would be cleared to let me through!'

'But since you're not,' Grace Collins said with a smile, 'we shall have to crawl yard by yard in patience!'

At last, however, the driver turned his wheel and drove under the arch and into the courtyard of Burlington House.

'There we are, ladies and gentlemen!' he said. 'The Royal Academy!'

Mr Collins paid the driver and, since it was a special day, added what was for him a generous tip. Then the four of them crossed the courtyard and climbed the steps to the entrance.

'Can you manage?' Chloe asked Simon.

'Perfectly well,' Simon said.

Going up steps was easier than coming down, but there were not many things now he couldn't do. He hoped the time wasn't too far distant when he could throw away his remaining stick.

They crossed the hall and walked towards the foot of a staircase. Chloe caught her breath at the sight of it. She had not known what to expect, but certainly nothing as grand as this, not such magnificence. They walked up the staircase four abreast, marvelling at the incredible flower displays on either side of them.

Nor, as they walked forward into the gallery, had she expected to see so many people. It was, after all, a private viewing. She had thought there would be small groups of selected people. Well, they *were* selected people. No-one, she had been told, would be there without an invitation.

The invitation to Chloe and the Collinses had come from Moira Portman, and they were to meet up with John and Moira in the gallery where the portrait was hung. Grace Collins was the first to spot the Portmans. They were standing at the far end of the gallery, part of a small crowd. Moira Portman was, for her, unusually smartly dressed. John Portman was always well dressed.

Grace Collins had said it would be a smart affair. 'Simon must take you into Brighton and buy you a new dress for the occasion,' she had said to Chloe.

And he had done so.

It became apparent as they drew near that the people around Moira and John were looking at one thing and as, suddenly, someone moved and Chloe could see through to the wall, she saw what it was, and stopped dead.

It wasn't true! It couldn't be true! But it was, and common sense reminded her that of course it was, because wasn't this exactly what they had been invited to see?

There she was, in her cream dress and headband – so real, so lifelike that she felt as though she was looking at reality, at herself as real as the self who was standing there, rooted to the ground.

Moira Portman turned round and saw them.

'Chloe! How are you? What do you think of it?'

Chloe moved closer, and the Collinses with her.

'It's quite wonderful! It's unbelievable!'

The whole experience was wonderful, dreamlike. She, Chloe Branksome, from Akersfield, Yorkshire, standing in front of her own portrait in the Royal

Academy's Summer Exhibition in Coronation year! And hung in the very best position. 'On the line,' Moira had told her when she'd given her the news – so that it was at eye level and could not fail to be a focus of attention.

'It looks different from when I saw it last,' Chloe said. It looked even better than it had then.

'It is different, in a way,' Moira said. 'I've done a lot to it since you saw it last.'

'I can see you've added the highlights, and in thicker paint,' Simon said.

'That's right,' Moira agreed. 'You work from thin to thick when you're painting a portrait. But I expect you know that?'

'I know next to nothing,' Simon said. 'But I do recognize it's a very good painting.' But nothing, he thought, could ever be as beautiful as the original; his Chloe, soon to be his very own Chloe. He reached for her hand and held it tightly in his own.

A man, accompanied by three young people who looked as though they might be students, had moved closer as Moira was speaking.

'This lady is quite correct,' he said in a voice of authority. 'You see, when you apply thick paint for the highlights, the paint also reflects extra light. Indeed, Rembrandt, whose use of highlights everyone knows, was accused of putting on his paint too thickly. But he was proud of that. Do you know what he said?' he asked his students. 'He said "I'm a painter, not a stainer!"'

He turned and spoke to Moira.

'This is a very good painting. Moira Portman. I don't know the artist at all, but whoever she is she has great merit!'

Looking at Moira as he spoke he became aware of the flush rising in her face until her cheeks were crimson.

'Oh dear!' he said. 'Oh dear! I do believe I've made a gaffe! You *are* . . .'

'Yes! I'm Moira Portman. And you haven't made a gaffe at all. You've paid me a great compliment.'

'Well it's kind of you to take it like that. And if we haven't heard of you until now, we certainly will in the future!' He held out his hand. 'Norman Manson.'

'I know,' Moira said, shaking his hand. 'I recognized you.' He was himself an eminent portrait painter, a Royal Academician of many years' standing, a frequent contributor to the Arts journals, a broadcaster.

Praise from Norman Manson was praise indeed. He was not known for being lavish with it. It made worthwhile all the hard work, all the niggling details, all the anxieties and misgivings which had led up to this moment. The checking of the tonal qualities which she feared she had got wrong; the correcting of the proportions when a mirror, held up to the work, told her she had definitely erred; the seemingly endless wait from submission day in April through all the stages of acceptance or rejection, wondering every day, through to the end, whether she would be asked to collect the painting because it was not acceptable.

And now here she was! And here her painting was! And here Chloe was, she suddenly remembered.

She took Chloe's hand and guided her forward.

'Perhaps you would like to meet the subject of the painting,' she said to Norman Manson. 'Chloe Branksome!'

'Ah!' Norman Manson said. He looked hard and appreciatively at Chloe. 'And now that I see the original I realize more than ever how good a painter you are, Mrs Portman. Not only have you captured your subject's beauty – which is considerable – but you have gone deeper.' He looked from Chloe to the portrait, and back again to Chloe. 'You have captured the person inside the beauty. Not to put too fine a point on it, you have captured the soul!'

'There was always something I felt I couldn't quite grasp,' Moira confessed. 'I still don't know that I did so.'

'Whether you did or not doesn't matter. What you've done is shown that there *is* an enigma. You've drawn our attention to it. We don't have to solve it. Who knows at what the Mona Lisa is smiling?'

'Thank you! Thank you very much. You've made me feel that perhaps there's some worth in my work. That means a lot to me.'

'There's a great deal of worth,' Norman Manson said. '*Portrait of Chloe* will be one of the important paintings of the year. It will bring you a lot of work, and if there's anything I can do, any introductions I can make, you have only to let me know. And now I must get back to my students.'

When he had gone Moira turned back to the rest of her party.

'Wasn't that wonderful? I'm so lucky!'

'It was well deserved, darling,' John Portman said.

'I echo that!' Simon added.

'I think it's just marvellous!' Chloe said. 'The whole day is marvellous. I never knew one like it!'

She went closer to the portrait, looked at it more intently.

'What's that little green sticker for?' she asked.

Moira looked slightly uncomfortable.

'It means it's not for sale.'

'You mean you're going to keep it?' Chloe was slightly disappointed. She didn't want it to hang in Blenheim House. Although she had no feeling whatever left for John Portman she didn't want her portrait in his house. If she couldn't have it herself – and she couldn't – she'd rather it went elsewhere – perhaps to a gallery.

'I'm not keeping it for myself,' Moira said. 'I did actually sell it before it was exhibited.' She looked over at Simon.

'Oh, very well!' he said. 'Chloe, *I* bought it! I bought it for you. It's to be your wedding present!'

They were to be married at the end of July. When they returned from their honeymoon – she had no idea where that was to be, Simon was keeping it a deep secret – Mr and Mrs Collins were to go to France to live permanently, and she and Simon would move into High Winds.

'What a wonderful present!' Chloe said. 'My own portrait. Where shall we hang it?'

'Over the mantelpiece in the drawing-room, of course!' Simon said.

'I rather thought in the hall,' Chloe said. 'Everyone would see it as they came into the house!'

'No, darling,' Simon said firmly. 'The drawing-room is the place!'

'I hope you two aren't going to quarrel about it,' Grace Collins said.

'Of course not!' Chloe said.

'Certainly not!' Simon agreed. 'We shall talk it over and come to an agreement.'

THE END

THE MOUNTAIN
by Elvi Rhodes

Jake Tempest spent the first twelve years of his life on the canals. Then, when his grandfather died, everything changed. His mam and he moved to Skipton, Mam worked in the mills, and they lived as best they could. It was there that she bought the picture of the mountain, and when she died it was one of the few things he took with him.

But the mountain was more than just a picture. It was a real place – Whernside – set amidst the rugged hill country of Yorkshire, and it was to Whernside that Jake was drawn, especially when he found they needed men to work on the new railway lines, cutting valleys, building viaducts, and carving a tunnel right through the great mountain itself.

As he settled into the new harsh life amongst the rough shanty villages of the railway workers, one woman lit his very existence – Beth Seymour. Beth was strong, brave, compassionate – and she was also married. Once she and Will had loved one another, but life for the rail builders was savage and coarse and Will Seymour was rapidly becoming brutalized by the manner in which he lived. Beneath the shadow of the mountain, in all its seasons, the passionate story of Beth, Will and Jake was played out to a dramatic climax.

0 552 14400 2

MIDSUMMER MEETING
by Elvi Rhodes

It was an unexpected legacy which brought Petra to the close village community of Mindon. An imposing stone house in the middle of the village, left to her by an old friend of her mother's, promised a very different way of life from Petra's lonely and unsettled life in Yorkshire, and she was immediately made welcome by the local residents – in particular, by the members of the local Amateur Dramatic Society. Presided over by the formidable Ursula, who liked to run things her way, the ambitious decision had been made (mainly by Ursula herself) to put on *A Midsummer Night's Dream* as the next production. Petra, to her surprise and pleasure, was put in charge of the scenery.

Rivalries, squabbles, love affairs and seething resentments threatened to scupper the production, and all Ursula's management skills were needed to prevent disaster. But Petra had more pressing things on her mind than the set designs. A mystery from the past had begun to haunt her – and the answer to that mystery might solve the puzzle of why she had been left such a beautiful house by a total stranger.

0 552 14715 X

SPRING MUSIC
by Elvi Rhodes

Naomi had been contentedly and, she thought, happily married for nearly all of her adult life when her husband Edward explained kindly to her one day that he had fallen in love with a twenty-six-year-old and wanted a divorce. She had to leave the comfortable home she had shared with Edward and their three children, now all grown-up, and move into a small flat in the middle of Bath. The dramatic change in her lifestyle threatened to overwhelm her.

But gradually Naomi began to appreciate the changes, and even to enjoy them. For the first time in her life she could do what she liked, and make her own friends. If these included men friends – well, why not? Unfortunately her children could think of many reasons why not, and Naomi began a battle to establish her own independence, and to persuade her family that she had moved into the springtime of a whole new life.

0 552 14655 2

A SELECTED LIST OF FINE NOVELS AVAILABLE FROM CORGI BOOKS